IDONIA
CREATION

RION DUNCAN

Rise Publishing

IDONIA CREATION

Rise Publishing

Edited by Evan Wheatley, Levi Sowerby, and Rion Duncan

The Library of Congress Cataloging-in-Publication Data is available upon request.

ISBN: 978-0-9988833-2-8

First Edition

DEDICATION

For Tiff who never gave up on me, Rue who makes me believe, my family who have always been there for me, and to everyone who ever dreamed of a world outside our own.

Author's Note:

The work you are reading is the original publication of my attempt at putting the world in my head onto the page. It is as imperfect as it is incomplete. I rushed this book into the world at the height of the pandemic's impact on my family's life. It wasn't ready to be released then, and it's only, almost, ready to be released now. At the time, my wife and I were battling repossessions, foreclosures, and more that felt almost inevitable, and I rushed this book into the world, hoping it would magically become a bestseller and alleviate all our struggles.

It didn't, obviously, but, possibly more importantly in the long run, it forced me to finally embrace the world I was creating and share it with everyone. This is not the proper version of it, and, to that extent, I am working on something better. It is not finished yet, but very soon there will be the appropriate version of this story for everyone to read. I'm not releasing the "title" just yet but suffice it to say it will be the "expanded edition" of *Idonia Creation.*

That is not the end, though. Far from it. Everything you read, everything you have experienced thus far, is only the beginning. There is so much more to come...

Yours in fiction,

Rion

I could no more tell you the tale of Idonia in simple form than I could explain the very nature of existence in a single breath. When you first heard it, the story would make little to no sense. It would be as if you were trying to put together a puzzle, only none of the pieces had faces and most were missing, and instead of an image for guidance, you were given a riddle. The more you heard the story, though, the clearer the riddle becomes, pieces start sliding into place, and you'll find the pieces you thought missing were right there in front of you the whole time, hidden just beyond your view. Before long, you will see it all clearly. You will see there never was a puzzle or a riddle or even a story. There was only ever The Story. Your story and our story, the story of all that is and all that was and all that will ever be. It is the story of existence, both eternal and finite.

Milas ~ Ann Terr 4th Section, 12th Version, Year 5188

PROLOGUE

NEVADOLIA

Milas stood on the terrace outside his solar overlooking Nevadolia as the ships docked. They were arriving. Soon his solar would be filled with his commanders and lieutenants as the final plans were laid, Nevadolia would begin preparations. Eons had passed since the Nalun and Ana'si last met as foes on the battlefields, but even a peace so lasting as this could not endure the forces it now faced. Samias and Milas' return had been prophesied before the ceasefire edict was even given, and their exile initially began. Despite their many variations, though, all the prophecies agreed upon one adamant fact: once the two finally returned, the war was inevitable.

Before the Ana'si could commit their total forces to the threat of the Nalun, though, they had to deal with the impending danger the Vigil posed. The Vigil's Watchers had grown too emboldened in his complacency, and Milas knew his failings had put more lives at risk than merely his own people. The fate of all the worlds was at long last being pulled into the Great War. Milas had failed to prevent the Watchers' surreptitious expansion just as he had been unable to thwart the Nalun's resurrection of Samias. He had thought the Vigil and the Nalun would both hold to the Treaty as he had held the Ana'si, and his misplaced faith was being met with its grave consequences. Milas had trusted the other Orders' leaders and never stopped to consider they might have rogue agents at work within them. His faith in his kin who led the Vigil and the Nalun had blinded him to what the members of their Orders were doing, and now he would have to guide his loyal Ana'si through the treacherous waters of all-out war with the Nalun whilst still deterring the Watchers ensuing advance.

He stared into the sky at the distant worlds and wondered what preparations they would be making. Inverna's broken pieces glowed a turbulent vermillion, as they had since The Fall. His heart still ached every time he looked upon them. It pained him even more to know that in the millions of years since Inverna's shattering, its people had still not evolved from their brutality. Content to live in darkness and chaos, their inability to overcome their tragic past had allowed Az'iel and the Jöltir to reform and return to power in their exile. A power that would no doubt shape much of the battles to come. Milas shuttered at the thought. He was as much responsible for the hatred boiling in Az'iel as anyone, and when the machines of war began thundering across Inverna, that hatred would be made known to all.

Pushing the thought to the back of his mind Milas watched the shattered pieces of Inverna in their broken orbit. No matter how well he came to understand it, the galactic dance of gravity and electromagnetic fields warping reality to their will never ceased to amaze him. Perhaps it even was the knowledge of it that made him so entranced. As the four large bodies danced their gravitational waltz around one another amongst the violent shades of scarlet in their gas clouds, they were quite a beautiful fiery spectacle. If one could simply forget Inverna's torment, they could lose themselves in the majesty of this fractured world. Its floating cities on the tiny fragments orbited their larger siblings like gorgeous satellites weaving through the pale gas clouds that swirled between and around the broken planet.

The clouds far out over the Greystone Bay coalesced and turned black, growing larger until the whole of Nevadolia was cast in their shadow, bringing Milas back to the present. A deafening crack sounded within the cloud, and a pillar of lightning hurtled towards the water setting the sky ablaze as it crashed into the waves splintering out in all directions. The dark figure began creeping across the water towards the bay. Milas smiled faintly, glad to know two of his prominent commanders had finally made their choice.

Sensing the approach, Milas turned to the door as his viceroy entered. "My Throne," Tavius bowed as he entered, "we have begun docking procedures as we speak. They should reach the Bay in short order. They have all been given leave to settle into their quarters before the meeting as per your request."

"My thanks, Tavius. Though I am certain, some will decline. Prepare some refreshments for the solar, please. I believe we will at least have three guests before this evening's events, and they have made quite the journey."

"Indeed."

Milas looked to the docks again. "Have any of our Traco relatives arrived unnoticed? I have neither seen nor sensed them."

"Just the one so far."

Milas turned, "Ah, yes. Of course."

"The others should be along shortly." Tavius continued, "They do have the longest travel after all."

"That they do," Milas replied, returning again to the terrace. "Make sure everyone's needs are met. They are, of course, free as always to make themselves at home while we await the final arrivals."

"At once. Will there be anything else, my Throne?"

"Just the refreshments, for now, Tavius."

With that, Tavius exited, leaving Milas with only his thoughts. Throne echoed in his mind. He had never liked the title, never wanted it. Ruling was a burden he never craved, even though it was his destined purpose. He knew one day soon that burden might grow exponentially. The Davpyr people, his people, were leaderless, as was the whole of Idonia. It would not be long before he would have to choose if he would take up his ancestors' mantle.

He looked again to the sky. Euern's lush forests and vibrant oceans painted its surface with vivid shades of blue and green that contrasted its fallen cousin so drastically, yet so perfect. How close the two worlds had once been, Milas feared how close they might be in the days to come. Even from his terrace, he could see the spot of scorched land where Euern's capitol had stood not long ago, the first spark of the fire that was this war renewed.

It pained him to think how many more cities, how many more worlds would burn before this war ended. This was a torment he had carried for so long, though, that he could not remember a reality without it. It was a part of him now, his responsibility, his punishment. Such was the nature of leadership, the constant weight of one's world bearing down on them. A weight Milas knew would grow even heavier before the war was over.

He closed his eyes to still himself and, upon opening them, found the distant light at the center of their system. A smile stretched across his face seeing the golden light from Leghtus wash over the city of Idonia and spread across the system, basking every world in its radiance. No matter how far he was from home, it was always with him.

At once, he heard a boom like thunder rolling in from the mountainside and felt the city rumble from the great wings billowing in the distance. Milas looked to the snow-capped mountains in the west to see the mighty Traco appear one by one over the ridge. Their massive, leathery wings flapped in unison as they began their landing formation. The last of his commanders would soon enter the city, and his guests would soon be at his solar. The fate of the Idonic lordship would continue to wait. For now, the Rising was at hand.

PART ONE
THE BROWNINGS

1
THE DAILY BREW

Ally woke to the sound of an alarm clock smashing against hardwood, followed by her friend's profanity-laced rant echoing down the stairs and through the hall. She lay back in bed, staring out the window as the sun began to fill her room. Another beautiful morning shone through the glass, basking her still bare walls and unpacked boxes in its glow. She could feel the light radiating on her skin, sending warmth flowing down her body. The robin egg blue paint Ally had put on the walls the previous week still looked fresh. The color poured into her eyes like that of a clear spring sky, flooding her senses, nearly drawing her out of bed. The endless mountain of covers seemed to suck her back in, though. That was the first night she'd slept with her new down comforter, which encased her that morning. Despite the racket outside her room from her friends getting ready for class, Ally saw no reason why she should leave her cozy little nest.

The University of Central Arkansas was a good school, Ally kept telling herself. Regardless of whether the statement was true, she still dreaded going. Erin and Rachel, two of her best friends that moved to Little Rock with her, seemed all too excited about going to class that day. "The first day of 'real' college," they kept saying. The three had spent the previous years completing their undergraduate degrees back home in south Arkansas. After graduating, they all decided to move to Little Rock together to continue their studies and finally move away from home, but they didn't realize what leaving home would genuinely mean.

They each missed it in their own way, but it wasn't the town they missed. It was the people they had left behind. Ally's mother, Mimi and Pops, and two of her cousins lived in south Arkansas. Mimi is what Ally called her grandmother since, at the time of Ally's birth, Mimi felt too young to be called "Grandma." Pops is what she called her grandfather because, well, Pops was just Pops. Erin's and Rachel's families were scattered throughout south Arkansas, the ones they knew at least. It was their roots. Leaving their families had been tough, but leaving their friends had been even harder. Between Ally's two cousins, Nick and Matt, and their brother-like best friend Thaddeus, the three girls were without their closest friends and family aside from each other.

Everyone swore moving would come naturally to the three of them, as they had always been adaptable. None of the friends realized how much they depended on Thaddeus, Nick, and Matt. Not to say that having each other as roommates hadn't helped immensely, but it just wasn't the same for any of them without the boys. Ally had been close friends with her cousins Matt and Nick since they were kids. Then, when middle school started, Ally made her first friends outside of her cousins in Erin and Rachel. Once Thaddeus came into the picture in high school, she had no closer friend. The six of them were practically inseparable until the girls moved away.

After finally coaxing herself out of bed, Ally began her morning routine and got ready for her first day. While that was not Ally's first "first day," something felt different. The three girls had not gone shopping to pick out brand new outfits for school, and neither Rachel nor Erin were worried about making a grand entrance. Instead, the day felt more like saying goodbye and getting ready for work at the same time. All of this came as a relief to Ally, who never liked being a center of attention. She preferred a corner somewhere at the back, away from everything. Most days, she wished she were utterly invisible.

They each put on their newfound favorite outfits, their comfortable clothes, their pieces of home. Erin put on the new slacks her mother gave her as part of her graduation gift, a collection of things a young professional would need. She paired it with a white V-neck and her grey vest with pale pink plaid stripes she loved. Her equally dressy counterpart, Rachel, wore her light-yellow sundress with white polka dots, her go-to summer outfit that complimented her chestnut skin. Even after years with them, Ally never knew how she managed to fit in with such girly girls. Her "southern belles," as she loved to call them.

There they were with their closets full of dresses and fancy clothes, with polka dots and paisley accents on their walls. And there stood Ally, with a room décor that looked as if she were opening an electronics store, rock posters still waiting to be hung.

How did we ever get here? She thought. Ally couldn't help smiling at herself in the mirror at the idea. Grinning back at her from the mirror was a nearly six feet tall, lanky girl who was a weird, even mix of clumsiness and athletic grace, wearing a Joan Jett shirt her mom had passed down, a pair of old jeans, and yellow Chucks. She was a nerd, not a fashionista; a rocker, sans bravado.

"We'll figure this out. We've made it this far." Ally said to herself, shrugging her shoulders and turning from the mirror.

Down the hall, Erin stared at her full-length mirror as she threw on necklace after necklace, trying to complete her outfit. "Too silver." "Too gold." "Too pink." One by one, she turned them down, telling herself she was unsure why she couldn't find the proper look. She dropped to the bed, burying her face in her hands as she inhaled deeply.

"Get your shit together, Erin." She said, exhaling deeply.

There was no point in acting like she was unaware. Erin knew why she couldn't choose, but she couldn't let her nervousness show. She was supposed to be the tough one. This was supposed to be easy for her.

Rachel found herself in a similar dilemma as she caught her reflection in the kitchen window. The two women stared at each other through the glass with confusion. Rachel observed how the woman's dark hair fell around her glasses and onto her shoulders, framing her face. She felt both old and young at the same time, lost between her teenage years and adulthood, and terrified at what the future may hold. She knew everything was going to change, no matter how little. All she could do was embrace it, so she arranged her face in a smile and finished preparing her shake.

A second later, Ally came downstairs, and the chatter began. "Why are you wearing that shirt, Ally?" Rachel practically shouted over the blender. "Don't get me wrong; I love that shirt. I just thought you'd wear your Marilyn. Isn't that one your fave?"

Rachel always made a point to be cordial.

"Eh, I do love me some Marilyn. Just felt like a Joan kind of day. Maybe next week. Besides, that's your favorite, Rach." Ally grinned as

Rachel returned the look. It was no secret Rachel loved Marilyn Monroe as much, if not more than Ally did.

"Yeah, I do wish your mom would get one made for me." She continued, giggling. "Christmas isn't far off, you know."

"I'll see what I can do." Ally replied with a smirk.

"Fu-huck that shit!" Piped the more foul-mouthed Erin as she reached the bottom of the stairs. "I'd be wearin' one of your Alexander the Greats! I mean, I would do damn near anything to have a shirt with my namesake on it, *Allyxandria*," she drew out the name with a devious tone, "never mind two of 'em." She paused thoughtfully before adding, "Well, if I had a namesake, that is. I wonder if in an alternate universe there was an Erin the Great instead."

Rachel nearly spat her protein shake out as she laughed. Making a scene was never outside Erin's capability.

"I will cut you." Ally gave Erin her coldest stare as Erin smirked. She knew Ally loathed being called by her full name.

"So, what was the provocation for profanity this morning?" Rachel asked, drawing out the words emphatically.

"Ha! Just realized what time it was and how much I still had to do. I'm here now, though, and that's what matters." Erin replied with her arms spread wide, gesturing to herself.

After Rachel finished her shake, they all meandered outside. That is to say, Ally meandered. The other two practically bounded. Ally's phone buzzed, giving her both a sense of relief and misery as she knew what it was, a text from each of the three people that mattered most to her; her mom, Mimi, and Thaddeus, all wishing her a good first day. Pops would have texted if he knew how. Nick and Matt would have as well if they ever thought about such things. She missed them all more than she wanted to admit.

"Thad said to tell you both that he hopes today sucks royally and for us not to be too anxious and just to enjoy this moment. It only happens once," Ally said to the group.

"Oh Thad, always the sweetheart," Rachel replied.

That day proved another scorcher, much to their confusion. Little Rock had just experienced the coldest, wettest, and most unpredictable year in the city's history. Still, the girls had seen nothing aside from typical weather since they arrived.

"Those people are some damn fools telling us the weather's been crazy here." Erin proclaimed as she landed on the sidewalk.

"True," Rachel added. "We haven't got a drop of rain, and I haven't stopped sweating yet, let alone got cold."

"Shit, I'd take some cold and rainy at this point. I'm done with this heat. So, where to ladies?" Ally glumly asked.

In unison, Rachel and Erin gleamed, "Daily Brew!" They both laughed, and even though Ally was dreading going to school, the thought forced a smile across her previously dull face.

The Daily Brew had become a routine stop for Ally and her friends since they discovered it. There were franchised java stops on busy corners, and niche hipster spots tucked all around town, but none of them could hold a portafilter to The Daily Brew. The shop was the quaintest little café nestled in an alleyway down the block from their house. It wasn't entirely on their way to school, but their arrival weeks before classes began allowed them time to search out the rough diamonds worth getting off the beaten path. Everything about it seemed to addict brewees harder than the caffeine in their drinks. From the low hum of customers, baristas, and machinery to the intoxicating aroma that suspended one's senses, The Daily Brew engulfed its visitors and loyal subjects alike in peaceful yet frenzied tranquillity.

Even from the outside, it was apparent The Brew was no run-of-the-mill coffee shop. While it was right in the heart of the business district, it was tucked down an alley on the second-floor patio of a skyrise. It had the appearance of a coffee shop that would have sat across the block from a fresh food market and right next to an old bookstore with a walk-up in between. The rich blue awning extending from the marquee and covering the patio stole everyone's sight from first glance if they made it down the alley in the first place. Even though red had long been Ally's favorite color, blue instantly became her favorite every time she laid eyes on the awning. She could not espy another color that could ever be more beautiful.

Beneath the awning, the wrought iron waist-high fence surrounded the deck and encased the matching iron chairs and tables, which were surprisingly comfortable despite not being cushioned. As soon as they reached the stairway leading to the brewery, they could hear the surreal hustle and bustle that was The Brew. Students waiting for school to start and locals meeting for morning coffee were relaxing outside on the patio as business types rushed in and out on their way to work. Once Ally heard them all, her stresses somehow melted away. After they passed the awe-striking entrance and lively conversations, a tea and coffee medley so sweet, bold, and rich they could taste it possessed the girls' senses. Cafés are widely known for that distinct coffee smell, but the instant the aroma of The Daily Brew filled one's nostrils, no other coffee shop would suffice. Closer to the door, the smell intensified as the sounds from espresso machines and blenders mingled with the warm hum of technology and softened voices. Where the patio met the shop were the store-long windows, tinted just enough to allow curiosity to take over.

Inside the shop, adults of all lifestyles could be found, from company execs working through the final details of their proposals to students getting started on research papers and everyone in between. Though it was much quieter indoors — the interior was a popular reading, working, and mild chit-chat area— it was still no library, at least not in regards to the noise levels. There was, in fact, a second-floor loft peering over the coffee shop lined with bookshelves. The girls had never seen anyone go up to the loft despite the staircase being openly accessible. It was almost as if it was only meant to serve as a backdrop for the coffee shop and not actually used. It only heightened the mystique of the Daily Brew. Orders being taken, given, and announced were the only sounds to be understood, but the soft buzz of conversation and machinery never ceased. The lounge brought an even sweeter scent with it, where the vanillas and caramels and cinnamon could be felt, wrapping them in a most sensual aura. It was a smell the girls wished could be folded up and placed in their pockets to be taken out and enjoyed whenever desired.

The menu would be like that of any other coffee shop if not for the oddly named drinks; names like *Stoni* for a Chai Tea Latte or *Lavyrja* for a Caramel Macchiato. These strange names made no sense to any of the frequent brewees, yet they held some significance to everyone without them knowing. What really drew attention to the menu, though, was the ghost-white driftwood-like slab it was carved into, and a tiny symbol of some type of bird with an illegible phrase emblazoned in its feathers etched in the bottom left corner.

A bar stood to the left with an adjacent order counter. There were a few tables, booths, and raised platforms, all of the same bleached white wood stylings as the menu in the lounge. Plushly cushioned sofas and chairs were scattered throughout, and planters hung from the walls and ceiling, making the interior a cozy indoor forest. Whether Ally and her friends wanted to sip their coffee over the lightening raucous of the patio or in the warming melody in the lounge, both places made them feel at home.

Once someone had been to The Daily Brew, it was with them everywhere. Each new building brought about visuals that were not that of The Brew. Other places brought about sounds that did not touch the soul and could not offer scents that encased one in ecstasy. The slogan made it perfectly clear, "Once you're in The Brew, The Brew is with you."

Though Ally's family had raised her to be religious, she had never felt very "spiritual," but as she approached the counter, something always spread through her. Oddly it just felt like she belonged. They each had their orders memorized, and before long, the baristas would as well. Rachel ordered her Iced *Stoni*. Erin and Ally's order was always a Vanilla and Caramel Latte, or as the shop called it, a *Milas*.

"Are you girls having your drinks here or taking them to class?" asked the cashier Denise, a lovely middle-aged lady who fit the coffee shop persona perfectly.

"To go." Ally replied.

"We need to get here earlier Monday, so we can have some drinks before History of Imperialism." Rachel said as they gave their orders.

"Yeah, because I'm sure as hell going to need some serious caffeine for that class once it picks up." Erin agreed.

That was undoubtedly the unique thing about The Brew. Time seemed but a distant concept, like the shop, was there forever and would be whenever people needed it. In the right corner sat their usual table, and for some reason, it was always vacant when they arrived. On more than one occasion, the girls pondered if it was mere coincidence or if that table had permanently reserved itself for them somehow. It was often one of the few empty tables, though the place also never got crowded, the girls noticed. Even when most tables were occupied, there were never more than a few people at any of them. Over the previous weeks, the three had watched people of all sorts visiting the Daily Brew. From the basic suits to the average boho, the Brew was a revolving door of eclectic characters, except there was nothing basic or average about any of them. Sometimes the three talked about it, sometimes they didn't, but they were all acutely aware that the people sitting at the tables in the Daily Brew didn't quite fit if taken out of the coffee shop. They only made sense there at their particular tables. In the far left corner, completely secluded, was the only table that always remained patronless.

"I really expected more people than this. I guess the school year doesn't really affect you?" Erin asked.

"It gets busier as the year goes on," Terry, the young barista, said as she made the drinks, "but it never gets too hectic. I guess because we're geared for the slow and steady while being surrounded by the hustle and bustle."

Rachel and Erin grabbed their drinks, both taking that first safe sip. "Mmm, God." Exclaimed Rachel as she drank her Chai. "Seriously, Terry, I've been drinking these for years, but like, what do y'all put in this?"

"For real. This place has the best damn coffee I've ever had. Hands down. Oralgasm!" Erin so graciously added.

Terry coughed out a laugh. "Lili is the mad scientist." She answered, regaining her composure. "You'd have to ask her. I just work the machines how she trained me."

Ally grabbed her Milas, "So this Lili, she's the manager?"

"Manager, barista, bus girl. You name it. She and her husband Marc own the place, but she works it mainly. He has his job, not entirely sure what. Their family's into all kinds of work, must be nice too 'cause they've been on vacation all summer. They go pretty much every year from what I gather."

"So she hasn't been here since we have?" Erin quizzed.

"Nope. Gets back, um, Sunday, I think?"

"Damn, must be nice."

"Chyeah! Especially when your husband's hotter than the steam in this place."

"Shut up." Rach doubted.

Ally's friends had been waiting all summer for this, finally moving out of the country to start a real adult life and meet someone sophisticated. Suave, sexy fantasies were all Ally had heard about the past three months, but Ally couldn't help feeling it was a bit of a put-on. She had no interest in adding any males to her equation, and she was in no rush to plunge her life into a serious relationship. Erin and Rachel talked like they did, but neither seemed to be making any effort.

Denise had caught on by then, "Ladies, he is completely gorgeous. Their whole family is. Just wait till you see Lili. She'll make you question your womanhood and your preferences all at once. Don't let their charm rope you in, though." Her voice carried a sense of motherly wisdom as she spoke. "They're all a bit rough around the edges."

The three couldn't help thinking there was much more to that statement. The friends were listening so attentively they completely forgot about their drinks. What Terry said next only fanned the flame.

"Rough around the edges is one way to put it." She began. "A family of ghosts is probably more fitting. Sure, all their family and friends are gorgeous. Guess money does buy looks. That or good-looking people get rich. I'm not sure which yet. Anyways, they all stop by from time to time, but four of them live here for the most part. So, you'll see them rather often. But seriously, all the erratic comings and goings, the random friends, family, business partners, or some combo of the three stopping by, and does anyone even know what 'business' they even do? I've worked here over two years, and I still don't know what all their family does besides this place."

"Going on three for me," Denise added with a smile, "and I couldn't tell you either."

"Yeah, rough around the edges is just the tip of the iceberg." Terry started back in a playful tone.

"I could handle a little roughness if I had to, though," Denise replied with a mischievous tone. "Just makes it more interesting. Beautiful, nice people with lots of money are boring without a little mystery. Most of them are too young for a keeper, but I'd give 'em a trial run." Said Denise, her smile turning mischievous for a bit. "I wouldn't want to hear that speech from Lili, though, so don't go getting any bright ideas, girls. There are plenty of worthwhile people to make friends with within this city, trust me. The Browning family is probably best left alone."

"We'll take your word on that." Ally said earnestly.

With that, they all grabbed their drinks and headed towards the door. Rachel and Erin instantly started discussing what the next week would be like the moment they left the shop. All Ally could think about was surviving the day, but part of her mind kept drifting to the strange family they were soon to meet.

They hopped in the car to head towards campus, and Ally began pouring back over her class lists and map while Rachel and Erin continued. They had already walked around campus the week before so they wouldn't look like first-year students walking around lost on the first day, but she still wanted a refresher. The girls all decided to pursue their graduate degrees in history together after the first two years into their undergraduates. It was something that interested them all and had such a variety of topics that they'd never run out of things to study. That was one core thread that tied the three together. They pined for knowledge. No amount of information was ever enough for them.

Not knowing yet on which field of history they would prefer to focus on, the girls entered grad school, taking a sampling of different topics that could work for whichever majors or electives they later chose. They'd discussed each course at length in setting up their schedules, and while they worried if they had taken on too much, they couldn't decide a class to give up. So, their schedule was set with History of Imperialism, Topics in European History, Asian History, and the one they were most excited for, History through War.

So many people they knew were bored by history, but they always found it fascinating and couldn't learn enough. None of them had fully decided yet what they would do with their degrees. They had discussed teaching, possibly museum curation, or even becoming actual historians. The one thing they knew was that they wanted to play a role in chronicling the story of humanity.

With a proper stroke of luck, they managed to get all their classes in the Monday, Wednesday, Friday blocks, so they had Tuesdays and Thursdays to study or do homework, or hopefully have some free time. As such, they had missed the official first day of school on Thursday, but the campus was just as busy nonetheless. The first day of class in college was even more laidback than high school was for them. Everyone knew they wouldn't be doing any work as the professor passed out the course syllabi and covered the schedules for the semester. That was for undergraduates, though. The three were anxious about what the first day would be like of "real classes," as they kept referring to them.

Much to their relief, though, the first two classes went by reasonably smoothly; a little more discussion about the nature of the course and what all they would cover, some simple introductory assignments over the weekend to get them started, but nothing too daunting.

The girls were most relieved to have a schedule of classes they truly cared about finally. They'd hated the layout of their core requirements so much in their first four years that they had purposefully scattered them out each semester. The need for such classes aggravated them, as they couldn't see how it helped them prepare for life after school. This was different though. Every class mattered, helped further their journey. As such, before they knew it, they were over halfway through their first day and heading to the cafeteria for lunch.

"Ok, can we agree that our bet on History of Imperialism being the toughest class paid off, at least thematically?" Erin asked.

"Yeah, that one is going to be a real struggle with what civilizations have done throughout the past," Rachel replied. "I mean, like, I feel like I'm going to be constantly debating in my head on where you draw the line on intervening in other people's situations in my own life."

"Same." Said Ally with a laugh. "I know both our Topics courses will be informative and all, but I feel like that one, and hopefully History through War will really get me thinking."

"I wonder how History through War is going to go," Erin added. "Cause with Imperialism it's 'of Imperialism' not 'through Imperialism.' So, History through War obviously won't be just general observations of war. Right? Am I way overthinking this?"

Rachel and Ally both chuckled. "Maybe."

Rachel continued, "We'll find out in a bit, though. It's that time, ladies."

Their first three classes had been in one of the campus' newer buildings, but History through War was on the next block nestled near the main road running by campus. It was in an older, more unique building that stood against the crisp, newly built ones. High arched windows and sharp peaks gave it a gothic look that was only heightened by the big oak tree out front and the curved staircase leading up to it, completing the haunted house of classes facade. Inside, they made their way upstairs to a small auditorium that looked like a vintage theatre with no balcony. There were enough seats to hold about fifty, but the students numbered closer to fifteen.

The girls took chairs somewhat in the middle, trying not to look too much like know-it-alls by sitting in the front or too much like slackers by sitting in the back. Blending in was Ally's secret talent, and she had perfected it. Following the trend of the other classes, they took out their binders, ready to receive a syllabus and take notes on any extra course-related items. Looking around, though, she noticed no other students had done such. Their bags were all zipped or latched, and they were just sitting attentively.

Suddenly Ally caught movement in the right corner of her eye and turned to see a youthfully vibrant-looking middle-aged man walking down the aisle. He appeared somewhere between thirty and forty with closely cropped hair, a salt and pepper goatee, and deep green eyes set behind thin rectangle framed glasses. The man wore a slate grey pair of slacks with a rich eggplant purple sweater over a matching slate grey button-up. As he reached the podium, he set his laptop bag at the base and immediately jumped into his lesson.

"What was the first war ever recorded?" He asked, leaving a trail of his British accent as he paused. "No one? I am Professor Charles Edmonton. Call me what you will. Professor, Charles, Chuck, Mr. Teacher Man; makes no difference to me. This class, however, is called History through War for a reason. We are going to work our way through humanity's timeline by covering major wars that shaped it. Naturally, we won't be covering every war, or we'd be in this class for the rest of our natural-born lives and possibly into whatever afterlife still studies war. No, we will be progressing through defining wars that shaped the world demographically, culturally, and politically. This is not your basic history class, so I do not expect basic students."

He paused for another moment studying the class. He knew right away, as did the girls, that no one in the audience took his words lightly. Everyone in the room knew what they were getting themselves into, everyone except the three friends sitting in the middle of the lecture hall.

"You will have a considerable amount of work to do outside of class, and hopefully, like your other classes, this work will matter. There will be no 'tests' this year, and your final will be a paper on a war of your choosing. The majority of your grade, aside from your final, will be from in-class participation and outside-of-class research. So, I ask you again, what was the first war ever recorded?"

No hands went up, but instead, one student, two rows up and a few seats down from them, answered, "The first known war to be recorded was some time around 2700 B.C.E. between Sumer and Elam. There had been constant fighting between tribes and city-states throughout the existence of the human race before that, of course, but this war was the first to be documented or at least documented and not lost."

"Thank you, sir. Surely this was common knowledge to most all of you in here, but I think I've made my point on how much your participation will count. While you are correct, this is not the first war we are going to discuss. No matter how many of you may or may not believe in it, we will be starting our semester with the war between God and the angels who were cast out of Heaven."

The mood in the room shifted a bit. No one seemed bothered but somewhat just confused by the development. Ally herself wasn't sure why he was taking this approach. Not that she had anything against it, nor did she figure Erin and Rachel would. They had all been raised in church, more or less. Even they felt it odd to have a history class start here, though.

"This will be a short section, I promise, just a lift-off for our class to get the mental gears turning. So, this weekend your assignment is to read *Paradise Lost* by John Milton. I don't care if you go buy the book, read it on the Internet, or however you want to go about it. Just get to a point where you feel comfortable talking about it. We will discuss it in class Monday and touch on some supporting pieces from the Christian Bible Wednesday, and then we'll start Sumer and Elam Friday. That's all for today. Everyone is free to leave."

Everyone grabbed their bags and began to stand up when he spoke again, "Oh, everyone except Allyxandria Carver, Erin Cartwright, and Rachel Harrison, that is. If you three would please meet me up here before you leave. I would like to speak with you briefly. That is all."

Ally's entire body tensed to the point it ached. Erin and Rachel met each other's frozen gaze. Why were they being called to stay after class and on the first day at that? They were terrified. What could he possibly have wanted to talk to them about so soon?

Everyone else made for the door as the friends grabbed their bags, tossed them over their shoulder, and headed to the front, swallowing the lumps in their throats as they did.

"I'm Erin." She said softly, taking the lead.

"And I'm Rachel, and this is Ally," Rachel added, gesturing to herself and Ally in kind. "You wanted to talk to us."

"Yes, ma'am. Thank you each for coming up. I hope I did not frighten you. I merely wanted to explain the nature of your situation. This is actually a doctoral-level course. Only graduate students under special permission as part of their theses are typically allowed to take this class, and even that is on rare occasions. To be frank, I am not quite sure how you three slipped through the cracks, but you are certainly not supposed to be in here."

Ally's gaze shifted, and her shoulders slumped a bit. Erin pushed her hands deeper in her pockets, trying not to feel defeated. Even Rachel's typical optimistic acquiescence seemed to waiver. Here they were about to get kicked out of class on the first day of school. How would they explain this to everyone? What would this do for their scholarships and grants? They had been so excited for History through War.

"Relax." Professor Edmonton said with a warming nod of understanding. "I'm not dropping you. Not yet, at least. As this class runs through the Fall and Spring semesters, it could potentially be used towards your theses in your final year or towards your doctorate should you choose that path. As such, I am going to give you each the opportunity to prove you can handle it. I will not be any lighter on you than I am on any other student, though. You will be expected to do just as much work, and if you do start slipping, I will promptly remove you from the course. It would be for your own good to keep it from affecting your transcript. Should that be the case, you would always be welcome back in a couple years when you feel ready. Do I make myself clear?"

"Yes, sir." The three girls replied in unison.

"Good. That's what I like to hear. Go on now, get out of here and enjoy your weekend." He said with a soft smile.

The friends nodded in agreement and turned towards the door. When they were about halfway out of the room, he spoke again. "And Ladies," they turned to face him, "I would highly recommend you get with some of the doctoral students to help you study with this one. You're going to need it."

"Thanks. Will do." Erin said for the group. With that, three exited the room and headed for the car in complete silence.

The three girls said nothing as they headed back to the house, each struggling in their own way. None of them wanted to be dropped from the class. This was the one course they'd been set on from when they first looked at the graduate catalog. *How had they even been able to register?* They each wondered to themselves.

Before too much time could pass, Ally's phone rang, taking them out of their dazed state.

"It's my mom." She said to the others as she answered her phone. "It's a good thing class didn't run late on the first day, Mom."

Despite her soured mood, she couldn't help smiling at the sound of her mom's voice.

"Oh yeah, didn't really think about that, but obviously it didn't. So, how's your day?"

"It's pretty good." She said, trying not to let her frustration show. "I mean, I can't say much about the classes since they just started, but they seem really interesting so far. How's life there?"

"Oh, pretty good. Been living it up since you left! Wild parties, staying out all night, you know, empty-nester stuff." Her mom gave a silly chuckle. "Took Lace for a walk after work. We just got back in. She misses you, sits in your room a lot, waiting for you to come home."

"Seriously, Mom, you can't tell me that. I already miss home as it is."

"Sorry. I know you're homesick, but you'll be back to visit soon. Don't let it get to you. Go enjoy the rest of your day. I just wanted to check in on you. Text me later, ok?"

"Yes, ma'am."

"Love you."

"Love you too, Mom."

Ally felt her eyes begin to water as she hung up the phone. She hated being so far from her mother. Not wanting to make the tears worse, she decided just to send Mimi a text saying her first day went well and asked her to tell Pops she loved him instead of calling. She did the same with Thad, but more because he didn't like phone calls than because of the tears. Her phone buzzed in reply from Thad just as Nick and Matt both texted asking if she was coming home for the weekend. It actually made her happy at how simple they were. No heartfelt expositions, just friends wanting to hang out. She wouldn't have them any other way. With heavy sadness, though, she typed a quick message back that she wouldn't be home until the following weekend and rubbed her eyes to clear the tears that were building.

"So, we're going to grab our books and get started on our homework right away, yeah?" Erin asked to break up the silence.

"Pass." Said Rachel, the second Erin finished.

"Hard Pass." Laughed Ally. "Friday night is for twitchy trigger fingers. Not epic poems about antiquity or divine order."

"Yeah, yeah, yeah. Well, you're not staying on there all night. We're going out and doing something tonight at least." Rachel stated.

"Fine..." Ally said, feigning resentment. She would get back online after they got home anyways. "Anything specific, or are we just winging it?"

"I'm thinking a movie downtown and maybe a pizza or three," Rachel suggested. "Sound good to you, Erin?"

"Suits me."

"Movies it is then." Ally said. "Before we get back to the apartment, though, I need a coffee."

"To The Daily Brew!" Erin said with mock bravado, striking a superhero pose.

2
HISTORY THROUGH WAR

Before the girls knew, the following Monday had arrived to the incessant blaring of their alarms. The weekend had flown by, and they had tried their best to make use of it. On Saturday, after stopping by The Brew, they dropped into the bookstore to grab copies of *Paradise Lost*. Eight dollars out of each of their pockets, and after about seven pages, they were all reading Wikipedia summaries and linking sources because they couldn't understand the actual poem.

They spent the rest of the weekend pouring over information to ensure they didn't look like idiots in the next class and risk sliding closer to the drop list. After two days of sharing notes and talking it through, the girls finally felt comfortable enough to answer questions without panicking, as they called it a night on Sunday. That didn't take the sting out of the six o'clock alarm, though, as each of them fought to get out of bed.

Getting up early so they could sit and have coffee for a bit was a motion Ally's brain supported, but, apparently, one her body did not as she stumbled to the bathroom, struggling to keep her eyes open. Quickly the morning routine began, though. Straightening her hair and putting on her makeup, she raced to get ready, and soon all the girls were downstairs and headed out the door.

The moment they exited the door, the crisp wind sent chills over the three.

"This must be the weather everyone talked about." Rachel said. "The clouds look like rain. God, it has to be like at least twenty degrees colder than last week."

"It's not freezing yet like they said, but it's only the end of August," Erin added. "If it keeps up like this, it'll be one cold-ass fall, and I don't even wanna think about winter."

"Yeah, it's gonna be cold as balls before we know it at this rate." Ally said. "I can smell the rain in the air, too. Did anyone check the radar? Should we grab our coats?"

Rachel had her phone out quick as a whip. "Nothing showing for me. Guess the clouds are just the precursor."

They were at The Brew in what seemed like no time at all. Each day the walk there felt quicker and quicker. Ally figured they were just getting accustomed to the walk. She certainly was not accustomed to The Daily Brew, however, as they rounded the corner to see its gorgeous blue awnings. It was the day they had talked about all weekend between study sessions. The girls paused for a moment, an air of nervousness settling over each of them. They then made their way across the street to meet the Brownings.

As the three girls approached the door, two new figures could be seen at the far left side of the counter. The girls held their breath as they opened the door to see a most beautiful young couple standing at the left side of the counter. The couple couldn't have been older than their late twenties or early thirties, yet they both had such a mature air even at first glance. It felt like they could have just as easily been Ally's parents as they could be her peers.

Marc stood a few inches shy of six feet with short dark hair cut in a close-cropped military look, dressed in a tailored suit of dark grey that complimented his smooth olive skin. Lili stood beside him, every bit his equal. The baristas had not exaggerated in the slightest. Her deep brown, near-black hair fell a few inches below her shoulders in the most subtle of waves. She was maybe six inches shorter than Marc, with her head just even with his shoulders. Her golden skin shone brilliant against her navy dress and complemented perfectly with the cream knit shawl she had over it. Together they looked like polished stone as if they were ancient statues brought to life. Lili stood next to him but at the same time was somehow part of him, as if they were one being.

They turned harmoniously to acknowledge the friends as they approached the counter. The sight the girls witnessed caused their breath to catch in their throats; it was their eyes. Their eyes were the same rich, deep, entrancing blue as The Brew's. A blue so pure and brilliant it looked as if God himself had taken a brush and painted their irides with the most brilliant blue watercolor in painstaking detail.

Their faces were like smooth porcelain that then broke into a smile. Marc's warrior-like armor seemed to shatter as his smile lit up the room, only to be matched by Lili's floral glow radiating warmth. This must have been the charm of which Denise and Terry spoke. Marc and Lili looked to be the nicest, most inviting people on the planet where just a second before a magnificent fortress had stood.

By the time Ally, Rachel, and Erin reached the counter, they had managed to wrench their eyes away from Marc and Lili as they went back to talking. *They were far enough away that if Ally and the others spoke quietly, Marc and Lili wouldn't be able to hear them*, they thought. So, amidst their ordering, they tried to slip in some small talk with Terry and Denise.

"Usual today, girls?" Terry asked with a grin.

"That sudden temp drop has me too damn cold for an iced drink today, Terry," Erin said. "You're going to have to make mine a regular Caffe Americano."

"What about you two? Swapping yours also?"

Ally and Rachel both nodded. Then they all three leaned in a bit closer to the counter and lowered their voices to a whisper. "So that's them, yeah?" Rachel started.

Denise leaned over, "Yep. Did we lie?"

"Not at all." Ally answered. "They're stunning. Do they always look like they stepped out of a painting or some courtyard fountain?"

"Every damn day," Terry said. "It's a bit infuriating, really. I've tried my hardest to look like that. It's just not happening."

"Oh hush, sweetie. You look lovely, and ya know it." Denise added. "They both smiled at you. That's pretty rare. Not them smiling necessarily. They just don't typically do so on first seeing someone. I've never seen them do that before."

"You mean they don't smile like that toward all the customers that come in?" Erin asked.

"Nope," Terry answered. "They're pretty reserved like we said. Lili does when she's working, of course. I mean, that's basic customer service, and Marc always smiles at us when he comes in, which makes working really hard sometimes, I might add. I overflowed two different lattes just this morning when he came in. That's nothing though, last semester, he came in one day and..."

"Terry, shush." Denise tried to stress her whisper as hard as she could. "They're not that far away. Goodness, gracious."

"Sorry." Terry giggled. "I get a little carried away. Anyways, y'all go have a seat, and we'll have your drinks out for you in a bit."

They all smiled and pulled themselves away from the counter, then made their way to their usual table. All of them looked like they were in a trance from Marc and Lili, and now they were all baffled, to top it off.

"Why did they smile at us?" Said Rachel, voicing all of their thoughts.

"Um, because I'm the tits. Hello? Have you met me?" Erin joked.

"OK, Erin. At least they like us, I guess...maybe." Ally said. "Oh shit. Game faces. Here they come."

They all tried to straighten up and look as pleasant as possible. The anxiety practically oozed off them and onto the table. Ally feared they would see right through her façade and know she was no one worth a smile.

Lili spoke first as Marc sat down, balancing three hot mugs like a veteran waiter. "Let us see, we have a Caffe Americano for Ms. Erin, a Stoni for Ms. Rachel, and it looks like a Milas for Ms. Ally. Does that sound about right?" Her voice was so soft and caring that of a mother's with only the faintest touch of a southern drawl coating an accent the friends had never heard before.

The girls all glanced at each other to see who would speak first. "Yes, ma'am. That's us." Ally finally said, partly in shock that she was the one who spoke up.

Marc spoke with a voice that sounded wise well beyond his years, "So Denise and Terry, tell us that you are our new regulars. How do you ladies find the place?"

It was like a young boy had been thrust into the military at the heat of war and came out a man far earlier than his peers. The girls were in a stunned silence till Erin spoke up, "It's awesome. Like really awesome. We basically come here like every day now. I've never seen a coffee shop like this."

"We are glad you like it so," Lili's voice rang softly in their ears. "Marc and I have worked very hard to create a unique and enjoyable experience here. It is always nice to see such satisfied guests."

"She gives me too much credit," Marc sincerely added, looking towards Lili with a smirk. "She is the one who works herself exhausted running this place. I am just here to help out once in a while."

Rachel finally found her voice, "Well, you've done a wonderful job.

We love the place."

"Thank you. Marc and I will let you ladies enjoy your drinks. Don't be afraid to ask if you need anything at all." That last phrase lingered in Ally's ears as Lili made eye contact with her. In that instant, Ally knew she meant just that. That Ally would be able to come to them with anything, and Ally somehow had a feeling she would be doing that a lot.

The two walked back to the counter and helped Terry and Denise prepare a few more orders while the girls sipped on their drinks. Then all of a sudden, Marc and Lili gave the slightest look towards each other, then the clock, and then said something to Terry and Denise as they began prepping two new orders.

Ally and the girls turned their heads towards the door and could see two figures approaching through the tint. They all thought these individuals must be their most consistent regulars if Marc and Lili both had the time they came in down.

The first individual came through the door and immediately stole the attention of everyone in the room without anyone even having to look his way. He was very tall and lean, with a regal presence about him so unfitting a man his age. He looked no more than his late twenties but yet seemed like someone you'd expect to be in parliament or running a Fortune 500 company. His blonde hair was all laid back, revealing a solid jaw and prominent cheekbones.

He wore a smile that looked so natural to him that Ally wondered if he ever took it off. His clothes were a bit loud and flashy at first glance, but it would have been weird to see him in anything else upon looking at him. With a pair of jeans custom-fitted for him and a bright green shirt with a colorful image of Mozart wailing away on an electric violin, he stood out from everyone in the room yet felt like he still belonged to the Brew's menagerie.

It wasn't until Ally saw his eyes that his place became apparent. A rich blue pair of eyes that even Eli would say looked beautiful were staring straight over at their table. *This was clearly what Terry and Denise were talking about*, the girls thought. A glance at the two confirmed it. Here stood this family they believed to be so captivating yet unobtainable, and the girls could see it as well. They were, all of them, beautiful beyond explanation, but at the same time, anyone could sense that roughness about them, an intense unapproachable aura that bordered on terrifying.

As soon as he turned his entrancing eyes and stunning smile away, the girls were lost. "Wow." Said Erin. "Just wow. I got nothin'."

"Yeah," said Rachel, "Adonis. He is some…." but before she could finish her statement, they were silenced again as the fourth member of the family walked in just behind the blonde-haired man.

This one differed from the rest of the family. He didn't request attention or admiration like the others. Something about him silently commanded it. It was as if a king had just entered a room full of lords, and his features were just as noble. His long hair fell onto his shoulders in deep brown waves of perfection, giving the appearance of a lion's mane that was the head of his pride. His smooth but strong jaw spoke clearly of his pedigree, and his cheekbones reflected such. His skin was paler than that of his family but with a golden glow that seemed almost unnatural, and yet he dressed in a manner that both complemented and disguised it. He wore a bespoke three-piece suit of smooth sterling grey with a matching grey-and-white striped button-up pulled together with a pearl white tie giving him a monochromatic look as if he were carved from stone.

Again, though, it was the eyes that set this individual apart the most, not just from the other customers but even from his family. They were not the brilliant blue of the other three but rather a near-white grey, which melded with his suit and skin tone. It was almost as if they had no color at all. Instead, what was so captivating about his eyes was the dark silvery glow around his eyelids. Scanning his family, the friends saw none of the others had this. He was the only one with this beautiful but empty glow; the Man in Grey.

This man did not smile as the first did, though he did not look at all upset or bothered. Instead, his face and his eyes looked like those that had seen bitter defeat and glorious victory, as they had been through war, death, and the deepest of betrayals and found themselves on the other side. Not the eyes of a man possessed, but of a man consumed.

Upon reaching the counter, he turned to Marc and Lili, and his stark expression gave way to a slight grin that sent chills down girls' spines and made them gasp for breath.

The men's drinks were already made, and Denise handed them over. The blonde man spoke first with such proper speech and utter charm and with a faint hint of some undetectable accent, "Thank you, Terry. You are as always a welcome vision to start the day." He continued to smile as Terry turned a bright shade of pink.

"As are you, Win." She said formally, smiling as widely as her lips would allow.

The other man didn't speak but simply gave her a very gracious nod and grinned once more. Taking their drinks, they headed over to the far left table that had always previously remained unoccupied.

"Ok, girls. Enough googly-eyed shit. We have class." Ally said as they all slowly came back to reality.

"No googly eyes here. Just getting some properly detailed files saved to the memory banks in case I need them on a cold, lonely night." Erin said, tapping her temple in reference.

Ally choked on her coffee, trying not to spit it out.

"No shit." Rach agreed. "Like seriously, what's the socially acceptable amount of time to wait after moving to the city before you set up a Tinder?"

"I just can't with you two." Ally chuckled, draining the last of her drink but stealing a fleeting glance at the two men.

The three grabbed their bags, but Lili stopped at their tableside with more drinks as they turned to get up.

"Hold on now, ladies," Lili spoke softly. "There is no reason why you cannot take a drink with you." Placing the go cups down on the table in front of their proper owner, she gave them a warm, knowing smile and a curt nod.

With that, she turned and walked away, and the three girls threw their bags over their shoulders and headed towards the door. There was an odd sense of protectiveness and awareness about Lili, coalesced with the family's reserved persona that gave the girls pause. Almost as if she knew what the three were thinking, but somehow she still seemed like she meant well. Everyone is protective of their families. This family, however, was something especially peculiar, and the girls could sense it.

The first three classes blurred, and lunch was spent in the student center instead of the cafeteria. The girls said nothing but rather sat in silence, deep in thought. Each of them had questions they wanted to ask, ideas in their heads they couldn't quite put into words, and none could find a way to voice them. In what felt like only a few moments since they arrived at the campus, they were already walking into History through War, taking the same seats as the previous time and getting out their binders to take notes. This time though, the other students were likewise. Mr. Edmonton made his way down the aisle and to the front of the room.

"So, everyone enjoyed our dear friend Milton's work, I presume?" He began with a brief pause for reaction. "No enthusiastic roar? No cheers from the crowd? Very well then, let's hear your thoughts."

One student in the front row bravely spoke up, "Well, religious connotations aside, I think it honestly represents the basis of many battles or wars."

"And that is?"

"Servitude and oppression. At the heart of most wars rests one side who believes they either are wrongfully subservient to the other or fear becoming subservient. On the other side, we see a group who thinks they are not oppressing the others but, rather, just doing what is right. In the American Revolution, the colonies believed they were being forced to serve England. England, however, thought they were treating them just as they did their own in Great Britain. You look at the expansion of the Mongol empire. The lands they invaded essentially became subservient, albeit with a bit more systematic approach to brainwashing said population. In World War I and II, we saw one alliance rise up that wanted to rule over the world, and another coalition formed that felt the former's rule would be unjust, and they would not be forced to serve in it. Same as we saw in Milton's work, rule or serve."

"That is one take. Very astute. Does anyone else have anything to add?"

Another student, a few seats down from the friends, began, "I think it also shows, as we all well know, the most common fact of history. The victors write the history books. Be it literal or metaphorical, we all know what the outcome of this 'war' was. We know which side wins, and thus we know how our world's history has been shaped in reflection, as many other wars have done so. There's no way of telling what pieces of our world's history have been lost because they were destroyed in the process of conquest or insurrection. The winner tells the story. That's how it goes."

"Another sharp take. Any other thoughts on the matter?"

"In agreement with what Nathan said," a young woman sitting next to the boy who spoke first began, "it shows really the basis for not just most wars, but all. Servitude may be at the heart of a lot of disagreements, but at the heart of them, all is belief. When one side believes something strongly enough, be it that they have the right to certain lands or dominance over a group of people or that they're in fact the ones being oppressed by the former example, and another side has an opposing belief sooner or later there's bound to be conflict."

"Bloody brilliant! I am going to love this class. All excellent points and, coincidentally, the main points I wanted to be made. Now I pose this question to you courtesy of Milton, is it better to serve in Heaven or rule in Hell? Now I don't mean in the literal sense. We're certainly not going to get into a religious debate. I mean, in the essence of the phrase itself, is it better to be a cog in the wheel of a great place, so to speak, or to be a so-called ruler in a lesser one, and by whose belief is one better than the other."

Suddenly a voice spoke up from the back of the room. It wasn't until hearing this voice against the professor's that the Welsh undertone became clear in Win's voice, "The true nature of the dilemma is not so much is it better to rule than to serve as it is, is to rule actually to serve."

The whole class turned to study the young man's profound statement and eagerly awaited what he said next. The girls turned as well, noticing that he was not alone. His brother sat next to Win, looking both attentive yet completely disinterested as if he'd heard this a thousand times before.

"Do elaborate, Win." Professor Edmonton said.

"By serving someone, you are meeting their needs and thus are their enabler, their source of power. In ancient times, many races worshiped the sun and the rain because they provided for their needs. One could say that the sun and rain were servants to those people as they provided the people's necessities, yet are they not also their ruler as they are the name in which the people worship. Throughout history, power has often been determined by the skill and number of a nation's military forces. Those soldiers who were in 'servitude' of their nation, are they not also the country's rulers in truth, as the nation's fate rests in their hands? In Christianity, Judaism, and Islam, a single deity serves the human race, giving them what they need and keeping them safe, yet that god is their ruler as well. So is to serve not to rule? Even in our modern times, people refer to elected officials as public servants, yet they are the ones who create the laws by which the citizens must all abide and even enforce said legislation. So are those public servants not then ruling over the population? Alternatively, as we've seen throughout history, the 'serving' class is typically more numerous than the 'ruling' one. When they realize the nature of their power and how they provide for the supposed ruler, they rise in revolt. Milton's work is not just a look into the archangel's tragic downfall. It is also a profound introspection of the human condition, posing questions about the power structures they create and the importance they place on said structures."

"A very insightful statement on the nature of power, indeed, Win," Edmonton said. "Does anyone have any comments on this? Anything they'd like to add?"

No one spoke up, so Edmonton continued discussing different aspects of Milton's Fall view. The girls took notes as best they could, trying not to lose themselves in the complexities of war. It was becoming evident very quickly this class was going to be more work than they were expecting.

"So, we're in agreement that Brew Boys are going to be our new study buddies, yeah?" Erin whispered to the other two.

"Edmonton did say to get help." Ally responded in an effort of nonchalance.

"I probably would've considered it without the impressive monologue, so I'm game," Rachel added, looking down at her notes to hide her whispering.

"Guess we know what we're doing after class then," Erin said

"Now, your assignment for tonight and tomorrow," Professor Edmonton said before the three even realized class was nearing a close, "is to briefly read the first few chapters of the book of Genesis. Skim through it, and then do some reading of the Second Book of Enoch and look up the stories of Inanna and Hattar online. These are all various takes on the so-called Fall. We will discuss the 'winner's' point of view on Wednesday and then jump right into Sumer vs. Elam, the heavyweight bout that began them all. Now get out of here! Go do whatever it is you do." Edmonton said with the wave of his hand.

On that queue, everyone took their leave. As the girls stood up and turned around, Win and Joshua were nowhere to be seen. They rushed out the door in an attempt to catch them, paying no regard to the spectacle they might be making. They needed help with that class, and those two seemed the most knowledgeable; at least, that's how they rationalized it. They knew something was odd about the family, but something in their collective consciousness overrode the warnings.

Hustling out the front doors, the girls scanned the horizon looking for the two men in the growing crowd, and without a word, the three split in opposite directions immediately. Heading along the left side of the building, Ally saw a head of blonde hair striding through the crowd and a near black mane atop a grey blazer next to him well in the distance at the end of the next hall as they rounded the corner.

She broke into a near jog crossing the campus, making it to the edge of the building where she last saw them. *What the hell am I thinking?* Kept echoing in her head. It was just one day of class, and she could see them Wednesday to ask. Rounding the corner, Ally saw the east parking lot with cars parked everywhere, countless ones coming and going. There was no hope of finding them that day. They would just have to wait and fall that much more behind.

Having a class-free day the following day didn't take away Ally's ingrained habit of waking up early. She pulled herself out of bed, did her morning routine, and headed for the door.

As Ally reached the door, it burst open, and a sweaty Rachel barreled into her, sending them both crashing onto the floor. Rachel pulled herself upright to look at Ally, pulling her headphones from her ears. "Whoa. Where are you off to so early? It's like two hours before your normal launch."

"I have to do some of that reading today, so I thought I'd head down to The Brew and have some coffee while I do."

"With you one hundred percent. If you can hold off for like fifteen minutes while I clean up, I'd be glad to tag along."

"Sure. I'll jump on and play a few matches while I wait."

"Cool deal. Want to see if Erin wants to join?"

Just then, the blaring of an alarm was halted by the sound of plastic crushing against hardwood.

"Never mind. We'll just fill her in."

A little more than an hour later and both girls were on their computers waiting for their coffee. They each pulled up different sites looking through stuff for their class, but both stopped what they were doing when Lili brought their drinks.

"Here are your drinks, a Milas and a Stoni, and how are we today?"

"Doing fine," Rachel said. "Um, I know y'all normally do free refills and all, but we're actually going to be here for quite a while today. Like maybe all day. Can we go ahead and pay for a few more drinks?"

"Do not even worry about it, dear. You may have as many refills as you please."

"Wow. Thanks."

"Mm. Double that." Said Ally as she swallowed her first sip. "So hey um, are your brothers going to be by today by chance? They're in one of our classes, and we could kinda use some help. Like a lot."

"They came through earlier this morning before their lessons. It is unlikely that they will be back through as they normally just go home or out to do things afterward." Lili said, sounding both sympathetic and a bit relieved.

"Oh. Ok. Makes sense." Ally replied, trying to mask her frustration.

"They will be here tomorrow, of course. What is the class?"

"Uh, it's a history course that covers world history as shaped by major wars that occurred."

"Ah, that is definitely one on which they would be knowledgeable. Our family is pretty big into historical events. That is, mostly, why we have the loft, in fact. It is full of history books, classical literature, basically any old writing that we could obtain. It is a bit of a family hobby, but those two go above and beyond. They are walking libraries."

"Awesome!" Rachel exclaimed. "You think they'd be up for helping some struggling students? The reading alone in this class is as much as our other courses combined."

"I would not want to speak on their behalf, but if I know my siblings, they likely will not pass on the chance to talk history with anyone. You fancy them, do you not?"

Ally froze as if caught in a trance. Rachel gagged ever so slightly on her coffee and did her best to recover and react calmly.

"You and your friend Erin?"

"Oh no, ma'am." Rachel began with a sputter. "They just seem like cool people, is all. I mean, y'all seem like cool people. Like, all of you. Yeah, I mean sure they're hot and all, and I'm sure they're nice, it's just not like that kind of liking. You know?" Rachel exhaled deeply. "Let me just stop."

Rachel looked away from Lili and stared at her coffee mug, trying to hide her embarrassment.

"Relax, relax," Lili said with a chuckle. "I meant no harm by it. On the contrary, your words and thoughts of my family are rather refreshing. Very few people look past our image to see us as kindred spirits. So, that you would feel that way about us is very kind. You may fancy or not fancy anyone you please, and if you wish your feelings to remain private, that is your prerogative. Mum's the word. I only asked out of curiosity and perhaps mild caution."

Ally jumped, in an effort to end the situation, "And that is totally understandable. They're your brothers, after all, so looking out for them is kinda part of the job. Our interests really are purely academic. Well, except maybe Erin." She added with an awkward giggle. "There's really no telling with her."

Lili smiled ambiguously, "While I appreciate your candor, you mistake my intentions. It was more out of caution for you ladies. Joshua and Win are more than capable of handling their affairs, and I would not stand in the way of them or you or anyone in those endeavors. You, three ladies, seem like very nice people, though, and while they are cool and nice as you say, they are not the cool and nice people of which you might think. Suffice it to say, their journey has been an arduous one thus far, and as such, they, along with the rest of our family, carry a certain amount of baggage with them. I say none of this in an attempt to steer you away from them or us. I merely encourage you to tread carefully. You may be in for a grave deal more than you might expect."

She looked the girls over knowingly but gave them a calming and encouraging smile all the same.

"Now, I can see you have research to do. So, I will leave you ladies to it. Feel free to browse the books upstairs if you would like as well. We do have quite the collection, if I might say, so perhaps something up there might help you. There is a bit of seating up there if you want to take your drinks and read, and of course, let us know if you need anything. We are always here."

She floated back behind the counter, and when Rachel assumed Lili was out of earshot, she turned to Ally, "Ok, first off, was I that obvious, Ally? Don't lie to me."

"Only to like ninety-five, maybe ninety-six percent of the world's population." Ally laughed. "Nah, for real, though, you were fine. I would have been a damn trainwreck trying to respond to that. You saw me. All I could do was sit there like a deer in headlights."

"Shit, I probably would have been better off doing the same with you. Seriously though, what's up with them?"

"I don't know. Something's off, though. I wish Erin and Thad had been here for that. Normally my BS meter is top-notch, but I can't get a read on them at all."

"Time to call in the sleuth?"

Ally chuckled, relaxing a little, "Not yet. Let's just get through the first week before we go that far."

"Fair enough. Plus, we'll be home this weekend, so we can tell him then if we feel like it."

Ally didn't reply.

"Yep, yep. Well, want to check out the loft in the meantime?" Rachel asked with her best attempt at a mischievous grin.

"Hell yes!" Ally exclaimed. "Wait, we should at least text Erin. I know she won't want to miss this."

As if on cue, Erin walked into the Brew. She headed straight for their tables after Lili gestured to her to do so.

"Sorry for being so behind," Erin said, sliding into a chair. "Did I miss anything? You guys done all the research yet, so I don't have to worry with it?"

Ally and Rachel looked at one another, unsure where to begin or who should do so, opening and closing their mouths as they both began to speak but paused, uncertain what to say.

"Alright, Stephen King, no need for the added suspense." Erin quipped at their prolonged silence.

"Tell you what," Rachel began as she saw Erin's drink heading towards them, "that's a lot to answer, but how about you grab your drink, and we'll all go up to the loft, like Lili suggested to do some reading?"

Erin stared at the two in puzzlement as Lili sat her drink down.

"Hi there, Erin." Lili said with disarming charisma, "No doubt Rachel and Ally will catch you up on our little chat earlier. I promise I am just as ferocious as they make me seem, and I will most certainly be keeping my eye on you."

Lili gave Rachel and Ally a friendly wink as she turned away.

"Upstairs," Erin said, part command, part request.

Grabbing their drinks, the three headed upstairs to the loft without a word. Reaching the landing, they were taken aback by bookshelves that seemed to stretch a near hundred feet back from the coffee shop, each one filled to the brim. Mounted against the side of the first bookshelf was a small touchscreen kiosk that caught their attention. Approaching it, they saw it was a simple search engine interface.

"So what, we just Google what we're researching?" Erin asked, her confusion growing.

"Beats me." Rachel said. "This is both the most weird and least weird thing so far."

Ally walked to the kiosk and typed "Enoch" into the search bar. A list of books in which Enoch was referenced appeared with a connotation by each explaining whether they were available in the peculiar library and, if so, where to find them.

Erin looked at Rachel and Ally incredulously. "Ok, I missed something."

3
THE LONGEST WEEK

Rachel and Ally recounting their morning with Lili turned out to be the easy part after the girls overcame the strange coffee shop library experience that had them questioning even more about this bizarre family. Erin, however, was less confused by Lili as she was suspicious. A fact she reiterated after dinner that night.

"Ok, so let me get this straight." She began as if she hadn't already discussed it with them in detail. "Lili essentially is the sweetest, most helpful southern lady who gives you all kinds of praise and thanks and even some helpful advice about class, but then gives the least veiled warning ever about her brothers. Call me crazy, but that just has passive-aggressive manipulation written all over it. She's clearly trying to scare us off from their whole clique while coming off like she's all nice. I don't buy it."

"Look, Erin," Rachel began, "I get where you're coming from. Really, I do. If I was in your shoes, I'd be saying the same thing. You know that. We have a link like that, but you had to be there. You need to just read her. Even Ally, who pretty much only trusts us, didn't have any alarms going off."

"That so?" Erin asked.

"Honestly, yeah." Ally replied. "There's obviously something odd about them. I'll give you that, but whatever it is, it doesn't seem bad, per se. I don't get any negative vibes from them."

"Erin, would you feel better if we had Thad check them out?" Rachel offered.

"No," Erin replied sharply as she shifted uncomfortably. "I mean, don't worry about it right now. I'm getting ahead of myself. We don't have to bring Thad in on this."

The girls often joked that their friend Thaddeus was an undercover detective hiding out amongst their family and friends for some decade-long sting operation. Untrue as it may be, he did have an interesting knack for finding things, especially about people. It was nothing more than extensive practice with search engines and social media and enough coding experience to crack into places that wouldn't get him in any real trouble if he needed additional information. Anytime someone in their group wanted to know a person's story, though, Thad figured it out.

"As if he would mind." Ally responded with a scoff. "You know he eats this kinda shit up."

"Let's just fucking drop it, ok," Erin said, desperately wanting the conversation to be over. "I'm just overreacting. Look, y'all wanna watch a movie or something before we have to call it a night?"

Rachel and Ally exchanged fleeting glances. Something was clearly bothering Erin, but neither friend wanted to press the topic.

"I'm not sure I'm good for a movie." Ally said earnestly. "You know my bedtime is like 9:25. I'd be up for an episode or two, though."

"Rach?"

"I'm game."

"Bet!" Erin exclaimed.

The following day came all too early, and everyone in the apartment overslept. In a mad rush, they went through their morning rituals. Rachel missed her run and protein smoothie, Ally had to skip straightening her hair, and Erin didn't bother picking out any jewelry aside from putting on her favorite bracelet. The three bolted for the door, hoping to make it to The Brew and class in time.

At The Daily Brew, Terry and Denise were as friendly as ever, but Lili was not around. The three girls ordered their drinks to go, as they were already running late. Rachel had already scanned the room to see the empty table on the left of the shop and was then staring at the door to see who may walk in next. As they grabbed their drinks, she hesitated as Ally did in spirit. Knowing they couldn't dally, though, she joined the other two in, heading towards the door. The door swung open gracefully, and Rachel held her breath.

"Good morning, ladies. Not staying today?" Lili asked, catching them off guard.

"No, ma'am. Late for the bundle of effin joy that is History of Imperialism." Erin said with a hiss. She was always that pleasant with little sleep, whether she liked a person or not.

"Well, I am sorry that you must rush. I will not keep you, though. Have a wonderful day." Lili smiled beautifully as she stepped out of the three's way. Ally and Rachel didn't understand why Erin disliked her, but it didn't seem to phase Lili one bit.

They slipped in the back of the class, trying to go unnoticed. Again the lessons flew by, lunch came and went, and the friends made their way towards History through War with newfound vigor. Back in their seats, they felt ready to tackle the class as they pulled out their binders finally.

"Alright, historians, who wants to begin this class discussion with your impressions? Keep in mind how much participation matters, and don't think I'm unaware of who speaks up. Theology talk, go."

A boy a few seats down from the friends was the first to speak up this time, "Sir, full honesty, I'm confused why you had us read Genesis for this assignment. The Fall of the archangel and his followers isn't even mentioned. And as for Inanna and Attar, they're both mythological tales from when humankind was trying to understand our planetary systems and make that all make sense to fairly primitive minds."

"Ah. So, you found precisely the reason why I assigned this to you. You won't find hardly any reference to this event in the bible, certainly not in Genesis. In fact, the pieces most historians and theologians attribute to the story of the archangel's fall are in Ezekiel and Isiah and the book of Enoch, if only a few verses at that. As I'm sure, all of you who did your reading noticed very little detail given on the War in Heaven, except that the archangel was arrogant and betrayed God and thus was cast out. The mythological readings, as you said, were humans trying to explain things beyond their current comprehension. If we were to believe this event actually took place, is it not strange there is so little record of it in the Bible and so very little material referencing it outside of that? There are numerous other religious texts, not just from Judeo-Christian beliefs but even Hinduism, Buddhism, and countless other religious beliefs, that have real-world historical events that coincide with said beliefs. So why would such a monumental war have so few corroborating stories? And more importantly, why is this relevant?"

Win's voice sounded through the auditorium again, commanding respect. The friends turned to see. His brother sat next to him again, looking just as disinterested yet attentive as he had two days before. Joshua didn't have on a coat that day but instead wore a soft yellow button-up with a grey vest and a grey and white checkered tie. Win's bright yellow shirt, which complemented his brother's, stole the girls' eyes away, though, and they couldn't help admiring his grey blazer that matched his brother's vest giving the pair a uniform, though, casual appeal as if they'd both been chosen to model a new spring line.

"Well, sir, you might ask why the nature of evil itself is not explained at all throughout the Bible. Humans are presented with all the different sins they are not to commit, but even most of that comes through various translations and interpretations. In actuality, what description of the archangel's evil are they given? Very little. The vast majority of the Bible's lessons are taught or interpreted after the fact. Only very little of the book gives explicit instructions. The rest came afterward. Therefore, it is relevant because this example gives the human race its building block for the rest of its history. History and thus historians seek to record events as they are happening, but it is in attempting to explain the complexities of past events that purpose and rationale are placed."

"Eloquently put Win, and spot-on. Some of my favorite discussions with you and Joshua have centered around this very aspect. This class seeks to explore history through the wars that shaped it, but there is one simple truth at the heart of history itself. It does not matter the course or the topic; there is one absolute in history. It looks at the world in the past tense. No matter how clearly and concisely any given event is documented, regardless of its magnitude, the record itself will only be the canvas upon which what comes after is painted. We have all heard that hindsight is 20/20, of course. This phrase is often used in the context of our daily lives and simple human experiences. History, however, is not all that different. Historians are constantly trying to apply their knowledge and understanding to a given historical event, to better understand and explain the event. The truth of history's tales lies with those who tell them."

Ally, Rachel, and Erin had been confused since Edmonton had first assigned them the task of researching the angels' fall and what possible context it could have for studying history. As Win and Edmonton's words soaked in, though, they realized how the professor had worked to lay a foundation for their further research. The fact that the victors wrote history was true long before Churchill said it. Edmonton sought to stretch the classes thinking even further to understand that people working to chronicle said victories wrote the history books, and with that, they held the truth.

The class discussion continued, probing various aspects of human intervention into history as the three friends worked to chime in and take notes where they could. They tried to have their bags ready as quickly as they could, so when Edmonton was wrapping up, they'd be able to make a break for it and catch Joshua and Win. "Ok, class. That will be enough for the day. You have but a little work to do for Friday. I simply want all of you to do some reading on the war between Sumer and Elam. Now you won't find a plethora of information, but you should get enough for us to talk about it Friday. Ready, break, or whatever."

The three girls stood and turned as quickly as they could, but the brothers were already gone. In file, they hastened for the door, working to be as subtle as possible. Reaching the outside, they looked left again where the two had gone Monday only to see their figures in the distance. Rachel raced to catch up and rounded the corner of the building to see a crowd of students with no sign of the Brownings.

"Shit!" Erin fumed as they caught up to Rachel.

"It's fine." Ally said, coming up behind Erin. "It's fine. We'll just catch them later."

"Yeah, it's fine," Rachel added. "At least we're still just doing reading. We haven't jumped into all the papers yet, Right?"

"Yeah. You're right." Erin agreed.

Still, their frustration grew even more, but they had no choice but to wait.

Thursday found the three friends studying at The Daily Brew yet again. The three had already plunged deep into their reading by the time Lili brought their drinks.

"I can see you ladies are hard at work, so I will not keep you. Here are your drinks, and just let me know if you need anything."

Rachel spoke first this time, "Oh Lili, you're fine. We don't mind at all, really. How are you today?"

"I am doing very well. Thank you for asking. I hope you are doing well yourselves?"

"We are," Ally said. "Just doing more research on ancient history."

"It never hurts to learn about the past. There is a great deal of ancient history out there that most will never discover."

"Hey, on that note," Erin began timidly, "like seriously, all jokes aside, do you think you could pass word to your brothers that we could really use some help with the class? The amount of reading alone is insane, and we're just in the first week."

Rachel continued sounding almost abashed, "To be completely honest, ma'am, we probably got in over our heads even taking this class. So any help would be great."

"Well, I respect you ladies being so honest about your struggles. That is no easy thing to admit. I doubt I see them today, but I will let them know you want to speak with them about it when I see them."

"Cool deal," Erin said in thanks.

"Enjoy your drinks, ladies." She added with a smile as she walked away.

With no time wasted, they went right back to their studying, only to learn how right Edmonton had been. There wasn't much information online aside from a few paragraphs. So the friends made their way upstairs in hopes the library of curiosities could provide some help. Reaching the kiosk, they typed in a search for the Sumer and Elam war resulting in a list of texts and references headed Kish-Elam, all of which were marked "digital record."

"Ok," Erin began in confusion, "how the fuck is this thing able to find stuff that don't even show up on the Internet."

"That is easier to explain than you might think." The friends all jumped as Marc appeared from one of the aisles.

"Holy shit, man!" Erin exclaimed, clutching her chest.

Marc chuckled softly, holding a hand up in apology; his other gripped a handful of books. "Terribly sorry, ladies. Please forgive me. I was merely grabbing a couple of books on my way to work."

"All good." Ally said, working to catch her breath. "Care to explain, though?"

"Certainly." Marc continued. "The search engine is from an open-source build that is customized to only search records of printed texts, such as books, historical records, even some scrolls if they have been digitized. It has an added layer of programming that allows it to display if we have a physical copy here in the hall or if we have a digital copy stored on our database. So whereas your search of the internet will query every online record that mentions a given topic, including articles about it, references to it in passing comments, and everything else, this kiosk is searching only a particular segment of data. So everything that exists on here could also be found on the Internet. You would just have to sift through more data. This simplifies that process."

"Wow." Rachel said in a stunned reply.

"Yeah, no shit, wow," Erin added. "So I take it you're the tech guru of the family?"

"I'm flattered, but I cannot lay claim to that entirely. The whole family played a part in this project."

"Wait, you built this?" Ally asked, both shocked and confused.

"We, yes," Marc emphasized. "Though, admittedly, Lili did most of the heavy lifting for this build. She and Win are probably the most skilled overall, but Lili has a real knack for archival queries."

"Wait, wait, wait," Erin said, gesturing with her hands to stop him. "No. Just no. There's no way your family builds a search engine database in your coffee shop and doesn't work for like Google or NASA or some shit."

"My dear, whoever suggested we do not work for Google and NASA," Marc replied with a coy smirk. "Our family does a variety of work as we all have an array of skill sets and interests. Just because a person enjoys one thing or is skilled at something, does not mean they can only do that thing ever. We own a coffee shop with a library because we enjoy coffee and reading. We can do that and do other things, too, though. Can we not?"

Marc's continued smiling gave the friends a calm, warm feeling they couldn't explain.

"If you say so," Erin replied, still slightly confused.

"Well, I thank you for allowing us to have our lifestyle then, ma'am." Marc's smile warmed. "I really should be going, but feel free to use the library. It exists for your use, after all. It is connected to our wireless system as well, of course. So any of the digital records available on the server are yours to read right on your phones, so long as you remain connected to the WiFi. Do try to have a good day."

The friends responded with a chorus of "you toos" as they waved goodbye. They remained there in stunned silence, briefly even after he was gone.

"Seriously, I'm not the only one who finds this shit weird, right?" Erin asked incredulously.

"Nope." Replied Rachel.

"Ditto." Added Ally.

"Don't suppose either of you want to leave, do you?" Asked Erin in reply.

"Not a chance in hell." Ally said without a chance.

"Not a snowball's chance." Rachel agreed.

With that, the three friends went back to the kiosk and began reading intently, their minds racing with ideas and curiosities.

After a long day studying for History through War and doing homework for their other classes, none of the girls felt like doing much of anything after dinner. So, the three friends found themselves in their respective beds scrolling on their phones well before they'd typically even consider getting their showers. The minutes slowly faded away, and the three drifted off to sleep until a crack of thunder shook the house so hard they felt it might fall apart.

They woke to see rich golden light shining through their windows and bolted from their beds. Each of them reached the hallway at the same time, but not one acknowledged another. The friends each walked in a slow, cautious stride to the stairs where they could see the light shining even brighter through the front glass. Without a word to each other, each girl slowly made their way down the stairs and towards the door. Erin reached the door first and slowly turned the handle to pull the door open.

The golden light filled the room, forcing them to cover their eyes as they adjusted. It was brighter than a midday summer, and the three struggled to adjust. Slowly, one by one, they made their way outside, stopping on the porch as the sight before them gradually set in. No longer were they on Rock St or even in the city of Little Rock or even on the same planet upon which they fell asleep, from what they could tell. Lush green mountainsides surrounded them with rivers flowing all around. Storm clouds hung along the ridges sending sparks of lightning across the summits and lighting the valley below.

Rachel was the first to step off the porch feeling the warm, flourishing grass against her feet. The three stood there in the grass for what seemed ages feeling it flow into their very being as if they were connected directly to the soil itself. They scanned the horizon, studying their surroundings as their minds began to adjust to this new reality they were seeing, and slowly it registered to them that there was no sky above them. Clouds were moving across overhead along with those on the mountain tops, but there was no color at all. No blue, nor grey, only stars in a dazzling clear sky as if they stood in open space staring out into the great cosmic beyond. There they stood, lost in time and space, in awe until a low rumble of thunder rolled across the mountains, reminding the friends of what brought them there initially.

Bringing their eyes back to the horizon, they saw the source of the golden glow curving from beyond the hills ahead. Slow was the trek through the valley as they soaked in every moment, each smell and sound, as the water flowed around them and the grass brushed against their feet and legs, sending sparks across their bodies and making their skin tingle. Flowers grew wildly amongst the valley blending their hues with the grass, a kaleidoscope of flora painting their path into a rainbow meadow. Each of the friends found themselves reaching out a hand regularly to let the flowers and blades of grass graze across their skin, entwining them with the world even more.

They steadily began to realize they were following the winding river course to the head of waterfalls as the source of the golden glow slowly broke over the horizon. A giant globe of golden, yellow, and orange rays peeking over the edge of the waterfall was calling to them, growing more significant still as they neared. It wasn't until they reached the precipice that the source came fully into view, shaking Ally, Rachel, and Erin to their core.

Standing miles off in the distance still was no orb of light, but the canopy of a great tree rising to the heavens, towering over the entire landscape around it. The tree stood taller than Olympus Mons and shone as bright as the sun, basking the world around it in a golden radiance that glowed into the empty space of the sky above. The source of the light they saw was that of the leaves on the mountainous tree, each glowing with their own brilliance as they danced together, creating their own gorgeous star at the heart of this strange world. Light shone in every direction as leaves were carried on the wind, making a light show unlike any in the known universe; each leaf its own spotlight and prism twirling amidst an endless open sky. Beams of light poured from the tree in every direction like mist rising above its canopy and raindrops falling to the ground below. The waters rushed by them, the grass blowing in the breeze brushed their skin, and the three friends stood there basking in the glow of the great tree as lifetimes passed.

As time passed, the world around the tree came into a blurry focus bit by bit. Slowly the limbs and trunk of the tree became apparent, its bark darker than onyx with the same golden glow coursing through the grain of its wood as if a mighty river flowed within, rushing beneath the bark itself. The friends stood in reverie, their eyes soaking in the effulgence, tracing the river of light through the tree's mighty branches that stretched out for miles, flowing from each individual leaf into a powerful current, streaming down through the tree. The trunk looked to span over a kilometer in each direction, the figure so massive it could likely house its own ecosystem, with its black and gold bark turning the mountain of a tree into the most gorgeous spectacle stretching thousands of meters down to the earth. At its base, the ground around it was fractured into monumental crystals, rising from the ground like a mountain range in dazzling shades of crimson, gold, turquoise, emerald, tanzanite, and countless other colors the girls couldn't even comprehend, reflecting the mind-bending light of the tree in a cosmic orchestra. Mesmerized as they were, Erin, Ally, and Rachel were further entranced watching the light of the great tree dance across the planes of the crystals, lost in its prismatic extravaganza as if seeing the Himalayas turned into a chromatic, rocky tapestry. The roots of the tree in its deep black wove through the crystals, the golden light pouring directly into the earth, flooding it with raw energy and shaping the crystal mountains which stretched outward for miles.

Time became a distant memory, all but lost to the friends. They stood on the cliffside, swept up in the melody of the rushing waters and windswept meadow as they watched the galactic light show play out before them, only barely beginning to realize that around the massive tree was an even more sprawling city, spanning endlessly across the world around the friends. Their eyes narrowed as they tried to focus on the city itself. As they began to see the city, their minds were torn asunder by a cacophony of ravens', forcing them to cover their ears and even close their eyes in reaction, feeling their skulls might split apart. When at last, the sound receded, the friends slowly opened their eyes. Before them on the cliffside stood a lone raven, so intensely black it was as if there was nothing there at all, but rather an empty void staring back at them.

The girls jolted from their beds Friday morning as each of their alarms echoed through the house in a chaotic chorus, all of them panting in a cold sweat as their bodies pulsated, sending shivers across their skin. The minutes passed by as the friends all sat in panic amidst the raging of their morning alarms. Slowly, steadily, they each eased their way out of bed to reach their phones, and the symphony died off at once into an even harsher silence.

The rest of the morning was closer to an out-of-body experience than anything they had ever known. The three friends each drifted to the showers to wash the night away and bring themselves back to life. It wasn't until they were downstairs together that they returned to a state of consciousness. No one mentioned the dream world, neither tree nor raven. No one said anything at all, but yet in the silence, the peace and relief washed over them. The gorgeous and terrifying vision slowly drifted away as all dreams do, and the friends found themselves excited it was Friday.

They were very hopeful they would meet up with Joshua and Win that day and be able to get their help with History through War. Regardless of whether that happened, it would be a good day because they were going home after school. They had been so busy with their classes that week that they had hardly talked to their family and friends. So going home would be quite a treat.

The three arrived at The Daily Brew late again after the peculiar night, so they had to get their drinks in a rush. Denise was working as Terry took their orders. "Running late again, I see. Still getting adjusted to the college experience?" Terry asked.

"I guess you could say that." Ally replied. "I think we'll be back on time next week, though. It's just been weird getting adjusted to everything and getting a proper night's sleep."

"I fully get you. It's not easy to adapt to new sleep schedules, new places, all that jazz. Hopefully, these will wake you up a bit. I hope you gals have a great Friday. Any chance we'll see you this weekend?"

"No, ma'am. We're all headed home for the weekend actually, holiday weekend and all." Rachel answered.

"Oh yeah, where's home?"

"Just south a bit. You know, out in the woods." Ally said with a faint grin.

"Well, in that case, y'all have a fun weekend, and we hope to see you next week. Don't have too much fun out in the woods." Terry finished with a shy giggle.

"See you, girls, next week! Be safe!" Denise called over the steamer.

"Thank y'all." Rachel said, and they headed for the door with no sign of Joshua or Win.

The first half of the day went by in a haze. The friends were so exhausted and ready to get the talk with the brothers over and head home, that they hardly noticed what was going on until they were sitting in History through War. Even once Edmonton came in, they barely caught a word he said. Despite all the reading yesterday and feeling prepared, the girls were just floating through the class. They weren't even sure how to catch the brothers until Edmonton gave them the break they needed.

"And that concludes our lesson for today. No homework over the weekend. Before you break into song and dance, let me assure you that this is only because it's a holiday and I'm not a complete monster. Joshua, if you would, meet me upfront after class. I'd like to speak with you for a minute. On that note, the rest of you get the hell out of my auditorium. I want to go home too."

That was their chance. Joshua would be upfront talking to Edmonton, and they could catch Win as he was waiting for his brother outside. The friends waited for Joshua to pass down the aisle then rushed out the door. Much to their dismay, though, they could already see Win well in the distance again. They would just have to wait until Joshua came out and talk to him then. Then Ally's phone rang.

"Hey, mom, I'm kinda busy. I'll call you back, ok?"

"No, we just got out of class."

"Alright, we'll be on the road in just a minute. I'll let you know when we are."

"What does it matter why? I have to ask my teacher something."

"Fine. We'll hurry."

Ally hung up her phone and swung around to her friends, hoping they hadn't missed Joshua coming by, but she was too late. He was already halfway across the yard, and Erin had taken off after him, refusing to let them get away this time. Ally and Rachel moved to catch up with her, the friends gravitating ever closer to this unusual family. They were slipping further and further in class, and it was only the first week. They needed the Brownings' help to pass. That's what kept echoing in their heads despite everything else. Erin made up some distance across the yard but was still a fair bit from him when he rounded the building. Abandoning her concerns of looking foolish, she began running, knowing she was about to lose him in the parking lot. He was almost to the street when she lunged to catch him. Erin grabbed his hand, "Joshua."

What happened next, Erin could not explain. An intense wave of pain shot through her body. For a moment, she thought she broke something while lunging after him until a deafening scream pierced her ears. Only it wasn't just a scream. It was her scream, but she wasn't screaming. It was resounding inside her head, and with it came another powerful noise she only briefly recognized. A blur of images flashed before her eyes at such a mesmerizing pace that she couldn't make out anything aside from a golden tree. Then it was gone. She was standing in the same spot, without a sign of anything ever happening.

Slowly he turned around to face her. Up close, he looked so much more imposing and powerful. His stare was unwavering and unnerving. Erin felt herself locked in it, unable to move. She lost all the words she had meant to say. Instead, she found herself studying him, trying to understand the expression carved in the granite that was his face. It wasn't anger. It wasn't hatred. It was bewilderment. Somehow her standing there in front of him defied everything he'd expected, and he was utterly stunned by it, his mind racing. Erin finally made contact with his eyes, those light grey eyes that looked so empty yet seemed to know everything. At once, they flickered, and a deep unrecognizable color began to swirl in them. Without a word, he turned as the car pulled up behind him, stepped in, and was gone.

4
GOING HOME

A mix of rage and confusion warred inside Erin. Her eyes stayed focused on the road as Ally drove, but her mind kept replaying the moment. It was the crescendo of an exhausting week that only exacerbated Erin's growing frustrations since moving. Ally and Rachel kept glancing at her in silence for some time before she drifted back from her thoughts, regained focus, and realized it.

"I just told you."

"Well, tell me again, Erin."

"I don't know how else to say it. He just stared at me. I don't know. It was like he didn't understand why I was there. He didn't even say anything, and then just turned and got in the car. They drove off like nothing happened. Why are we still discussing this, Rachel?"

"I just don't get it. It seems so weird."

Rachel had no idea how true her statement was. Erin held out the detail about the strange jolt of pain she received when she touched him and the way his eyes swirled with some deep darkness.

"I'm sure you just startled him. I mean, Lili had to 've talked to them by now. What blows my mind is the car." Ally said, trying her best to shift the topic.

"No joke. That was a Roadster, wasn't it?" Rachel asked.

"Chyeah. That's like a quarter mil base. I don't even think they were in production yet. I don't know if I was more upset that we didn't get to ask for their help, or that they drove off without me getting to look at the car longer." Ally joked.

"Where do people their age even get money like that? I mean, we all knew they were pretty well taken care of, obviously, but damn.

That's next-level money."

"Trust fund babies," Erin muttered. "You two are really getting off on this too much. They're a couple of rich kids in a pretentious family that thinks they're God's gift to Earth, and try to play it all off like they're sweet and caring. They need to get off their fucking high horse, and you two need to quit being a couple of naive little shits."

"Well, somebody's had a fun week." Rachel snapped back with an icy glare. "You pissed about this, or is there something else you wanted to talk about?"

An awkward silence hung in the air. Erin refused to meet Rachel's gaze.

Ally broke the silence in an attempt. "Maybe they don't have any parents. Maybe their parents died, and their inheritance is how they have so much money. I mean, it's not like we know these people."

"Exactly. We don't know them, and they're trying really fucking hard to keep it that way in their ivory tower."

Rachel read Erin's face. "Clearly, The Brew is doing decent, and after hearing Marc talk, they probably got all kinds of shit going. Maybe Lili and Marc bankroll all of 'em. Or maybe what Ally said is right. We have no idea, and while yeah, they're a bit odd, it's not like they've been rude to us. We shouldn't jump to conclusions just because they got money and are different than us."

"Oh, come off it, Rach. Do you hear yourself defending people we barely know? And Ally, inheritance, really? People with a simple inheritance aren't driving around quarter-million-dollar cars. That's some trust-fund baby shit right there. Lili is clearly fake. I don't know how you two don't see it. Who the fuck knows what Marc's deal is, and the other two are a couple of ostentatious douchebags. Did you not see the way they walked into the coffee shop? They didn't even acknowledge the presence of anyone in the room. It's as if they exist in a world of their own. That's not just a coincidence. That's a personality trait."

Erin clenched her jaw tight to stop the raw fury that was washing over her from pouring out. She could feel the lump rising in her throat as her eyes threatened to water. Her frustration at the Brownings was only mild annoyance, but it pushed her nerves to the brink on top of her real issues; issues she refused to share openly with Rachel and Ally.

The rest of the drive home was silent. Ally never thought only a few weeks after moving off together she would already be fighting with one of her best friends. She knew there would be growing pains with moving in together, but she always told herself those stories of people growing apart after school wouldn't apply to her life. After all, they'd already made it through college together. She had no interest in new friends, and she would keep all the friends that she had. That's how Ally told herself it would work, and she reminded herself of it to calm her mind.

Rachel fought the urge to speak multiple times. Erin was the firecracker, Ally the stoic. She was always the calm and compassionate one, and the silence from the friend's squabble tore at her. Erin needed comforting. Rachel knew that, but Erin wasn't going to say it. So, Rachel sat in silence, willing her friend to find peace.

After almost two hours with just the music playing, the trio rolled into town. All three had hoped they would feel instantly better, but the truths of that week continued to gnaw at them. Rachel's family lived right down the street from Ally, so Erin's house on the other side of town was their first stop. Ally pulled her car up next to Erin's driveway.

Erin exited the car without a word but turned back as she closed the door. "I'll text ya." She said before the door shut, but the words were softer than before.

"Don't let her get to you. You know she's just salty, Ally."

"I don't see why. She'll come around, though. I hope."

The two friends both exhaled deeply, letting their minds relax before pulling back out onto the road.

"So, are you jealous?"

"Of what?" Ally asked in complete confusion.

"That they have the car you want?"

"Oh, blow me." Ally laughed. "My Jeep is just fine, thank you. There's a ton of cars I want. I don't think I could write a list of all the cars I want. I'm not going to get all huffy just because some dumb boys have one of 'em. Real talk, I'm more bummed that they didn't say anything. We really do need help with History through War. I'm trying not to stress it, Rach, but this class is killing me. I can barely keep up with this reading, and it hasn't even got going yet. Don't act like you can either."

"Think of the upside. We don't have any homework in his class this weekend, so failing miserably can be fixed next week."

"Wow, now that you put it that way, I feel so much better. Thanks a million, Rach." Ally's voice dripped with sarcasm.

"I know you're stressed. I am too. Here's an even better upside. We don't have class Monday since it's Labor Day, so we can at least relax for a nice long weekend, and then get back to the grind on Tuesday or Wednesday. That better?"

"Much. I actually like the sound of that news. Now get out of my car, hussy." Ally laughed as she pulled into Rachel's driveway.

"I'm sure your mom will want all your time tonight, but we should all get together tomorrow. Mi madre would love to see you. Oh, and you can bring the boys if you want."

"You mean I can bring Thad."

"And I'm getting out of the car now."

Rachel closed the door, and Ally eased back out into the road. Putting it in drive, she felt her heart jump a little. She was almost home. She tried not to show it, but she was so very homesick. Being gone for three weeks had felt like a lifetime for her. Though the boys were the main thing Ally kept thinking of, she missed her mom dearly, and as soon as Ally pulled into the drive, she saw her on the front porch.

"Why, hello there, stranger. May I help you with anything?" Her voice was strong and soft like only a mother's could be.

"Yeah, yeah, yeah. I missed you too." Ally said as her mom wrapped her in a warm embrace like a momma bear snuggling her long-lost cub. Ally's family didn't hug, but when they did, they meant it. "So Mom, how much you been cryin'?"

"A little bit earlier when I realized you were coming home, and I wouldn't have the place all to myself this weekend. I had to cancel the kegs and margarita maker, postpone the strippers and the fire-breather. The neighbors were thoroughly disappointed. Not sure how I'm going to make it up to them."

"You didn't have to cancel all that because of me. I could've stayed in my room playing games. You wouldn't have even known I was here. Traditional Friday night back home." Ally and her mom smiled as they made their way up the steps towards the door.

Right as the door opened, a scurry of feet against the hardwood and excited barking created a welcoming chorus as Ally's Malamute flew through the house. She threw her front paws on Ally, almost knocking her over as she began licking her arms and face.

"I missed you too, girl." Ally laughed as she tried to keep her footing. "Alright, alright. We'll play in a bit, Lace. Let me put my stuff down. Goodness."

Ally's house sat on Denison Ave, against a thick forest of loblolly pines that nestled right up to one of the many rivers carved through Southern Arkansas. She stood in the foyer for a moment looking through the house and out the bay windows at the trees, petting Lace's head absentmindedly. She had so many memories there, yet all of a sudden, it felt so foreign. What had only been three short weeks away felt like ages to her then, and Ally felt like a stranger in her own home.

"Are you going to stand there all night, or are you going to come have some dinner? I already have the table set."

"Smells yummy. What'd you make?"

"Biscuits and gravy."

"With the maple sausage?"

"Do I make it any other way, or have you been gone so long you forgot?"

"That's what I'm talking 'bout. Always on your A-game."

"Comes with being a mom. So, tell me everything since you haven't texted much this week."

"Oh lord, where do I begin? Well, the coffee shop I told you about not far from our apartment, it's called The Daily Brew. You'll have to come up and try it. They have the best coffee in the world, and we're basically there every day now. It's owned by this young couple named Lili and Marc."

"Oh, you've met the owners? That's interesting."

"Yeah, I'm not sure if they're from here or what. They talk real proper but also very casual, and are always very friendly, but they both have a sorta accent I can't place. Like they feel like they're from somewhere else, but still kinda have the whole southern hospitality thing going. Regardless they're cool as hell, although a bit intimidating."

"How so?"

"Well, they're kinda odd. They're very nice, attractive, have a lot of money apparently, but we can't figure them out. Like they own the coffee shop, but I mean their brother who's in our class has a freaking supercar. A coffee shop ain't paying for that. One of those blessed families, I guess, but it just doesn't add up. Something about them is just off."

"Ah, so you have a crush on the boy in your class who has a nice car? Here I thought you were going off to grad school, not back to high school." Her mom teased lovingly.

"Ha, ha, Mom. If you must know, there's two of their brothers in our class, and yes, they are both quite the lookers. That's not the point, though. We haven't even met them yet, only Marc and Lili. It's something else about them. They're very nice, but it's like there's something they're not saying."

"Now Ally, you know as well as anyone that all families have their things they like to keep private. We're no different. It's not like we go around introducing ourselves in regards to your dad."

"My sperm donor, you mean."

"Allyxandria, you know what I mean. Just because they don't lay all their cards out there on the table doesn't mean their secrets are bad."

"Yeah. What if they are, though? What if they're hiding something that needs to be hidden?"

"Well then, I trust I've raised you well enough to make the right decision. Like it or not, you're going to have to make a lot of big decisions in the years to come. I may not always agree with your choices, but you have to do what's right by you."

"Thanks, Mom."

"Anytime. So how are you and the girls liking your classes?"

"Oh, Mom, they're so much fun. I've never learned so much information at such a brisk pace. It's crazy. The best class, though, is the History through War one I told you about. It's a lot different than I thought it was going to be, a lot of outside research. In class time is mainly spent in discussing different views and aspects of what we found, like analyzing what moved and motivated the various parties in the given war. We started off by reading Paradise Lost along with a bunch of pieces from the Bible and ancient texts and talking about the War in Heaven and the Fall of Satan."

"Oh wow. That sounds rather different." Her voice conveyed her clear disapproval of history lessons improperly teaching about religion.

"It wasn't really like that. It was meant to introduce key aspects of history and war as we see it. The teacher is amazing, though. You'd love him. He's got a English accent, but I'm not sure yet where he's from exactly, or how long he's been here. Anyways though, he knows his shit, and even though he's pretty hardcore on us about working a lot, he's cool about it. We are falling a bit behind, but we're going to meet up with some of our classmates Tuesday or Wednesday, hopefully, to see about getting some help. Mr. Edmonton suggested that in fact. I don't remember if I told you, but this is actually a doctorate-level course. My biggest problem is going to be that the grading in the class is all based on participation in the discussion. You know I can't speak in front of people like that."

"Says the woman who's rambling so fast she can barely catch her breath."

"Yeah, yeah. This is us, not a room full of strangers."

"I know, baby. Just speak with this professor and let him know how you are. You aren't the only person to come through his classes that can't do public speaking, I'm sure."

Ally and her mother continued talking about school and the city as they ate. Her mother, of course, wanted every detail and hung excitedly on every word as moms do. Though she tried to play it off, the mom in her wanted to be there with Ally. She wasn't the only one wishing that, but Ally knew she had to walk this path on her own.

After a movie with her mom and Lace, and a couple of hours of video games, Ally decided to call it a night. Once she finally got still in bed and Lace got settled in next to her, the images of that day came flashing back in front of her eyes, and all the questions she had been trying not to ask followed. *What was going on with Erin? Did she really have such disdain for the Brownings, and if so, should Ally be concerned too? What were the Brownings hiding after all?* Those were the thoughts that sent Ally off to sleep and littered her dreams.

It was past midnight when the light knocking wrapped at her door. He was later than she'd hoped, but that was to be expected given the situation. Being home meant slipping back into their old routine. After graduating high school, her parents opted to move her into the room over the garage to give her a sense of the freedom and responsibilities of adulthood. It was also, she knew, so that she could have dates over without having any awkward tensions of being in the same house with her parents.

This was different, though. He was different. If her parents knew he'd been coming over for some time now, or even worse if her friends knew, they wouldn't hear the end of it. They would constantly be bombarded with questions about how serious it was and where they saw it going, and what their plans were. They weren't ready for those questions yet. They weren't even prepared to ask those questions of themselves. They liked being with each other, and they wanted to spend as much time together as they could. After that, everything became far more complex than they were ready to address. So, these late-night rendezvous were all they had, and since she'd been away the past few weeks, they hadn't even had that.

He wrapped his knuckles lightly on the door a second time. She was purposefully waiting, letting the anticipation build. She could see him through the glass shifting his weight from side to side. The lights were left off, so he might think she'd fallen asleep. Making her way to the door, she wondered how long he'd wait, if he'd knock again, if she could keep him waiting. Outside, he turned like he was about to leave but paused at the top of the steps. Turning back, he knocked lightly one final time. She opened the door before he finished knocking and pulled him gently inside.

"Don't say a word." She commanded him. "I'm still mad at you."

"Yes, ma'am." He whispered.

"I don't care if it's been almost a month; I still want that massage you promised me first." She said as she led him across the studio apartment towards the bed.

"Yes, ma'am." He whispered again.

She stopped on a dime and turned, grabbing him by his lapels and pulling his lips to hers. Running her fingers through the back of his hair, she kissed him deeply, pressing her lips so tightly against his they tingled, a wash of pain and pleasure sending shivers down her body. The days and weeks apart had been excruciating. She'd longed for this, needed to feel his skin against her own. She grabbed his hair firmly, pulling it tightly as his fingers dug into her shoulder blades, squeezing her against his chest with fervor, echoing her thoughts with his actions. Where minutes before an entire world existed outside, now there was only that one room, only those two people, only that moment. His fingers moved swiftly but delicately up her shoulders, tracing along her collar bone, gliding up her neck, until he was gently cupping her cheeks in his strong hands. He knew what that did to her, and she could feel the chill creeping down her spine. Parting her lips, she slid her tongue forward and slowly traced his lips. Caressing them as his tongue rose to meet hers. They moved in perfect harmony, a natural rhythm they kept without effort. Her hands moved back to his lapels, pulling him even closer still to her. Sliding her hands under his jacket, across his lean, sinewy chest towards his shoulders, she pushed the coat off, letting it fall to the floor. With that and a quick, playful bite of his tongue, she pushed him back away, grabbing her robe in a fluid motion and softly pulling it off her shoulders. She let it fall slowly to the floor, revealing every inch of her smooth, bare skin to her lover.

"I told you," she glowered, "not to say a word."

He motioned an imaginary zipper being closed over his mouth, made a locking gesture with his fingers, and flicked the pretend key across the room.

"That's better." She replied and motioned to the bed.

It wasn't until the sound of laughter and yelling from downstairs woke her that Ally snapped back to reality. They had already arrived. Ally flew through putting her makeup on and barely straightened her hair. She threw on some jeans and a t-shirt and rushed downstairs with Lace at her heels to join breakfast. The smell of pancakes and bacon grease grew stronger as she neared the kitchen. Ally turned at the foot of the stairs to see four of them sitting at the table and the fifth plopped up on the counter.

Three lanky boys had made themselves at home in her kitchen along with her grandparents. Mimi and Pops sat at the table with Matt and Nick. Though two years apart, Matt and Nick could have easily passed for twins, both with their shaggy brown hair about ear length tucked underneath a backward cap. If it weren't for Nick's pierced ears and goatee, he would have looked just like his younger brother Matt. Both were wearing the same shirts they had clearly worn the day before and didn't care at all about it. Mimi wobbled up from the table to give Ally a big hug. Pops just gave her a big smile. He was more the quiet, strong love type than the hugging type.

On the counter rested the leanest of Ally's three boys. Even though he was only a few inches shorter than Ally and the same age, if it weren't for Thaddeus' scruffy face, he could have passed for fifteen as tiny as he was. His brown hair looked just the way it did a few weeks before but was adorned with a new hat from one of his online sneaker boutiques, no doubt. He wore a plain coral V-neck with a pair of cut-off jeans only someone his size could make work, and his crisp grey and white checkerboard vans swung back and forth against the cabinet door as he munched on a strip of bacon.

"Sup skank?" Nick gladly welcomed Ally home as Mimi released her from a hug.

"Not much, jackass. What about you punks? Does the asylum know their three stooges escaped?"

"I resent that statement." Said Thad, pointing his bacon at her. "I happen to be on certified leave for the weekend. These two nimrods, however, I am not associated with." He waved the bacon in their direction.

"Would you two be nice to your cousin for once?" Mimi huffed at Matt and Nick in an altogether non-threatening tone.

"Glad to see y'all have missed each other so much. Now, how many pancakes does everyone want?" Ally's mom said as she started grabbing out plates.

"However many you've got batter for, ma'am." Thad hopped off the counter and took a seat. "So Ally, you know what's coming. Spill it."

Ally went into yet another explanation of all the things she'd been doing in Little Rock while they ate. She told them about The Brew, Marc and Lili, her classes, and how Rachel and Erin were doing. She didn't dare mention Joshua or Win, though. Her boys were nice enough, but they could be cruel at times, especially about guys. Ally knew the field day they'd have with the friends meeting some new boys, so she just skipped right over that part. They waited until she finished to start all their jabbering.

"Sounds like we need to make a visit to Little Rock next weekend," Thad said. "I'm curious for an insider's tour. Plus, I do love good coffee."

Matt and Nick didn't look as sold. "Eh, I'm sure it's alright. I don't think I feel like driving out there just yet, though. Gotta get the lease prepped too. I'll just get the play-by-play from Thad." Matt explained.

"I'll come eventually," Nick added. "Workin' at the shop this weekend, though."

"Always the pud," Thad replied. "Anyways, I think I'll go for a walk. Gotta work off all those calories. I'm trying to watch my figure, you know."

"You need to," Nick said. "You're getting a bit pudgy around the middle."

"Yeah, yeah," Thad said, letting his northeastern accent slip just a little. "Any of you lovely ladies care to join? Mimi, Mom?"

"Such a charmer, but I have a kitchen to clean." Replied Ally's Mom.

Lace let out a loud bark as she began hopping around the kitchen.

"Lace! My girl. I knew you wouldn't let me down. I'll go get your leash." Thad laughed as he patted her on the head.

"I'll tag along." Ally said as she stood from the table. "Lord knows I need to with all this food I've been eating lately. You two know where my room is and how to work everything. Feel free to do what you always do."

"Thanks. Not that we were really waiting for your blessing, more just for you to leave." Matt and Nick both laughed.

"You two be safe." Mimi cautioned, always the worrier.

As they started to leave, Ally went to get her hoodie thinking she was back in Little Rock. The last week had been the beginning of the cold everyone spoke of, and she hadn't thought about the fact she was back at home. After putting one foot on the stairs, it hit her, and she turned to see Thad's bewildered face. Ignoring him, she went straight out the door.

"Not even gone a month, and you already forget which way the door was?" Thad jeered as they reached the sidewalk.

"Ha. Ha. No, it got crazy cold last week, so I'm used to going out with a hoodie."

"Ah. Gotcha. So anything you want to add about your new town, now that Tweedledee and Tweedledum aren't here?"

"You know it's creepy when you do that, right?" She paused for a response, but Thad just smiled expectantly. "Well, for starters, I wasn't fully honest about the family that owns The Brew."

"You mean they're not as wicked cool as you described them?"

"Oh no. They seem pretty cool. It's just, there's something more. I tried to talk to mom about it, but she just blew it off. There's something they're not showing, though, something wrong."

"Hm…" Thad began. "Maybe they're robots, like androids from the future come back in time. Have you thought about that? Oooh. Or maybe, maybe their ghosts, or assassins. Ghost assassins would be badass. Even better, maybe they're like demon hunters. Demon hunters are cool. I'm going with that."

"Hardy fuckin' har. I'm being serious, Thad."

"Right. Serious face on." He gestured to his face. "I'm still banking on Demon Hunters, though. So, real talk, do you think they're actually bad people, or they're just trying to cover something up?"

"No. I'm certain that Marc and Lili are good people. Though they're certainly a peculiar couple. I think they may just have some secrets about their family. Mom figures it's no different than our situation in principle. She's probably right. It's the others I'm not so sure about."

"Others? What others? You didn't say anything about others at the table."

"Yeah, well, that's the other part. There are these two guys."

"Ah. I see why you skipped that inside. So what's up with them?"

"They're Marc and Lili's brothers. Younger brothers, I assume, but it's kinda hard to tell with them. I'm really not sure how old any of them are. One seems like our age or maybe a bit older, Win. The other, I think, is a few years older than him. His name is Joshua. They're in our History through War class, and we're trying to get them to help us study because it's a bitch of a class. Both of 'em though, there's just something different about them. They feel much older and more mature than they look, kinda like that person you went to grade school with, but then by the time you're seniors, they're already like an adult. If that makes any sense, and I'm not so sure if they are the good kind of people Marc and Lili are."

"What makes you think that?"

"Well, their behavior aside, Lili. She kinda warned me and Rachel that if we tried to get to know them, there would be a lot more to deal with than we realized. It wasn't like a big sister not approving kind of thing either. She seemed more worried about us."

"Think about what you're saying, Ally. You said they seemed much older and more mature than they looked, and Lili is clearly warning you that getting closer to them would mean having to deal with some serious issues. They're clearly android demon hunters from the future. There's no other explanation."

"Wait, when did the demon hunters and the androids become one storyline?"

"I'm editing as I go here; stay with me," Thad smirked. "For reals, though, they've probably just had a rough life. You and I both know that different things can happen to cause people to have to grow up sooner than they planned. Maybe that's what happened to these guys. I'm not telling you not to get to know them. I'll agree with Lili, though. Be careful and be open-minded. You're probably walking into some new territory here."

"Thanks, Thad. I'm glad you decided to walk. I'm sure I'm overreacting. Just skittish is all. I mean, the five of you are the only friends I've ever really known, and even y'all took about a decade to get comfortable with. Getting to know new people isn't easy for all of us."

"It's not always easy for me either. I just can put the mask on pretty well, and don't sweat it. I knew you'd have more to say than you can say in front of your cousins. I've been doing this for a few years now. Give it time, though. If they are good people, you'll be fine, and if they aren't, you'll figure it out. You got this."

"If you say so."

"I do. So Rachel is interested in these guys too, I take it?"

"Yeah, pretty sure she's actually crushing on Win. The one that's our age or so. I'm sure you could still get her back, though, if you wanted to bad enough."

"How many times must we go through this, Ally? I like Rachel. I love her. She's a great girl. We had a wonderful run, and it didn't work. We'll be friends forever, but that's all there is for us. Besides, I'm just not looking for a relationship right now."

"You do realize I know the truth, right? She's in grad school now, Thad. We're almost out into the real world. You had better buck up your courage soon, or someone's going to snatch her up. And let me tell you, Win is some stiff competition, buddy. You might wanna act before he takes interest in her too. You could do so at lunch today, because that's where we're going."

"Oh, for fuck's sake. You're kidding me, right? You know I hate dealing with her parents. Not cool, Ally. Not cool."

"I make no promises that her parents won't try to arrange your marriage for tomorrow, but you can probably bet that Erin won't be there. We kinda had a fight."

"Oh wow, I'm sorry, Ally. What happened?."

"It's not your fault. Maybe it's just a episode. She'll come around. I hope. It was actually about the Brownings too."

"Really? What's her take?"

"Well, she thinks they're pretentious and spoiled, but it was way more heated than just that. I mean, we know other people that are really well off, and she's never had an attitude towards them."

"Look, even though I pick at her a lot, I still like her well enough and don't want you guys fighting. I'm sure you'll figure it out, though.

You all care for each other too much to let some time-traveling android demon hunters come between you."

"You're having way too much fun with that."

"Fine. Think we ought to start heading back?"

"Yeah. They'll be joking enough as it is. Were you for real about coming to visit next weekend?"

"Totally. I genuinely want to see this place, and I certainly want to meet these people after all this talk. I'm pretty sure I will be making the trip alone, though. I love your cousins to death and all, but they're both a couple of wet blankets for the most part. Not sure how long I'll be able to stay, though. I mean, you do have roommates."

"Yeah, they really can be. Hopefully, they'll come visit eventually. I know Rachel wouldn't mind at all if you crashed a night or two, or ten. I'm sure Erin will be in better spirits by then. Regardless I'll definitely have to show you around and introduce you to some folks."

"I'm curious most about this Joshua character. You didn't really mention much about him, but I did hear your breathing pick up when you mentioned his name."

"How the hell can you hear my breathing pick up?"

"I didn't. It was a bluff. You do admit then that your breathing picked up, though?"

"I hate you."

"So are you going to humor me, or am I going to have to find out about him when I get there?"

"I don't really know too much about him, to be honest. Just what he looks like and somewhat how he acts. Hell, I haven't even heard him talk. He seems very quiet and reserved, but it may just be because I don't know him. He's insanely intimidating, though, more so than his brothers and sister. He seems, I don't know, untouchable."

"So intimidating and mysterious, is he brooding too? You almost have the hat trick."

"Very funny, sir. I don't even know him enough to know if he's brooding, but he at least doesn't look it, thank God. I mean, he smiles at least."

"Well, let's solve the mystery of them then." He said, pulling out his phone. "Any weird spelling in their names?"

"Um, I don't know. I mean, they're all pretty common names. How many ways can you spell Mark, Lilly, Joshua, and Win? Not to mention Brownings."

"You'd be surprised with people, man." He replied, typing the various names in searches and swapping between apps to cross-reference. Thad went silent as he worked aside from the occasional, "Huh," and, "Ok, then." Finally, after minutes of searching, Thad turned to face Ally.

"This just got good." He said with excitement glowing in his eyes as his lips curled into a smirk.

"Well, enough with the build-up. Spill it."

"Nothing." He replied. "No social media accounts for a single one of them, not even a mention that I could find. I even pulled up the Daily Brew's pages, and they're not even mentioned in the reviews or the about section. Do you know who has absolutely zero presence on the Internet?"

"Probably smart people that want privacy. I'm half tempted every day to delete my apps."

"Yeah, but there's a difference between leaving social media or not being very active, and being completely absent from the Internet entirely. There's only one type of person I know that does that."

"Who's that?"

"Androids from the future."

"Oh, dear Lord." Ally laughed, burying her face in her hands. "I hate you." She said with her voice muffled by her fingers. "I really fucking hate you."

The smile on Thad's face radiated with his elation. "You know what this means?"

"Wait," Ally cut in, "I thought they were android demon hunters?"

"I'm workshopping that part still. I'll get back to you. Being super serial, though, do you know what this means, Ally?" His voice trembled with anticipation. "I have so much research to do. My week is booked solid now. Oh, thank you, sweet, amazing Ally!"

"Oh Thad, please no." Ally lamented, knowing her friend's proclivity for sleuthing.

"Oh-ho, no," Thad replied, his voice still shaky. "This is too damn good, Ally. I've never had one this fun. I get to go through property records, registration databases; oh, this will be so dope!"

"Thad, seriously," Ally wavered, unsure if she wanted Thad to venture down this rabbit hole yet certain she wanted to know what things he might find. Finally, after a long pause, she exhaled a deep sigh, "Fine. Do your thing."

5

MEET THE BROWNINGS

Ally woke that Tuesday to the sound of Rachel blending her protein shake. She was already back from the gym and showered, so Ally started getting ready to walk with her to The Brew. The drive back to Little Rock had been calmer than the trip home. None of the friends mentioned their conversation from the previous drive, and Erin seemed in a better spirit. Though she didn't speak much to the effect, the friends only had the idle chit-chat here and there. The group felt closer to normal than they had, though, and Ally hoped Erin would join them at The Brew once she was up and going later.

To Ally's surprise, though, when she arrived downstairs that morning, Erin was reading on her tablet, ready to go. The walk felt much colder than the previous week as a crisp breeze with the scent of Autumn swirled around them. Ally thought she might need her pea coat by the first of October at the rate it was going. For the first time since moving to Little Rock, they opened the door to an empty coffee shop aside from Lili, Denise, and Terry working behind the counter. Lili was exceptionally vibrant that day as her skin seemed to radiate light throughout the room, her dark complexion set beautifully against her orange dress.

"Well, hello again, ladies," Lili said as the friends made it to the counter.

"Hey, gals," Terry added. "Haven't seen you in a few days. How was your weekend?"

"Not bad." Ally said. "We just hung out with some friends and our parents. You know. Normal weekend."

"That sounds most enjoyable. My family visits are too few and far between, but I do enjoy them when we can. My brother is supposed to come by sometime soon. Are you staying in today or getting it to go?"

"Oh, we're staying here," Rachel replied. "Study day."

"Sounds good. If you would just have a seat at your table, and one of us will have your drinks right over."

"Oh, do you want us to pay before we leave then?" Rachel asked.

"No, ma'am," Lili interjected. "Your drinks are of no charge today. Consider it a welcome home treat from us."

"Wicked. Thanks." Ally exclaimed.

The friends took their seats and made for their computers, but Lili had their drinks over before they could even get to them. Every day she amazed them with how fast she could make coffee, but that day was almost instant. So much so that Ally was compelled to ask how long she had been doing that as she couldn't help wondering if Lili had already prepared them.

"How long have you and Marc had this place, Lili?"

"It has been in our family for quite a few years now. Why do you ask, dear?"

"Just curious, really. You run this place so smooth. I figured you had to've been at it for a while."

"Well, I am very practiced at it." Lili smiled coyly. "I have been making espresso routinely for almost as long as I can remember, even before we had this place. Though in truth, the secret is in the coffee beans themselves. They do all the work. I merely mix things. Do you ladies need anything else?" She added with a soothing smile.

Erin spoke as Ally drank, "No, ma'am. We should be good. Thank you, though."

Ally and Rachel couldn't help noticing the suspicion in Erin's voice now, though the malice was no longer prevalent.

"Very well then. I need to get another order ready, so if you need anything at all, just let me know. It is not like I will be very far away after all." She smiled as she turned towards the counter. The three friends shared a brief glance before looking up to see Lili was already prepping the next drinks just as they caught the door opening in the corner of their eyes.

In walked Win with his hair somewhat ruffled but with an effortless grace that still dripped with charm and beauty. He was followed by

Joshua, who was as dressy as usual with a soft grey blazer over his turquoise blue and white striped button-up and grey tie, a matching pair of grey slacks, and oxblood monk straps completing his ensemble.

No sooner had the door closed than they were on their way to their table. It wasn't until about halfway there that Joshua paused, ever so briefly glancing over his shoulder towards the three. He didn't say a word or make the slightest indication before continuing his walk, but Win turned on his mark and headed straight towards the girls. Joshua, however, detoured over to greet Lili and grab his drink. Win was dressed up a little more than his usual t-shirt that day, sporting a thin navy v-neck cashmere sweater that clung to his body. Rachel had commented before that his muscles had muscles, and from the look of him up close, that was rather possible. Win's incredibly sculpted figure only added to his alluring presence. *Adonis*, the friends thought collectively. His blue eyes gleamed with a fierce intensity as they met Ally's, Rachel's, and Erin's each in turn. His lips parted, revealing his stunning smile, causing each of the girls', even Ally's, breathing to stutter as their nerves began to build.

"Good morning, ladies. I trust you are each doing well?"

None of them knew what to say. They were in complete shock as to why he was standing in front of their table. This was no teenage crush that had the friends' tongues gripped by the same silence. It was as if they were physically incapable of speaking to him. Rachel managed a nod first, her cheeks visibly flushing with heat, Ally seconded, whereas Erin sat transfixed, but tried as the friends might, no words came out.

"Joshua and I have noticed your growing regularity here, and Lili told us a fair deal about you. We would like to cordially request your company at our table today if you would be so kind." Win said with a casual gesture towards their table. "If you wish to decline, though, we would be most understanding and wish you a wonderful day nonetheless. So, what say you?"

Reaching into the deepest parts of her mind to force words, Ally spoke up, "We would be delighted. However, we do have work to do, so I'm not sure as to how long we can join you." She didn't know where the words came from, but Ally had never spoken so correctly in her life.

"That is perfectly fair, ma'am. He and I would be more than happy to help you with any work you have, if you would like. I do not mean to boast, but we are both well versed in several subjects, heavy readers and all."

Rachel finally found her voice and replied, "Absolutely lovely." Win and Ally both looked at her with bewilderment. "I mean, that would be absolutely lovely of you and your brother to help. We actually could really use some help with History through War. You guys are in our class."

"That sounds absolutely lovely indeed." He teased. "I recognized you from class, naturally, and Lili mentioned you want some assistance. I did not wish to be too forward, though, by jumping straight to that. We can begin whenever you please. What about you ladies? Will you be joining us to study also?"

Without even a word, Erin and Ally rose, grabbed their bags, and suddenly floated away from the table. They weren't walking towards Joshua. They were gravitating to him. They couldn't do anything to stop themselves, even if they had wanted. He had something they each needed, different though it may be. He knew something they each had to know, and they couldn't keep from being pulled to find out what.

In what felt like the blink of an eye to the friends, they already were at the edge of his table. Rachel had not even managed to stand yet as she watched her friends drift across the room. There Ally and Erin stood face to face with him. He met their gaze with an intensity they had never known possible, reaching into the depths of their souls, pressing their minds with questions unknown.

His scent wrapped around them even amidst all the smells of The Brew, a distinct aroma of cherry blossom and the color black, laced with a hint of guilt. He rose, gesturing with his hand to the seats across from him, his lips parting in a faint smile as the words formed, "Please," his voice came soft and low, "have a seat." There was a sense of sincerity and security in his words that drew the two friends in and put them at ease. As they took their seats, they saw Rachel, Win, and even Lili transfixed on them and Joshua as if witnessing the end of all things or the beginning of everything.

"I am certain You have many questions for me. Let us begin with the formalities, though. My name is, well, people call me Joshua as I am sure you well know."

"I'm Allyxandria Carver, but everyone calls me Ally. And this is…"

"Erin, Erin Cartwright. It's nice to meet you."

"I assure you both the pleasure is all mine. Thank you for joining me today, and Erin, I believe I owe you an apology and explanation for my actions last week."

Erin was startled to see him address the incident so quickly. Part of her had even wondered if he would acknowledge it at all or just pretend it never happened. She could feel Rachel and Win approaching but didn't look towards them. Instead, her eyes locked with Joshua's. She searched for that strange swirl of color that she caught the previous time, but there was no trace of it. All she saw were grey eyes, both cold and warm simultaneously, with an endless depth to them.

"You startled me." He began again; all eyes now locked on him. "I did not see you coming, and upon you reaching for my hand to get my attention, I was completely taken aback. Typically, I am very perceptive, yet somehow you managed to sneak up on me despite actively trying to do otherwise. It was, strange, really. I hope I did not frighten or upset you with my reaction. I have been told my stare can be rather, unsettling," his lips curled in a slight smirk, "and I am sure the look on my face probably puzzled you too. I do hope I can make a better second impression than my first."

Erin looked down to avoid his gaze. Even without the shocking sensation and awkward standoff, she could hardly handle looking into his eyes. There was something in them she was not ready to see. Working to put her thoughts in order, she scanned the table, looking for a distraction. His hands rested on the table across from her, and Erin's eyes caught on a ring he wore on his right middle finger. The metal shined with an unusual sheen, black one moment then white the next as if it had no actual color, but artisan hands clearly crafted it. A lion's head, like that of a medieval seal was brilliantly forged into the center of the ring, giving Joshua even more of an obscure persona.

He followed Erin's eyes to the ring as the other friends followed and lifted his hand in response. "It is rather ostentatious, I know." He said as he twisted his hand around so they could see it. "You could call it an heirloom if you like, though I do not know if that properly describes it. It is one of the few things that remains of a dying generation."

"I'm sorry." Erin swiftly apologized, though secretly glad for the distraction. "I didn't mean to stare. It's a very nice ring."

Joshua let out a soft laugh. "Thank you. There is no need to be sorry, though. You are not the first to stare at it. Not too many people wear rings like this, I suppose. So, is there nothing you wanted to ask of me the other day?"

"Why didn't you say anything?" Erin blurted out without thinking.

"I wanted to speak. I did not know what to say, however. Try as I might, all words escaped me, and that is not something to which I am accustomed. So, when neither of us spoke, I did the only thing I could think to do." He paused and gave Erin a very genuine smile.

Somehow, that answer was enough. Erin couldn't figure it out. There was still something there, something deeply troubling, but she knew in the very fiber of her being that it was nothing of malice or contempt from this increasingly strange man with whom she and her friends then sat drinking coffee. Ally and Rachel both took long draws from their drinks, watching with intense focus at the conversation unfolding. They both had countless questions running through their minds, but they could not concentrate on anything but the interaction at hand for some reason unknown to them.

"Is there nothing else?" Joshua asked, bringing Erin's mind back to that day.

"Um, not that I can think of. Oddly."

"May I ask you a question then?"

"Sure."

"Why is it that you sought us that day? Lili told us you wanted our help with the class, but that does not adequately explain your behavior. You could have easily waited for us before class, asked Lili for our numbers, or gave her yours, yet you chose to do none of those things. Why is that?"

He scanned the friends' faces hoping for some insight into their psyche. All three of the girls shared glances as they sought themselves to answer his question. None of them were able to find it, though. There was a place in their minds that held the answer. It was buried so far down they couldn't reach it, though, or they weren't yet ready to.

"I honestly don't know," Erin replied shakily. "Really."

"It's weird," Rachel began attempting to shoulder some of Erin's struggle, "we just didn't think about it. Like even amongst ourselves, the topic never came up. Waiting for you after class or crossing paths with you here were the only things we thought of."

The friends couldn't help questioning themselves at that point. *Why had they gone about it so obtusely? Why didn't they just take the direct and straightforward approach?*

Joshua seemed to consider this too as he studied them. A silence that felt eternal to the girls on them as Joshua and Win sat in contemplation.

"Very well then." Win said, breaking the silence. "Nothing more to be done about that."

"Indeed," Joshua added with a brief smile before he looked out the window, still clearly considering something. He tapped his fingers once on the table, the final piece sliding into place in his mind, and turned back towards the friends sharing a fleeting glance with Lili along the way, "Win and I would be glad to help you with anything you need. If I may, I would presume Win's speeches in class prompted you to seek us. He and I have studied a large swath of history. One might say it is a hobby of ours, though that may not be quite adequate. It is a most fascinating topic. Humanity unknowingly writes some of the greatest tales imaginable simply by living out their individual lives. War, in particular, is one topic in which we are considerably knowledgeable. The machinations of individuals or small groups that propel an entire society or civilization into armed combat for a nearly incomprehensible amount of reasonings is truly astonishing."

The friends were so wrapped up in Joshua's words they didn't realize Win and Lili were still transfixed on the group. A sharp tension hung over the room. Without hesitation, Joshua gave Win and Lili passing glances. Whatever the look meant to them, it caused them both to relax as the tension dissipated. Joshua turned back toward them, and a smile spread across his face, the most beautiful smile they had ever seen. It was a soothing, bright smile full of warmth and charm, but at the same time, it was very sure of itself and seemed to be hiding so many things.

Without the slightest acknowledgment of what had happened, Joshua continued, "Where or when would you like to start?"

The friends looked back and forth at one another to see who would speak until finally, Rachel took the lead.

"Well, I mean, we already covered the war between Sumer and Elam, but we could hardly find any info. Most of the stuff we found actually came from the little library upstairs. I'm not sure where he is taking us next, but we've been at a loss so far. I want to speak up in class because I know he's all about participation, but it's kind of hard to say anything when you don't know anything."

"The first war ever recorded, so they say. Yes, always a fun place to start a discussion on warfare. From what I know of Edmonton, which is a fair deal, he will not spend much time on lackluster battles. He will only cover wars that shaped our world's history, so there should be plenty of information to find the rest of the semester. I have noticed, of course, that none of you speak up in class, which is something Charles does not take lightly. He, Win, and I are all close, though, so we will see what we can do about getting Charles to forgive you on that aspect. As you may have noticed, I hardly speak as well, though Win usually does enough for me."

Win gave a faint, knowing grin and winked at them, sending chills across their skin.

"Thanks. That'd be awesome." Ally said, joining the conversation. She was terrified of public speaking, and the thought of not having to talk in class brought a wave of relief. She paused for a moment, looking down at the table before finally asking, "What did you mean 'so they say?"

"I beg your pardon?" Joshua replied with genuine confusion.

"You said that was the first war ever recorded, so they say. What did you mean by 'so they say'?"

Win's smile faded slightly as he met his brother's gaze, but it didn't disappear entirely. More so, it seemed the two were sharing in a moment of curiosity and intrigue.

A grin crept into Joshua's lip as he replied, "Just that there were other wars, of course, wars that were, some belief, removed from the annals of history. Some call them myths. Others call them legends. They have been lost and forgotten or changed throughout the sands of time. Few, if any, exist who know of their true nature, but their echoes can be found rippling through many of the things humans believe to be true in this day and age. That is not really a topic for a first study date, though. Your current task is knowing what to learn for the next class after all."

"We'd really like to hear more, though. Wouldn't we girls?" Ally asked, turning to her friends, who all nodded in agreement.

"Yeah, you seem to really care about it," Rachel replied.

"And so you shall," Win responded with his smoldering grin. "In due time. We are very passionate about it, but now is not the time for such talk. Let us just get you ready for class tomorrow."

"Trying to build up suspense, or just trying to seem mysterious?" Erin asked suspiciously.

"My deepest apologies, ladies." Win began. "We truly do wish to help as you requested. If we withhold anything from you in the short term, I assure you it is for your better understanding as time progresses. Information is a layered puzzle. Each piece connects to a previous thread that ties together the understanding. What do you say we agree to set aside another time for further discussion of this topic?"

The friends studied one another, questioning themselves and each other as to if the agreement suited them.

"We accept the terms of your agreement, sir," Erin spoke for the friends. "Don't go thinking we're going to forget or let you back out, though. You're on the hook now."

She gave them both a piercing stare but accompanied it with a charming grin to which both men smiled in return.

"Glad we could reach an arrangement," Joshua said. "Then, for now, you are content with learning about the Battle of Megiddo, correct?"

"Um, is that the next war?" Rachel asked with genuine confusion as her mind tried focusing on why they were talking to the men in the first place.

"Well, it is actually the first battle recorded in what is considered 'reliable' detail. It gives a better portrait of how wars are documented and detailed. That is where Charles will likely stop next before leaping into bigger wars. He always wants to make sure everyone understands the foundation of what he is trying to teach."

"I can see why y'all get along. You two seem to know as much as he does."

"As I said, history is something of which we have learned a great deal. Though I would say, he has studied more. Now. the Battle of Megiddo was fought between Egyptian forces led by Pharaoh Thutmose III and a large group of Canaanites led by King Kadesh. Most sources claim it was on April 16th, 1457 BCE, although others say 1482 or 1479. In truth, the best records indicate it took place on April 12th, 1463. Most records say that there were between ten and twenty thousand troops under Thutmose III and between ten and fifteen thousand troops under Kadesh. Digging deep enough, though, you will find the most accurate accounts list both forces numbered around twelve to thirteen thousand."

"Wait, wait," Erin stopped Joshua as her friends frantically rushed to take notes, "how the hell do you know all this?"

"How, is immaterial." Win replied. "As he said, we are students of history. It matters not how we know; it matters that we know. Shall we continue?"

"No, I'm not quite sold yet." She continued to object despite grabbing her tablet while doing so. "Why are you guys even in this class if you know all this stuff?"

Joshua's reply was leveled and concise. "While we may know some things, or even a great deal of things on a given topic, to think we know everything and thus seek not to learn more would be a betrayal of our species' fundamental nature and an acceptance of eventual oblivion."

Tried as she might, Erin was unable to muster any witty rebuttal. Joshua's profound statement tugged at her core as she too understood that insatiable quest for knowledge, the need always to discover something new and foreign. The three friends were always that way; it was one of the fundamentals that drew them together. They were all constant learners, explorers of the mental frontier ever seeking new information, and there they found themselves amongst their kind with that peculiar family known as the Brownings.

So, the day continued with Joshua and Win recounting great historical details. On more than one occasion, one would grab a book from upstairs to further elaborate on a topic. Customers came and went, all while the friends were wrapped up in the tales. They were trying their hardest to absorb everything the two were saying. However, something about them made it hard for the friends to focus, yet at the same time made them strive even harder to learn. Had Ally's stomach not began to rumble, they may never have known it was already evening.

"It sounds as if someone has had all the studying she can take for one day." Joshua smiled.

"Wow," Ally began, embarrassment flushing her face, "I guess so. We got so caught up I didn't even realize all I had for lunch was a muffin. An incredible muffin, I might add. Which, by the way, how does your sister do it?"

"She is incredibly gifted with what she does." Win replied. "Lili has always loved to cook, but baking, in particular, is her specialty. You could probably all use some real food by now, though, I would imagine."

Erin was the first to reply. "I'm hella hungry. I had no friggin' clue what time it was. You ladies wanna head back to the apartment to grab some food?"

"I have a better idea." Win broke in with his devilishly charming smile. "How would the three of you like to join my brother and me for dinner tonight? Joshua, are you not rather hungry?"

Joshua swallowed softly, then grinned as he spoke, "I could certainly eat. Have you had Brave New Restaurant since moving to town?"

"No, but uh, we'd love to go," Rachel replied before either friend could say otherwise. Blushing in realization, she backpedaled. "Isn't that right, guys?"

Ally and Erin made eye contact, sharing in their conflicts. Rachel had not been affected the way they had yet. She was still looking at the whole situation as meeting new friends. Thanks to Thad's discussion and Erin's strange encounter with Joshua, they approached the family with a newfound sense of caution and unease. Even still, something kept pushing them forward.

With a faint nod of acknowledgment at one another, they agreed in unison, "Sure."

"There is only one small problem." Win said with a hint of remorse. "Our vehicle does not exactly have room for five. Would you like to meet us there, or..."

"Oh, I'm sure we could squeeze in the back seat." Ally cut in without hesitation, hoping for any chance to ride in it, even if it meant being cramped in the back seat.

Both Joshua and Win let out a slight chuckle. "While we appreciate your easy-going demeanor there, our car actually has no back seat."

Ally sighed, unable to hide her disappointment, but before any alternatives could be presented, Lili chimed in, "You can take mine. We can swap for the night, if you like. Joshua, you have to drive, though, and you had better take care of it."

"Why does Joshua have to drive? Do you not trust me, Lili?"

"I trust you fine, Win. I just trust Joshua more. He is a bit more responsible when it comes to driving than you are, and I would like to keep my trade-in value on this one." With that, she and Joshua tossed each other their keys. He was already heading for the door, a smirk on his face.

"Oh, betrayal! Cruel, cruel betrayal. What an agonizing beast you are." Win feigned dramatically.

"Oh, hush. No one is buying that, nor would they care if they did." Lili replied dismissively.

"Sure. Let Joshua drive. It's not even that fancy anyways." Win said to her with a wink of his glowing eyes and devilish grin as he motioned the girls towards the door.

"Do not make me hurt you, Win. You ladies enjoy your dinner, and if you have any trouble out of them, just let me know."

"We will behave, mother." Win said snidely, closing the door as they exited onto the sidewalk.

6

A BRAVE NEW DINNER

Even though night had yet to fall, it was already dark from overcast, looking as though it might rain at any minute. The girls pulled their coats tight, following the brothers as they rounded the corner to the parking lot where Lili's car was. There were a few cars in the lot from surrounding businesses' overflow, but Joshua unlocking the door told the two girls which car was hers. As soon as they saw the lights flash, Ally slowed with caution, afraid to approach Lili's Model X. She wanted to run her hands down the deep navy finish and slip right into the leather seats. She cursed her love of cars under her breath.

"Should we, like, wipe our feet off?" Ally said.

"I assure you that is not necessary. It has all-weather mats, for starters, but we also are not that uptight. Just make yourselves comfortable." Joshua said as the falcon wing doors rose to let them in.

"Would one of you care to sit upfront?" Win asked graciously. "I can sit in the back."

The friends paused awkwardly, not sure how to respond. Growing up, they'd always been conditioned to sit in the back, and even as adults, they were accustomed to doing so when riding with someone else. They looked at each other, searching for an answer or an inkling of who would sit upfront if they said yes.

"Maybe next time," Erin replied for the group. "No one called shotgun, and we don't want to have to rock-paper-scissors it to add complications. Thanks, though."

Ally climbed in first, making for the third row to avoid a debate in selflessness of who would do so. Rachel and Erin both eased into their chairs, sitting nervously as they were unsure how to close the doors.

Much to their relief, the doors closed almost automatically as they got comfortable.

Uncertain what to discuss now that they didn't have class as a topic, the girls sat stunned in silence until Rachel made a move to break the quiet, "It looks like rain out tonight."

"No need to worry. It will not rain tonight." Win stated succinctly.

"If you say so. Those clouds don't look like they'll hold off much longer, though."

A smirk spread across his lips. "Trust me. There will be no rain. I am sure you ladies heard about Little Rock's crazy weather as of late. It looks like rain almost every day now. It primarily just gets progressively colder, though."

"Which is crazy, because it wasn't all that cold the first couple weeks we were in town. Never mind the fact that Arkansas essentially has eight-month summers then a couple months for spring and fall." Erin said, finding her nerve again.

"That has been the case for some time, but just in the last few years, the area has seen an interesting increase in cold fronts. The meteorologists seem to be fascinated by it. So now, while it gets hot in the summer, autumn sets in swiftly, and it tends to get cold rather fast." Said Joshua as he pressed the pedal to turn, and the girls felt the strange sensation as they were pressed into their seats without delay.

"I guess that makes sense. Hey, do you guys always talk so properly?" Rachel asked.

"It is just our nature. It mainly comes from traveling routinely and dealing with frequent travelers. We come across several different languages and speech patterns on a constant basis, so we work to be very concise and articulate so as not to have any miscommunications." Joshua continued as he pulled into the restaurant parking. "If it bothers you, we can speak differently. Is there anything in particular about our vernacular that you dislike?" The car rolled to a stop, and Joshua put it in park.

"Oh no. It doesn't bother me at all. I'm sorry. I didn't mean to sound like I wanted you to change how you talk. It's just different, especially around here." Rachel apologized as they all stepped out.

Joshua laughed knowingly. "We get that sometimes. If ever it becomes a perturbation, feel free to request we speak otherwise. It matters not to us." Joshua politely stated as they walked towards the entrance.

"Genuinely, Rachel, do not feel bad. You are certainly not the first person to comment on our speaking. Many people are thrown off by it." Win added.

"Ah, Mr. Browning and Mr. Browning. How are you this evening, Joshua? Win?" The host of the restaurant opened the door for them all before the girls even realized what had happened.

"We are doing very well, George. How are you and the family?" Joshua replied with the air of a visiting dignitary.

"We're doing well as always. I wish we'd known you were coming. I'll have Lauren get your usual table ready if you don't mind waiting just a moment."

"Actually, George, that will not be necessary this evening. We will take whatever table is available. Thank you, though, for being wonderful as always."

"If that is your preference. Will it just be the five of you, or will Marc and Lili be joining?"

"It will just be the five of us. Lili is closing the shop tonight."

"I admire her workmanship. Running a restaurant is a tricky business, but she does it flawlessly. Lauren will seat you, and I will check in on you briefly. Chef is at work with a few orders, but I'll be sure to let him know you're here. He wouldn't want to miss you."

"Thank you very much, George. After you, Lauren." Joshua replied as a tall, slender young woman appeared with dark blonde locks flowing over her shoulders.

"Right this way, gentlemen." The woman said, giving them a gleaming smile as her blue eyes sparkled and gestured ahead. The friends followed behind Joshua and Win, feeling more out of place by the minute. "Here's your table. Now, before we get started, Josh, I have to tell you that Rock Town is about to release their anniversary edition, but we were able to get our case a little early as a special treat. This year's is a single malt that's been finished in cognac casks, so I definitely think you'll like it. The nose has notes of almond and vanilla against tart apples. The initial palette will be the strong wood spices, but that will quickly change to notes of tobacco, jam, and licorice. It's one of their best yet if you ask me. Neat?"

"Lauren, you know me too well."

"You're just lucky like that." She replied with noticeable confidence, "Now, Win for you, we have a fresh batch of their Feast in the Field if you would like to try that with your martini. The botanicals in this year's would pair nicely with a tiny splash of cherry juice too."

Win smiled with all his charm, "What on Earth did I do to deserve such a wonderful person like you?"

"Oh, Win, ever so sweet. If only." She returned his smile with compassion. "Sadly, as you know, you are quite literally not my type. I can at least help you drown your sorrow, though."

The two shared the warmest of smiles with one another, so content with their friendly banter.

"As for you ladies," Lauren said, turning to the friends, "I must apologize. Typically it's ladies first, but these two are easy to sort out quickly, whereas the three of you are a mystery. So, what's our poison? Wine, whiskey, or maybe something unique."

The three friends paused in confusion. They were still adjusting to being of age. There was wine and some assorted brews back at their house, but they were still at the point where they had to show their IDs anytime they bought something. Being asked for drinks upfront was foreign to them.

Erin recovered the quickest, "I'll take whatever red blend you recommend for now."

"The Sienna from Ferrari Carano. Can't go wrong there. I'll bring the wine list over as well so you can browse around, though. And you two?"

Ally replied next, "Um, I don't really like anything too strong. I'm pretty much your standard light and sweet kinda drinker."

"Nothing wrong with that, ma'am. Well, if you want some flavor without the kick, you should really try our Strawberry Lemonade Spritzer. It's somewhere between seltzer and cider. We make it fresh in-house. It's pretty tasty."

"Alright then. I'll try that."

"You got it, and for you, ma'am?" Lauren said, meeting eyes with Rachel.

"I'm slowly working my way through new breweries. Got anything local on tap?"

"You know it. Lost Forty, Flyway, Stone's Throw, plus a few from up north. We have out of state too. Got a particular type you're feeling?"

"Uh, a pale ale of some kind sounds good. Surprise me. Not too citrusy, though, please."

"Ale drinker and adventurous. That's my kind of lady right there. Alright, that's a Rock Town Anniversary neat, special martini, Sienna, spritzer, and brew of my choosing. I'll be right back with that and water for the table." Lauren shot Win another playful smile as she turned and headed towards the back.

"So I take it you guys come here often?" Erin asked, wasting no time.

"Every other week or so." Win replied. "Depends on our schedules. Our family enjoys the place, and we have known Mr. Brave and his family for some time now."

"Wait, so the owner's name is Brave?" Ally said with a chuckle as the joke clicked.

"Yeah," Win began, "he found it pretty clever. It would be hard to argue he was wrong. Many people have commented on it over the years."

Lauren slid menus in front of them almost imperceptibly.

"So, what are you guys like, the first family of Little Rock?" Erin quizzed, though her tone had shifted from aggravated caution to genuine curiosity.

"Hardly." Win replied. "We manage a few small businesses around town and are known in certain circles, but there is no seat at the Governor's table for us or anything like that. We tend to keep to ourselves. We are merely very personable with those close to us."

He met Erin's gaze, seeming to recognize her apprehension. Somehow his knowing gaze actually put Erin at ease instead of concerning her. There was honesty in it.

"Alright, here are your drinks," Lauren said as she placed them. "Do we want to get started with something light to eat, or have we been too busy chatting to think of food?"

"Oh, dear. I haven't even looked at the menu." Ally replied.

"I can save you the trouble to start at least," Joshua said before the friends could open their menus. "Do you ladies like cheese, mushrooms, seafood, or all of the above."

"Ally doesn't do seafood, but she can eat her weight in cheese. I probably could, too, if I'm being honest. I'm not big on shellfish, but Rach is." Erin replied, summing up their preferences.

"Lauren, you think you can make something work?" Joshua turned to the waitress with a knowing smile.

"Most certainly. A small selection of the baked brie, mushroom tart, and some of the crab cakes should do quite nicely."

"As always," Joshua's smile widened, "you are the best."

"Oh Joshua, you know flattery will get you nowhere except everywhere you want. I'll get those started for you."

They both grinned as she walked away.

"You two are quite chummy," Erin stated without subtlety.

Joshua seemed to miss the implication entirely and replied, "Yes, I suppose so. We have known each other for some time now. She is practically part of the family at this point."

"So," Rachel began, looking to swiftly change the subject, "Since you know the menu so well, what all's good here?"

"Well, the good news is you can hardly go wrong." Win began. "If you like wild game, the Duck with Duck is incredible. Alternatively, if you would like a meat-free option, the Mushroom Wellington is delicious. Both the filet and lobster salads are fantastic if you want something lighter, and everything else I didn't mention is also amazing. As I said, it is hard to go wrong. They are one of the best restaurants in town for a reason."

"Oh my," Rachel sighed. "Guess this'll be a tough choice then."

"Not for me," Erin replied. "I'm going straight for the Mixed Grill. Getting me a nice helping of it all."

Ally was at a complete loss. She had rarely ever been to a fine dining restaurant, and certainly never one as nice as that. She combed the menu looking for something that wasn't too expensive or too cheap that she could mostly understand the description, finally deciding on the half chicken, figuring it would at least be a tasty middle-of-the-road option. Ally felt more out of place by the minute.

"Well then," Rachel replied after a bit of hesitation, "I'm going with the Lobster Salad as Joshua recommended. I'm trusting you here."

"I assure you that your trust is not misplaced." Win said, smiling.

Erin and Ally both sipped their drinks in unison, watching Rachel's reaction, letting the silence linger. After a brief moment, Erin broke the quiet, "So, you said y'all are fairly involved around town. Are you from here, or just transplants?"

"Something like that." Win answered. "Our parents live upstate part-time. It is just Joshua, Lili, Marc, and myself that live here for the time being. Where not from here originally, though, I would imagine you guessed. We all moved here quite some time ago. Lili and Marc have been here for the most part, but our family also has property in the Northeast, where our parents stay when working and not in the Ozarks. We all go out there pretty frequently. Joshua and I just moved back here, though, last year."

"Northeast?" Erin asked. "You mean like Jonesboro?"

Win chuckled, "My mistake. I meant Northeast as in the Northeast United States, New York specifically. That is where we moved when we first came to the States."

"Hold up," Erin began, "you mean to tell me you moved from New York, to, of all the places, Little Rock? Not saying people don't move from New York, but of all the places you could move, seems odd you'd end up here."

"I suppose it could," Joshua replied. "It often seems so when people move from a place that is perceived to be a cultural epicenter like a major city. People have been moving from place to place throughout history, though. Humans, by their very nature, are nomadic, even if they sometimes forget that. It is hard to say why we moved here specifically, though. We felt called to this place is the easiest answer, felt a great sense of possibility here, and so far, we have found that to be true."

"That makes sense, I guess." Rachel began. "I mean, we moved here from just a couple hours south. Arkansas is all we've ever known, so for us being here seems like a big deal yet also seems like Podunk compared to some places. Our friend Thad lived in New York when he was a little kid, but his family moved here because of work. He's been here so long now we kind of forget he was even from there. What makes anybody live anywhere, though, I guess."

"Yeah, different strokes for different folks," Erin added. "So, you said when you moved to the states, where were you from before that? Your accent sounds kinda British."

Joshua and Win both smirked.

"What?" Erin asked. "What'd I say?"

"Nothing." Win replied. "Just the accent bit. It never gets old hearing the term 'British accent' since Britain is not specifically a place. I, for example, am from South Wales, so my accent is Southern Welsh, which is a bit more musical than most in the Isles. Grouping the various accents is easier for description, but it would be like saying someone from Texas and Boston has an American accent when those two sound considerably different. The UK alone has dozens of accents, not to mention all the former colonies' accents. You can thank the British Empire for making that so tricky, though. In contrast, Professor Edmonton's accent is known as Received Pronunciation or just Standard English, which is basically everything you are probably used to hearing. If BBC had its own accent, that would be it."

"I wouldn't have even said there was a difference between how you and Edmonton sound." Rachel said in confusion

"It's like those YouTube videos you see where people do fifty different accents or whatnot," Erin interjected. "Even listening to them in order, I can still hardly tell the difference."

Before the conversation could continue, Lauren appeared with their appetizers. "How is everyone enjoying their drinks? Ladies, did I do alright?"

"Great." Ally replied.

"Couldn't have asked for a better wine," Erin said. "Great body, not too heavy. Smelling it just makes me want chocolate."

"Glad to hear it. How about your beer, ma'am?" She asked, fixing her gaze on Rachel.

"Excellent. You've got great taste."

"Oh, I know," Lauren replied, giving Rachel a longing wink that made her flush with unexpected excitement as she shifted in her seat. "How about you two gentlemen?"

"As always, Lauren," Win began, "you do not disappoint."

"That I don't." She replied to him with a mischievous grin.

"I have to say, Lauren," Joshua stated, "I believe this may be their best anniversary release yet."

"Five for five. That's what I like to hear. Did we want to go ahead and get dinner ordered, or would y'all like some time to snack and drink before we do?"

"Ally, did you get a chance to decide what you want?" Joshua asked without hesitation.

"Oh, um yeah." Ally replied, surprised he'd been so attentive to her. "I want to do the Half Chicken, please."

"Great choice." Joshua and Lauren said in unison before smiling at each other.

"And I believe Rachel was wanting the Lobster Salad and Erin the Mixed Grill, was that right?" Win asked.

The two friends responded in agreement.

"All excellent choices, ladies. You'll be impressed for sure. And you two are doing the usual; I take it?"

"But of course," Joshua replied, still smiling.

"Alright then, with that, I'll take my leave." Lauren gave a faint curtsy as she left.

"What's the usual?" Erin quizzed.

"Whatever Chef prepares." Win said. "Everything they make is fantastic, so we just let Peter decide what he feels we should eat."

"What if it's something you don't, though?"

"That has yet to happen, so until then, we embrace it."

"You're braver than I am."

"Well," Joshua added, "it helps when you like virtually any cuisine. So we are fortunate in that sense."

"Gotcha. Whatever works for ya."

"So," Ally began, anxious to get back to the conversation, "you said you're from England originally. What part?"

Both brothers looked at each other as if trying to decide who should explain. Without any audible decision, Win began, "Um, yeah, so I am originally from Wales. I grew up there for a time and then started traveling back and forth to the City of London with the family business. We were there until I went through university, and that is when we started moving around. Once we landed in the states and put down roots in New York, we traveled around to a number of the major cities, getting a feel for the place, until we landed here. Now we live the two-city life in America and occasionally pop off back to England. We spent quite a bit of time traveling checking into different schools, but we made some memories along the way as well."

Win chuckled a little bit as Joshua smiled, clearly knowing what his brother was thinking. Ally was having a hard time deciding what to think. Her friends' and family's thoughts that these men had a brutal youth seemed ever more unfathomable, but it was apparent there was something they weren't saying. She could tell by the look on Erin's face her friend felt similarly.

"We were spending more time in New York the past couple years. It was not until we learned of Professor Edmonton's arrival that we decided to return to Little Rock. You see, I studied under Edmonton while I was in London, and Joshua and I were very eager to take his class here. Upon learning the news, we enrolled in UCA, and the rest, you know."

Erin's curiosity and suspicion had matched Ally's. "You keep saying I, instead of we. Joshua, are you not from England? Is that why your voice sounds different?"

"Yes and no, respectively. My family was originally from Eastern Europe. We somewhat made our journey across Europe until we arrived in London, and that was when Win came along. He is a bit younger, so England was mostly all he knew. As for the accent, all the moving around blended my voice around until it became what you hear today."

"So, who's the oldest?" Erin continued probing.

"Well," Joshua began. "That depends on your definition of age. Whether you define years lived compared to lived experiences compared to the knowledge obtained, a person's longevity and lifespan could vary greatly. Alas, though, I feel as if we have only talked about ourselves. What about the three of you? What are your stories?"

"There's not really much to tell." A mesmerized Rachel spoke up. "We've known each other since grade school, grew up in the same town, done pretty much everything together, including moving here as our first place of our own. Nothing fun like traveling the world. I bet you guys speak a ton of different languages, huh?"

"Traveling can be nice." Joshua "It is not always quite what you think it to be, though, and yes, we do speak a few languages. That, however, is a show for another time. The food is here."

Just as he said that, Lauren popped up behind him, "Josh, how do you always hear me coming? One of these days, I'll sneak up on you."

He smiled a wicked yet beautiful smile, "You carry your weight on your left side but the tray on your right arm. The offset causes a sway that makes a distinct noise. That, and the general aura of suaveness radiating from you."

Was he lying? Ally certainly couldn't hear that. She looked at Erin, attempting to read each other's expressions. Was this just an incredible bluff, or was he somehow that attentive? Or was it something else entirely. Ally couldn't decide, but the plate of food stole her attention, and she didn't care.

"Well, Josh, I'm very flattered that you pay that much attention to me, though who could blame you," Lauren said with a wink at him that sent waves of jealousy over the friends they couldn't understand. "I'll have to start paying more attention to you. If you need anything, I'll be by in a bit. Enjoy your meals."

With that she left, the eating began, and the chatter gave way to the tune of the mouth-watering chicken stuffed with Boursin cheese and roasted in garlic caper au jus, bacon and smoked gruyere potato au gratin, sizzling pork tenderloins, apple brandy roasted potatoes, tender beef medallions topped in a red wine glaze, succulent shrimp and fennel risotto, buttery lobster and lump crabmeat, stuffed quail, duck sausage, and more being savored harmoniously.

"Ok," Rachel said, taking a break from her Lobster Salad. "I gotta say you two just earned yourself the spot as my food tour guide."

"I am certain that Joshua and I could show you a few places to dine that you would enjoy."

"We have been eating around here for some time. We know the layout pretty well. You are welcome to join us for dinner with Marc and Lili Friday night. It is somewhat of a tradition." Joshua said.

"I don't know if I'd feel right intruding on your tradition." Ally said with genuine confliction. "We can just let y'all do your thing. We wouldn't want to get in the way of family time."

"I insist. I promise we will not bite. Except for Win, maybe." Win smirked at his brother's remark. "Marc and Lili have already taken a liking to you anyways. I am sure they would love for you to join us."

Ally was about to throw out another stubborn refusal, but Erin beat her to the punch. "We'd love to join you. Don't mind, Ally. She always feels like she'll 'get in the way' like a stubborn ass. You kinda have to beat her into submission from time to time." Erin smiled her evil grin at Ally. She knew how much Ally hated to be called out on that.

"Well, we will do our very best to make the three of you feel at home, and I assure you, Ally, you most certainly will not get in the way with my family. Lili and Marc are both quite anxious to know more about you."

"That they are. Plus, you hopefully have noticed their polite demeanor towards you by now. Our family may be a bit unapproachable, but they are all mostly nice. The fact that Lili and Marc are already so chatty with you should be a sign they like you. We just tend to keep to ourselves." Win added.

"Tell me about it." Erin wished she could snatch the words out of the air and put them back in her mouth before Joshua or Win heard her.

"So you have noticed that my family is somewhat reserved," Joshua said with a look on his face that showed no surprise at all. It looked as if he knew all along that Rachel had thought that. He seemed as if he knew the answer to his question before he even asked, "What is it about my family that makes you think such?"

Erin fidgeted in her seat. Rachel and Ally both watched in horror as if a traffic accident were unfolding before them. He didn't seem angry, but that made it worse. He was very calm and at peace even though she thought his family was somewhat stuck up. Win was no different. He finished his bite of chicken and washed it down with a sip of his martini, utterly unphased by the girl's comment.

"I just meant that your family doesn't seem to associate with many people. Almost as if you don't want to be approached. Not that that's a bad thing."

"There is no need to backtrack. You said what you said because it is what you felt. I promise you are not the first to find my family unapproachable or even pretentious." Joshua smiled beautifully, putting the friends at ease, but the tone he spoke with next only enforced his seriousness in the statement. "Have you stopped to think, though, that perhaps my family appears unapproachable for a reason? You've been asking questions of us all night with open admiration. I know that you are likely thinking how amazing our lives are with the lavish traveling and the well-to-do family. However, I assure you that our journeys were not the fun-filled movies you may be envisioning, and our wealth has not come without a price. We have sacrificed a great deal to be where we are, and that is not without its consequences. If my family seems unapproachable, it is simply because they do not wish anyone to share our troubles." He stopped to stare at each of them. The look on his face told the friends they would do well not to ask too many questions. The line of his pursed lips curled at the edges. "Would any of you ladies like dessert?"

Right as Joshua said that Chef arrived. Ally and Rachel were so entirely stunned by Joshua's stern words that they didn't even notice his again impeccable awareness that someone was approaching.

"Now Joshua, you know that's supposed to be our job to ask. But first, did you ladies enjoy your meals?" He said as he ushered someone over to take their plates.

"Absolutely." Rachel said. "It was delicious. We'll definitely be coming back."

"Fully agreed," Ally added. "Possibly the most incredible thing I've ever eaten, but I don't think I have room for dessert."

"I'm with her. The deserts look amazing, but I'm already on the verge of meat sweats, and I still need a to-go box. Next time I'll have to eat something smaller, so I have room for dessert." Erin added.

Both Joshua and Win looked as if they had not scratched the surface of their hunger, but Joshua declined. "I think we shall pass as well. Thank you, though, Peter. As always, it was sublime. Excellent selection tonight."

"Well, that is always good to hear. I'm terribly sorry I'm just now getting out here. Hopefully, next time I won't be so busy and can come chat some more. I'm glad you girls enjoyed your first visit. We look forward to seeing you again. You'll have to try something different next time to get a feel for the menu. Joshua, Win, it's always a pleasure." With that, Peter left, and the two men stood up to leave.

"Um, don't we need to pay?" Ally said, reaching for her wallet in her backpack.

"What self-respecting individual could possibly let their guests pay on their first visit?" Win replied. "They run our tab automatically. Relax." He smiled, and they.

"Now, do we need to take you, ladies, home or back to your vehicle?" Joshua asked.

"Oh crap. Uh, we just walk to the Brew. We don't really live far enough to drive." Ally replied.

"Then we shall drive you home. Where do you live?" Joshua asked as he pressed the button to raise their doors.

Erin gave the address before asking, "So what exactly does Marc do?"

"I beg your pardon?" Joshua asked with genuine confusion.

"Well, we ran into him in the library upstairs at the Brew. He explained to us how the library search thing worked, but then he got all cryptic about what he and y'all do. It was weird, to say the least. Y'all aren't in like some secret government agency or witness protection program or some shit, are you?" Erin asked, only partially in jest.

"I can assure you none of our family are in witness protection, thankfully, and that none of us work in the government. We have and do, however, on occasion work on government projects. Marc, in particular, is a freelancer. So while I am unaware of what exactly was said, I would imagine Marc was just being funny considering what he does and for whom can vary from day to day."

There was a rigid uniformity to Joshua's explanation like he was reciting a script he'd memorized and delivered countless times over.

Erin and Ally both sensed it. Rachel, however, was busy absorbing every bit of information the two men were saying, cataloging every piece should it ever become practical.

"You said we in regards to the work," Rachel interjected. "Do you two both work with him, or was that just a general statement? Just curious what all you do along with school. The schoolwork alone is enough to wear me out."

Win answered, "Should a given contract require one of our skill sets, we will. That is very situational, though. We all have some overlapping skills, but it is not all that often they are all needed in conjunction. What Joshua meant by we is that each of us individually has worked on various contracts over time. Usually, they are concise jobs that may only take a week or two to complete, if not less, so the work comes and goes."

"Follow-up question," Erin began with noted sarcasm, "are all of you enigmatic intentionally, or is that just a genuine coincidence you don't realize is occurring?"

"You know," Joshua replied, "I think it is a bit of both. We are often intentionally cryptic or enigmatic, as you say, and have been historically, to the point I believe it often happens unintentionally simply because we have practiced being ambiguous so long."

There was a faint level of humor in his voice, but Ally and Erin couldn't tell if it was genuine or sarcastic.

"Anyways," he continued, "I believe that is about all the mysterious deflecting we can do for one evening given that we are almost to your house.

As they turned onto the friends' road, Ally was surprised. She cleared her throat to be the first to thank the two men, "It was a real pleasure hanging out tonight. Thank you both for having us." She tried to sound as proper as she could.

"Are you guys staying for a bit?" Rachel added.

Erin and Ally both inhaled, deeply unsure if they wanted the two men to come in or not. Part of them was still wildly curious about this strange set of siblings and their family, but still, some portion was screaming to flee.

"Win and I appreciate your hospitality, but it would be inappropriate of us to do so on the first outing."

"Couldn't agree more," Win added. "Thank you greatly for the offer, though. Perhaps next time. Besides, we would do best to return

Lili's car tonight rather than tomorrow. Have a wonderful rest of the evening, and hopefully, we will see you tomorrow."

"Fair enough," Erin replied. "It really was a fun evening. Thank y'all for taking us and humoring us with our interrogations."

"I assure you the pleasure was ours." Win replied, graciously bowing.

"Cool deal. See you tomorrow." Ally said as the three friends exited, and the car rolled off into the black of the night.

"So, we gonna talk about all this?" Rachel asked, all her sense of awe and wonder removed.

"Oh, most definitely," Ally began, "but I say let's wait till after tomorrow's hang out and have a collective conversation. Deal?"

"Deal," Rachel answered.

"Suits me," Erin replied. "I think my brain has processed all it can for one day.

Once in her room, Ally grabbed her phone and began the evening text log with Thad.

"What's up jackass?"

"Not much wench. Just playing. Wanna jump on?"

"In a bit. Let me get ready for bed."

"Lame. I'll play a few more matches then. I just went 32-1. How's your night been?"

"My day/ night was fine. Hung out with Joshua and Win…."

"Holy shit. I knew it was just a matter of time. Haha Let's hear the details?"

"Ugh. I knew you'd be like this. What do you want to know?"

"I told you, everything. I'm still building my dossier on them, so any information is helpful. Are they still as unsettling and unapproachable as you thought?"

"Honestly, even more. Turns out they've basically moved all over the planet. In addition to being pretty wealthy they all work in super clandestine jobs, and they own up to their intimidating nature. What all have you found on them?"

"Nothing I'm discussing via text. Besides, I'm still researching. I'll give you the full debriefing when I come up this weekend. So where all have they lived?"

"Well, Win was born in England when the family lived there, and before that the family lived somewhere in Eastern Europe where Joshua was born. He didn't say where exactly. I'm still not sure yet about Marc and Lili. They didn't join us. The family originally moved to New York when they first came here. They still have a house there. Then on top of that they spent a few years traveling all through the US."

"From Eastern Europe to England to here? Man, talk about some nomads.

That's pretty wild. It's cool to have some fellow New Yorkers around at least. These guys seem to be one anomaly after another, though."

"If I were to guess I'd have thought they were foreign exchange students. I didn't even tell you about the new car, Model X. That's Lili's though we had to take it so there'd be enough room."

"Hey, I can respect their style at least, even if they are uppity."

"Eh, they're not as uppity as I thought, at least not in hanging out. They're super down to earth once you actually get around them. They're just very proper and such. They both admitted that their family is unapproachable. Joshua even said that his family is that way for a reason and got a bit defensive."

"Oh really? What'd he say?"

"Basically that everything they had didn't come easy. He made it out like they tried to keep people away for their own safety. Don't ask me what that's all about."

"Told ya. They're android demon hunters. That's why they want to scare people away."

"You are such a effin dork. Are you ready to play yet?"

"Yeah. Let me grab my headset. Hey what was the name of the coffee shop they own? I wanna do a little research on it to go with what else I'm working on."

"If it'll make you feel better. It's called The Daily Brew. To my understanding it's owned by Marc and Lili Browning, but it may be in their family's name since they said it'd been in the family for some time. Send me an invite loser."

Ally stayed up playing with Thad for a couple of hours, before calling it a night. The topic of the Brownings didn't come up much as they were busy calling out enemies, cheap kills, and clips they needed to save but never would. By the time she turned off her system, Ally could barely keep her eyes open. She curled up in her sheets, closed her eyes, and fell right to sleep.

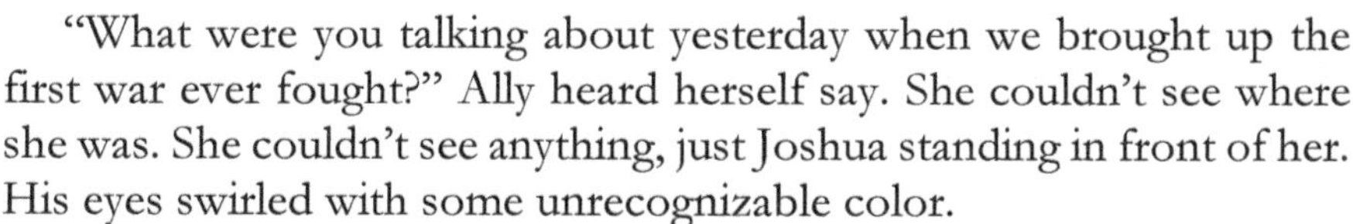

"What were you talking about yesterday when we brought up the first war ever fought?" Ally heard herself say. She couldn't see where she was. She couldn't see anything, just Joshua standing in front of her. His eyes swirled with some unrecognizable color.

"Why do you want to know? Are you certain you are prepared for the response?" His lips curled into an evil smile as his eyes turned fiery red, and his appearance continued slowly shifting until the man she knew was gone entirely. Before her then stood a hooded figure, its robe covering one arm. Mighty pauldrons emblazoned with symbols she couldn't make out covered its shoulder, and she could see intricately crafted gauntlets hiding the figure's hands. Underneath the cowl of its hood, nothing was visible save two brilliant, fiery orbs that served as eyes. From the hood flowed a set of golden locks aglow in the darkness that rested on the figure's chest.

"There are things in this world that mean you harm Allyxandria Carver. There are those that mean to kill you. Are you prepared to die, Ally?" The voice had changed and carried tones that were metallic and hollow.

A rush of pain shot through Ally's body. Something excruciating pulsed through her veins. It flowed through her body until it gripped her heart. She knew she could not fight it, but she must. The pain rang out in her head. She wanted to claw her skin away to make it stop, but her body had been consumed. Ally took a deep breath as death began to grip her.

Suddenly the voice came from all around with a sense of infiniteness, as if coming from light-years away and was all-encompassing.

"Nigh is the hour of The Raven and The Lion.
The Frost sets in as the Storms coalesce.
Slow, steady doth beat the Drums of War.
The Mountain rages as the Great Tree beckons.
With fire and fury beat the Wings of the Wind.
The River rises and carries forth unto Oblivion.
Stars will fall. The Heavens will burn.
Gods will crumble as the Void reaches out.
Seek not the end. The Rising is at hand."

7
ANCIENT HISTORY

The cold air accompanied the friends on their way to The Daily Brew, reminding them they were never alone in their new city. The three girls shuffled along from their house to the coffee shop after another day of class.

"You think they'll be there?"

"I don't know, Rach." Ally replied as the three walked to The Brew from their house after getting home from class. "I hope so, considering we still need help with class and have a million questions about them, but I hate to assume last night is going to become a regular thing. I mean, if you didn't pick up on anything else last night, surely you caught the 'danger, danger' vibe."

"Well yeah, I caught that, but we're just being friendly, right. Surely being friends isn't dangerous?"

Rachel's voice betrayed her. She was hoping for the previous night's events to become an everyday thing, but she was just as concerned as Erin and Ally. The friends had not talked about their day with the Brownings before school that morning. Each had their concerns as it was clear they were heading down a slippery slope. Ally, of course, didn't mention her dream. That would just make matters worse, and she still wasn't even sure what her dream was. A warning? A prophecy? Try as she might, her brain couldn't even process it. It was more specific and obscure than anything she had ever experienced, but she knew she wanted to learn more without question.

Further yet, Joshua and Win weren't in class that day, much to their shock. Edmonton didn't comment on it, but there was a noticeable difference in the classroom air as if the lesson had waned gradually in some way. Despite having been told the night before they would see

Joshua and Win the next day, the three friends couldn't help wondering if it was a diversion.

Erin pretended like she didn't notice Rachel's concern or have her own, "Yeah, you're probably right. We'll find out in just a bit, though." The three friends approached the doors to The Brew together and took a deep breath.

Relief and surprise settled over Ally, Erin, and Rachel as the doors opened to show Joshua and Win standing at the counter talking with Terry, Denise, and Lili. The relief and surprise were immediately replaced with nervousness, though—the exact mix of emotions from the day before and their morning talk. None of the friends could place it. There was a war going on within their minds, with one side demanding they get away from this family, whilst the other felt inexplicably drawn to them as if they all belonged. Together, they walked towards the counter with caution.

Win was the first to speak, "Good afternoon, ladies. How are we today?"

Ally relaxed, "I'm fine, Win. How 'bout you?"

"Wonderful as always seeing your lovely face." For once, he didn't seem to be pouring on the charm. His words seemed sincere. "Rachel, I trust you are doing well also?"

"Hell yeah," Rachel swore, a rare thing in mixed company. "I could go for something to drink, though. Of coffee. I meant coffee. I mean, I like a drink and all, as you of course know, but I just meant now that I would really like a coffee."

Win, and the friends, for that matter, couldn't help smiling as she blushed, "Shall we get to studying while we await our drinks then?"

"I'm followin' you." Rachel began to glow as she followed Win to their table.

As formal as usual, Joshua had a faint grin as he watched his brother and Rachel walking towards the table. "Ally, Erin, I assume you will both be joining us too?" Joshua's voice wrapped Ally and Erin in it. Here they were, two of the most skeptical and cynical people they knew, and this man and his family were somehow steadily disarming them.

"I suppose." Erin knew her façade was as transparent as freshly cleaned glass.

Once the three reached the table and joined Win and Rachel, Ally immediately asked her question while she could.

"So how come y'all weren't in class today?"

Win didn't even hesitate, "Sadly, we had a meeting run over. We would be about ten minutes late, but we know how much Edmonton hates having his classes interrupted. So, we messaged Charles to let him know and headed over here instead."

Joshua picked up immediately before one of the friends could reply, "Given how frequently you visit here, we figured it safe to presume you would eventually make it here after class. Fortunately, Edmonton sent us today's discussion already. If it pleases you, we can go over today's lesson to make sure you are comfortable with it?"

This was Ally's chance. "Actually, I'm pretty sure we're all set on today's lesson. We'd really like to know more about the wars you spoke of yesterday; the ones that have been removed from the history books and few people are alive that know. You did say we could discuss that today, after all."

Erin couldn't help beaming in pride at Ally. She hadn't wanted to do the exact same thing, and for once, Ally beat her to it.

"I had hoped my warning yesterday would have sufficed. I do not feel it is the appropriate time for me to begin telling ghost stories and ancient myths when there is much work to be done."

"We don't have class tomorrow." Erin joined in to support Ally's moxie. "We can study then, and we actually wanna know these ancient myths. It may have escaped your purview, but we are, after all, students of history. All of it interests us."

"Right, you are there, but unfortunately, we will not be able to study tomorrow. This Thursday is Zoo Day."

"Zoo Day?" Rachel said, channeling the three friends' collective confusion.

"Yes, ma'am," Lili said as she set their drinks down. "Our family is, well, let us say, rather involved in the zoo. We take turns going on Thursdays as best we can. It is nice to see the animals, and we like to know that our money is being put to good use for them. Conservation is vital to us, to say the least."

"That's really amazing." Ally said without filter. "Like really. You guys are rather incredible. I love animals. I wish I could contribute like you."

"We are not so incredible." Lili sat down at the table with them. There was a calm to her statement that seemed to cover up some truth. "We are just doing our duty. Those animals need people to look after them. Humans have a responsibility to look after this planet and all its lifeforms, and you can contribute. They actually love visitors, and zoos do thrive on attendance."

"Oh, I love going to the zoo," Erin added, not able to contain herself. "I love the zoo, period. I have to agree with Ally, though, it's really great what you do."

"You should join us tomorrow then." Win said, grabbing his and Rachel's drinks. "We would welcome the company, and as patrons, our guests get in free."

"We would be honored." Ally said, wondering who spoke. That was her voice, but the words were all wrong.

"Very well then," Lili said, smiling at the friends, then fixing Win with a glare before turning to Joshua. "Do you need to borrow one of our cars, or do you want to take the –"

"We will take one of yours." Joshua cut her off without even making a glance towards her. "Shall I come by tonight to get one of them?"

"That is perfectly fine. Just let yourself in if Marc or I am not home."

"Do you think Marc will be home late tonight?" Win chimed in, breaking the awkwardness. "I would like to speak about some rendering issues I have been having."

"There are only a couple days left on the project, so I would expect it will be eleven or twelve most likely."

"Well, then it looks like I will be coming over around eleven or twelve. If that is ok with you?"

"As if a lack of invitation ever stopped you before," Lili said with a smirk that suggested he frequented their house.

"Splendid." Win smiled at her with the dangerous smile he had as he rose and walked behind the counter.

"Feel free to help yourself, Win. It is not like my job is to get people food and drinks."

"I would not want to put any more work on you than was necessary, Lili. I mean, you are ever so busy." Win grinned ever so evilly as Lili's eyes burned with rage. That mother stare that no matter how little or sweet the woman giving it is, everyone in the room cringes with fear. Joshua and Win just chuckled, though. It wasn't that they thought the stare was empty, just that they were accustomed to it.

The friends looked back at Joshua to see him still smiling broadly as he looked towards them. "My family may be unapproachable, but they are still very much a family."

Win made his way back to the table as Lili threw a muffin at him. Without even turning, he threw his hand up and snagged it. Then he spun to face her with the same mischievous grin plastered on his face.

"I can tell. That's the first time I've ever seen y'all be, normalish." Erin said, smiling to show she meant well, and Joshua returned the smile, so she began again. "So, what was the deal with cutting off Lili there? What was she about to say?"

"It might seem trivial to you possibly, but I do not particularly care for my possessions to be discussed for everyone to hear. I prefer to keep most things to myself."

"Must be one hell of a garage then." Ally said.

Joshua's lips curled on the right side, feeling slightly complimented and slightly amused at Ally's words.

"So," Rachel began, "you meticulously dodged Erin yesterday on what Marc does, but after Win's comment, things are even more obscure. What does Marc do? And, better yet, what is your relation to Marc even?"

Win smirked as he took a bite of his muffin.

Joshua let out a soft chuckle as he answered, "Well, Lili is my sibling; therefore, Marc would be my in-law by legal definition. Marc and Lili, however, have been together for so long, and Marc has been such a huge aspect of my family, that I honestly just see it as yet another member of the family. As for employment, I already stated that Marc is a freelancer. Being as that is obviously not a detailed enough answer, to be more specific though Marc builds graphic engines. The project Marc is currently finishing, ironically as Erin quizzed, is for a government training program. I am not allowed to disclose the details. His business takes all manner of contracts, but video games and movies are his personal favorites."

"He makes video games and movies? That's wicked." Ally said, completely stunned.

"No, ma'am. Marc just builds the engines companies use to make games and movies, among other stuff. Though, I can easily say that making the products themselves is not at all out of the realm of possibility if Marc wanted to do so."

"I would imagine so if he has those kinds of contracts. What was that about rendering issues then?"

"Oh, that?" Win replied. "Well, I am currently designing a puzzle game for my own amusement. I recently ran into some rendering issues on one of the stages, and, being that Marc built the engine I am using, I figured best to have the creator take a look at it."

"Wow," Erin said with unexpected fondness. "Your family gets stranger by the day. In a good way. Like I wish we had cool stories like that."

"I would not say 'cool' is the proper term to describe us, but thank you nonetheless."

"So, what's the game about?" Ally asked in earnest.

"Um," Win began, unsure what to say, "in essence, it is an actual four-dimensional chess system, but then each stage only has certain pieces and dimensions in play. Rather odd, I realize."

"Wait," Erin said incredulously, "you're joking, right?"

"Joking how?"

"4D Chess is just a phrase based on the concept of chess with added layers and moves not expected. How would you make an actual game of it?"

"Well, you are familiar with regular chess, yes?"

"Obviously," Erin replied snidely.

"That is played in two dimensions, obviously. Three-dimensional chess has already been demonstrated and showcased in previous iterations. Even now, there are computer simulations that include the fourth dimension. Consider how a tesseract is a four-dimensional representation of the cube. Similarly, chess can function in a similar capacity. What I am working to do, though, is build a series of puzzles from that concept. Imagine, for instance, if you had a series of chess games where you only had certain pieces you could use or plays you could make. In a very scaled-down example, that is what I am doing."

The three friends were perplexed as they worked to understand both what Win was explaining and how or why this would be something of interest to him. When he was just an eclectic history buff, it was one thing. To add his interest in chess, puzzle games, and coding, he became a new, yet unknown, thing entirely.

"Guess your brother was speaking more broadly when he said you can do and enjoy more than one thing." Ally said, remembering Marc's statement.

"Thankfully, that is very true." Win replied. "After all, we are all more than simply one thing. No one thing can define us. We are all amalgamations of all things that make us. Were someone to be defined by only a singular thing, well, that would be a deplorable state of existence."

The friends let his words sink in, searching themselves to see what different aspects and characteristics made up their whole self and finding in the process how right Win was. They were each more than the sum of their parts, and they never had to extrapolate that out to an even larger scale as they were seeing with this family.

"Two questions," Erin asked, part incredulous, part curious. "First, what all else are you guys into? Second, do you sleep at all with all the shit you do?"

Win laughed as he worked to reply, "Well, sleep is certainly the 'shit' we do the least, but we do rest on occasion, yes. As for your other question, there frankly is no limit. We are, each of us, lifelong students in a sense, ever studying and researching any new thing we can. There almost is no field in which we do not have some level of interest. We try to learn everything we can about physics, biology, chemistry, transportation, sports, politics, psychology, honestly anything. Some of our favorite things to study are cultures of the world, religion, and history. It is a truly fascinating topic, how humanity grows and evolves over time. Society is the single most complex organism in this known existence. What is there not to love about learning everything you can of it?"

"Wow." Erin began with profound awe. "You're not joking. You guys really are just giant data sponges, aren't you?"

"That is one way to put it," Joshua replied with calm fervor. "It all flows together. History, religion, science, politics; they all shape and mold one another. It is a never-ceasing development as the entire world warps and shifts with each new discovery and how that reflects things learned or experienced in the past. Humans are continually rewriting everything they know."

Ally chewed the inside of her lip in hesitation. This was their opportunity.

"So, do these intricate human histories have anything to do with the myths and legends of ancient lore you say some still believe?"

"Not relenting on that, are you?" Joshua more stated than asked.

"Not a chance," Erin said, reminding him of her promise.

"Are you truly that adamant to hear some silly old fairy tale?" Win asked sarcastically.

"Absolutely," Rachel replied in earnest.

The three friends were resolute. Something drove each of them to understand.

"How is this for you?" Joshua began. "I will tell you the very beginning of the part that is mine to tell today, and if you have questions, I will answer them. Then if you truly wish to know more, we will go from there. Does this suit you?"

The friends' eyes all met in agreement.

"Sounds fair enough." Ally replied.

"As you wish. Naturally, you have each studied history extensively, or you wouldn't be in Edmonton's course. Have you ever read the Bible, though? Or rather, do you believe it?"

The friends were puzzled.

"Yes," Rachel replied. "Not cover to cover, but I mean, we know most of the stories from growing up in church. I think I can safely say for all of us that we believe it's true, at least the majority anyways."

Erin and Ally nodded their agreement.

"So, then you know of the angels and their place? Why Adam and Eve were cast out of Eden, and why God came to Earth as Jesus? You know of the world's end as told in Revelation?"

"Yeah, for the most part, I guess," Rachel replied again.

"And what of Adi Parashakit's commands to Brahma? Do you know of Nana Buluku's birth of Mawu-Lisa? Are you familiar with Takamagahara and the journeys of Izanagi and Izanami? And what about Lingbao Tianzun and the works of the Three Pure Ones? Or what of Kāne and his separation from Po?"

The friends were beyond perplexed, trying to follow along with where Joshua was going.

"Um," Erin began. "I think I can safely say we have no idea about that."

"And what of mythology? Greek, Egyptian, Norse. Do you know or believe any of them?"

"I know a little about Greek and Roman." Ally replied. "We studied them in high school, but I wouldn't say any of us 'know' mythology. As for believing it, I personally can see where they got a lot of their ideas, but they were just ideas."

"What if I were to tell you every story of creation, every religious and scientific explanation of this existence were all tiny pieces of a much larger tapestry that few could even comprehend? Would you scoff, or think us mad? Or would you begin to question the nature of your reality?"

Joshua's eyes flashed brilliantly. He meant every word of what he said, and somehow the three friends knew it was true. Like nothing ever before, they could feel the truth touch the very fiber of their beings. They had to know more, had to know what secrets he possessed.

"What do you mean?" Ally asked in barely a whisper.

"I mean that the story you say you wish to know is a most beautiful and tragic one, that explains the very nature of this world and its place in the universe. It also tells what is to become of this existence eventually. This story will not end the way you wish, for it will end the way it must. The way it was meant to end. In this life, there are worlds within worlds and stories within histories. This tale is one of many parts, each with its own troubling piece, and it is a tale of many peoples, each with a more horrible reality, and most with the darkest of secrets; secrets worth dying, secrets worth killing. The laws by which I am bound are simple but fierce, and their consequences are grave. I cannot divulge any information until its proper time has come, and not all parts are mine to tell. If ever these rules are broken, it will cost all our lives, and many more. If I am to tell you this tale, everything you know about this world and this life will change, forever. Are you truly prepared for that?"

The friends wanted to laugh. His words sounded so absurd, but the look that his face held was in no way joking. This was why they were being pulled towards him, why they could not turn away. This is what he was hiding that they needed to know. They had to choose. The friends searched each other's faces. They knew without a doubt that there was no deceit in his voice. Whatever he was about to say was real to him. He truly believed, however unreal it seemed. Were they prepared to make that commitment? Did they know the weight their choice would carry? Was the choice ever even theirs to make, or had fate already made it for them? These were questions that should have taken weeks of search and reflection to answer, but that searching had been done without them even knowing. They already knew their answers the moment they asked the questions. Without a second thought Ally's, Rachel's, and Erin's lips parted as the words flowed out.

"Yes." They replied in harmony. "We are prepared."

"If you so choose," Joshua replied, turning to meet Win's eyes and then Lili's before nodding and turning back to face the friends.

"From its very dawn, this world and this known universe have been but a piece detached from its original form. A greater whole exists in a higher realm, and this universe is merely cast-off existence. This higher realm was created by a group of supreme beings of infinite power. They made and shaped this great world together, coalescing all the needed elements to foster abundant life. A single being of indescribable power was leader and lord of this group of Celestials, a being known as Vox Ramus. Vox Ramus was a being of balance and wisdom, whose sole focus was creating a world for creatures that would grow and evolve infinitely until they too would rise to the state of the Celestials. This work would take eons to accomplish. Alongside Vox Ramus was a partner and companion Freyðr, their commander Theus; who oversaw the transition of life, Andurin; who terraformed the atmosphere, Mjirgovair and Tempe; the partners who oversaw the seas and the storms, Hån; who guided the geology, Ygrivem; responsible for metamorphosis, and Vanakus; the child of Vox Ramus and Freyðr. Together this group created an entire existence, and its heart was the world of Idonia.

"The Celestials knew their time with the world was limited, and they would need help both completing their work and maintaining it after they were gone. Vox Ramus knew, however, that alongside Freyðr, they could create nothing in their likeness as it would disrupt the balance they had worked so hard to create. Vox Ramus had already given everything they could to the world by pouring their essence directly into the heart of Idonia. This essence coalesced within the world, creating fusion and spawning from it the great tree that would bind and stabilize the entire world and everything connected to it, Leghtus. This great tree would power the entire world, providing life for all, and around it would be formed the heart of the Idonic realm, a massive expanse spanning out for thousands of miles and the pantheon of civilization.

"Thus, it was left to the others to bring about their finest creations, the Ancients. Andurin created the mighty Traco as wardens of the sky. Comprised of six races, the Traco were the wisest of the Ancients, and each race upheld an aspect of virtue within the Idonic society. Mjirgovair and Tempe together mothered the Nuati, children of the storm and sea. They would help mortals brave the waters and, along with the Traco, carry them on their ventures into the skies. Ygrivem created the most enduring of Ancients who could take on any corporeal form, the Secarno. They would serve as guides to mortals everywhere, forever helping them along their journey.

"Theus, the noblest and powerful of the remaining Celestials, sought to create beings that would be their ever-present light in the darkness, a beacon for the whole world to see and know that there would always be hope. Thus, Theus' first creation was the Davpyr. Theus took from the Earth their two favorite stones, diamond and obsidian. Theus shaped these two stones into eight beings of four races, four of each from their own images, and imbued the new lifeforms with part of their own essence, giving part of their life to bring the Davpyr families into existence. The Resharim, the Netiziath, the Salarinde, and the leader of the four, the Daevon. Gifted with as much of Theus' abilities and knowledge as an imperfect being could be, this race would help all other creations throughout their existence. The Davpyr were to teach others, to impart their knowledge to them all as became necessary, and to usher each creation on their journey to The Rising."

Ally's fist clenched at the word as her blood ran cold; flashes from the previous night's dream danced before her. She was shocked to glance down and see that both Erin's and Rachel's fists clenched as well.

Joshua spoke again, breaking their silent panic, "Are you each alright? You seem a bit uneasy."

They shared glances, unsure what to say. Each was searching the other's eyes, trying to understand what they were experiencing.

"Um," Erin began shakily, "I'm good. We're good. It's just, uh, a lot to take in."

Erin looked to her friends for assistance.

"Yeah, you're kinda like creating or recreating an entire, I don't know, religion, history, something that we have literally never even heard of," Rachel added.

"We're trying to follow." Ally said. "Truly. It's just. This is a lot to understand. Please, continue."

"Are you certain? We can stop and discuss it again another time, or never discuss it at all if that is your preference."

"No." The trio replied, more firmly than any of them had wished.

"Honestly," Erin spoke for the group, steadying her voice, "we're good. We want to hear what you have to say."

With that, Joshua took a large drink from his mug, gave a swift glance at Win, and began again. The friends sat mesmerized as his words washed over them. They didn't know what was real and what was fantasy. He spoke with such certainty that it seemed he held the history of the world. They had countless questions with more forming by the minute but were unable to ask any. They were entranced. As Joshua continued, his words formed the scene in front of their very eyes. The lines of history blurred away as they saw this new world unfold.

"At the epicenter of Idonia, Theus made sacred a special part of the world and gave it to the Ancestors as their holy domain. Within it, the Ancients created a hallowed mecca amongst the mountain tops that ranged forth from the roots of Leghtus, with sprawling courtyards reaching out into the valleys and pressing against the mighty river that flowed through the immaculate city. The Celestials waited until the Ancients had completed this metropolis to usher in their second creation, the mortal races. For each Ancient race, a mortal one was made in their image, and thus the city of Idonia became as vibrant and full of life as the world around it. For millennia the Ancients and mortals worked side by side to bring the Celestials' vision into focus. New life was discovered and created as the mortals bore children, bringing new joy and wonder into the world. In time the Ancients themselves discovered how to create life fashioned after them, a feat the Celestials knew meant their world would indeed continue to grow and thrive. These Children of Ancients, Gurén Liber, would carry the world of Idonia, and all those yet to come, into the Void beyond.

"When the Gurén Liber came of age, they each took with them a seed of Leghtus and multitudes of mortals to venture out into the great expanse around them. Their civilization spread throughout the world of Idonia as each group built new cities best suited to their interests. The era that followed was known as the Age of Discovery. With the mortals alongside them, the Ancients explored the vastness of this massive world, learning everything they could from it and the Celestials as they sought to understand their place in the universe. The various cities grew into massive hubs of information and trade. Research and discoveries were shared throughout Idonia as the citizens moved throughout the world, creating a living web of knowledge and wonder."

Joshua paused and looked towards his brother with a bit of sadness on his face. "I think that is enough storytelling for me for one day, though. May we save any further questions for tomorrow?"

The girls were taken aback by Joshua's sudden mood change. Jolted out of this fantastical world he was describing.

"Um, sure," Erin replied with confusion.

"That's fine," Ally added, not able to hide her disappointment.

"Yeah, if that's what you want. I kinda need some time for everything to set in anyways." Rachel added sadly, but she smiled as she grabbed her drink nonetheless.

"Thank you. If it is all the same to you, I think I am going to skip dinner tonight. I really would just like to go home." Something about the tale troubled Joshua, but the friends were at a loss as to why. "What time should we pick you up tomorrow, or would you rather meet us here?"

"Well, I'd kinda like to grab some coffee before we go," Rachel began, "especially if it's going to be so freakishly cold like it is."

"Does the cold bother you?" His words were directed at Ally, but his gaze rested on Win. Joshua looked back at her, eagerly awaiting a response.

"It's not so much that it bothers me per se," Rachel replied. "It's more just that I'm always cold."

"Same," Ally added. "I like the idea of the cold, comfy sweaters and scarves all layered, but then the cold actually gets here. Then I'm basically a popsicle for a few months."

"Not me," Erin interjected. "I love the cold. Cold days and rainy days are my favorite weather." Joshua's lips curled into a soft smile. Erin continued, "So we'll meet you here tomorrow? What time?"

Joshua rose from his seat as Win did the same, and Lili pushed two to-go drinks to the counter's edge. "Shall we say nine? If that is not too early?"

"Nine works," Erin replied for the group. "Thanks for the story."

"Thanks for listening. I thoroughly enjoyed it." He smiled weakly and headed towards the door, grabbing his drink on the way.

As he reached the door, Ally snapped back to reality. "Hey, wait. That story, you said that the world we know was just a cast-off from a higher realm of existence, this Idonia as you call it. If that's the case, how were we separated?"

A solemnity crept into Joshua's, Win's, and Lili's eyes as they looked at one another knowing looks, before Joshua turned back to the friends.

"A cataclysmic event known as The Sundering. The death of Vox Ramus shattered the world of Idonia with force so powerful it ripped through space and time, sending the fractured remains tumbling through the Void, splintering out, forming new dimensions. One such event created the universe we now inhabit, the Big Bang."

8
THE RAVEN MAN

The three friends walked home from the Brew feeling the cold air press against them, their ever-present new friend.

"So, are they crazy?" Erin asked with doubt in her voice.

The three friends walked home from the Brew feeling the cold air press against them.

"Are we?" Rachel replied, searching herself for the answer. "Just being frank. I mean, we're the ones sittin' here listening to the man. They've given us pretty much every chance possible to run away, and yet we persevere. So they can't be much crazier than us if we're going along."

There was a long pause as the friends considered Rachel's words. The streetlights cast an ambient glow across the sidewalk, sending their shadows dancing through the crisp autumn night. The trek from The Daily Brew to their home was a simple, peaceful one. A handful of quaint apartments were scattered along the path, along with lovely pre-war dwellings in all their majesty. A stroll through masonry, young and old, echoed the changing of the seasons.

As the friends walked, they reflected on the day's discoveries. This strange family to which they were being drawn grew more enigmatic by the moment. Each of the three searched themselves, trying to understand and rationalize what they were feeling.

"Then again," Rachel continued, breaking the silence, "every generation of humanity has thought they had things figured out, only to learn they were laughably wrong. Millenia ago, we were certain that the moon and sun were gods, sometimes even lovers that were stuck in some eternal struggle. Now, we know the sun is a giant ball of gas powering our solar system, and the moon is a massive hunk of rock that smashed into us and got swept in our gravitational pull. Judeo-

Christian teachings told the world as we know would be roughly, what, six thousand years old in our current era, yet we now know that our planet alone has existed for billions of years. Hell, it took us until the last few hundred years to even discover the outermost planets, and not too terribly long before that we were certain Earth was the center of our universe." She paused, her breath wavering as she spoke the last of her thoughts. "Imagine what we'll be wrong about tomorrow."

"Maybe them." Ally said, surprised at herself. "I'm not sayin' I believe what they're sayin'. I think we can all agree, though, that they most certainly believe it. It goes against everything I've ever understood of our life. Quite frankly, it's almost too big for me to even try to understand. It's like I think about it, and my mind just can't process it fully. We know what we know of our life, our world," she sighed, "shit, our existence from what we were raised and taught to think. Anything outside of that just feels... impossible. Rach is right, though."

"Damn," Erin said incredulously, "I really thought in movin' away, you know, goin' out into the big world beyond, that whole couple hours away from home we went, I really thought we'd meet new people that believed different things. I was thinkin', that would be like maybe, atheists or Hindus or Muslims. I didn't think we'd be getting to know, Idonians? Idonics? Idons? Fuck, what do we even call them?"

The friends had reached their home and were making their way inside as the crisp air bid them goodnight.

"Well," Rachel replied with certainty she didn't realize she had, "we call them Joshua and Win and Lili and Marc, and so on. I don't know how to frame what they believe. I don't believe it, but they don't believe what we believe either. So I gotta respect that. For all their efforts to keep us at bay, I don't feel threatened or concerned by them. It's strange, really. I've never felt more uncertain about anything in my life, and yet, I've never felt more at ease as I am around them."

Erin and Ally stopped just inside the entrance at Rachel's statement. They understood completely. Each of them was confused, terrified to a degree even. Somehow though, they felt confident, sure, that they were doing the right thing. No matter how strange it seemed to them, they were walking down the path meant for them. The friends lingered there in the entryway of their home for a moment, letting their thoughts settle.

"Alright, ladies," Erin said finally. "I think it's off to bed for me. In case I don't say it enough, or ever, I can't thank y'all enough for being here with me. I'm an asshole. I know that, but y'all love me all the same. That's special. Real talk."

The friends each smiled at each other briefly. Their bond was special. All of them knew that even if they never spoke about it. They were family, to their very core. No amount of struggles, mishaps, and peculiar new acquaintances could ever change that, and it was something they were beginning to understand was true of the Brownings as well. Without another word, the three made their way up the stairs to their respective bedrooms, finally turning in for the night.

Erin sat in her room, trying to collect her thoughts. The day had been overwhelming, to say the least. Everything had happened so fast. She could still see the story Joshua told her laid out right in front of her eyes as if she were standing in Idonia herself. Beautiful stone walls stretched along the mountainside with the mighty river flowing through the valley, and the enormous tree known as Legthus towered above, reaching so far into the sky it seemed endless. At the far end of the city, the mountains gave way to sharp cliffs where the river tumbled down into the fields below. Erin could see sprawling courtyards of beautiful trees with leaves of lovely green and every shade of fall. A crisp wind blew, and deep purple leaves swirled by her feet from one of the nearby trees. She felt herself walking towards the tree. The wind picked up, and she felt her hair whip around her ears. The sky began to darken as she neared the tree. Then a voice could be heard against the wind as if the trees themselves were speaking to her. "Erin Cartwright, what are you doing here?" Erin stood there frozen. *How could they be aware of her presence?* Then the voice came again, "Why are you here?"

"Erin!" Ally yelled again as Erin snapped back to reality. "Not that you aren't welcome, but it's a bit creepy when you just waltz into my room without speaking. What are you doing?"

"Uh," Erin said as she looked around the room. She couldn't tell Ally the truth. "I'm really not sure. I was in my room just a second ago. I guess I was, like, starting to doze off and walked in here thinking it was the kitchen or something."

"Ok, that's weird as shit, but not as weird as anything else lately, I suppose."

"Yeah, I suppose so. Anyways, my bad. I'll, uh, get back to my room now. Erin turned to leave, but something stopped her. "Hey, while I'm here, I wanted to apologize for how I acted this past weekend. I was a real flitter, and I had no right to be. I don't know what came over me." She lied. "I guess I'm just having a harder time adjusting to being away from home and everyone than I thought I would. Still, you guys didn't deserve that, and it's not like I'm the only one of us here moved. I just want you to know; it had nothing to do with you or us or any of what's going on with us being here. This is great. I love being here with both of you. It's just an adjustment. Are we, like, still cool? No hard feelings."

"Erin, I've known you for most of my life. One little crazy outburst isn't gonna change us being friends, especially when being the crazy one of the group is kinda your thing. Besides, Rachel and I just chalked it up to you bein' about to start anyways." Ally replied, smiling wickedly.

"You're twice the asshole for that, you know," Erin said, pointing at Ally. "Once simply for saying it, and the second because you know good and damn well that doesn't happen with an IUD." She continued as sincerity crept into her voice, "I'll give you, though, I was crazier than my normal. Which by the way, the stuff I said about Joshua and Win was completely out of line. Yeah, they're rich. I mean, there's no real hiding that. They aren't jackasses, though. They seem like decent people. Sure they're secretive af, and I'm pretty sure they're into some shit they straight up don't want anybody knowing. I don't think they're bad people, and I'm delighted you and Rachel have somebody to crush on."

"What?" Ally said with a jerk. "I'm not crushing on anyone. Have you met me? I don't crush on people. That ain't me."

"Wow. You almost convinced yourself for a second there," Erin replied with heavy sarcasm. "I've seen how you look at Joshua. Ally, you are way more badass and hotter and cooler and everything else than you ever let yourself think. If you thought you were a quarter as awesome as you are, you'd be impossible to live with. Don't be stupid. Go for him."

"I'm not even going to discuss that." Ally shifted her feet awkwardly, trying to change the topic. "So, are you excited for the zoo trip?"

"I am, but I'm also a bit anxious. These people are something else. On that note, when I gave my epic apology to Rachel earlier, though, she asked if it would be cool for Thad to come up this weekend. Looking to solicit his sleuthing skills on the Brownings?"

"Oh shit. I completely forgot to ask you about Thad coming up. Erin, I am so sorry. We all agreed to have dinner with the Brownings Friday too, and I didn't even ask. What the hell was I thinking?"

"Well, the dinner situation is easy. We'll just tell Joshua and Win that we already made plans for our friend to come into town this weekend. See if that's ok with them, and if not, then we postpone. No big deal. We got that."

"I guess you're right. Granted, I still have to see if Thad would be ok with that, and that still doesn't address whether or not you're cool with Thad coming?"

"Really, Ally?" Erin said incredulously. "It's Thad. He's the most laid-back person in the world. I'm sure Thad would be all over dinner with the Brownings. As for me, I can get along with Thad just fine. I know we get on each other's nerves and give each other a lot of shit in the process, and yes he annoys the fuck out of me. It's all good, though. I'm sure we can survive a weekend without killing one another."

"Yeah, I guess you're right. On both accounts. I just never know with the two of you. I know you guys joke a lot, but sometimes it seems more serious than joking. Oh man, I didn't even think about how awkward this will all be for Rachel. You'll think she'll be ok with everything?"

"What do you mean?" Erin said, deeply confused.

"Well, Thad is her ex, after all. And while I have no feelings whatsoever towards Joshua, I think it's pretty obvious to everyone Rachel has a hardcore crush on Win. You don't think that'll be strange at all?"

"Thad is an ex, yes, but just one of them. Yes, they were together the longest, but that was also years ago, and she's dated other guys since. Well, tried dating at least. I don't think the others fell through because she's still hung up on Thad, though. I'm pretty certain they've both moved on."

"If you say so." Ally said, still not convinced. "But I guess it doesn't matter really. If they both want to go to dinner, then that's on them."

"Sure is," Erin replied, letting Ally have her moment. "Well, then. This has been fun. Now, if you don't mind, I'd like to read a bit before bed, and I would bet you have some game to play. So, I'll just sleepwalk my happy ass back to my room now." She said with a smirk and a spinning hand gesture towards the door. Ally laughed as Erin started on her way out.

"Oh, and Erin," Ally said, "It's good to have you back to normal." The two smiled as Erin closed Ally's door.

Ally whipped out her phone as Erin headed back to her room. *"You online?"* She typed out to Thad and tossed her phone on her bed, grabbed her cup, and refilled it from the bathroom sink just in time for her phone to ring with a response. Walking back to her phone, she grabbed her controller and turned on her system.

"Well, I'm not at work or in class. I'll let you do the math." Thad replied. Ally didn't even need to check her friends list to know he was on. Her system dinged with an invite as soon as it powered up. She grabbed her headset and accepted the party invite. "So, what are we playing?" Thad asked.

"Actually, I have a pretty crazy story to tell you, but there's no way I'll be able to tell it while we're in a game."

"Fine. Let me finish my match, and I'll back out. Then you can chat all you want. This had better be good."

Soon Ally was fast into retelling the story the friends had heard from Joshua. After several times of telling Thad to "just be quiet and listen," she finally reached the end of the story she knew thus far. "So, what do you think?"

"I think," Thad said with a long pause following. "I think it sounds pretty damn insane, but," he paused again, "to be honest, it's no more insane than any other story we have of creation. I mean, from Greek Mythology to modern religion, there are some pretty wild tales of how things began, and all of them take a pretty decent amount of faith to believe. My question to you is, do you think Joshua believes this to be true, or do you think it's just a cool story he came across?"

"I can tell you with near absolute certainty they believe every bit of it. You should have seen the look on his face, on Win's face, even Lili at points. There was no doubt in it at all. He knows more too. This isn't just some simple tale of the first days of man. There's a lot more they're not saying, and we all wanna know what. Do you think we're crazy?"

"Yes, but I thought that before all this. Try keeping an open mind, please." Thad's voice was so genuine it startled Ally. "I know you're very 'open-minded' in general, but I know you can be set in your ways too. Hear what he has to say, and listen to what Rachel and Erin think. You three, you're about as close as it gets. If all of you are in agreement on something, it's probably legit, but if one of you has concerns, all of you should. Maybe it's not all that crazy after all. Maybe there's some truth to what he believes. I'm not telling you to believe it yourself. I'm just telling you to be accepting that he believes it and see what that means for you. Ok?"

"I will, Thad. Don't worry. It's like we talked about when I was there. I can tell they're good people. They're different, I know, and they believe things that are very different. If something is truly of concern, though, one of us will sense it. On that note, have you found anything worth sharing?" Excitement rose in her voice at what Thad may have discovered.

"Yes, and no." He replied ambiguously. "Nothing I'm sharing via chat, though. This is definitely an in-person discussion. Don't worry. I'll bring my notes."

Ally could hear the unease in his voice discussing his research and realized it had been there the whole conversation. She had missed it entirely at first, but something was troubling Thad. Whatever it was, though, it wasn't enough to say yet, and she knew better than to press him.

"Well, that actually brings me to my next question before we play. How would you like to have dinner with them Friday when you come up? You could see how your data checks out in person."

"Um, what?" Thad replied, taken back.

"You see," Ally paused, "we may have kinda, slightly, maybe forgot that you were coming up this weekend whenever Joshua invited all of us to dinner with them this Friday. So, we sorta told them yes."

"I could sit here and give you endless amounts of shit for forgetting about me, but, seeing as I'd genuinely like to meet them after all this mysterious teasing, I'll let the fact that you are all selfish, love-struck tramps slide this time. If it's cool with them, of course. I don't want to just barge in without their ok."

"We may be forgetful, but we're not inconsiderate, Thad." Ally said, refusing to acknowledge his accusation. "We'll ask them first. I just wanted to make sure you'd actually be ok with it before the whole thing is decided on. Oh, and do you by chance have anything nice to wear?"

"Nice? What's wrong with a pair of 'nice' jeans and a 'nice' t-shirt?

We're not attending a gala, are we? We're having dinner. Or are you just ashamed of my attire?"

"Don't be a dick. You know what I mean. They're just fancy kinda people. I feel awkward as hell around them as it is. I was just giving you a heads up."

"I know, and I'm just giving you a hard time. I'm just going to wear something I'd normally wear for going out. I'm not going to get all dolled up, but you know I'm not trying to be a slob. You shouldn't misrepresent who you are just because they're kinda fancy, though. You're a 'jeans and t-shirt' kinda gal. There's nothing wrong with that. Besides, I'm pretty sure from what you've told me Joshua and Win won't mind."

"About that. It won't be just Joshua and Win there. It's a family dinner, so Marc and Lili are coming too."

"You did that on purpose."

"I may have left out a few details upfront, but you've agreed to go, so why back out now."

"Whatever. I'm not mad. Just let's me see if my research holds true even more. Still, dick move. So are we playing or not?"

Down the hall, Erin was getting ready for a nice hot shower. She wanted to wash the stresses of the day away. It wasn't that it was a bad day, but she couldn't help feeling exhausted from it. The stories, the visions, the weekend that loomed ahead, it was all too much for her. The more Erin tried to understand things, the less she understood, and the lines between reality and fantasy kept blurring. She tilted her head back and closed her eyes to let the water rush over her face and down her body. When she opened her eyes the shower was gone.

There she stood in the middle of the luscious courtyard once more. She looked down to see a soft, silken dress that fell just above her knees, showing her silky, smooth legs and bare feet. The wind blew, sending leaves rushing across her feet, and light from Leghtus cascaded all around, basking the courtyard in its ethereal radiance. She turned and headed up the steps out of the courtyard. Passing through the gate, she found herself surrounded by a maze of tall stone buildings; castles turned skyscrapers. She spun to find the entrance back into the courtyard, but it was no longer there.

She sauntered forward, making her way through the alleyway formed by the first two buildings. As she got closer to the odd structures, their soft grey tone gave way to a blackish grey, glassy rock with a smoky haze to it. She felt a chill around her feet and looked to see a thick fog encroaching. The sharp caw of a bird made her jump, and she looked up to see a massive, jet-black raven resting on the first awning of the tiered building. It stared sternly at her with its empty black eyes. She felt a darkness coalescing as a presence settled behind her. The hairs on her neck stood as an ominous chill crawled down her spine. The air around her grew cold, and her breath began to fog. Petrified with fear, she forced her eyes away from the raven. Unable to move her body, she slowly turned her head to see what was there, only to find the fog.

The raven cawed again, but when she looked, it was nowhere to be found. The fog crept around her ankles, making her shiver. Erin looked downed to see a faint golden yellow light in the ground beneath the mist as if the light were part of the stone walkway itself. She followed the shining beacon in the earth, desperately seeking an exit to this labyrinth. It took her winding through buildings as the fog thickened. The caw of the raven continued, but she dare not look for it. A thick swirl of fog blew across the ground, making her lose sight of the light for but a moment. She froze.

Erin looked up to find herself at the edge of a black forest. Dead trees were all that could be seen for miles. Was this the courtyard from whence she had just come? What had happened to its beauty? Erin stood rooted in the spot, staring into the abysmal, black forest. With terrified reluctance, she turned to see what became of the immaculate Leghtus, only to be horrified at the sight of its massive frame laid bare, fragile, and sickly where once the most glorious sight she had ever witnessed stood. Where was the beautiful Idonia she had found earlier?

Another heart-wrenching chill ran down her spine. This time, though, it was not the fog. Something, no, someone was breathing on her neck. Erin felt the cold breath of death against her skin. She could feel the life leaving her body. Afraid to move, but knowing she must, she twitched the fingers in her hand. There was still life left in her. She cringed her toes and let her knees bend just a little. Her legs still worked. Balling both her hands into fists and gritting her teeth, she moved her left foot slightly. She must turn and face this monster. Erin would not let her story end without facing her death. She moved her right foot a little more, then her left, then her right again. Her face was still stuck staring at the forest as she moved her left foot once more. One more step and she would be completely turned around with nothing to see but death. She moved her right foot and snapped her head forward.

There was nothing but the golden yellow light in the stone walkway and the soft grey castle spires she had passed. Erin caught her breath. She had nothing to fear. Her mind had been playing tricks on her, the fog getting the best of her. She unclenched her fist and forced a deep breath into her lungs. A wave of relaxation rushed through her body as she felt the life return. She turned again to face the courtyard, knowing that its beauty would have been restored, but it was still just black with death.

Caw! Another scream from the raven she could not see, and something began to move in the blackness. Glossy black eyes lit up throughout the forest, moving closer, gaining speed. Before she knew it, a sea of black flew from the forest. Feathers rushed past Erin knocking her to the ground. She lay there with her eyes closed as she heard the ruffle of feathers moving behind her. She jolted up to see the forest still dark as before and spun back to the streets to see a most terrifying sight.

The fog, the black, the cold grip of death had returned. The murmuration flew rapidly down the street from where she stood, circling about each other until they began to take form. Black shoes could be seen through the fog at the bottom of their swarm. It stepped forward with a hideous clack against the stone, and the bottom of black pinstripe pants could be seen emerging from the flock. An umbrella cane extended from within the murder of ravens and struck the ground with a sinister crack. Another foot extended forward as the tails of his black suit coat became visible. He was coming for Erin. The cane moved forward again, and a skeleton thin white hand could be seen extending from the sleeve of the tailcoat. Another step ahead, and his entire body was visible with the small black swarm of ravens circling his head. He then stopped and clicked his cane again. The flock formed his head slowly, and the multitude gave way to a deep black top hat that cast the creature's face in shadow.

Another caw echoed through the woods as the first raven took its place on the man's shoulder. He was no more than ten feet from Erin, yet she still could not see anything but darkness shrouding his face. He tilted his head up, and a devilish grin could be seen shining through the black. Then he spoke with a haunting whisper, "Erin Cartwright, Death is nigh."

9

ZOO DAY

Erin jolted out of bed, searching the room for the Raven Man. Nothing was there but darkness. She couldn't even remember how she got to bed, just the shower and then Idonia. She grabbed her phone. 3:46 am. Her body was still exhausted, and begged for sleep, but her mind was racing. Why did the beautiful Idonia change into that hellish forest? What was that golden yellow light that was part of the stone? Who was the Raven Man, and why was Death coming?

She sat in her bed, rolling the thoughts around in her head. She closed her eyes, hoping to drift back to sleep, but the blood-curdling caw of a raven kept jarring her awake. After a time, Erin slid to the edge of the bed and slowly placed her feet against the cold hardwood floor. Grabbing her cup, she made her way to the bathroom to get some more water. After filling it, she threw a quick splash on her face hoping to wash away the terrible dream. Then her eyes made contact with themselves in the mirror.

"Look at you. Normal girl, normal life. What could Death possibly want with you?" Erin couldn't help but laugh. *Talking to yourself in the mirror about Death coming for you, yeah, that's totally normal.* She thought. Grabbing her cup again, she headed back to the bed and crawled in, pulling the sheets tight up around her neck. She grabbed her phone and checked the time once more. 4:48 am.

That was impossible. She had just walked into the bathroom to grab a drink. There's no way she stood talking to the mirror that long. She unlocked her phone and typed out a quick text.

"You awake by any chance?"

"No. So go away."

"For real. I need to talk."

"Fine, fine. Go ahead. I'll do my best to respond."

She proceeded to text him the dream in just enough detail to get the point across. Then her phone sat dark for a minute.

"Ok, to be honest compared to your dreams of your teeth falling out, this one seems kinda cool. I mean, you had a badass dude made out of crows. That's pretty kinda kickass right?"

"Thanks a lot jackass."

"Geez. Fun switch off. My bad."

She was typing out an apology, but before she could, another text came through.

"Look you just heard probably the craziest story you've ever imagined and were thinking about it hardcore yesterday, plus you've wanted something weird to be going on from day one. Clearly your dark, twisted mind got the best of all your thoughts. Ravens are often espoused with death, obviously, but they also carry meanings of wisdom. There's other stuff too, but I'll have to look it up when my brain turns on. It's strange, I get it. The mind is capable of all kinds of stuff. If you're still worked up about it in the morning though, ask them about it on your Zoo trip. Sadly this is one thing I can't really do much about other than being your sounding board, but I'll gladly do that as you need.."

"Maybe you're right." She typed, loving and hating how his logic could always get through to her.

"Of course I am. I'm always right. (Insert smirk here) Now please ma'am, may I go back to sleep?"

"Of course. Good night, and thank you."

"Always."

With that, Erin laid her head back down and tried to get another couple of hours of sleep. She wrestled with the thoughts in her head, trying to push them out and let sleep in. Try as she might, though, flashes of Idonia kept racing through her mind. Beautiful trees in every shade of autumn, stunning gothic stone architecture that looked like it were built eons in the future with golden yellow lights built into them, darkness taking over, a thick fog settling in, the beautiful forest turned black, a flock of murderous crows, and then it. The Raven Man. Its face unnoticeable but with a smile of pure evil. Its slim skeletal figure and a voice like acid on metal.

"Bah, bah, bah," sounded her alarm. 7:00 am already. She could hear shuffling and mumblings in the house as well, so her friends were awake. *Had she even managed to fall back asleep?* She had no idea. All she knew was that she never wanted to see Raven Man again. There was a more critical issue at hand, though. *Should she tell her friends about the dream? Should she tell Joshua? Was it even possible to do one without the other? Or should she just let it go and think only about the story from the day before?* Then it dawned on her that she had not thought about Joshua's tale of Idonia. She had thought of no questions. This is already shaping up to be a great day. She thought.

An hour later, she was downstairs as Rachel was drinking her protein shake. It was apparent Rachel had spent a little extra time getting ready that morning. She had curled her hair, which she never did unless she was going to some special event. She had picked out her favorite sweater and even took the time to put on her fancy make-up. Rachel was a naturally beautiful person. Ally and Erin both saw it. She was one of those bare minimum types that always managed to look incredible even when they did nothing at all, but when she wanted to be, Rachel was absolutely stunning.

"I'm sure the penguins will love your look today, Rach," Erin stated with a smile, never missing a chance to tease her friend.

"Ha. Ha." Rachel gave her a stern look. "Is there something wrong with just wanting to look nice for the sake of looking nice?"

Ally had come downstairs by then and started fixing a bowl of cereal. Their kitchen was probably the most excellent room in the apartment with soft, antiqued white cabinets wrapping the walls, top-end stainless steel appliances with more functions than they could imagine set into the cabinetry, dark granite countertops, and a giant island with a bar in the middle. They never got over how amazingly fortunate they had been to have the place. Rachel stood next to the fridge while Erin took her seat at the bar in one of the wooden barstools stained ebony with a soft blue cushion that matched the pale blue towels hanging from the stove.

"So let me get this straight," Erin began, "you did your hair special, did your makeup special, and put on your favorite sweater just to go to the zoo?" Rachel's cheeks flushed. "Damn, somebody's dying to go to pound town." Rachel spat her protein shake all over the grey tile floor in embarrassment as Ally giggled, partly embarrassed with Rachel, partly amused at the truth. "What? I'm just saying if you wanna jump his bones, then do it. Hell, I would if I were you. He's fuckin' hot, Rach. Like, 'fuck him' hot."

Sex was a topic that was private for Rachel. She was no stranger to it and would talk about it occasionally, but she wasn't as cavalier about it as Erin. Granted, Erin wasn't shy about anything. Ally often laughed or smiled as a deflection. If Rachel was private about sex, Ally was an encrypted message.

Rachel was regaining her composure as she wiped up her spill, "Look, nobody's 'jumping bones' anytime soon. I don't think. I just want to look nice. Ally got more fancied up than she normally does, and you get all chatty around him. Why can't we talk about how both of you want to get some from Joshua?"

Rachel's and Erin's eyes met briefly before Erin took a good, long look at Ally's outfit as she chewed her cereal. "Well, it's quite simple, really." Rachel had just finished cleaning up and threw the paper towel away while she downed the remains of her protein shake, hoping to have it drunk before Erin made another joke. "Ally's far too traditional just to let Joshua into her pants, even if he is all suave and debonair with an insanely sexy, dark, and mysterious thing going for him." Ally blushed, a little insulted. "Which, of course, brings us to me. I, unlike Ally, am far too aggressive and tumultuous, and frankly, probably, way too obnoxious to garner his interests. So, you're barking up the wrong tree, Rach. We are impervious to the Browning Boys, so to speak."

Reading both Rachel and Ally, Erin paused, hoping that she hadn't, like all too many times before, reached the point of inserting her foot into her mouth. She was ever the instigator, the firecracker of the group, but she never meant anything but love for her friends.

"Besides, we all know Ally's immune to persuasion. I mean, she hates romance and all that stuff, plus she doesn't get all weak in the knees and forget how to talk." Ally smiled in reply. "Now you, on the other hand, Rach, are a completely different story." Rachel flushed again as she knew she was back in the spotlight, and Erin was right. "You're like the ultimo romantic and get all hung up on guys, and Win, woo girl, has way more than enough charm to make your panties just fly off. Like, they'll just disintegrate."

Rachel's dark complexion turned a deep shade of red. It was a good thing Rachel finished her drink when she did; otherwise, she might have been cleaning it off the tile again. Erin had managed to thread the needle. She'd made precise observations of both her friends, but nothing too direct. It was a constant balance she worked to maintain.

Ally couldn't help but giggle at Erin's comment, though she spoke up quickly to save Rachel anymore blushing, "On that note, we should really get out of here. We wouldn't want Rachel's boyfriend to be kept waiting." She gave a friendly smile to Rachel, letting her know that she meant no harm by it.

The moment they got outside, Erin realized she'd forgotten her phone, an infrequent occurrence for her. Rare enough, Ally and Rachel both checked their pockets, too, after Erin went inside. Luckily, they had remembered. The two stood on the front porch debating whether or not to go back into the warmth while they waited. They each yawned in turn. Neither had slept well, clearly.

Ally took the chance to press Rachel about what Erin had said, "So was she right? Do you wanna jump his bones?"

Rachel didn't answer right away. Instead, she stared down at the ground for a stretch.

"Would you think I'm being I said I don't know?" She finally responded. "Like, the attraction is there, but, I don't know. It's not that kind of attraction, I don't think. I'm not sure if he's my," she paused searching for the right word, "type."

"Rach, I'll never think you're too forward if you're responsible about what you do and doing it with someone you care about, and I'll never think you're too reserved. I really thought, it's dumb, I guess, I thought for some reason you and Thad might still have something."

"Ally," Rachel began calmly, "I love Thad. He loves me. There is nothing but love and respect there, and yes, if I'm being unusually forthright, he was most enjoyable at absolutely all of the 'bone jumping' things, and, if life were somehow different, I would welcome that any time if such a thing were feasible. It's just not what life has for us. He's not the person for me, and I'm not the one for him."

"Wow," Ally interrupted, "ok, um, I mean, I guess I knew it sort of, but I don't know if I need to actually hear that about my best friend."

"Our best friend, Ally." Rachel said in an aggravated yet calm and caring voice. "I know he's your best, best. He was your first real best friend that you could actually do all the things you like together, but he's all of ours too. I mean, you know we were together, of course. We're not now, but we still love each other, and we're still friends. All of us are. You, me, even Erin. Despite that they both kinda hate each other, they really are friends too. Sure, you have the longest connection and have the most in common with him. I mean, do you know how weird it was all those years through high school when he wouldn't respond to a text because he was playing with you and your cousins? It was definitely a learning experience. That's gone now, but those experiences aren't. Sure, that time has passed. We don't talk as much as we did then, but we still talk regularly. We're still friends. Yeah, sure, I think Win is hot. I mean, who wouldn't? Erin might be a jackass, but she's not an idiot. I'm not about to try and find some temporarily closed exhibit at the zoo so I can try knockin' boots with him."

"You're not wearing boots," Erin said as she came back outside. "Not saying you can't knock some things. You do you, bro. I'm just saying you aren't wearing boots, so you may need to come up with a different phrase for it. I'd say Netflix and chill, but that'd be kinda hard at a Zoo. Maybe a roll in the hay?"

Rachel flushed again, "And with that, let's get to the Brew."

"Agreed." Ally replied. "So, did anybody think of anything to ask them? I slept like shit last night, so I pretty much got nothing."

"Same," Erin said, not wishing to go into any details.

"That makes three of us then," Rachel added. "Like, I had, have even, a million things rolling around in my head. For some reason, I can't formulate a single one into something I want to know."

"I'm right there with you." Ally said. "I want to know everything. I want to understand it all. I just can't think of any ways to ask them something specific.

"Well, broads," Erin began, "guess we're just going to be winging it today."

With that, the three friends headed down the coffee shop alley to meet the family that would forever change their life.

The girls opened the doors to see Joshua and Win standing at the counter. Win approached with his charming grin on full blast, holding his drink as well as Rachel's and Erin's. "Good morning, ladies. I trust you each got a good night's sleep in preparation for today." He handed Rachel and Erin their coffees in turn and glanced back and forth at the friends awaiting a response.

No one spoke. Confusion and apprehension settled over the friends. None of them wanted to say how they slept, but they also couldn't think of what to say instead or who should say it. All they could think was just how wrong he was, but none of them were going to discuss it.

Joshua approached, extending a cup to Ally, but his look was much more solemn than Win's. His gaze seemed fixed on a point past Ally, outside the Brew. Did he sense their apprehension? The look on his face suggested just that, but he grinned at Ally nonetheless.

"Yours wasn't quite done when Win grabbed the others. Is everyone ready to go, or do you need anything else?"

"Um," Erin began, still in a dazed state from the lack of sleep, "I actually could really go for something to eat really quick."

Ally hadn't realized how hungry she was until then, and Rachel, despite her shake, was surprisingly so as well.

"I could go for food too," Rachel added. "Mind if we grab a quick bite?"

"Well," Win began, "if you ladies are peckish, we could stop on the way, could we not, Joshua?"

"Certainly. Have you tried The Root yet by chance?"

"Oh yes!" Ally said enthusiastically. "Well, we've had dinner there. It was great. We didn't realize they did breakfast."

"They do indeed. If that works for everyone, then." He said as he pushed open the door and gestured outside.

As soon as they slipped in the car, Ally and Rachel felt the warm leather's soft embrace. Heated seats were one modern comfort they so deeply loved. Ally realized then just how observant Joshua was to have remembered their cold nature and have the seat warm and waiting. "Damn. He is good." She thought to herself.

As soon as the doors closed, the friends' minds were already working through thoughts about Idonia, trying to think of a question. Rachel, though, was too quick for Ally and Erin. As soon as the car slid into motion, Rachel jumped on the opportunity.

"So, Joshua, I have a question for you about your story."

Joshua stared out the window briefly before turning out into the street. Win stared out of his passenger window with a humored expression on his face.

"Well, Rachel, what would you like to know?" Joshua's voice was welcoming but cautious.

Rachel hesitated. She clearly was taken aback by the brothers' reaction along with her friends. "My main thing, you named and described a few different, Celestials as you called them; the beings that created the universe as you said. And you said each one was, I guess in charge of, certain things. Is that like in Greek Mythology how Poseidon controls the seas, and Hades rules the underworld?"

Both men grinned faintly with mild amusement.

"Not in that sense, no. They each worked on things collaboratively as they saw fit within the group. It is not as if one of them was solely capable of a given task like how Zeus 'made lightning storms.' Think of it more like a specialist. A welder probably could have been a carpenter had they studied that craft instead, or a microbiologist could have been a marine biologist had they gone down that path. The Celestials each did what they were best suited to do."

The message struck the friends as odd. They'd never heard someone reference seemingly supreme beings with such reverence and yet use such simple analogies as an explanation.

Erin spoke before Rachel could continue, "So there's no like god of this, lord of that in what you believe? No angels and demons watching over things or trying to sew evil?"

That seemed to be the ticket to snap Win out of his endless stare. "Humans have no need for demons or spirits. They are plenty evil on their own and more than capable of tempting themselves and each other. The fact that humans even made up such figures throughout history is frankly pathetic. People need to grow up and take responsibility for what they do."

The friends were taken aback. They had never heard any of the Brownings speak with such ferocious contempt in their voice. Joshua gave a nod towards Win as if that would comfort him. Strangely enough, it did. Win took a deep breath and began again.

"I apologize for my outburst. It just angers me that humans are constantly looking for someone to blame for their problems. Humans are fully in control and should be held fully responsible for the good and the evil they put into the world. People get treated unfairly, cruelly at times, entire groups of people even, and that happens at other people's hands. Humans seek any number of reasons to excuse or justify their behaviors instead of merely admitting that they, and only they, were responsible."

Erin sat back in silence. Ally and Rachel imagined what she must have been thinking. They figured it probably wasn't too different from their own thoughts. It was such a simple concept, yet none of them could quite grasp the idea of a world without a spiritual evil. They knew that none of them were the most devout of purists when it came to their faith, but they had never really met many people who presented such starkly different beliefs.

Sensing their discomfort Joshua jumped back in the conversation,

"I think that should suffice for moral and religious discussions for the day. It would be a tragedy to blow through most of the divisive topics in a single outing. Then we would be left only with politics. Is there anything else you would like to know?"

His question wasn't directed at either girl, giving them each a chance to ask anything they wanted. Erin knew what she wanted, but she wasn't sure how to word it without giving herself away. Instead, she threw out a mildly joking question to buy herself time.

"Well then, who are you voting for this November?"

"Come again?"

"Well, you said all we'd have left was politics. So what are your politics?"

Win gave Joshua a knowing smirk.

"Interesting approach, trying to tackle religion, moral quandaries, and politics all in one gathering. Are you sure you do not want to save something for the next visit?"

"Trying to decide if there's going to be a next visit," Erin replied sarcastically.

"Well, then you will be disappointed to know we do not vote, but we can save that conversation for another day as it never fails to be an underwhelming one."

Win chuckled softly as a grin spread on Joshua's face. Clearly, there had been several instances where that very topic made for intriguing situations. Erin wanted to reply. She wasn't all too concerned with their political stances, but more so, she was surprised at how nonchalantly they addressed it. In an ever more politicized climate, it was strange to see people be so insouciant. Silence filled the space for a time. Erin worked on what she wanted to ask, slowly working up the nerve.

Before she could, though, Rachel was onto her next question. "What were the different families like?"

That was one question neither Ally nor Erin had considered. They were both so fixated on knowing what the city and its creators were like they had barely thought about its inhabitants. Ally and Erin were glad to have Rachel there to bring up things they hadn't thought to ask. That was why the friends loved each other so, they each brought something different to the group that made them better as a whole.

Joshua's face showed no surprise as if he knew that question was coming. "The four families of Davpyr were each their own species in a sense, as were the mortals made in their image. The Resharim were very tall, lean and fair. Most were known to have soft blonde or white hair, though it is said that some of their lineages had been known to have deep auburn and brunette hair. Their skin was the palest of the four races, which allowed them to blend in with the snowy mountains of Idonia that would become their home. High-set cheekbones, sharp ears, and orb-like eyes gave their faces a sage appearance, which echoed in their personalities as the Resharim were above all things insatiable academics. Their lives were dedicated to the pursuit of knowledge, seeking to document everything they could of the world and catalog it in Idonia's great library. These traits led them to a close relationship with Andurin and the Traco, as the groups worked together in their pursuits for intelligence.

"Aside from their physical attributes, the thing that most separated the Resharim and Netiziath was their mastery of atomic manipulation, or Incarnum. All of the Ancients were capable of manipulating the world around them, but none took to it like the Resharim. These Ancients could conjure fire out of thin air, call down lightning from the sky, or even cause a flower to bloom in the palm of their hand from nothing but a pebble. The other Ancients and even the mortal races would obtain such prowess in time, but the Resharim were naturally adept at such things. Their power of Incarnum was matched only by their beauty, as none of the races were fairer than the Resharim and the Netiziath.

"The Netiziath channeled Incarnum with more physical prowess and were athletically unmatched. They were just as fast and nimble of runners on the ground as they were gliding through the trees that would become their homes. They had a way with flora and fauna that the other races could not even fathom. They were one with the world, not merely in tune with it. Leaping from limb to limb with spear or bow in hand, they were the apex predators, yet they did not hunt for sport or out of malice. Every Netiziath knew their connection to the living beings around them, each an integral part of the cycle. Reverence of their fellow lifeforms was a basis of all the Ancients, and the Netiziath were the paragons of such. Each life form had an essential role, and each was part of a more excellent balance to be maintained. Similar to their snowy relatives, they were lean and agile, but whereas the Resharim were built for navigating treacherous mountain slopes, the Netiziath were the epitome of the spry swiftness the forest required.

"The Salarinde were the strongest and arguably most courageous of the four races. Instead of taking to the beauties of snowy mountains or lush green forests, they found their peace working within the earth itself, which drew them even closer to Hån, whom they worked alongside, channeling their Incarum to forge the magnificent underground world where the Salarinde would study and hone their craft. They took great joy in their ability to manipulate the earth around them and bring forth its inner form. As such, what they enjoyed more than anything was building things. It was said that no creature was ever more at home than a Salarinde was turning the stones and crystals provided by Leghtus into majestic wonders of infinite possibilities. Despite being the shortest of all the races, the Salarinde overcame any obstacle with their brilliant engineering prowess and raw strength. It was even said they themselves held up the mountain out of sheer force of will. Their love of stone and metal and their time spent studying it turned their skin shades of ashen grey, but their eyes still shone as brilliantly as the crystals around them."

The three friends were deep within their own minds envisioning the world Joshua described and were caught off guard when his speech shifted rapidly.

Joshua pressed a button on the steering wheel and said clearly and firmly, "Message the Zoo and let them know we will not be there for a bit still."

An electronic voice with soft cadence replied. "Very well. Should I request to reschedule the usual activities also?"

"If you would please inform them we will not partake in the usual activities today. This will be a regular visit."

"It is done."

"Ok," Rachel began, "so I get your car talking and all. That was some next-level response, though."

"Yeah, Alexa and Google ain't replying with that shit," Erin added.

"I am sure they will be soon." Joshua smiled while his brother sat chuckling. "It is just a Beta version of an upcoming prototype smart system. Marc assisted in the development, so we were fortunate enough to utilize the source code. The base format will likely be worked into several integrations, so this one is just specific to our settings."

"What all can it do?" Ally asked, her curiosity growing with the family's strange business dealings.

"Well, I could spend all day showing you a tech demo of it, but that would probably get boring. For a start, it is integrated with all our communication systems and our smart home setups, so it can easily carry out multiple processes across each user. Though the voice recognition and heavy processing require a home server for this build, it is quite hefty. Undoubtedly, all the cloud corporations will easily capitalize on their incredible server capacity to offer it to end-users with a much easier setup and interface. In short, what you just witnessed was merely it recognizing my voice and then searching through my contacts, calendars, and communications to determine what a viable response would be. If I were to ask it something simplistic with no additional data points, such as 'where is the nearest gas station,' it would respond no differently than any connected device. There are many other things it can do, though. I would just have to show you at our house."

"What's your house like?" Rachel asked innocently.

Joshua and Win both looked at each other with a grin.

"Perhaps one day you will see. Enough of that now, though. Now is the time to eat." Joshua laughed as they pulled into the parking lot.

The Root was a delightful farm-to-table cafe nestled in the heart of Little Rock's SoMa district right across from a creamery, a corner store and tea house, and a local bakery. With a makeshift collection of second-hand chairs and tables and a mouth-watering menu prepared entirely in-house, from grinding the beef for burgers to their own pickling, it gave the comfortable feel of being invited to someone's home for dinner rather than going to a restaurant. The breakfast menu was full of homemade biscuits, farm-raised eggs, locally grown mushrooms, and everything in between, providing a guaranteed joy for any and everyone.

The parking lot was small, jutting up against a colorful mural featuring different food items dancing across the neighboring building. Only a few cars occupied the lot, but many more people were scattered about the patio and inside the cafe.

As they approached the door to the restaurant, Joshua and Win began to slow as their brows furrowed. As Joshua opened the door for Ally, she could see what the brothers apparently saw through the windows. There was a beast of a man yelling at the employees at the counter because his order was taking too long. Win turned to Joshua with a languid expression, "Shall I, or would you like to handle it?"

"I will take care of it," was all Joshua said as he made his way towards the counter. Ally, Rachel, and Erin stood in shock as the event unfolded before their eyes.

"Excuse me, sir," Joshua spoke politely but incredibly forcefully as he reached the angered man who didn't even notice Joshua and continued his tirade. "I said excuse me, sir." Joshua's voice got louder and more powerful, commanding everyone in the place's attention and respect.

The man who must have had six inches and a hundred pounds of muscle on Joshua turned to see him standing there very casually in his sleek blazer and button-down with his wavy hair resting on his collar. The man raised his voice in a failed attempt to match Joshua's authority. "Listen, pretty boy; I'm damn certain I wasn't talking to you. So turn the fuck around and walk away before I have to rearrange your face in front of your boyfriend over there." The man gestured to Win, who couldn't keep a short laugh from escaping. It was clear neither brother was intimidated by the man. On the contrary, they both seemed rather amused yet exhausted, though only Win laughed.

The man turned around to begin yelling at the cashier again, but before he could speak, Joshua's voice thundered down on him. "That is quite enough, sir. It is time for you to leave."

The large mass of a man spun on his heel back to Joshua as the blood rushed to his face and the veins bulged in his neck. "Listen here, pipsqueak. I don't really care for some douchebag kid who finally got a gym membership thinking he can tell me what to do, and I'll leave here whenever the fuck I want to. Now beat it, you little son of a bitch." The man threw his right hand forward to shove Joshua's shoulder. The second he connected, Joshua reacted in a blur of speed as he grabbed the man's arm, spun him around, and slammed his face down on the counter with so much force that a crack went down the edge.

Holding the man's arm behind his back, Joshua began again with the same calm as before, "Now there are two lessons you are going to leave here with today. The first is that you will never again lay your hands on someone unless you are both fully aware of the consequences and prepared to deal with them. The second thing, and this is the most important one, is that just because you are self-centered and egotistical does not give you the right to be condescending to people you think beneath you. These individuals are hard at work providing you a service. A little patience and appreciation is not a hard request."

The friend's eyes were transfixed on the scene in front of them in awe, but Win just gave a lackadaisical smile as he typed something on his phone.

"This is what is going to happen," Joshua said as he leaned down towards the man's ear. I am going to release you, and you are going to apologize to this young man for ruining his day."

Joshua released the man as he promised and casually stepped back.

"I… I'm, s-sorry." The once towering man said to the cashier, taking deep breaths.

"You leave now," Joshua said with an undeniable tone that made it a statement of fact, not a command.

The second the man exited, Joshua's smile and peaceful demeanor returned as he turned to the cashier. "I give you my deepest apologies for having to see that." His voice grew louder but remained just as soft as he addressed the entire restaurant that was now watching. "I am terribly, terribly sorry all of you had to sit through that incident. Please go back to enjoying your lunch and your day." He lowered his voice back to normal and began talking to the cashier once more. "I will be paying for a replacement counter, as well. It is the least I can do to make up for my actions."

The cashier just smiled. "Are you kidding me? That was awesome. That dude comes in here all the time, and he always finds something to gripe about no matter what we do. If it were up to me, I'd let you guys eat for free for what you did."

"I am flattered, but that is not necessary at all. The less that is said about this, the better." Joshua said as he slid a strange coin from his pocket and placed it on the counter. It was obsidian black with a pearlescent orb in the center from which three golden etched lines, resembling circuitry, curved outwards, forming a triskelion. The cashier took the coin without a word as if nothing had happened.

"Would you ladies care to order?" Win asked, gesturing towards the counter.

The friends were hit with a wave of confusion at what had occurred. They had never experienced so many emotions at once. In the blink of an eye, they went from respecting Joshua for standing up for the cashier to fearing his ferocity, back to the ever-present feeling of mysterious intrigue of who this peculiar family was. Not wishing to draw any attention to the matter, though, they step forward to order their breakfast.

"I apologize for the incident," Joshua said as they selected a table and sat down.

"It's ok." Rachel said shakily. "You were just trying to stand up for someone."

"True," Joshua replied. "We are not ones to sit idly by in the face of injustice. I had hoped it would not escalate, however. It is unfortunate that you had to witness that, for the man's sake and my own. Sadly, some people need more than just firm words to correct their actions."

"You gave him some firm correction, alright," Erin said with a smile. "That was dope as dicks. I thought y'all were about to have a full-on brawl."

Win couldn't help smirking at Erin's reaction.

"I assure you it would not have come to that," Joshua said with a polite smile. "Right then, what else would you ladies like to discuss? How are you finding Little Rock? Is it to your liking?"

"It's been nice." Ally answered for the group, actively hoping to turn the conversation back to Idonia. "Our house is awesome. The people have been enjoyable, and we've really had fun getting to know the place. To what you were discussing earlier, the Davpyr, you only described three of the races. That leaves one left, right? What were they like?"

Joshua's face lost some of its luster as he began again. "Ah yes, the Daevon, the leader of the four races. They were neither the strongest nor the fastest nor the most attuned to their Incarnum. Instead, the Daevon were a balance of them all; somewhat rugged and muscular, yet equal parts wisdom and grace. They served as an intersection of the other families, a harmony amongst them, but it was their drive and intellect which made them so notable. They were, above all else, fighters, conquerors, not just physically but mentally. Every situation was a strategic battle they sought to overcome. The entirety of existence was a puzzle they were driven to solve. The Daevon were loyal and devoted to their relatives at all costs and would do anything to see them thrive. It was for this reason that the Resharim, Netiziath, and Salarinde all chose the Daevon to lead."

Joshua's voice fell silent, and a somber look took over his face. It was clear that something about the Daevon troubled him. The friends could sense this in him. Ally attempted to delve deeper. "So they were chosen to lead? The way you told it yesterday, I thought they were just created as the leader of the four."

Joshua's face twitched as if he was choosing his words carefully, but his eyes gave nothing away. "No. The other races wanted the Daevon to rule as their leader. They felt the Daevon had the clearest outlook on how the world should be governed. That outlook was to not govern the world at all, but rather to let the world govern itself. At least, that is how things were in the beginning."

"What do you mean how things were in the beginning?" Ally pressed harder.

"Nothing. I am just rambling at this point. Are you ladies not getting bored of this fable by now?"

Ally didn't want to let it go, but Rachel's excitement blocked her from it.

"Dear God, no!" Rachel exclaimed, giving away a little too much of her joy, causing Joshua and Win to both chuckle.

"I mean to say," she recovered, "that it's an engrossing tale, and I think I speak for each of us when I say we're curious to learn more is all."

Win, still chuckling, responded, "I see. Well, is there anything else you would like to know? Storytime will be over soon. Our food is almost here, and then it's off to the zoo."

Erin saw her chance and seized it while Rachel was recovering. "What was Idonia like?" She asked rather forcibly, giving away that she had wanted to ask that for a while. Win turned calmly to look at Joshua, and even though his expression was mild, it was as if he felt the concern on his brother's face. They could both sense the despair in Erin's voice, signaling something was awry.

Joshua's voice was cold and concerned as it came across. "As legend has it, Idonia would be about the size of a small country. Most of it was made up of dense forests, tall mountains, and beautiful rivers, but there was every biome imaginable. High in the mountain ranges was a sea of snow-swept peaks and a mighty river flowed through the landscape from high in the mountains to the sandy beaches of the coast. I would venture to guess that you are talking about the city at the heart of Idonia, though. Correct?"

Erin tried to backtrack and sound only mildly interested, but she couldn't help noticing her friends mirroring her expression. "Yeah, I suppose. I mean, I was curious about where the people all lived. What was that place like?"

It was clear her act wasn't fooling the brothers, but Joshua played it off as if it did. "I told you yesterday of Leghtus and the land around it. Stretching beyond Leghtus were sprawling courtyards whose trees were covered in leaves of all different colors, spread about like an autumn rainbow leading up to the City of Idonia. Rows upon rows of towers spaced throughout flowing greenways rose to the sky. The buildings were unlike any the human world has ever or would ever see. They were part ancient stone architecture, part synthetic organism growing from the world itself, but yet completely separate from either. It was as if they existed at the dawn of civilization and in the most distant of futures simultaneously, an architectural tapestry woven together from the raw energy Legthus poured into the ground reaching towards the heavens. The one thing, though, that made Idonia amazing beyond comparison, was the glorious golden light that flowed from Leghtus into the very ground itself, connecting the world and glowing throughout every street and building in the land; a golden light against the black and grey monumental structure of the Idonic system."

That was it, the description for which Erin had been searching. The buildings Joshua described weren't quite what she saw in her dream, but they were close enough that it was clear she didn't just imagine things. The light, though, the magnificent golden light that ran all through the city, was unmistakable. She wasn't crazy, or maybe she was, but either way, Erin knew she had seen Idonia that night before in her dreams, and she had a powerful feeling it would not be the last time she saw it.

10

DINNER WITH THE BROWNINGS

The rest of the day passed with little talk of Idonia or the Davpyr, much to the friends' dismay. The zoo proved to be a pleasant trip. Joshua and Win listened as the friends took turns telling the siblings about their lives before Little Rock, their families and friends in south Arkansas, and why they were studying history, among other things. Surprisingly, the friends were very exhausted when they arrived home and moseyed to their rooms without much discussion.

Erin sat on her bed, rolling her thoughts of the day around; Joshua's swift deterrence, the Davpyric families of Idonia, and most of all, the city from her dreams. Unbeknownst to her, down the hall, Ally was doing the same thing. She sat on the edge of her bed, twirling her phone between her fingers, debating on whether to text Thad or not. She feared he would grow tired of her constant nonsensical ramblings, but she unlocked her phone nonetheless and typed a quick message to see if he was playing.

Setting the phone down, she walked to her window and looked outside. Even from her room, she could sense a chill in the air as her eyes drifted towards the street light, where, as she focused, a raven gently landed and met her gaze. Chills ran through her body as if someone had poured ice water into her veins. Her phone dinged, and she jumped in fear, her heart racing. When she looked back through the window, though, the bird was gone. She checked her phone to find a text from Thad then grabbed her controller and headset to fill him in. After a few minutes, he was caught up on the entire day's events.

"Well, if you're asking my opinion, which you never do, I think Joshua seems pretty badass. Don't tell me you've never wanted to eff some dude up for being a dick. We all have. Joshua just obviously has the guts to act on it. Hell, you said yourself the guy deserved it."

"It's just weird to see someone carry out the thoughts so many of us won't, especially to that degree. I mean, it's one thing to politely ask someone to calm down. It's a whole other to bash somebody's head into a counter when they start an altercation. I guess you're right, though."

"Of course I'm right. I always am. Loading in, by the way." As the match loaded, they kept talking. "Now, as for the feathered friend outside your window, I think you're just seeing shit." Ally tried to cut in, but Thad stopped her. "Hold on a minute. I'm not saying you're crazy or anything. I'm sure there was a bird of some kind. I just don't think some aviary fiend is stalking you. Could you even tell what kind it was?"

"No," Ally said, questioning her own memory.

There was a long pause as Ally let everything sink in. She knew he was right, but she didn't want to believe it. As much as she wished there was something spectacular happening, she knew it was just her mind playing tricks on itself.

"Look, whatever is going on in Joshua and Win's life has obviously made them very different than us, but they're still just people. So what if they believe something different than you do. So does every other religion and billions of other people throughout time. Don't let it get to your head. It's just your imagination getting you worked up. They're just stories."

Thaddeus was always the pragmatist. Ally tried to be too, but her level-headed, open-minded approach had never really been tested to the lengths it was since meeting the Brownings. Thad was right about one thing, though. They did see the world differently, much differently.

"Speaking of the Brownings, are you ready to have dinner with them tomorrow?" Ally's voice gave away her smile.

"Are you excited to see me awkwardly introduced to your boyfriend and his family?" Thad laughed, knowing he had turned the spotlight back to Ally.

"Real cute, Thad. Real cute. Just be ready to see what they're like in person. You can find out first hand what I've been talking about."

"Oh, I'm ready. Trust me, I am. I'll leave here about two-ish when I get done at work."

"Whatever. Watch the guy on the awning."

Ally turned the conversation back to the game as the two continued their match. Once they were done playing, Ally got her shower and went back to the window. She stood there staring at the streetlamp where the raven had been, or rather where she thought it had been. In bed, she tossed and turned all night, unable to get to sleep without visions of the last few days' and nights' experiences coming back to her.

Downstairs the following day, Rachel and Erin were equally exhausted, but neither led on.

"You look like shit." Erin bluntly stated as she ate her cereal. "You stay up all night playing?"

"Shockingly no. I just couldn't sleep. No reason in particular." She lied. "Just one of those nights. You girls about ready to get some coffee?"

"Let me grab my purse, and I'll be ready. You look like you could use it quick." Rachel said as she darted up the stairs.

Erin drank the milk from her cereal bowl as she walked over to the sink. Wiping her lips, she looked at Ally. "Real talk, you alright?"

"Yeah. I'm good. The past couple days just got to me a bit, I think."

"I gotcha. If you need to talk, just let me know. For real."

"Thanks. You ready to go?"

"Shit yeah."

"So when is Thad getting here?" Rachel asked as she descended the stairs.

"He's leaving around two, and with the way he drives, he'll probably be here a little after four. Better question, though, is where is he gonna sleep." Ally locked the door as the girls walked down the front steps.

"With you naturally. He's your 'buddy', after all." Erin looked over her shoulder at Ally with her sarcastic smile.

"Oh shit, it's got jokes. I didn't know it had a sense of humor." Ally's words were as cold as ice.

"Hey, somebody's gotta be the fun one of the group. Seeing as Rach is too modest, and you're too busy being the awkward one. So that only leaves me. Glad I could be of service." Erin gave a slight curtsey as she walked.

"God, now I'm ready for Thad to be here so you can torment someone else." Ally shot back, and Erin just laughed.

The day blurred past as the girls got their coffee and went through their classes. Much to the friend's surprise, Joshua and Win were not in History through War when they arrived. Mr. Edmonton gave his lesson like normal, but he seemed to focus on the trio of friends and the two empty chairs behind them the entire time.

"Now, for this weekend's assignment, I'm going to mix things up. I know the class is about war, but for the next couple of days, I want you to look at singular people or groups who waged war on humanity compared to situations where organized government structures did so. To put it more plainly, as you all looked confused, I'm speaking of situations of large-scale murder, be they serial killings or individual events such as a particular terrorist attack, compared to an act of genocide. I want you all to research an individual historical figure or sect that used their connections, influence, and power to committed mass murder in our world's history, along with one carried out by a political group that wasn't necessarily tied directly to a specific war. Now I know this is a rather odd assignment, but I'm sure it will be an enjoyable break from your current studies."

His eyes rested on Ally's for a brief moment as he paused. Everyone in the class jotted down the assignment, but Ally sat transfixed on Edmonton's eyes; light grey that looked completely empty yet eternally driven stared back at her.

"I'm sure most of you are wondering why I'm assigning this to you, but you will have to wait until next week when we discuss it. You want to think about situations that had large-scale effects. So an example I'll give that is not to be used is the deportation of the Crimean Tatars under the Soviet Union. Avoid the obvious ones, of course, so all German-occupied Europe is off the table. As for the individual or small group attacks, you have free reign. I want you to focus on why each of your two examples did what they did. Were they acting out of some zealotry? Were there inciting incidents? Were they seeking revenge on certain people or demographics for a perceived injustice or inequality, or simply seeking control and dominion? Whatever you can find. Then look into the greater ramifications of their actions; what additional incidents did it spur, was there backlash or retaliation, etc. We are still in a history class, so try not picking anything too recent. Take the time tonight or tomorrow to look up examples from each category that strikes your interest, gathering everything you can, and then have a five-page paper ready by Monday. That is all. Enjoy your weekend."

His eyes fell upon the friends one last time as everyone grabbed their bags. They rose slowly to leave, and he broke his gaze as they reached the door though Ally glanced back over her shoulder and saw his grey eyes still on them as they let the door close.

The ride back to the apartment was in silence. They even skipped The Brew right after class so they could take Thad when he arrived. Each regretted the choice. At least coffee would have provided a distraction from Edmonton's ominous stare. They just kept telling themselves Thad would be there soon.

It wasn't until almost five that Thaddeus finally arrived, and the girls were all relieved to see him. Ally and Rachel were in the kitchen when the doorbell rang. A shuffle came from upstairs that said Erin was about to head down. Ally unlocked the door and pulled it open just enough for Thad to make it in.

"Took you long enough." She teased.

"Eh, I felt like going the speed limit. New drive and all. So this is the place, huh?" He sat his bag down by the end of the stairs and walked into the kitchen where Rachel was.

"Pretty cool, isn't it?" Rachel asked, getting up for the tour as she gestured to the house. "How was your drive?"

"It was fine. No muss, no fuss. I like the place. Granted, I kinda figured I would from the description. Kitchen's spacious enough."

"Hey, chicks gotta eat ya know." Said Erin as she reached the bottom step. "Sup bitch?"

"Oh Erin, how I've missed your eloquent vernacular. Do the guys on the street corner enjoy it as much as I do?"

"Eh, you know there's not really a lot of talking in my line of work."

"I'll keep that in mind next time I'm in the market."

"Psh. You can't afford it."

"You're probably right. Overpriced product and all. So, you gonna give me the tour, or are we just gonna talk shit till dinner?" Thad and Erin both smiled at each other as Ally and Rachel laughed.

"Oh, also, I just parked on the street out front. Is that cool? I'm not trying to get towed."

They assured him it was fine, and the three girls showed Thad around the kitchen, living room, and back patio. The backyard was small, but charming with a covered walkway between the house and the detached shop. A privacy fence encased the yard, and there was a cozy firepit which the friends still hadn't furnished with seating options. Then they headed upstairs and showed him their rooms one by one.

"So who won the rock, paper, scissors war to have me sleep in their room tonight?" He said with a smirk.

"None of us were willing to risk losing and having you sleep with us, so the couch graciously volunteered itself," Erin responded without missing a beat.

"Awesome. Couches love me. So what are we doing till dinner, Alls?"

"Actually, dinner is at six, and since you took longer than expected, we probably better get going soon."

"Alright," Thad began, "so do we want to discuss what I've learned since you came back before we go or on the drive, or do you want to wait until we're done with dinner to go through all that?"

The friends froze at his words. They knew Thad eventually would dig something up to tell them. None of them knew what to expect, or what they hoped, or feared, it might be. They each shared uncertain glances with one another.

"Well," Erin said finally, "let's hear it."

"Alright," Thad began, "the first thing I kinda figured out when you guys were down last weekend, but I can confirm now with almost absolute certainty that they have no presence on social media whatsoever. Now, sure that could just be them being private. While it may seem unfathomable, some folks just don't care about being online, but it gets better. The Brew has pages. Claimed and verified pages as well, not just the ones that pop up regardless. Despite that, though, there's not a single mention of Lili or Marc or any of them anywhere. Not in the descriptions, not in reviews, nothing. It's like The Brew is just a normal business, only they don't exist."

"Ok," Rachel replied, "that's weird, right? Like that's weird as shit. I'm not the only one thinking that?"

"Yeah, I'm with Rach on that," Erin added. "Although, could it be that we're actually like the only customers they've gotten to know? I mean, even Terry and Denise said they don't really talk to anyone."

"Maybe," Thad answered. "In searching, I did see people saying stuff like 'very nice lady' and whatnot, that didn't have a name or anything. So it's possible, but we're talking about some slim chances here. There's more, though, and this is where it gets very intriguing."

The friends listened with bated breath.

"I looked into business and property records. That was the one thing I knew had to have a paper trail of some kind. Sure, you can choose not to have a social media account or have your website registration listing set as private, but you can't own and operate a business in the middle of a major city with no records of any kind. Fortunately, I was right there. It's not that kind of weird. I was able to find the business info on the Secretary of State site, but it wasn't listed in their name. All the paperwork leads to another business that owns it, and another that owns it, and another, and so on. The records go on and on; there's a dozen or more different listings, forming this web of paperwork. I still haven't found all of them. I don't know if I can even, but the furthest I could peel things back led to a company called the Harbilin Corporation."

"Harbilin?" Ally said in confusion. "That's an interesting name. I've never heard of anything close to that."

"You can imagine why not, after all that. What's crazy, though, is the company has to be massive. Massive enough, we should know of it. I'm not even from Little Rock, and I could probably name half a dozen major businesses in the area. Nothing like this, though. So, I pulled up property records of places owned by the businesses I've found thus far, and it is absolutely staggering. For example, that nice office building The Brew is located in? Yeah, they don't just lease the spot with the coffee shop. They own that whole thing. And that's just the tip of the iceberg. Just on the records I've found so far, they may own half the city, and that's just here. I haven't begun looking into other places, but with the fact they're not from here, there's bound to be more."

"So," Ally began in confusion, asking more out of curiosity than actually expecting an answer, "what does that mean for the Brownings? Do they work for this company, do they operate it, what?"

"That's a question I'm still trying to answer," Thad replied in defeat. "The Brownings pop up on a couple of company records here and there in some of the more recent filings, but it's very few and far between. I've looked into a handful of the other names that have appeared, but they all lead to the same results as trying to find stuff on the Brownings. Zilch."

"You said these various companies own maybe half the town, yeah?" Rachel asked. "If that's the case, how come no one else has talked about them? I mean, even if you are a super private business, you can't buy a big building or let alone renovate one, and the news not be covering it. How does that not get out?"

"And now you've made it to my favorite question," Thad answered with excitement. "None of this I looked up is hidden, really. It's not hard to find. Yeah, sure, I had to spend some hours going through a bunch of sites and queries, but countless people can do this. It's all public information. Anyone at any time could go find, literally, any of this, and yet, no one does. It's like people see the web and just walk away, not even wanting to try. And for being super private, they don't really act all that private. They drive around in fancy cars, they're on a first-name basis with the chef at one of the most acclaimed restaurants in town, and they smash people's heads through counters. It's not like they're trying to keep a low profile, but yet a lower profile than they have couldn't exist. You girls really outdid yourself with this one. This family is top-notch weird af. I can't wait to meet 'em!"

Thad's smile was full of anticipation as he radiated enthusiasm, and somehow the three friends couldn't help feeling some of the emotion spread to them. Despite everything their week had brought, everything they learned or dreamt, they were still compelled to unravel the mystery of the Brownings.

Their drive to Brave New Restaurant was a quiet one. The friends could sense that as excited as Thad seemed, he was also very nervous about meeting the elusive Browning Family, and he wasn't alone. While the three knew the Brownings, each outing was a new adventure, and this one brought the added intrigue of meeting the parents. As soon as they pulled into the parking lot, Ally spotted Lili's vehicle and drove towards it to park.

Upon rounding the corner, though, Thaddeus blurted out in response to the cars parked next to it, "Shit, I don't think my fancy car statement covered it?"

The friends couldn't agree more. Lili's seemed modest in comparison to the rest of the family. Ally followed more luxury car accounts than she cared to admit, and even she didn't recognize all of them. She didn't have to know the makes and models to guess the collection easily topped the seven-figure mark.

"I wouldn't park next to them, Ally. Their cars might eat yours."

Ally scoffed at his remarks and patted her steering wheel, "He doesn't mean it, sweetie." She put the car in park right next to Lili's and turned to Thad, "You can walk home if you like."

"Just being honest. Let's just go meet y'all's new boyfriends already."

"I'm going to murder you before this trip is over." Ally replied.

"Get in line," Erin added.

The group walked down the sidewalk and up to the door to find it open and George anxiously awaiting them.

"Welcome back again, ladies, and you must be Mr. Thad. Is that correct?"

"Whoah. No need for the Mr. You can just call me Thad. Nice to meet you, man." Thad held out his hand, motioning Ally to enter first.

"Come right this way. Lauren will take you to the Brownings' table. If you need anything, please feel free to ask." George bowed graciously and as his Lauren approached.

"Hey there, gals." Lauren's blonde hair was curled into ringlets, draping her face and showing off her gorgeous smile. "You ladies look stunning tonight." She gave the girls all a knowing grin, lingering a second longer on Rachel's flushed grin. "That would make this gentleman Thad, I presume? Pleasure to make your acquaintance."

"Pleasure's all mine," Thaddeus replied, slightly amused.

He leaned closer to the friends on the way to the table Lauren had pointed out and whispered, "Are they always so formal here? I mean, I feel like I should have a tie on."

Ally looked back at him, "It's just part of the Brownings effect. You'll see."

As the group neared the table in the farthest corner of the building, they spotted Joshua and Win, who stood at their approach. Noticing this, Marc and Lili stood and turned to them as well. The last two to rise were facing away from the friends, and all that could be seen was the backs of their bright, near ice-blonde hair. None of the friends noticed how tall they were sitting down, but as the pair stood, they saw that the woman must have been almost six feet two, and her husband was every bit of six feet six. The man's hair was combed back, not unlike his son Win's hair. The mother's, though, flowed in soft waves down to the middle of her back and shined against her soft, mint green dress, which dazzled brilliantly against her dark skin. The friends felt as if they were watching the world in slow motion that day as the couple turned to face them. Their faces were both beautifully chiseled in their unique way. Together they looked as if they stepped forth from Nordic mythology, he the brave Viking, and she the brutally gorgeous Valkyrie.

Strangely enough, it was Joshua that spoke first instead of the parents. "Ah, this must be Thad. We are so pleased you could join us. This is my family." Joshua's arms swept open in a mass gesture showing off his family. It was the first time the friends had ever seen Joshua in anything but a suit as a subtle grey V-neck clung to his frame. His forearms looked like he could as easily be a pro baseball player as he could a college student, and his biceps threatened to rip at the seams in his sleeves even though it was loose throughout the waist. Despite being the shortest of his family alongside Marcus, he was still one of the biggest. As he brought his arms back in his chest pushed against the fabric of his shirt, and even the muscles along his neck could be seen protruding from his collar. Were it anyone else, the friends would have thought Joshua a gym fanatic, but instead, he came across like a warrior as if everything about him was by design. Decorating the muscles protruding from his neck was a thin strip of leather and the black beads of a necklace, but they disappeared under his shirt. Surveying the family, it was evident that all the men had the same leather strip hidden under their shirts, but neither of the women did.

One by one, Joshua introduced his family to Thad. "This is my sibling, Win." Joshua gestured to Win, who stood at his right. Win wore a bright blue shirt that was as loud as the shirts he usually wore, but he didn't have a hoodie or blazer on over it for the first time. As he extended his hand forward to shake Thaddeus' it was not his chiseled muscles that caught the girls' attention, but rather the massive silvery tattoo of a bird emblazoned in flames with two words worked into the burning feathers. It was the same symbol the friends had seen on the wooden menu at The Brew.

"Nice to meet you, man," Thad said as he shook Win's hand, studying every aspect of him.

"This lovely couple here is Lili and Marc." Joshua pointed his hand across the table where Marc and Lili stood.

Thad walked over and shook both their hands. "It's good to meet you too. So, is the Lotus out there yours?" He said to Marc as he released his hand.

"Actually, no." Marc and Lili laughed softly, knowing Thad made the apparent guess. The girls had been wrong too.

Joshua spoke again with a knowing smirk on his face, "Thad, Ally, Rachel, and Erin, I would like you each to meet Ceph and Lavy, the owners of the Lotus."

The friends looked at their faces directly for the first time since they arrived as they took turns shaking hands. His was very rugged and chiseled, long with a strong jawline and slender nose. Hers shared the long, slim structure but with a much softer feel despite her sculpted cheekbones. It was their eyes, though. Their eyes burned with the same vivid blue as Win's, Marc's, and Lili's. Not Joshua's, though. His were the only ones the shade of steely grey.

Ceph spoke with a soft authority that almost neared that of Joshua's voice. "It is a genuine delight to meet you, ladies, finally. Our family has told us a great deal about you. And Thad, which I am guessing is short for Thaddeus, I have heard only a little about you, but I can tell from your reaction to our family and the reputation of the company you keep that you will be a wonderful friend. My wife Lavy and I are thrilled to meet you both."

"I am delighted each of you could join us tonight," Lavy added in a silky voice. "It is not very often either of those two brings friends around." Her voice had a sharpness at the end with motherly insinuation as she looked over at Joshua and Win.

With that, Joshua motioned to the seats next to him, and everyone sat down. Marc playfully nudged Win as they were doing so. The friends were glad to see that the Browning family was somewhat typical after all. Erin was even more interested, though, to see the silvery tattoo poking out of Marc's sleeve on the inside of his bicep. She could only see half of it when he pushed his brother, but it was almost certainly the same one that Win had. *Was it some kind of family crest*, she thought. Something like the family ring that Joshua wore. *If so, though, why did Joshua not have one as well?*

It wasn't two seconds after they sat down that Lauren was at the table. "Ah, Dr. Browning and Dr. Browning. When did you slip in? I didn't even notice you were here with your family. Lavy, dear, you look as beautiful as ever." Lauren's words came off very clearly with a deep admiration for her and her entire family.

"And you are as kind as ever, Lauren. You're one to speak on beauty after all." Lavy said, flashing a dazzling smile that lit up the room. "We snuck in while you were away from the door."

"Always trying to be sneaky. I knew one of these days you'd manage it." She gave them a playful wink. "And Marcus, Lili, why did you not join your brothers and their dates the other night?"

The word echoed through the friend's head over and over. *Dates.*

None of the girls quite understood it. *Was that a date, and if so, who was on a date with whom?* The friends pushed the thought to the back of their minds.

"Oh, I wanted to join Lauren." Marc began. "I just have a huge project currently. To be honest, I should not even be here tonight, but I cannot exactly say no to the family." Marc smiled his brilliant smile as he looked at each of them thankfully. Whatever dark past it was that Joshua mentioned, it clearly brought them very close together.

"And Lauren, you know full well I was working, my love," Lili added with a wink. "You know, given the opportunity, I would not miss a chance to help you put these two in check." She gestured to Joshua and Win."

"Work, work, work. Posh, posh." Lauren smiled jokingly. "Speaking of, let me get back to my job. Usual drinks for everyone?" She said, looking at the Brownings and seeing their nods. "Now, you four. Ladies, same as last time, or want to mix it up?"

Erin and Ally both agreed in unison.

"Something different for me." Rachel began. "Still your choice, just swap it up. I trust you."

"Dangerous words there," Lauren smirked. "I'll try not to disappoint, which leaves you, sir. What's your poison?"

"Um," Thad began, uncertain, "I'm not sure. What do you recommend?"

"Well, let me get a look at you." Lauren began. "Yeah, you're usually a Jack and Coke type of guy, but that's just not gonna cut it here. So I'll do you my take on a Manhattan with some of our Rock Town Bottled in Bond that we infused."

"If that's what you're pouring, that's what I'm drinking."

"A man after my own tastes," Joshua said, giving Thad a curt nod as Lauren left to get the drinks.

"So, Dr. Browning and Dr. Browning," Thad began, excited to get to the bottom of the Browning family mystery, "what is it you doctors do?"

Ceph smirked knowingly as the rest of the family laughed to themselves, "Lauren always insists on the formalities. Most people do not refer to me as Dr. Browning. That would just be Lavy. I am not that kind of doctor. I work in medical research; thus, I have a doctorate. The actual doctor in the family is this wonderful person." Ceph touched his wife's arm gently. The look in his eyes said it all.

They had clearly been through hell and back, and his love for her would never die.

"That's really cool. You guys are like two sides of the same coin." Thad's observation was so simple yet so beautiful that the whole family looked as if they'd blush, but the redness never came, just the eyes searching each other's to show how special it made them all feel. "So what type of doctor are you, Dr. Lavy?"

"Please, just Lavy. Any friend of Joshua's is a friend of ours, and my friends and family do not call me Doctor." Her voice was comforting, like only a mother's could be. "I work in advanced triage and neurosurgery. So I handle patients who've been injured and are at risk of losing brain function or nervous system issues, as well as certain cases where the damage is already thought to be permanent. My team is usually the last resort for most patients."

The group of friends was utterly taken aback.

"That's incredible. You're like a hero." Rachel said.

"Thank you, Rachel, but I am just a doctor. I am no hero, merely someone trying to help where they can, while they can."

The friends began to see the Brownings in an entirely different light. They saw how unapproachable they were. They heard the warnings to stay away. Joshua told the friends his family had been through many bad things, but that day the group saw them for what they were; a family who had been to war and made it through more united than ever, loving each other and willing to do anything for one another.

Sensing that Lavy didn't like the spotlight and knowing all too well how that felt, Ally changed the subject, "So Ceph," She stumbled over the name awkwardly as she fought not to call him doctor, "what kind of medical research do you do? Like pharmaceuticals or therapy?"

The smiles and laughter died away slightly, and a severe look took over Ceph's face. "I am not at liberty to discuss the nature of my research. I apologize for the secrecy, but my obligations demand it is for the best. All I can tell you is that I do research dealing with biological adaptation." The faces of his family made it clear they all knew exactly what he did but would never discuss it. If any one thing defined the Browning family, it was their secrets and their ability to keep them.

"Enough about us, though." Ceph sensed the shift in conversation. "Let us hear about you. All we know of your group is what we have been told. We prefer first-hand accounts."

The friends all looked at one another. No one knew who should go first. Knowing how much Ally, Rachel, and Erin had likely shared thus far, though, Thad jumped in to spare them. "There's not much to say, really. I live a couple hours south, where they're from. I'm currently going to school for computer engineering. I'm not exactly sure what I want to do with it just yet, but I love programming. So we'll see."

Marcus and Win lit up when he said that. Win looked to his brother as if asking permission to go first. Without even a nod, Win somehow sensed the ok and began, "What all have you done? What is your preferred field? Marc and I could easily give you some pointers and introduce you to some people who could help? Perhaps maybe even bring you in for some contract work, if you know where you want to be?" Win realized he was loading a lot of questions into one go and stopped.

"I've actually put a lot of thought into it, but I still don't quite know. I mean, if I'm being honest, the pipe dream would be space. Literally, anything I could do to work in space travel, I would be all over, but that's one tough break to get. Plus, I don't know where I would want to go, and the choices are kind of limited. I'm from New York originally, so I'd love to be back there. That's not really feasible, though."

"Well, if you decide that is something you want to pursue, we would gladly help any way we could." Win said with a flare of a smile that a child gets with a new toy.

"I'll do some research and get back to you," Thad responded with utmost confusion and excitement.

"So, where in New York did you live? Ceph and I have a home in upper Manhattan, but we both work down around Midtown." Lavy's voice was sweet and modest yet deceptive. She made a point not to say precisely where in Manhattan they lived or worked.

"Oh, I'm from Brooklyn originally. Greenpoint, back before it was Greenpoint." Thad never talked much about his life before Arkansas. "I lived there with my mother until high school when I moved in with my grandmother down here."

That was the same story any of the friends got whenever they asked about his life in Brooklyn. That was all, though. Thad never visited his mom, never talked about his mom, never even acknowledged her existence. They never asked why.

Lavy's maternal instincts were showing again as she sensed

something wrong, but before she could speak, she froze. It was as if there were a voice inside her head telling her not to ask what she was about to ask. Joshua was fixated on Lavy intently but sincerely. Lavy leaned back and began rolling the thoughts around in her head of what to say instead.

"Well, if you are ever in New York again, please feel free to stop by and visit us," were the words she chose. "We always enjoy the company."

The rest of the dinner went on with the typical conversation. The friends all said simple things about themselves; hobbies, interests, and such. They asked questions of Ceph and Lavy, and the rest of the family, trying to understand them in any way they could, but were met with guarded responses or artful dodges anytime they drew near to something of consequence. The Brownings were polite and courteous at every turn, showing genuine interest in each of the friends and at all times indicating the skilled navigation of master tacticians. The Brownings were a fortress of a family.

11
LIFE IN THE SHADOWS

The sun hung low over the city and was setting rapidly, sending shadows of office buildings dancing ahead of them. A cool breeze was in the air, and the friends could feel the freakish cold they'd heard so much about on the horizon. The drive home from the restaurant wasn't long, but it was long enough for the night's events to weigh on them.

"So," Thad began, breaking the long silence hanging over the car ride home, "quite frankly, I don't know if they're more or less intimidating after meeting them."

"You can say that again," Rachel added.

"No shit." Erin continued. "I mean, every fucking response sounded like it was rehearsed to perfection. They didn't stumble. They didn't hesitate. Yet somehow, they felt so goddamn genuine it was agonizing. They're the nicest fucking people I've ever met, and I'm damn near terrified of them. Shit. Thad, I really thought you'd be the weirdest person I'd ever meet. I'm beginnin' to think I was wrong."

The sun hung low over the city and was setting rapidly, sending shadows of office buildings dancing ahead of them. A cool breeze was in the air, and the friends could feel the freakish cold they'd heard so much about on the horizon. The drive home from the restaurant wasn't long, but it was long enough for the night's events to weigh on them.

Thad may not have heard the stories the girls did directly, but he got enough in the relay of information that he wasn't far off from them. It had been affecting them each differently. Their thoughts, their moods, their dreams were all swirling about with a mix of emotions that they could hardly understand and pieces of a puzzle they couldn't seem to solve. With each step they took closer to the Brownings, the murkier it all became.

City lights came on across the town as Little Rock took on its second life. The bridges would light up soon after for their evening dance across the river that ran right through the heart of the city. Bands would then be tuned up in restaurants down in the River Market. The friends kept saying they would go down there one night and listen, but they had yet to do so and would not do so that night. Too many other things flooded their minds.

"Sorry to disappoint," Thad replied. "Though, admittedly, I don't really think I could do much to compete with this lot. They're insanely cool. Right? Yes, they're proper. Yes, they have things they won't talk about, which I can totally understand, but at the end of the day, they really are a badass family. Aren't they?"

"Yeah," Ally cut in, "and that's what I hate about it. It's so much easier when it's clear-cut. This one, though, I'm just not sure. Hell, the mom's a doctor in triage. You don't get much nicer than that, and yet here we are."

"Yeah, it doesn't make any sense." Rachel said, dismay and frustration apparent in her voice. "Their secrets seem like they have secrets, and yet all we've seen is them be kind and gracious. Even the incident at The Root with Joshua was him standing up for someone, and I feel like that could've been far worse if he'd wanted it so. What, do we think they're incredibly polite because they're serial killers or the Illuminati?"

No one answered for a spell. If the question remained unanswered, then it couldn't be wrong or right. None of the friends knew what they wanted the truth behind the Brownings to be. They were each intrigued beyond compare, but that was part of the mystique. Uncovering the truth would mean facing it, and they weren't ready for that. What they were or weren't prepared for was irrelevant, though, for the answers would come regardless.

"So Thad," Ally began, "what's your take? You callin' off the search on them since they're so cool?"

"Oh hell no. I'm still sticking to them being demon hunters from the future." Thad joked, opening his door as they arrived home.

"And just like that, you're back to being the weirdest person I know," Erin said mockingly.

"Fuck yeah!" Thad exclaimed, thrusting his fist in the air. "Got my title back. You Brownings ain't got shit on me."

Ally, Rachel, and Erin couldn't help laughing at their dear friend. As crazy as the night's findings had been, they were still able to find humor in things. They supposed that was a good sign.

"Real talk, though," he began again, seriousness back in his voice, "I'm going to keep looking into them. Yeah, they're super nice and cool and all, but we all know they're hiding something. I want to know what it is."

"Agreed." The three girls agreed in unison.

With that, the group headed into the house in hopes of finding some distraction from the Brownings.

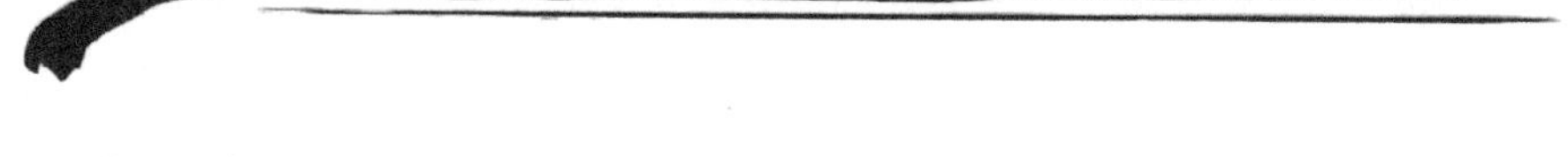

Over in downtown, dark clouds formed overhead as the woman made her way down the street. The cold was setting in faster each day. It wouldn't be much longer before the hazy chill covered the city throughout the day and night, making her endeavors far easier. She hated having to wait until nightfall to go about her business. It made her feel wrong, and wrong is the one thing she knew, beyond a shadow of a doubt, she was not. Nothing had ever felt so right. She was finally being true to herself, and it was euphoric.

The man wasn't far ahead of her. She kept enough distance between them that no one would take notice except him. That was part of the game, the part that made it fun. She needed him to know she was there, just out of reach. It was what made all the stealth worth it in the end. She hated having to hide what they were doing, but she'd found a way to make it entertaining.

A crisp wind blew, and she breathed it in deep down to her core. The first leaves had begun to fall from the trees. It was her favorite time of year. A season of change, and that particular season felt long overdue for her. She kept pace with the man as she watched the leaves fall. They were perfect as they danced through the air, the physical embodiment of the beautiful passage of time. For so many, autumn meant the end of vibrant life as the world turned cold, rendering all of its creatures dormant. She knew better, though. All things must end. No matter how long the season, nothing lasts forever, and the death of one thing paved the way for the next. Her. The season she was in had lasted a lifetime, and she was finally ready to change that.

The man crossed the street, but she didn't move to follow. He was almost home now. So, instead, she continued nonchalantly down her side of the road as she watched him. A trolley languidly passed between them, distracting her briefly. She had come to appreciate the city. It was still not to her preferences, but she came to admit it wasn't without its charms. She'd visited a number of the local restaurants and was very pleased. The denizens she'd come across had all been welcoming, and on more than one occasion, she had felt briefly at home.

She suppressed the thoughts anytime they arose, not wanting to let herself get attached to the place. It was the people that mattered. The city wasn't hers. Hers was far away, back where her family missed her. She missed them, too, no matter how much she tried to ignore it. All too often, she would remind herself that it wouldn't be long before she saw them again. Her time in the city would be brief, and she shouldn't feel remorse for making the most of it. That was the point, after all, the reason she was there.

It was about the experience, the journey, getting to know the city and, more importantly, its people in the time she had there. The most important of those people, though, was him. He was the first, the first of the journey she was on. He wouldn't be the last she knew. That knowledge brought her both joy and sadness. She wanted to cherish the moment she was in, but she also was excited about all the moments still to come. The seasons were indeed changing, and she was ready for that. Soon the world would go dormant as it prepared to usher forth new life, new seasons, new journeys to be had. For the moment, though, she was happy to live in the space between; that time when the last season of adventure and wonder had not yet ended, and the new one was just beginning.

She stopped on the sidewalk and leaned against the building, knowing he was almost to his door. Hers was just around the corner so that they wouldn't be far, and she mustn't wait much longer. Her new season was almost at hand, and he marked the solstice. Everything was about to change, and her new life would begin. As he opened the door to his walk-up, he looked back over his shoulder to where she stood, leaning against the building as a smile spread across both their lips for a brief moment before they parted ways. The time was almost at hand.

Ally, Erin, Rachel, and Thad were spread across the sofa and loungers that furnished the living room sifting through potential movies to stream for the night, but none of them could find anything they cared to watch. Try as they might to push the evening's events from their heads, it just refused to work.

"Alright, y'all, let's face it," Erin began, "we're not making any progress, and I think we all know why. So here's the deal, either we just call it a night and go to bed, or we throw on some background music and start working through this shit."

The room was silent in response. Neither Rachel, Ally, nor Erin liked the idea of heading to bed and the potentially horrible dreams that awaited them. Still, any deeper excursions into The Brownings felt only certain to exacerbate their problems. Thad was at a loss as well. His inquiries into the Brownings had started as sport. He enjoyed combing through the internet looking for fun, hidden facts about things, but the more time he spent looking into the Brownings, the less of a game it became. There was something massive at the heart of all the strings upon which he was tugging. Something that actively didn't want to be found, and the more he uncovered, the less certain he became that he wanted to know what that thing was.

"How about this then," Thad began after the silence stretched long enough to break his indecision, "I'll pull up all the stuff I found so far, and we can all sift through that. Additionally, though, I think we should also take some time to look into some of the tales they've shared about their beliefs. Figuring out who the hell these people are is a huge interest to us all, and if we can learn anything more about what they believe, maybe that can give us some insight. I will forewarn you, though, if it's anything like everything I've looked up so far, it'll be a lot of dead ends. What do we say?"

The three friends exchanged glances. They knew the answer, but no one wanted to say. The precipice was upon them.

"Okay." Rachel said finally. "We do this."

The friends each grabbed their devices as Thad began sharing out data he'd compiled, and the group was soon combing through property records and business records, working to match up who owned what and how each branch was connected to the others. Slowly a pattern began to form as certain companies arose that were shells over specific groups. However, even as they connected the dots, it still gave them no new insight into why the companies were formed, who was involved, or what connection the Brownings had to them. The Brownings name only showed up on a handful of the smallest companies within the seemingly endless conglomerate. All of those records were relatively recent compared to the much older companies in the collection.

Once they had the pattern of company structures roughly outlined, the group split off into different directions, with Thad looking into records in other states, Erin and Rachel going over properties owned by the companies in Arkansas, and Ally trying to find anything about Idonia online. None of them made much progress, though.

Rachel and Erin went through page after page after page of properties in Little Rock, chasing down what they thought were convincing leads only to have one or another go nowhere. The best they could deduce was that the majority of downtown was owned in one way or another by the ever-illusive Harbilin Corporation. There seemed to be no rhyme or reason for collecting properties and businesses they owned, though. The two found everything from office buildings scattered across town to random apartments to abandoned warehouses along the river with seemingly no connection whatsoever.

Thad was having even worse luck plowing through state site after state only to find more of the same random selections of businesses. Most states only had a few here and there, but there were always some, and none of them had any logical collection to another. Anywhere there was a dense population of people, there were anywhere from a handful to a dozen of affiliated companies, all owning several properties for no discernible reason at all.

"Hey guys," Ally finally said out loud, grabbing the group's attention. Hours had drifted by without hardly a word until she spoke. "So I officially can't find anything on any of the stuff they've told us online. Literally, the only thing I can find at all is baby names, that I'm pretty sure no one actually has ever used, and some kind of herbal body cream. I don't think that's anything to do with them. I've tried every word and phrase I could remember that they've said, spelled every way I can imagine, and I got a whole lot of nothing. I think we've managed to discover the one topic Google literally has no record of."

She tilted her head back and pinched her nose in frustration, rubbing her tired, watery eyes.

"Well," Rachel began sardonically, "we've found some beneficial information. The foundation owns our house our scholarships are through, which is truly shocking considering that living here was kinda part of the whole scholarship in the first place."

The house had been an unexplainable blessing for them, part of a series of such blessings that had allowed them to attend UCA in the first place. Their financial aid had all been provided through a private scholarship at the school and allowed them to rent an apartment off-campus, so they didn't have to worry about random roommates, which they knew was a rare feat for graduate students. Moving to a new city and living with strangers would have been more than any of them could handle. They looked for a place near campus initially, but once they were awarded the scholarship and informed the house was part of the package, the choice was clear. Ally personally had never been keen on the idea of living in the city, but Erin and Rachel convinced her to embrace it as the move was supposed to be a chance for them to all try something new and find themselves. It was only a thirty-minute drive to campus, and they would be going against the flow of rush hour traffic, so it wasn't a bad commute. Much to Ally's surprise, she instantly loved the place. It was everything the friends needed, and all the things they wanted, rolled into one.

"Even more informative is that the house next to us is the childhood home of a former governor," Erin added, slouching her shoulders in defeat.

"Really?" Thad said with mock interest.

"Yup," Erin replied. "Pryor. Small world, huh."

Rachel and Erin both sat back, feeling the same exhaustion Ally had shown.

"Sure is," Thad interjected. "Small enough that I can tell you the Haribilin Corporation has businesses in probably every state. I haven't actually checked them all, but every one I have is connected. That's all I've found, though. No headquarters, no personnel listings, not even a company motto. I guess it would just be, 'we own a bunch of shit.' Not sure how that would look on the business cards, though."

"I mean, I'd be cool with a business card like that." Ally scoffed. "Real talk, I think I'm done. My eyes are killing me, and all we've done is dug a deeper hole."

"Yeah I'm getting tired myself," Thad replied, "and you guys are kind of sitting on my bed. So, I'm bound to your decisions. We can come back to this when we feel more functional.

Erin and Rachel agreed, and the three friends began gathering their things as Thad adjusted the couch for him to sleep. After a round of goodnights, the girls made their way upstairs. Ally stopped at the top of the stairs where her door was as Rachel and Erin continued down the hall towards theirs with brief goodnights exchanged. After her nightly routine, Ally pulled the blankets up tight around her and drifted off to sleep.

In a dark room, the woman waited impatiently for their secret rendezvous. "Took you long enough." The woman whispered as he entered the room. "I had to start without you." A faint moan escaped her lips as her fingers got carried away, caressing herself. "No worries, though." She told him as she gently slid her fingers up from between her thighs, slowly across her abdomen, until they found her breasts. Cupping them gently, she squeezed, letting out another soft moan, and bit down on her bottom lip as she locked eyes with him. "You can pick up where I left off." Biting her lip even harder, she took the firm nipple of the breast she was cupping between her thumb and index finger, pinching hard and causing herself to gasp for air while never taking her eyes off his. She spread her bent knees apart only the slightest bit to tease him, raising her free hand to gesture him forward.

He dared not keep her waiting, but he moved as slowly as he could manage without annoying her. That was part of their forbidden dance, the power struggle that breathed life into their secret romance, each toying with the other, acting controlling and submissive, whichever way they could to counter one another. It was the balance they struck that made their time together electrifying. She loved to be bossy until he made her quiver. He loved for her to dominate him until she begged him to take control.

He stepped closer to the bed, slowly pulling his shirt up and over his head. The glow from the streetlamps outside danced across his lean body. She pinched herself even harder. She wanted to scream at him, command him to take her then and there, but that wasn't how the dance went. They had to cherish it, take their time, and play their part until neither could take anymore.

A bead of sweat ran down her neck as she watched him unbutton his pants. He took his precious time as he slid them down over his chiseled thighs. She loved his body. Most never saw it. To the outside world, he seemed average, but she knew that when the clothes came off, his true nature showed. His lean, sculpted frame bulged as he pulled the pants from his legs and tossed them aside. Even in the darkness, she could see him swelling in his trunks. He knelt on the bed beside her and began gently kissing her upright knees, working his way slowly down her thighs as he gripped her calves and gently massaged them. She worked to control herself.

"Just your hands for the moment, sir." She said, grabbing him by the hair pulling his face up towards hers. "For now, I want your tongue right, here." She said, drawing her finger down her tongue and bottom lip.

The second his tongue touched hers, she wrapped her lips around it, pulling him into her. He grabbed the back of her neck, matching her intensity as their tongues caressed. He placed his hand on the inside of her thigh just above the knee, and she shivered with anticipation. Grabbing his hair tighter still, she commanded him to continue. His hand slid down her thigh, slowly, methodically tracing fine lines across her skin, teasing her as only he could. Her impatience rising, she grabbed his hand, sliding it the rest of the way down until he found her, already moist with anticipation.

She released from his kiss, gasping for air. She hated how much she had missed him, and yet she loved nothing more. Her heart raced to have him in her arms once more. His index and ring finger tracing her edges as his middle drifted between them, gently opening her. She pulled him so close her lips touched his ear as she let out an ecstatic moan, urging him onward. He loved when she did that. It sent chills down his spine, and he responded in kind, running his thumb softly over her sweet spot at the very moment he slid his finger inside her. She let out a purring moan before gently biting his earlobe and sucking slowly.

His fingers moved in concert with one another, his thumb rhythmically massaging her sweet spot as he slowly thrust his finger in and out, going slightly deeper with every push. His lips moved first to her ear, kissing then licking her earlobe. He whispered softly, sending shivers down her skin before he moved down her neck. He knew every centimeter of her; where to place a soft peck, where to caress with his tongue gently, and where to bite so that she would choke back a scream of pleasure. His lips and tongue traced down her collarbone as her fingers increased their tempo, thrusting harder and pulling her hips into the motion.

By the time his mouth reached her breasts, she could barely contain herself. His lips parted as he pressed them softly against her skin. His tongue traced her circles around her nipple, teasing her as he did. His fingers raced, keeping rhythm with her thrusts, as he placed his other hand on the small of her back, pulling her into each motion. He ran his tongue over her nipple as he took it in his mouth and sucked softly. Her breath quickened, and her back arched with each rhythmic thrust as he sent her cascading over the edge.

Ally was running, running through darkness. A branch from a tree scraped her as she ran by and she felt the warm blood dripping down her skin. It began to sting, but she knew she had to keep running. She didn't have to look back. She knew who was chasing her. The flock of crows grew closer and closer until her foot caught a root and sent her flying forward onto the leaf-covered forest floor. They were damp and cold against her skin, but she didn't let the feeling linger as she rose to run again.

On her feet once more, she saw the flock was gone. She no longer was in the forest but instead in the middle of the mighty city with its gorgeous skyrises stretching for miles amidst lush greenways. She had a sense she'd been there before, but at the same time, it felt utterly foreign. It felt hollow, like the life that once flowed from the vibrant place had been slowly siphoned away. She looked to the horizon for the enormous tree which anchored the world, longing to see its fiery leaves glowing against the sky. To her horror, the brilliant glow of the tree was gone, and the once dazzling leaves had turned an ashen grey.

A chill crept down her spine as a faint breeze blew around her. She could sense the figure looming behind her. There were no ravens about, no wings rustling. No, this was the other one, she knew. Even without turning, she could see his hooded form in her mind, the terrifyingly radiant eyes glowing at her from under its cowl, and the feeling of imminent doom that emanated from it. She turned slowly, again refusing not to meet her own end head-on.

She stared deep into the abyss under the figure's hood, locking onto the glowing orbs set within it. Fear gripped her heart. Not at her own peril, but at that which she saw within the figure's eyes. There was pain, agonizing pain within them; pain they had caused, and pain they had endured. They were eternal, infinite, knowing no limit to the destruction and desecration that could be. In that moment, they were the once beautiful Leghtus turned to ashen grey death, the once vibrant galactic metropolis made hollow and barren. They had witnessed Time, destroyer of all, as it carried through endlessly, existence after existence rising and falling, blinking out into the ever-present nothingness of the Void.

She could hear the screams of infinite worlds ending, feel the terror as they ripped apart, atom by atom, lost to the sands of time. The words came to her without warning, and she spoke them clear as crystal. "Nigh is the hour of The Raven and The Lion."

With that, a caw sounded through her mind. She blinked, and the hooded figure was gone, leaving her alone in the dying forest once more. Looking to the skies, she saw the ravens perched on every decrepit branch, staring back at her as one. The Raven, she thought, yet no Lion. And the words returned, "Nigh." The caw resounded in a cacophony around her, shaking her to the very fabric of her being, threatening to tear her asunder.

Again, she turned and fled, fleeing from her imminent doom. The ravens took flight once more and gave chase. She bound through the forest, willing herself forward faster and faster, knowing that He was close behind. The ravens coalesced into a singular swirl of feathers as they pushed closer and closer to her. Ally leaped over a fallen tree in her path with agility and grace she knew she didn't possess and landed on the other side in a swift recovery as she pressed further onward. Then, without warning, the flock descended, crashing into her with a force she knew not possible and sending her flying forward.

She shot out of bed the second she hit the ground. Gasping for breath, she looked at her arm where the tree had cut her; of course, there was no blood. How could there be blood, she told herself, panting. She was only dreaming, but only dreaming didn't change the burning in her throat, though. It wasn't the burn of a parched, dry mouth. No, it was much more. It felt as if molten metal had been poured down her throat. Or poured from it, she thought as the words echoed in her head again.

She reached for the water on her nightstand, hoping to squelch the burn, but felt nothing except the wooden top. She had never grabbed a cup before going to bed. Grudgingly, she slung her feet out of bed and let them hit the cold floor.

She tried her best to be quiet and not wake any of her housemates. She didn't even bother turning on a light as she felt her way down the stairs. In the kitchen, she simply cracked the fridge and let the light spill out on the floor. It was just enough to see the cabinet where the cups were. She snagged one and closed the fridge, not even bothering to fill the cup downstairs at risk of waking Thad.

At the foot of the stairs, a sound sent chills down her spine. Panicked breaths followed by a faint scream. It wasn't just a dream. It was a sign. Raven Man had come, and now he was in their home. This was all her fault was the only thought filling her brain. She should have told them about her visions, the dreams. This was more than just some fantastical story from some enigmatic family. It was manifesting within their reality. She pushed her fear down and darted up the stairs dropping her cup. As she topped the stairs, she saw nothing but pure blackness. She made to break into a run, but before she could make the first bound down the black hallway, three words stopped her dead in her tracks.

"Oh God, Thaddeus."

12
THE MORNING AFTER

Ally braced herself against the wall for fear she might faint. The whole world seemed to unravel before her. She felt like she was losing her mind thinking that some supernatural horror was in her house. She felt foolish for not knowing that panicked breathing and a faint scream of terror was actually heavy breathing and a scream of ecstasy. Most of all, she felt embarrassed that she was no more than ten steps away from walking in on Thaddeus and one of her friends, and yet still, her dreams had happened. The visions did occur, and those two realities warred in her mind.

She turned slowly to go back to her room, but as her hand reached her doorknob, she remembered why she left her room in the first place. The cup was at the bottom of the stairs still, so she carefully slid down, grabbed it, and eased back up to her room. Once she had a glass of water down and a fresh one, in case she woke again, she laid back down in bed. Her dreams were an incoherent blur of the hooded figure with infinite eyes, her dear friend Thad, and the flock of ravens all bleeding together, intertwining until all three felt like one unified nightmare.

Restless as she was, Ally was thrilled when morning finally arrived to greet her. She was out of bed well before the rest of her friends, she assumed, and began getting ready. Without delay, she sped downstairs, hoping to find an empty couch so she wouldn't have to be the one to address the situation. As long as Thad and her friend came downstairs together, she had nothing to fear. Much to her surprise, though, Thaddeus was still fast asleep on the couch.

Ally began to race back through the previous night's events. Had she imagined them? Was she asleep the whole time? She walked closer to the couch to get a better look. It was really him—no imagining that.

Thad, however, who usually slept with his shirt off, still had it on that morning. She was surprised to see him so modest. Even if he was asleep in a house full of girls, it was just his friends.

Thad shifted, startling Ally. She scuttled into the kitchen swiftly, hoping he wouldn't know she had been peering over him. Ally loudly grabbed a bowl down from the cabinet as Thad sat up. She didn't bother being quiet while pouring the cereal and milk. "Sleep well?" She asked, trying not to give away that she suspected anything.

"Not too shabby." He said, rising from the couch and joining her in the kitchen. "Your couch is actually pretty comfy." He grabbed a bowl from the cabinet for himself.

"Yeah, I guess. Still not as comfy as a bed." Ally felt a bitterness rising in her voice. *Why am I bitter*, she thought. Her friends were both adults, and certainly not maidens. *Was she angry that her best friend was having sex with one of her other best friends and not telling her?* She thought back to how Thaddeus had told her about back when he and Rachel dated before Rachel did. *How could he have told her, though?* It had just happened the night before. *Or was it that morning*, she thought. She didn't know what time it had happened. Still, it wasn't Thad not telling her either. *So, what was it?* She thought.

Thad sat there staring at her blank expression sensing something was awry. He sat the cereal box down. "Got something on your mind there?"

Ally snapped back from her thoughts. "Huh?" She paused, looking at him. "Oh no, I just zoned out, sorry."

"Bullshit, Ally. I know you better than anyone. If something's wrong, talk to me."

Too late. No sooner had the words left Thad's mouth than the top stair creaked under someone's weight. Ally's eyes shot to the stairs, wondering who it would be. Ally processed the odds of the person walking downstairs being the owner of the voice she heard the night before. More than likely, if Thad had slept with one of them, that person would be the last one to come down as they would be more tired, but both Rachel and Erin liked to sleep late, so that could offset everything.

Then she thought of the possibility of who it had been. *Were he and Rachel getting back together after blowing it off all this time?* There was merit to that argument, she knew. When she thought about the potential of it being Erin, though, she couldn't bring herself to it. *Sure, the constant teasing sets it up nicely*, she thought, *but then both Erin and Thad would be doing that behind Rach's back too.* That seemed a bridge too far in Ally's mind, for either Erin or Thad. Ally was sure it was Rachel, but then she wasn't sure if it was even real at all. The night before, she would've sworn that it was, but the night before, she also would have sworn Raven Man or the horrifying figure that kept wandering into her dreams were coming after them.

Ally's attempt at guessing would have been pointless regardless, as both Rachel and Erin walked down the stairs together. She went back to eating her cereal as the three said their good mornings. No awkwardness could be sensed between any of them. Was she the only one who found the whole situation weird? *Surely, if Thad slept with Rachel, she would have at least given him an awkward glance, and surely Erin would have heard them in the night too.* That's what Ally told herself, but Ally was the only one who seemed even to be aware of anything. She felt like she might actually be losing her mind.

"So we're going to get coffee like two minutes ago, right, because my brain is about to blow my skull to shit," Erin said with no humor in her voice.

"Amen to that," Rachel added. "I don't remember the last time I felt this out of it in the morning."

Still no sure sign from either of them. Ally didn't care, though. Whether she imagined it or not, Ally was going to spend all weekend figuring out if it was true. Thad was the only one who sensed something was amiss with Ally, but she wasn't going to let that get in her way. Then it dawned on Ally; she was just as tired. Both Erin and Rachel talked about how exhausted they were, and she didn't stop to think about how tired she was. She wondered if they were all drained for the same reason. If none of them had slept well. Ally began to wonder if any of the previous night's memories were correct. She looked to her room and questioned if there was even a cup of water up there, or if it had been there the whole night, and she'd never even got up.

"Hey!" Thad was yelling at Ally. She had zoned out again. "You going to snap back to reality and answer the question?"

"Uh, what," Ally rubbed her eyes, "Sorry, I must be a bit out of it too. What was the question?"

"We asked how long it would take your zombie ass to get ready." Erin's voice was joking but sharp.

"Give me like five minutes to go throw on some different clothes," was all she said in reply as Ally left the room and headed upstairs. She had no idea what that day would bring, but she knew for what she would search. What she would find would only be another mystery for her to solve.

Once ready, the four began their trek to The Brew, still showing no signs of awkwardness or awareness even.

"Have y'all wanted to just do something crazy since we're not at home anymore?" Erin said as they rounded the corner across from The Brew.

"Like what exactly?" Ally asked, hoping it was leading to something profound.

"Well, there are three things I've been wanting to do for a while." Erin paused as she checked the street before crossing. "I'm really ready for a new tatt. Yeah, I've got the little one, but I want something new. I want to get my lip pierced and, or my nose. Not really sure. Just something I've always considered, and, strange as it may seem, I really want to do a Mohawk." The girls stopped just outside the door in shock at Erin's statement.

"And, your mother would kill you if you did any of those," Rachel responded to Erin's wish. "Except that tattoo, if you kept it hidden."

"Maybe, but I mean, they gotta be ok with us doing our own thing at some point. Our school's being paid for by scholarships, same for the house, and my car's paid off, so it's not like I'm a burden on them anymore. As long as we're not banging every guy in Little Rock or selling crack off our back porch, I think they'll understand." Erin smirked, knowing how much her mother would hate all three of the things she wanted. "Eventually."

Ally couldn't help but wonder if the "every guy in Little Rock" line was meant to be a crack at Rachel for sleeping with Thad or wanting to sleep with Win. That confused her even more. Rachel had essentially said she was into Win. Thad and Rachel both seemed to take it as just another one of Erin's snide comments, though. Ally was beginning to exhaust even herself and gave up the hunt for a minute, because as much as Erin tried to keep the tough-girl persona, Ally knew what she really wanted that day was a friend to support her.

"I think you should go for it." The other three stared at Ally in disbelief. "I'm not saying like today necessarily, but if you really want to do that, then why not. I'd say start small, probably with a tattoo you can easily cover up or a piercing you can take out. Probably oughta save the Mohawk for last. Sure it's hair, so it'll grow back, but there won't be any hiding it at first."

"Ya think? Because I totally planned on doing the 'hawk and getting the side of my head tatted to start with." Her voice was so full of laughter Ally couldn't even attempt to take it seriously. Behind that, though, was a look in Erin's eyes that said what she meant, Thanks.

When they opened the door, four friends stopped their conversation and looked forward to see a peculiar man dressed in all black standing in line in front of them. He looked as if he had just left a funeral, but he was on his phone, and the person on the other line was talking very loudly about some shipment being delayed.

A quick wave from Terry and the girls led Thad over to their table to await their drinks. No eyes left the funeral salesman as they walked. He was neither tall nor short, but he had an air about him that made his height indifferent, an air of power. The group could see his square jawline decorated with a neatly trimmed beard from the side on which they sat. With his hand pressed against his phone, the group could see a very ornate gold ring on his middle finger that complimented his dark complexion beautifully. His jet-black fedora and black-rimmed glasses only serve to complete his morbidly handsome ensemble. He stepped aside to let another couple order since he wasn't finished with his call and switched his phone to his left hand, revealing his most peculiar feature; a striking tattoo of a pair of bright blue lines running parallel down the man's neck as if they were part of a circuit.

With the man still yelling on the other line, the funeral salesman spoke with the firm voice of the man in charge, "Stop talking." His voice carried an accent both cold and rigid. "Can you even begin to comprehend how much work goes into properly transporting these things? Don't even try to answer the question, because I know you don't. You know why you don't? Because that's my job. Your job is simply to make sure the shipments arrive on time. That is all. This conversation's over." He abruptly hung up the phone and placed it in his suit pocket. Taking off his glasses, he saw the four friends watching. He folded his glasses, put them in his pocket, and gave a charming smile to the friends and a nod of his head.

Stepping to the counter, he showed his charm again, "I'm dreadfully sorry at keeping such a lovely thing as you waiting. The work of an honest businessman is never over." He smiled at Terry as her face turned bright red. Ally figured that she would be more prepared with Win's constant compliments, but clearly, she wasn't. "However, my work will be over around, say, six o'clock this evening if you're free for dinner."

Still blushing, Terry tried her best to play coy. "Actually, I don't get off until seven. Sorry."

"How fortunate for me, I don't have to return to work until ten at the earliest." His smile grew as he pulled a pen from his pocket. "I tell you what. Don't decide just now. Think about it. Here is my number." He said as he wrote it on one of the sleeves and slid it across the counter. "When you get off at seven, or whenever it is, text me if you're hungry. If I don't hear from you, I'll know to go back to work."

Terry grabbed the sleeve and placed it in her pocket. "So, are you here for coffee, or did you just come to give me your number?" She said, trying her best to sound smooth, but failing terribly.

"Honestly, I came to see if the Brownings were available. I haven't even looked at the drinks." He glanced at the all-white hardwood menu behind her and let out a breath of a laugh. "How fitting of them." He spoke as if his mind were elsewhere. "I'll have a *Milas*, and do you know if they'll be in today?"

Terry's face had gone bleach-white, and the friends couldn't blame her. The Brownings were troubling enough on their own. Someone coming to call on them was another thing entirely.

"Lili's not scheduled today," Terry began with a faint tremble, "but her brothers normally come in."

"They're all going out of town today." Thad's voice rang out, shocking the girls at the table. He stood and walked over to the counter so as not to have to yell. "They're supposed to be gone all weekend. They told us at dinner last night. We were all going to eat again tonight, but obviously not with them leaving."

"I see. They must have left for the match. Makes sense. You're a friend of theirs; I take it?" The man extended his hand, and Thad saw the sword inlay on the ornate ring as he accepted the shake.

"I wouldn't go that far yet. I just met them last night, but things seemed to go pretty well. Name's Thaddeus, but all my friends call me Thad."

"Pleasure to meet you, Thad. My name is Avram Vanitote, but the few friends I have call me Van. Oh, and if you've already made it to dinner with the entire family, that constitutes you as a friend in their book. You're probably the first person they've had dinner with in five years or more. The Brownings and I go, well, way back. Hell, I feel like I've known them for hundreds of years." He laughed at his joke.

"Shit, if I made it to the friends' list with the first dinner, that must make my friends Ally, Rachel, and Erin almost family. They've already had like three dinners and a zoo trip."

Terry slid Van's drink across the counter and leaned over to listen. He smiled at her as he took a sip. "Really now? That's pretty impressive. I take it; those are your friends over there?" He smirked at the girls who were still staring at him.

"That's them." Thad spun around to point them out. "The tall glass of water is Ally." Ally gave Thad her screw you smile. "She's crushing on Joshua," Thad added in a whisper. "The adorable one in the middle is Rachel." Rachel waved and smiled as big as she could. "She's crushing on Win." He whispered again. "And the one who looks like she might murder me for whatever I'm about to say, that's Erin." Erin raised her middle finger to Thad before smiling flirtingly at Van. "And she's now crushing on you and Joshua. Funny how the world works, huh?"

"Quite so. It looks like a fun group you have there."

"Oh yeah, hanging with them is a blast, let me tell ya. Speaking of, since we don't currently have dinner plans, and Terry here obviously wants to have dinner with you but is a bit shy," Thad smiled at Terry, giving her an, *I got your back*, wink, "why don't you two just join us for dinner tonight?"

"You know what, that sounds like a riveting plan." Van clapped Thad on the shoulder. "If Terry is interested, of course." He turned his charm on Terry, who only had to blush to agree. "Then it's settled. How about we meet at the distillery just down the way for drinks and grab something in SoMa? You lot pick the dinner spot, and since Terry has my number, she can just text me when she gets off at seven. Or was it six?" His smirk made it clear he knew Terry got off well before then. "I'll see you at the distillery, but for now, I must get back to work." He flashed a smile once more at Terry before turning to leave. "It was a pleasure semi-meeting, you ladies. I look forward to dinner." He waved at the girls as he exited the building.

Thad made his way back to the table. "I like this town. I think I'm going to be coming here a whole lot more often." His grin showed his pride in his latest actions.

"A, you're a dick." Erin cut him off. "2, what are you doing setting up dinner plans with a stranger we just met?"

"Well, see, he's friends with the Brownings, so I thought you guys might want to get to know him a little better. I mean, unless you guys want to consult the long list of their friends, you know, to get more information on them. Oh wait, he's the only friend they have that we know of. Not to mention we found a whopping jack shit last night. Besides, I thought you might want to ask where you can get a tattoo like his."

"Hey, that neckpiece with the cyborg lines looks pretty damn hot if you ask me. Wouldn't you agree, Ally?" Ally's smile was the only answer Erin's question needed.

"I just wonder how far down his body they go." Rachel injected.

"I bet you do, Rach." Erin grinned as Thad and Ally both laughed. Heat rushed to Rachel's face, but she smiled back.

"So, what are we doing till this evening then?" Thad asked.

13
ROCK TOWN

The girls spent the rest of the day showing Thad around some of their favorite spots in Little Rock; the Fold, Loblolly, the Arkansas River Trail, and more. They even took him to the college after lunch. Thad was amazed he'd lived just a couple of hours south of there for years and seen so little of what the town had to offer. After they were back in town, Rachel texted Terry to find out if she was ready. An hour later, the four friends arrived at Rock Town Distillery to see what the Brownings' surprising new friend had in store.

"I'm still not sure about this guy." Ally confessed as they walked towards the door. "I mean, don't get me wrong, I'm sure we all want to know what's going on with the Brownings, but we don't even know this dude."

"Hence why we didn't invite him over for dinner," Thad said, opening the door. "Look, we're meeting at a public place full of other people hanging out and going to dinner after. The guy is obviously a friend of the Brownings, so how is this any crazier than the dinner we had with them last night?"

Ally tried to calm herself. She couldn't place it at the time, but something about Van set her on edge. He and Terry had yet to arrive, so they went ahead and got a table and left word. A few minutes later, a figure draped in black stepped into the distillery, escorting a very elegantly dressed Terry.

"Moment of truth, Ally. Should we jet out the back door real quick?" Erin nudged Ally to show she was teasing.

"Oh, would you two shut up? He seems like a perfect gentleman."

Rachel said defensively.

"In case you didn't notice Rach, he kinda has a date," Erin smirked.

"How about all of you drop it. They're heading this way." Rachel shushed the others and waved to Van and Terry to call them over.

"Is this your first time checking out the distillery? I love this place." Van said as he pulled Terry's chair for her.

"First time, actually." Ally replied. "Though I have had some of their stuff in cocktails before."

"Yeah, I actually had a special kind of Manhattan last night that the waitress at Brave New Restaurant fixed up for me with their Bottled in Bond that was supreme."

"Oh, that would've been Lauren for sure," Van replied. "She's a wizard that one. I don't know if they have anyone quite like her here, but they nonetheless have some mighty fine drinks. Have you ordered yet?"

The friends all shook their heads.

"Oh, how delightful." Van's smile radiated with charm. "Anyone have any special flavors, requests, or anything they'd like to avoid?"

They were all somewhat overwhelmed, even Terry.

"Um," Erin began, "honestly, we're still kinda gettin' the feel for things. High school and college drinking isn't exactly fancy stuff. Pretty sure all of us are used to well margaritas and watered-down Coke and rum."

"Yeah," Terry began, "I had a martini once that was pretty good, but it's mostly white wine for me."

"Very well then. Hey Phil," Van said with a smile to the man at the bar, "Could we have about four or five of Sorcerer's Stone, Illustrated Man, Once Upon a Thyme, and, uh, Lemony Snicket for the table, please."

"You got it, Van." The man said in return.

"That man's a true gent. I don't know anywhere else that'll whip up group drinks so graciously. Everyone can somewhat sip and share. At least this way, though, it's only about two or three drinks per person, so nobody's getting smashed before dinner. Plus, you get to try a few things. See what you like. So, tell me a little about yourselves. I'm anxious to get to know the new acquaintances of my closest friends."

Erin spoke for the group to save Ally and Rachel the trouble. "Well, we're all from Podunk, a couple hours south of here. The girls and me were born and raised there. Thin man over here moved there from

New York right as we were starting high school, and we've been stuck with him ever since. He and Rach used to date, and, if we're being honest, everyone still thinks they have a thing for each other and just refuse to admit it." Rachel rolled her eyes with as much contempt as she could muster as Thad shook his head. "Especially her parents. Granted, right now, she's hard up for your friend Win, and my girl Ally here is about the same for Joshua. That's pretty much the basic rundown of our group. Oh, and the final two members of our crew are still back home, and we haven't hung out much since we got here. Any questions?" Erin's spiel left Ally and Rachel as flush as could be. Even Erin herself was blushing a little. Thad just sat giggling.

"Wow. No, I think that pretty much covers it for right now. Once I finish processing all of that, then I'll see if I have any more questions." Van laughed. "So, how did you get to know the Brownings?"

Ally jumped in before Erin could embarrass her anymore. "We have a class with Joshua and Win. We were having a hard time keeping up, and the professor suggested we get help from some of the other students. It's a doctorate-level course, and we're only working on our grad degree currently. So, we asked Joshua and Win if they'd help us study. Don't let Erin play it up for you too much, though. That was just earlier this week. Since then, we've just kinda gotten started to know the Brownings and all. They're very," she paused, searching for the right word given the company, "interesting."

Terry spoke with confidence for the first time since Van arrived, "Interesting doesn't even begin to describe them."

"Whatever do you mean, darling?" Van asked, sounding both concerned and intrigued.

"Oh, nothing. They just seem," she paused, losing her nerve, "very different is all. Not in a bad way. I mean, I work for Lili, and she's as good to me as could be. Marc is lovely as well. Joshua and Win are hard to get a read on, but they seem alright. It's just something about them all, something, like I said, different."

"That's because they are very different," Van replied reassuringly. "They're an exceptional group of people."

Thad's curiosity broke in, "What do you know about them? What's your story?"

"I know virtually everything about them. They've been a major part of my life for quite some time."

"How's that?" Ally asked. "I mean, you clearly sound like you're not from here, but neither are they. So how have you known them for so long if they're from all over, and you're from wherever you're from?"

Van took a sip from his Sorcerer's Stone and ran a hand over his beard. "Mmm. I do love the lemon oleo-saccharum they make for this. To answer your question, though, yes, the Brownings nor I am from here, nor did we meet here. Our paths crossed elsewhere."

The entire group listened intently, waiting to hear more of the mysterious Brownings and their equally mysterious friend Avram Vanitote.

"I met them in England. That's where my family lived and worked originally. My mom moved to Germany when she found out she was pregnant with me. She died when I was four, and I moved back with my family in London. I met Joshua and Win when I was six years old. I had no idea they would change my life forever." He stopped and stared out the window as if he were searching for what to say next. "I'm going to get a refill real quick if you don't mind."

He paused for a moment as he finished his first drink. The friends tried theirs along with him. Ally could already tell she wasn't a fan of bourbon, but she tried another sip anyway before sliding hers to Erin. Terry's response seemed similar to Ally's, and she was glad she wasn't alone. Erin, Rachel, and Thad, on the other hand, thoroughly enjoyed theirs. Van stared at the other drinks left as he decided which to drink next. After a brief moment, he grabbed the Once Upon a Thyme and took a sip.

"I apologize if I seem weird in talking about them. I'm sure you're anxious to know more. It's just, not all of their story is mine to tell. Joshua and Win always looked out for me when I was little, kept the other kids from picking on me and all. It wasn't until I was eight that I met the rest of their family. You see, I wasn't exactly allowed to be around them. My family and their family were, um, what's a good term for it, rival families. Business tends to do that to people. I can still remember the first time I had dinner with them. Cepharis and Lavyrja were so nice to me I couldn't believe it." He scanned their faces and saw the confusion. "I'm sorry, they probably just introduced themselves as Ceph and Lavy to you. It's much easier to say."

"Yeah, they did. I can see why, though. I probably would've pronounced it wrong. So why were you shocked at how nice they were?" Thad asked.

"As I said, our families were rather opposed to one another. I was told terrible things about them when I was young. I never understood how my family could say such horrible things about such wonderful people—taking Win in off the streets, saving Marcus from a hell hole of a life. Those kinds of things more than counter the awful lies my family told me. Don't get me wrong, they're no saints, but they're pretty fine people."

"So, wait, I just assumed Marcus had married into the family, and are you saying Win was adopted?" Ally's confusion only grew.

Van finished drinking his Once Upon a Thyme as the friends sipped along. Ally and Terry enjoyed it much more with its floral notes from the gin melding with the lemon, but not nearly as much as the Lemony Snicket they tried next. It was like drinking a Lemon Drop that was coated in strawberry. The two girls caught each other's reactions, as the tartness made their cheeks pucker, and smiled. The others followed along as they listened to Van.

"I'm sure you've noticed that none of the family looks related. That's because none of them are. They're living proof, though, that blood doesn't define a family. Ceph and Lavy can't have kids of their own. Joshua was the first addition to the family when they were very young. Lili was never really theirs but rather a close friend of Joshua's. When her family died, Ceph, Lavy, and Joshua were the closest thing she had left to family. Joshua found Win, kind of like he found me. Win was a kid growing up in the dark alleys of London, and they gladly brought him in. Marcus, they met while they were doing business in Italy. Again, at Joshua's bidding, the family welcomed him in too. It was a beautiful day when they brought him home. Lili was older than him by a couple of years, but they all saw it that day. From the moment their eyes met, everyone knew." He smiled with a look full of love and compassion. "Those two will die hand in hand."

The entire table sat in silence. They had all been suspicious of the Brownings; they had each thought the family was just wealthy and arrogant at points. They even accused them of having some terrible, dark secret, and there was the dark secret they sought. The Brownings were orphans and runaways that had made it through all of that together and on top. They finished the last drink of their Lemony Snickets, feeling the sourness sting at their remorse.

"So, Joshua is the reason why they all wound up a family, basically?"

Erin asked with more compassion than her friends had ever seen her show.

"Yes, ma'am. It may not seem like it to look at him, but Joshua is the glue that holds their family together. He found Ceph and Lavy, and they couldn't say no to him. He befriended Lili and Win and convinced his family to take them, and he was the one who insisted they bring Marc back from Italy. It was even his idea to come to America and get away from their old life in the first place. It wasn't until they came here that they took up the name Browning. Marc and Lili were married at that point, so they all just took the name and presented themselves as one big family, which is what they are. They figured it was best to leave their old names behind them. Start fresh. They could find new connections and opportunities, forge a whole new path. They wanted to make a decent, honest life for themselves here, and that's just what they did."

"So Browning isn't really their last name. Huh." Ally said, feeling mildly insulted. The friends all did, but they knew they should have expected such. A family of immigrants, banded together in the new world, a common last name like Browning was a perfect choice. A new life where they could blend in without concern and build an entirely new world for themselves.

"It is their real last name here. That's all that matters."

"What did their last name used to be?" Thad pried for more information.

"I already told you not all of their story is mine to tell. If they want you to know about their old life, then they will tell you."

"Fair enough. They already seemed like awesome people to me; now they're all that and more." Thad smiled with content.

"I don't mean to be intrusive," Terry's sweet voice broke in again, "but do you know the legitimacy or legality of the work they did before? I mean, they are nice people. It's just I've seen some things that raise questions, and you said they left their old life behind. Was their old business involved in anything bad?"

Van's face turned very fierce in an instant. "What do you mean by anything bad?"

"I don't know, really. I've just heard them making phone calls and arranging meetings that didn't exactly sound right. I remember hearing Joshua saying on the phone once, 'The family won't approve.' I walked away from the table, so I didn't hear anymore."

Van's face was cold and calculated, his eyes empty, but his words were genuine when he spoke. "That's a different family. Moving to a new world and erasing your past to start over isn't an easy thing to do. Sometimes deals must be made, and while the Brownings may be good people, not every family in this world is, including some of the people they work for. Don't go worrying about those calls. You have great people looking after you. I wouldn't be here if it weren't for them."

"Thanks. I'm glad to know it's not them. I really like Lili, and the rest of the family is always very nice to me, especially Win." Terry blushed as she smiled.

Van laughed. "Of course he is. Win's nice to everyone."

A flicker of confusion shot across Rachel's face, and Ally quickly moved to change the topic. "So, what brought you to Little Rock from London?"

Van began sipping on his Illustrated Man along with the friends trading theirs around. It made for the perfect finish to the series of drinks. A rich, chocolatey bourbon drink that made like a dessert for the evening of drinks, one that even Ally somewhat enjoyed.

"The Brownings did so by way of New York at first, of course. I finished up my schooling when I was sixteen. They'd already been here a couple of years at the time. Not long after I finished up, I received a letter from Joshua saying he had a job opportunity for me. I was supposed to join the family business, but I had long since relinquished any obligations to them. I disappeared into the night and wound up in New York City with the Brownings. I haven't seen my family since, and I doubt I ever will. My life and my work are here now."

"We, um, accidentally heard you talking about your work, when we walked into The Daily Brew earlier. You were on the phone. What exactly do you do?" Erin leaned further in to hear.

"Ah yes, that lovely phone call." He grinned confidently. "I handle transportation for several companies. The companies we work for own a number of production facilities in the states and abroad. That was the shipment you heard me talking about earlier. I've been in the position a while now. It's not as glamorous as you probably think, though. I spend all my time making certain incredibly fragile or volatile things don't get destroyed in transit and getting in arguments with the companies carrying the shipments when they don't arrive on time. I'm just a glorified inventory manager."

The friends all laughed in agreement, but they all sensed the modest cover-up, not unlike the Browning family. Van was clearly well to do in his position, but he would never admit to it. The luxurious watch on his wrist only added to the fact as he glanced down at it.

"Speaking of my glorified inventory job, I really must get back to it. I'm terribly sorry to miss dinner. Drinks lasted far longer than I expected, but I have some paperwork I must tend to before a shipment goes out tomorrow. I'll give you a ride home if you like, Terry, but if you want to stay for dinner with them, I fully understand." He stood graciously nodding to the friends for their company.

"I'm actually rather tired already. Being at the shop all morning and now this, it's a busy day. I think I'll just ride with you and call it a night. Maybe order some late-night takeout I'll regret." Terry said, rising to join him.

"My apartment is in New York, but I have a room at the Capital Hotel downtown when I'm in town. Perhaps we can do this again sometime?" He pulled from his pocket four business cards and handed them to each of the four still seated. "If you ever need to get in touch or want to plan another evening, just shoot me a text."

With that, he spun on his heel and headed towards the counter. He slipped a strange coin from his pocket just like the one they saw Joshua use just days before and handed it to Phil before he escorted his date towards the door.

He stopped a few steps away from the friends and turned back, "I like all of you. I'm glad that you weren't scared away by my friends. It'd be nice if you stuck around for a while. I will say this, though, I've long since been ok with who they are and what they do. I hope you can do the same. Good evening."

"Night, guys," Terry added sweetly.

The ride home was silent. All four of them were letting Van's words sink in. They still didn't know what to think about the Brownings. Clearly, they had done many good things, but the friends couldn't help wondering what past they had left behind. Understanding them grew more difficult by the moment.

Once they got inside the house, Thad reopened the conversation, "So are we going to talk about this, or are we just going to act like we still know nothing about them?"

"There's not much to talk about. You heard everything we did, and all it does is make everything else we've found even stranger. What else do you want to know that any of us could possibly tell you?" Ally's voice showed her frustration with the weekend. She had learned a plethora of new information about the Brownings, only to realize she still knew nothing.

"I just wanna know why Van wrote down his number to give to Terry if he had a business card in his pocket with the number." Rachel's comment lightened the mood as they all smiled.

"I can answer that one for you," Thad replied. "If he had just handed her a business card, it wouldn't have felt personal. By writing it down, he took the time to show he genuinely wanted her to have his number. I'm sure she'll be using it often." He chuckled to himself.

"Oh, shut it, Thad. Not everyone's as easy to get in bed as you, I'm sure. Van might actually have morals." Erin's playful tone brought a calm back to the evening. They were stressed, all of them, but somehow, they felt they would be ok.

"Well, you guys can all think what you want. I'm going to get ready for bed, and yes, I know I'm an 80-year-old woman for going to bed this early, and this 80-year-old woman has had two more drinks than she can normally handle. So, you can suck it." Ally made her way to the stairs until Thad's final question stopped her.

"Why do you think he didn't mention anything about Idonia?"

The room fell quiet. Ally turned back to the kitchen where her friends stood.

"Either he doesn't know, or he doesn't know that we know. If I were to place a bet, it'd be on the latter. Guess we'll find out if we hang out again. Night guys." With that, she ascended the stairs to her shower.

Ally had to fight herself to sleep, battling her mind to let go of all the thoughts from the last week. Everything about the Brownings only confused her more and more. They still had the paper due for Professor Edmonton, and she was at a complete loss on what was going on with her friends or if she was indeed losing her mind. A mere week into knowing this strange family, and already her life seemed to unravel before her in a way she couldn't understand. She closed her eyes and begged for sleep to come.

When she finally managed to drift off, she found herself in Idonia once more. Only everything looked different somehow. The architecture was still the same, and the mighty tree stood towering above the landscape in the distance. Only, it wasn't the same tree. The colors had changed. Instead of the massive black tree with leaves of golden fire, she saw an equally beautiful white hardwood trunk growing from the ground where it had splintered the earth into gargantuan crystals, and atop it were vivid blue leaves all aglow hanging from its branches. The lights that ran through the city connecting all the buildings to the courtyard at the center were the same blue. She followed the glow with her eyes as it flowed away from the tree, and what she saw took her breath away. Far in the distance behind all the buildings stood a gorgeous mountain of a tower rising thousands of feet into the sky. Black and white stone interlaced around the blue lights running up the tiers of the tower.

A cold wind blew, and Ally sensed she was not alone. On the ground before her, a single, massive raven landed and met her gaze. "Ally Carver, Death is coming."

14
THE LABYRINTH

The four friends each rose at their own leisurely pace the following morning. No one in the house on Rock Street had slept well, their dreams filled with visions of otherworldly cities, hooded figures, and flocks of ravens. None of the friends spoke a word of this to the others, though. Each of them felt isolated like they alone were losing their grip on reality, unaware that they were all entwined in their journey.

They each went about getting ready, still in silence. The girls dressed and did their makeup as much as they felt like. Thad packed for his departure, feeling more like he was leaving home than returning to it. He had missed his friends dearly, but it wasn't until being there with them that weekend he realized how much that meant. The entire time they had been gone, the emotions were slowly mounting. Every week that passed without them, he'd felt less and less like himself.

When they'd returned to visit, the relief he had felt was indescribable. He thought it would be alright for that brief moment, but when they were gone again, that emptiness grew ever vaster. It filled him with guilt and confusion. It felt a betrayal to Matt and Nick, and even his grandmother, to not feel at home with them, but still, that didn't change what was missing. It wasn't that Ally, Rachel, and Erin were missing from his life. A part of him was missing, and it wasn't until he was getting ready to leave that he understood how much a part of him they were.

He had no choice but to leave. His grandmother still needed him. There wasn't a place in Little Rock for him just yet, and he couldn't just abandon Matt and Nick. His school and work could go with him wherever he went, but they could not, especially not his grandmother. That was the most important thing for him still. She didn't have much longer, he knew, and she still needed him to take care of her until then. He knew at that moment, though, change was on the horizon, and nothing he could do would slow its arrival.

"Would you guys like to grab coffee with me before I head out?" Thad asked, finally breaking the silence that had filled the house that morning and hoping to prolong their time together as much as he could.

"Actually," Rachel began, her brilliant idea forming as she spoke, "that's a perfect plan. God, we're idiots. Why didn't we think of this before. We still have that paper for Edmonton we haven't finished. What better place to work on it than a coffee shop with a creepily effective library system?"

"This is why I love you, Rach," Erin exclaimed.

"Ditto," Thad added. "Because that also gives me the perfect chance to see if I can't find anything else on the Harbilin Corporation, or if nothing else Idonia perhaps. What better place to look than in the belly of the beast?"

"You sure about that, Thad?" Ally asked cautiously, her dream from the night before still tugging at her mind. "I mean, after everything this weekend, are we sure we want to keep tugging at strings?"

The question wasn't simply directed at Thad. Ally was asking the entire room, herself included. The slope they were on grew slipperier by that moment, and they each knew they were running short on chances to turn back.

"I still want to know more," Thad said resolutely. "Everything I've heard, everything I've seen, I want to know what's goin' on. So, I'm going to keep lookin'. If you guys aren't comfortable with it, I fully understand. I won't bring any of it to you, if you don't want."

"I do," Erin said with no hesitation. "Look, I like these folks. I really do. The only thing stranger than the stuff they believe, though, is everything else about them. I wanna know what's what. It's not even about gettin' to the bottom of things at this point. I just want the truth, whatever it is."

"I don't know what I want." Rachel said with deep sincerity. "I mean that in general, but especially with this. I still don't know where I'm tryin' to go, or what I'm tryin' to do. All I know, is I feel right doing this right now, all of this. Being here with y'all, goin' to school, getting to know the Brownings, it all feels right. That's the best I got."

The three looked back to Ally awaiting her response.

"It was already a yes for me." Ally said with honesty she didn't know she had. "Despite everything, it's been a yes for me this whole time. I don't know what's goin' on, honestly. I don't know what to believe, but I don't even think I have a choice anymore. I mean, I think I already made it. Just wanted to make sure I wasn't the only one."

"Alright then," Erin said with a smile. "We do this."

"We do." Thad agreed, sharing her smile.

Rachel and Ally smiled back in agreement.

"Well," Ally began. "We're burnin' daylight. Let's do this."

Within minutes the four friends were outside on their way to The Daily Brew.

"So real quick," Rachel began, "let's talk about what we do know. We know they've kinda been all over, but clearly, the move to the states was a big one. New name, new everything. Van made it seem pretty clear he doesn't have any dealings with folks back where they're from, but the Brownings have straight up said they still have stuff going on overseas. So it's not like they fully cut ties, yeah?"

"Well," Thad began, "I know less about them personally than any of you, obviously. What I do know is what I've found online. The few company records we could find mentioning them were both fairly recent and smaller compared to everything Harbilin has going. Maybe that's part of the deal? They wash their hands of whatever they were doin' back in Europe; Harbilin gives them a new deal stateside to help out?"

"Some of them," Erin interjected. "I mean, Ceph and Lavy's work at the hospital surely is just cut and dry."

"True," Thad replied. "That could just be fortunate skill sets, though. Yeah? You got two people that have a ton of medical knowledge, so use some connections for a job?"

"Maybe." Ally agreed. "It's kinda hard to tell, though. It's all just shots in the dark without knowing what they did before or what exactly they do now. I mean, Joshua and Win talked about Marc's freelance work, but that could easily all be going through Harbilin. Hell, far as we know, Van works for Harbilin too."

"Shit," Erin said. "Good point. He did say Joshua helped him get started here, and working in transportation could mean transportin' literally fucking anything."

"Not wrong at all." Thad concurred. "You know, my android demon hunter theory is still holding pretty sound so far."

"Oh dear God, I'm gonna hit you." Erin sighed as they climbed the steps to the coffee shop.

Inside they found Terry behind the counter looking as chipper as she was tired.

"Hey Terry, still recovering from a fun late night?" Erin asked playfully, turning Terry a brilliant shade of crimson that made even Erin embarrassed.

"No ma'am," Terry began, "Just not really a hard liquor kinda girl. The drinks were good, mind you. I'm just not really used to it, so recovery is a bit rough."

"Fully understand." Ally said in consultation. "I'm right there with you. So how was your night aside from the drinks?"

"It was very nice. I, um, don't get out much, really. Bit of a homebody, I guess you could say. So it was fun getting to dress up and go out for a change."

Ally felt her connection to Terry growing even more potent. While she had no interest in "dressing up," as Terry said, Ally did fully understand the joys of getting out once in a while, even as an introvert.

"It's always good to get out," Rachel replied. "How about Van? Think there's a second date in the future?"

Terry flushed again, "He was quite the gentleman. I won't lie, I was a bit worried he might be a bit more, um, forward perhaps. I was pleasantly surprised, though. After picking me up on the way there, he just asked questions about me. What I liked doing in my free time, how I enjoyed the city, stuff like that. Afterward, too. I was extremely nervous. I'm terrible at first dates. You know, do you hug, shake hands, kiss. It's just exhausting. Fortunately, none of that was even an issue. We talked some more as he drove me home, and then when he walked me to my door, he took my hand and kissed it before he bid me goodnight. It was really quite charming."

There were clear signs of excitement in Terry's voice, and the friends could each sense it. Terry was still new to them, a potential friend in Little Rock they'd yet to understand. In that moment, though, they felt a kindred spirit.

"Well, it sounds like a wonderful evening, if you ask me. Hopefully, there's many more to come." Erin said with intentional modesty to make amends for her previous statement.

Denise walked over with impeccable timing. "Oh, there will be. Don't let her fool you. I'd say she's downright smitten with the man if I know her at all."

"Denise," Terry said with an embarrassed glance.

"But enough about that," Denise said with a grin at Terry. "Y'all did come for drinks as well, yes?"

"We did indeed," Thad replied, not wanting to embarrass Terry any further.

"And to study for a bit, as well," Ally added. "We have some papers due for one of our classes, long papers. So we were going to check the books upstairs to see if we could find any help. If that's alright."

"Of course, dear," Denise said with a loving smile. "That's why all the books are up there after all. Frankly, it's a shame they get used as little as they do."

"She's not wrong," Terry added. "During breaks, I love to just pop up there for a bit and find something fun to check out. It's always sad for me when people don't go up there. Guess that's part of it, though. Times change."

"Not for me," Thad said defiantly. "Give me something tangible any day of the week. Sure I may work on my computer all the time, but I'd rather hold a book than a tablet anytime."

"Yeah," Rachel agreed, "that's pretty much all of us. We're history buffs, after all. If we didn't like weathered, old books, we'd be rather out of place."

The friends chuckled in agreement before placing their orders and heading upstairs to begin their quest. Ally, Erin, and Rachel set off to find examples to use for their papers. Ally knew without question she wanted to include Alexander the Great as one of hers if she could find some way to make it work. It was far-fetched, she knew, but she couldn't help but appreciate the macabre humor in using her namesake as an example in a paper about genocides and mass murders. Erin and Rachel, however, were working with completely blank slates as they began compiling options to use.

Thad, on the other hand, was the most purpose-driven of them all. He knew exactly what he was looking for, and for the most part, he knew where to begin. After the friends showed him to the kiosk, he was fast at work, looking for any reference he could find of Harbilin. An hour passed, then two, and before he knew it, his stomach rumbled, begging for food when he'd made no progress at all. He was happy to see his friends were each making ample progress on their papers, but he had hoped to at least find something. He knew before he had started the chances were slim given the nature of the collection, so he finally accepted defeat and went downstairs to get a quick bite.

"Hello, again, handsome." Denise greeted him as he reached the counter. "Find anything good to read?"

"Well, not yet, but I'm pretty sure I've been wastin' my time with what I was trying to find anyways. So, I figured I'd grab a sandwich and another coffee."

"Oh, that's unfortunate." She said in an apologetic tone as she prepared his drink. "What were you trying to find? There's a ton of books up there, but it's basically just the history section. So you may have to settle sadly."

"Yeah, I was thinking the same thing. I was trying to find if there was any info on a really old company that was here in Arkansas, but there doesn't seem to be much about small history bits. That's alright, though. I have other stuff I could try instead."

"Well, I wish you the best of luck then, sweetie." She said with motherly love in her voice as she handed him his coffee and sandwich. "Let me know if you need anything else."

"Will do." He replied with a big smile before heading up the stairs.

"Yo, Denise rocks." He whispered to his friends as he passed.

"Yeah, she's hella cool." Rachel agreed as the other two nodded, still entrenched in their work.

With a fresh coffee and fresh mind, Thad began his next search. He finished entering the term "Idonia" and was taken aback the moment he hit submit. Dozens of references popped up that were located within the physical library, and more than double that was stored digitally on the server. He had fully prepared himself for more disappointment and was so thrilled to be wrong he didn't know where to begin.

"Um, guys," Thad said with a tremor of anticipation, "I think you may wanna come see this."

The friends dropped their work and shot over to the kiosk immediately.

"Whoah," Erin said, simply and effectively communicating what they were all thinking.

"That's a lot of results," Rachel added.

"Not really." Thad corrected as he filtered through the results. "It looks like it's mostly papers and other publishings that are referencing the same thing. Look."

He pointed through a handful of results that all had quotations referenced to the same book, *Primus Stella: The God Star.*

"It looks like all of them come back to this one book, but yet, the book doesn't show up in the results itself."

"Okay," Rachel said, taking point, "divide and conquer strat. Ally, you take the first three references, Erin the next, and I'll work the ones after that. Thad, start combing through everything you can, trying to find the actual book."

The friends wasted no time copying the results they were assigned and making their way into the labyrinth of books to locate them, which was no simple task. The library had no set organizational structure. Each book had a handful of possible locations it could be located at any given time, if not more. Thad continued sifting through the results only to find more and more results referencing the same thing. After a few pages of similar results, he took out his phone and typed *Primus Stella* in a quick Google search; no books manifested. He followed it up with a quick search on the ISBN registry, still nothing. He went back to the kiosk on a whim and searched for the book directly by name again, skipping to the very last page of results. At the very bottom of the page, he finally found the book itself, buried at the very back of the results. *Primus Stella: The God Star.* No author, no publication date, nothing. Just the title and the indication it was on hand in the library. He took a picture of the exhaustive list of possible locations, closed out the search, and set off through the aisles.

Ally found her first two books with ease, but the final book proved quite the challenge. The lack of organization made the process daunting, as that particular book had eight potential locations. She finally found it on the seventh try. Rachel's search proved the complete inverse, spending almost half an hour on her first book, only to find the second and third both in their first possible location, which worked out to the benefit of the group as Erin was still working on hers when Rachel and Ally finished. They helped her search the remaining possible locations, and the group reconvened at their tables.

"Where's Thad?" Rachel asked.

"Down here." They heard from within the labyrinth and set off to find him.

"What'd you find?" Erin asked when they finally found him.

"Well," Thad began, "nothing so far. According to the kiosk, there is a copy of the book in the library, but there's more than a few possible spots."

"How many?" Ally asked.

"Thirty-two," Thad said in exasperation.

"Fuck me," Erin said, matching Thad's mood. "Alright, split up the rest."

Thad sent the picture of the list to their group text. "I've been going in order. I'm on thirteen currently, so you guys pick what you want from the last twelve or fifteen. Surely it won't take long to find it."

He wasn't wrong about the time, but he was wrong about finding it. A few minutes later, the friends regrouped with nothing to show for their time.

"Are we sure that was all of them?" Rachel asked as they regrouped.

"Yep, Positive," Thad replied. "And on top of that, you guys missed seeing the search process. It was the very last result in the queries despite having all those references. It also doesn't exist anywhere else on the internet that I can find."

"So we're looking for a book that doesn't exist. Awesome. How perfectly fitting." Ally said, the frustration in her voice evident.

"Well," Rachel said, pointing to the other books, "we at least have these we can look through."

Laying on their table was a collection of various astronomy and physics books on planetary studies, solar observations, and compiled research projects on the universe.

"Alright," Erin said with no excitement, "everybody grab a book. Let's get started."

With that, the friends set off through the books in search of Idonia. Flipping through page after page after page, they delved deeper into the unknown. Minutes turned to hours as they worked their way through every book, searching for any references they could find to *Primus Stella*, hoping it would have some information about the things they had learned from the Brownings.

"Alright, I got something," Erin said, waving her hand at the others.

"Hold on, one sec." Rachel said, flipping frantically through the pages of her book. "I think I may have too. Just a sec. Yep. Got it. What's yours say?"

Rachel shuffled over to Erin, along with Ally and Thad, holding the place in her own book as she did so.

"Look," Erin said, spinning the book and pointing where the friends should read.

Primus Stella: The God Star discusses the early formations of the universe and forms an alternative theory to current scientific stances and religious beliefs held widely throughout human history. This work is notable in its comparison of Po as endless black chaos, which could be perceived as a black hole or the emptiness of space, and the ensuing act of Kāne realizing his existence and thus separating himself by sheer force of will, which it correlates to matter that is expelled from stellar masses when they collapse into a black hole. While the work is strictly theoretical, its depiction of an original stellar form of Vox Ramus, whose mass is referenced as being hundreds if not thousands of times that of IC 1101, whose eventual destruction would fracture the system of Idonia to the extent of creating alternate existences is compelling. Were a star of such magnitude to indeed exist, its eventual end would no doubt be of a scale we are not yet capable of understanding and, in theory, be possibly capable of creating entirely new dimensions or universes of existence.

The friends all stood in confusion as they read the brief reference repeatedly, seeking more understanding. The book continued with potential explanations of such an existence, but it veered into heavy technical terms, and none of the group could properly follow.

"Okay," Erin began, "that was a lot of words that I don't understand. The only thing that made a connection for me was Po and Kāne. Joshua said something about them in his weird little questionnaire the other day, yeah?"

"Yes, he did." Ally answered flatly. "I remember Vox Ramus as well, of course."

"Yeah," Erin replied deflated, "the one whose death he said created our world."

"Hey Ally," Thad cut in, "what did you say they called beings that created Idonia? Celestials?"

"Yeah."

"Well, there you go. Celestial is used as just another term for a star. Do you think he was just being poetic?"

"I mean," Ally began, "religion throughout history is poetry practically. Am I right? Just look at Greek or Norse mythology. We call it mythology, but just a few thousand years ago, it was believed as doctrine. All of the stuff you read about it is poetic. That's the way people talk about religion, at the end of the day, no? The Big Bang supposedly created our universe, but nobody has any idea what caused it. What more fitting way to explain it than with another poetic tale."

"Well," Rachel said, "if you want more blends of poetry and science, I think you're in luck."

Rachel opened the book she was holding where she'd marked the reference point. The friends gathered around it and read another take on how *Primus Stella* gave an in-depth alternative to the Judeo-Christian belief of God speaking the universe into existence by saying, "Let there be light" as a simplified metaphor befitting the understanding of humans of that time. It went on to define the Idonic system in which Vox Ramus existed, a stellar body which is reckoned to be thousands of times the size of Sagittarius A*, which was torn asunder when Vox Ramus went supernova, warping spacetime and creating entirely new dimensions.

The friends sat in silence for a time. Having read each of the references and thinking about the other books, which undoubtedly included more of the same information, their minds struggled to process the data. It was written clearly before their eyes, but it was as if some piece of their mind was simply unable to properly catalog the information as if a machine programmed to sort squares and triangles had suddenly been given a circle and knew not what to do. The friends felt minuscule and fragile like the world was pressing down on them with such force they might be crushed at any moment. The silence held as minutes passed.

"So why can't we find the actual book?" Rachel said finally, breaking them from their trance.

"What?" Thad said as he came to.

"*Primus Stella.* All of these books supposedly reference it. We've just read two direct references, yet we can't find the actual book. How can a book be referenced if it isn't even a real book?"

"That," Thad began, "is an excellent question. I can tell you with quite a bit of confidence it can't be found online anywhere, which only leaves one possibility. It has to be in here somewhere."

The friends turned and stared into the labyrinth of the library, a blend of fear and exhilaration gripping them tightly. They had checked every place the book was supposed to be to no avail, but the book was definitely there. Each of them could feel it in their core. Somewhere, deep within the shelves of that seemingly infinite library, were the answers to all the questions echoing within their minds.

"Well," Erin said, "looks like we have a new homework project."

The day was waning fast, though, and the friends' new project would have to wait while the girls finished their current one. They took notes of the books they had before returning to the locations from which they came, and Thad said his farewell much to his dismay. The friends stayed at The Brew most of the day, working tirelessly to finish their papers. Finally, a few hours after Thad was gone, they finished their work and headed to the house.

It was still reasonably early, but the friends were all exhausted from the busy weekend, lack of sleep, and sheer overload of everything they had experienced. So, they each made their way to their respective rooms to wind down for the night. Ally loaded up a game to play for a bit. It was the one surefire way to take her mind off things she knew. Erin wanted very much to read, but her mind was grinding to a halt from the day's activities. Instead, she flipped through her streaming options for a bit before settling on reruns of Frasier.

Rachel sat on the edge of her bed, uncertain what to do with her evening. She was tired enough she wanted to go straight to sleep, but she feared what may come. The weekend had taken its toll on her. It was refreshing having Thad back around and saddening as it was a reminder of what things were like when he wasn't there. She felt terrible for feeling that way as her two best friends sat mere rooms away, but she couldn't help it. He was the missing piece of their puzzle. She knew that, just as she knew there was nothing she could do to change it at the moment. She pulled out her phone and sent him a message asking if he made it home safely before falling down the social media feeds rabbit hole. Minute after minute went by without her actually registering a single post she was seeing. Her mind was elsewhere, and it wasn't long before elsewhere was all there was.

Rachel found herself yet again in Idonia, or that's at least what she thought. The tree was different again, though. She was standing in the courtyard with another massive white tree towering overhead with foliage of the deepest red flowing down from it. She turned to look opposite the center square for the tower she'd seen before, but none stood. Instead, she saw rows of houses and buildings growing taller in the back. She could hear the sounds of children laughing in the distance. The wind blew and sent leaves flying all around her. She closed her eyes and let wind envelop her. Sticking out her hands, she felt leaf after leaf brush against her skin.

When she opened her eyes, she saw the bright red light that led from the child of Leghtus throughout the town. She followed an immense shaft of red light into the sea of buildings. It wound through amaranthine house after amaranthine house until she was surrounded by castle-like structures all around. Though she couldn't see anyone, she could hear families playing and people walking around inside all the houses and buildings. She kept following the sizeable red light to see what all life it was powering.

After a short while, she broke through the buildings and saw a massive track suspended some hundred feet in the air and running outside the city walls. She followed the route and the red light back into the city to find a massive station with what looked like steam stacks rising hundreds of feet into the sky. An enormous staircase split in front and led up to the sides of the building. A fountain stood in the middle with the sculpture of a gorgeous woman holding a trident-like spear in her right hand. Her face was soft and full of youth. Her hair was short, cropped well above her eyebrows. She stood strong and proud, the personification of war and beauty. Her left hand was engulfed in flames as if she herself wielded it as a weapon. Even in stone, her eyes seemed to glow with passion. Rachel couldn't help but envy this marble woman.

Without warning, a crash of lightning streaked from the sky. Rachel ducked and closed her eyes as the brightness threatened to blind her, and when she opened them, she was looking down at the ground in the courtyard. As her eyes began to focus, she saw the red lights lighting the path from the mighty tree into the city. Then another shade of red came into view. A red liquid began to spread, rolling down the steps of the courtyard. Rachel leaned down to get a closer look and froze. Blood was flowing through the courtyard. She looked around and saw ravens circling overhead as body after body littered the ground with their throats slashed open and a dagger buried in their hearts as their blood poured forth onto the floor around them.

15
SEARCHING FOR GHOSTS

Rachel woke in a cold sweat, gasping for air as she gripped the sheets. Reaching a hand up to wipe her face, she felt tears on her cheeks along with the sweat. She wasn't sure how long the dream had lasted, how long she stood amongst the bodies, but clearly, it was long enough to have sent her body into a state of panic. Climbing from the bed, she made her way to the bathroom and splashed cold water on her face, hoping to wash away the fear that gripped her. She stood in the dark silence for a moment feeling her breath rise and fall as her nerves settled.

Crossing back over to the bed, she grabbed her phone to check the time before she climbed back under the covers, only to be disappointed to learn there was no time for that. She had already overslept her alarm. She pulled herself back off the bed again and made herself get dressed for her morning exercise. It would have to be a quick one, she knew, but she couldn't let herself get derailed. Her gym was located in the same building as The Daily Brew, which made it an ideal distance for a quick jog there and back for a brief workout.

She needed it that day especially. Rachel hadn't always been a fitness person. She was active growing up and participated in athletics in high school, but she had noticed over the years of college her body was slowing down in a sense. She didn't have quite as much energy and didn't recover quite as quickly. Over the summer before moving to Little Rock, she decided on a new routine, and as with anything in Rachel's life, once she got started, it was permanent. More than anything, it was the mental aspect that she enjoyed. It challenged her, focused her mind, and gave her a safety valve to release stress.

That morning it was all about the stress. A way to clear her mind of anything Idonia or Browning related and let her body purge itself. She wanted to work out longer than she could, but her alarm went off, letting her know it was time to head home. The run back was freeing. She felt the weekend drifting away behind her with each step, and by the time she arrived at the house, she was finally ready to begin anew for the week.

It wouldn't last long, though. After her shower, Rachel headed downstairs to make her smoothie, running late still and working to catch up. Ally and Erin were already gathered downstairs waiting on her, both chatting idly about their terrible night's sleep yet again as they scrolled through their phones. Not wanting to take any longer, she decided to grab a protein bar instead of bothering with a shake, but what happened next killed her appetite entirely.

"Holy shit." Erin's voice grew hollow as she slammed her phone down on the table. "You guys look at this!"

Ally and Rachel leaned in to read the article Erin had pulled up on the local newspaper site. The headline said it all, "*Little Rock Man Murdered.*" Rachel wanted to look away but couldn't do so as she and Ally leaned closer to see what else it said.

> *"Johnaton Pruit was found dead in his home this morning when his friend came to get him for their morning jog before work. Police say there was no sign of a struggle, but it was apparently no accident as the man's throat had been slit, and a knife was lodged in his chest where he was stabbed in the heart. Police were most concerned by the stab to the chest as the coroner's office gave the laceration on the man's neck as the cause of death, worrying them that perhaps the murder was premeditated. They searched the house but found nothing was missing or tampered with, so the police believe this to have been an attack of homicide at the moment. Mr. Pruit, aged 28, has no known family, so if anyone knows the individual, the police ask that they please come forward. The police are doing everything they can to find out what might have motivated the attack. Officials hope to have a full report soon."*

Life drained from the friends' faces. Murder wasn't something unique to the city they knew. They remembered a few from back home, but they were rare, to say the least. It was the nature of the murder, though, that struck the friends. They knew they shouldn't be scared, but the elaborate method was horrifying to consider. Rachel couldn't help but find herself back in the courtyard of her dream the night before. Rachel knew this was not a coincidence, *but what was she to do.* She couldn't just go to the police and explain how she'd seen that in her dream the night before. Rachel felt sure she couldn't tell her friends either, which left her no choice but to keep it to herself and act like it wasn't a big deal.

"Well, guess we knew the reality of living in the city would have to set in eventually. Wonder what that poor bastard did to piss someone off that bad." Ally's voice carried fake confidence, but it was enough to set Rachel at ease at the distraction.

"Yeah, I guess you're right. It's not like I expected there to never be a murder here. Still, just didn't expect one so gruesome." Erin said, her voice resonating with fear.

Rachel wanted so much for it just to be gruesome and not something she had seen foreshadowed. She thought of the man in the article. He was no one to her. Even looking at his picture, he was a complete stranger, yet she felt like she knew him. For all, she knew he was one of the countless bodies she saw dead in the courtyard the night before. A shiver ran down her spine. The protein bar still laid on the counter as the friends walked out the door.

The crisp air met them outside. It was far too cold for the time of year it was, yet still, the cold was there. The walk to The Brew was a silent one. Everyone wanted to say something to comfort the group, something to take away the fear that gripped them. Each one opened their mouth to speak more than once, but nothing was said. Instead, they just walked, each thinking of the poor soul they didn't know who had been so brutally executed.

As such, the friends walked along in silence, unaware that eyes were fixated on them, every step they took, every awkward twitch, every concerned look towards the others. They were being studied, and were completely unaware.

They had hoped that entering The Daily Brew would prove a much-needed lift to their spirits, but much to their dismay, a gloom had settled upon the coffee shop they could sense. It was the strangest feeling they'd had since first discovering The Brew. It had always radiated with an otherworldly warming and calming aura, but that day their spiritual oasis felt almost foreign with its bleak and empty state of existence.

"Did y'all see the news about that man Mr. Pruit?" Denise asked with sorrow in her voice as they reached the counter.

They each gave soft confirmations that they had.

"It's so tragic," Terry said in a solemn voice. "I mean, what could a person do to deserve such a thing."

"Nothing I could possibly imagine. You know he'd been through here?" Denise said to the girls. "Mind you, I couldn't tell you a thing about the man, but I've seen him a time or two come in to get a coffee. Crazy world."

"I thought I recognized his face. That's just horrible. I sure hope they catch the cruel bastard who'd do such a thing."

"I'm sure they will," Denise reassured her. "Just give it time."

"You're right," Terry replied. "I wish Lili was back, though. At least then it wouldn't feel so dreary in here."

"She's not back?" Erin asked, finally contributing to the conversation.

"No, ma'am," Denise answered. "They were heading out of town for the weekend; for some reason, they haven't returned yet. Said it may be sometime next week."

"Not soon enough, that's for sure," Terry added with a notable sadness in her voice.

For a brief moment, the friends thought about what would have kept the Brownings away, and all at once, they reached the same hypothesis; Harbilin. The Brownings had been intentionally vague about why they were leaving. While at first, the group assumed it was merely a family trip, the events of the weekend and the unexpected trip extension seemed less and less likely to be a simple weekend getaway.

The friends floated through the rest of their day thinking of how strange everything was that they'd experienced, and the day only grew stranger when they reached History through War only to find a notice on the door that class was canceled for the week. Professor Edmonton had to fill in for a colleague at a conference last minute. They were instructed to email their papers and begin researching the Warring States period. Thus the three friends returned home after checking in with Thad to let him know of the day's stirring developments. Thad had considered driving back to town for a moment given everything that was happening, but the friends assured him everything was fine and he should wait and come up the following weekend.

At home, the friends sat in a daze, unable to come to grasp everything that had occurred. Thus the week went. It was the least amount of words said in the house since the friends had arrived. They came and went in collective silence. They attended class, spent free time combing the shelves of The Brew searching for the book, and meandered throughout the house in a fog. They had no luck in the library, remembered virtually nothing from their classes, and by the time Friday arrived, not one of the friends could honestly say what they'd done with the week. It was one of those periods that simply passed by without notice. The one positive any of them could find was that they hadn't had a single strange dream the entire week.

It wasn't until they received a message from Thad early Friday afternoon stating he was on his way that the friends began to come out of their fog.

"Um," Erin began in confusion, "so what exactly are we doing this weekend?"

Ally couldn't help but think how much her life had changed. Just a few months ago, every weekend was the same. Friday night was game night with the boys. Saturday night was girls' night. Now her boys were nowhere around. Girls' night was essentially every night, which effectively made it no night. Despite that, though, all she could think about was where the Brownings had gone and what they were doing amidst all that was developing. Things were changing, and the friends all knew it.

"What does everybody want to do?" Rachel asked.

"I don't know." Ally replied. "Should we see if Terry wants to do something? She has seemed pretty lethargic all week. Like I'm one to talk."

As much as Ally just wanted to go back to her old life, she thought maybe having more than just their usual crew around could help drown out her thoughts. Fittingly she then saw the business card sitting on the counter from the previous weekend.

Before she could even say it, Rachel caught her eyes and agreed, "You want to?"

"Want to what?" Erin asked.

"Rachel wants to text Van and see if he's still in town." Ally replied jokingly.

"Hey, you were lookin' at the card too. Don't act like you weren't." She slapped her hand down on the card and snatched it up.

"Works fine for me," Erin said. "Just so long, so long as we're not going near anyone that might kill us."

The police report on the murder hadn't brought anyone closure. There were still no leads to go on and no new developments. As far as anyone knew, Mr. Pruit had been killed by a ghost.

"Well, I would hope none of our new acquaintances are into the whole ritual killing scene." Ally said disdainfully. "Besides, I'm not sure one dude constitutes the need to worry just yet."

"Never know," Erin said mockingly. "Might have been the Brownings sending a message to someone that the family didn't approve."

Humor was Erin's defense mechanism for everything, even morbid things.

"Oh, so we're friends with the mafia now, are we?" Ally said, matching Erin's mocking tone.

"Van is still in town, and he and Terry both said they're up for hanging out tonight if you two are done with the hitman discussion." Rachel said, cutting off her friends' exchange.

"Sounds good." Ally said. "Should we just meet them at The Pantry to grab a bite to eat before we go catch a movie?"

"Suits me," Erin replied. "Anything to improve on this long-ass week."

"Damn, ain't that the truth." Rachel said as she replied to Van and Terry, respectively.

"Alrighty then." Ally agreed, feeling some life returning to her. "I'll text Thad and get ready."

"I'm glad you decided to put my card to use. Thank you for the invite." Van said as he and Terry met up with the friends.

"Yeah, Van and I were already talking about how we should all hang out again, so it's cool you guys were wanting to hang too." Terry smiled so sweetly and innocently. Ally couldn't help thinking there must be no one in Little Rock more adorable than her.

"We all had fun last time. Seemed fitting to invite you out again." Erin said. "So, what brought you back to town so quick?"

"Well," Van began, "I haven't managed to leave yet. The shipping fiasco I was dealing with last weekend still hasn't been resolved. The shipment is down at the docks waiting for the paperwork to clear. I've been down there every day this week to no avail."

"Bummer, man," Thad said. "It's fun we at least get to visit some more, but that still sucks."

"It is, but as you said, I at least get the joy of spending more time with all of you. I'm not sure when the next chance to do that will be after I head out, so I must enjoy it while I can. How was everyone's week?"

Van seemed completely unphased by anything that had happened, *and why shouldn't he be* the friends thought. He wasn't the one going through what they were. None of the friends wanted to talk about their weeks, and they quickly glossed over what they referred to as an uneventful few days.

"So," Rachel began to change the subject as she took a sip of her drink, "Terry, tell us about yourself. We spent the whole last visit talking about us and Van. What's your story?"

"You really want to know about me?" Terry blushed, rather astonished that they cared. "There's not much of a story, really. My family moved around a lot as a kid. We moved here just a while back, and when they moved again, I decided to stay, so I found a place here. It's just a cozy little apartment, nothing fancy. Van said it was nice. I still keep in touch with my parents, though. I'd be lying if I said I didn't miss them. They live in Florida now, but I get to see them from time to time. My brother is with them too, but he's supposed to come visit sometime soon." She felt like she was talking too much and stopped to take a drink.

"I didn't realize Van had seen your apartment. That's interesting." Erin teased Terry.

Her face turned bright pink in response. "Oh, dear. Not like that. He just came by to pick me up before our date. I mean, not like a date, date. Just he saw my apartment again when we hung out last weekend. Not like that, though. He just came inside. It wasn't like, oh dear. I should stop talking."

"Relax, Terry." Ally said, feeling her pain. "Erin's just kidding with you. Trust me; it happens all the time with our group. Don't sweat it." She smiled politely at Terry to tell her it was ok to calm down.

"Yeah, that's just Erin for you," Rachel reassured her. "She's relentless. She still picks on me about Thad, and now she even picks on me about Win. Just the other day, she said I'm just hooking up with them both until I can decide which ones better in the long haul. I don't even know what that's supposed to mean."

Erin laughed at her joke, and Ally, Van, and Thad couldn't help joining.

Terry smiled, still slightly blushing as she spoke, "I'm glad to know I'm not the only one who gets picked on for stuff like that. But, yeah, that's pretty much all there is to know about me. Pretty dull, I know. Van's story last week was much better."

Van smiled at her flattery. Even though she was far too embarrassed to admit it, Terry was quite smitten by Van. From the look on his face, he knew it too.

"Speaking of stories, Van," Ally began, seeing a chance to press the issue, "do you know anything about Idonia?"

The smile left his face in an instant. His eyes locked with Ally's in search of what she knew. The look of bewilderment on Terry's face made her seem perplexed. Van's stare said more, though. Almost as if he were telling Ally she was wrong for asking in front of Terry. He studied her face and then scanned the others to see they were all of an accord.

"I don't know nearly as much as Joshua and Win do, which I'm guessing is who told you. I do know a fair bit, though. I'm also going to guess that they impressed upon you the importance of how these things are divulged. Thus, I'm not just going to go about discussing things they would not." His voice was a stern reprimand.

Ally felt slightly insulted, but more so, she felt naive for thinking Van would just open up and explain the whole thing to them. She knew if Idonia was as sacred to him as it was to the Brownings that he would never break that honor. Still, the friends needed information, so she decided to try a different approach.

"They told us that only certain things were theirs to tell and that they would only divulge things in a certain order. I wasn't about to ask you to tell us things they wouldn't. I'm really just curious about the Sundering. That was the last thing Joshua told us, aside from some stuff he and Win explained about the Davpyr. They didn't really talk much about the other races. All of that is super interesting. The Sundering, though, that's kind of all that affects us?"

"To say that's all that affects us is a vast oversimplification of things, but that's beside the point. Terry here still doesn't know what you're talking about, and it would be rather rude for us to start having a conversation about something that excludes one of our guests. So it's probably best if we just move onto something more relevant." Van replied politely, trying his best to dodge the situation entirely.

"I think I kinda know what it is." Terry chimed in, giving the friends some hope yet. "It's like their religion, isn't it? I've only heard them mention things about it here and there, and going by what you're saying, it seems like that's what they believe. It's what that symbol on the menu at work is from, right?"

Van shook his head, knowing he had no argument that they would believe. "You can call it a religion if you like. That's probably the closest word to explain it in a way you each would understand, but the symbol doesn't represent Idonia, at least not in that sense. Idonia is a world and a system. The symbol represents an Order, and that is all I will say of it."

"What happened after the Sundering?" Rachel's words were calculated. She wanted to know precisely.

"What did he tell you of the Sundering?"

"That the death of Vox Ramus destroyed Idonia," Ally replied, "from which new worlds were created."

Terry listened intently at that point, clearly learning more than she'd ever heard before from the Brownings.

"No," Van began, "Joshua wouldn't have said 'destroyed.' You're trying to jump to explanations on your own. No, he would have said something like, broken apart or…"

"Fractured," Erin said definitively, cutting Van off.

"Yes," Van replied with a charming smile, "fractured. That's much more Joshua's language and much more accurate as well. Idonia was not destroyed. Yes, it was torn apart, but pieces of it were massive enough to stay intact and hold themselves together. The cities the Gurén Liber had made with seeds of Leghtus were able to hold firm, but they were torn apart from one another, cast adrift in the growing void. It's said to have taken millennia before they were able to reform, but their connection to one another was never lost. No, it was bound by something much more powerful than the world itself."

He paused for a moment as he took a drink, "It's a very human thing, you know, to jump to the conclusion you did. We learn of a world beyond that of our own that sparked our beginning, and immediately we focus on the 'our beginning' part. It's a perfectly natural response. As humans, we're limited in just how far our minds can reach, and it's much easier to focus on a story of our creation than it is to focus on the creation of something much larger."

A silence fell over the table as Van's words took root. He was right. They had been looking at everything as an alternative explanation of things they loosely knew already. Terry's face was entranced as she listed, trying to piece together what else she didn't know.

"I'll answer your question, though, the question you actually meant. That doesn't mean it'll be any easier to process. The fragments of Idonia that were indeed torn apart were done so with such force that it tore the very fabric of reality, tearing open entirely new realms of existence and carrying with it all the building blocks of life. One of these such realms was ours, some fourteen billion years ago, and here we sit talking about it now. Without the Celestials and Ancients driving the development of our universe, it formed at its own basic rate, building life as best it could from the remnants of the shattered world. 'The nitrogen in our DNA, the calcium in our teeth.' Sagan really was a poet, whether he knew it or not."

The friends all shared glances with one another as they worked to understand everything Van was saying. It was as if neither he nor the Brownings had any realization of how outlandishly perplexing the things they said were. Van sat there across the table, slowly nursing his Manhattan, discussing the destruction and formation of entire universes as nonchalantly as if he had told the group what the weather was like on his last trip home and what he had to eat along the way.

He seemed to have no awareness of the fundamental reality in which the rest of them lived, and the friends realized the Brownings were no different. At that moment, Van's previous statement began to make sense, that calling it a religion would be the closest thing they would understand. It was something that the Brownings and Van simply believed to be true, so why would they talk about it in any way other than a simple conversation.

"Well, that's about enough cosmological discussion for one night. Partly because it is not my place to tell you anymore, but more importantly, we'll miss the movie if we don't leave soon. So everybody up." Van grabbed his jacket as he stood, making it clear the discussion was over, and they needed to move.

The four friends followed Van and Terry to the theater. They only stood in line a short while to get their tickets as cars rolled by on the street behind them. The friends were completely unaware of the eyes that continued to watch from the shadows, continued to study them. It was a rustic theater they had found a few weeks before, the kind that only showed old movies or put on special events like Rocky Horror Picture Show. No stadium seating or any of the fancy new features. Just an old theater with a raised stage and velvet curtains lining the sides with the balcony seating up top. The friends loved it. As much as Ally and Thad loved their technology, and Erin and Rachel had to have the latest gadgets, they all wanted the old-world charm any time they could get it. It was about the experience.

Erin and Terry got outvoted and were forced to endure a classic horror film. Inside, the theater was cold, but that was to be expected. It smelled of endless popcorn and had the slightly sticky floors that made noise with each step. Thad, who was endlessly hungry, opted for some cookie dough bites while Rachel worked her way through some Skittles. Ally skipped the soda she desperately wanted because she already felt full but couldn't resist sharing some of Erin's popcorn, though most of it ended up on the floor from Erin jumping at every scary bit. Ally noticed at one-point Terry had her face buried in the shoulder of Van's blazer. The other four seemed to be the only ones that watched the entire movie—a fact the friends didn't let Erin live down when they got outside.

"Seriously, Erin, you were jumping at parts that were just dialogue. For a minute, I thought you were just trying to find an excuse to get rid of the popcorn and not feel bad that you wasted the whole bucket." Ally's jeer sent a round of laughter through most of the group.

"Hey, I don't blame her. I was scared the whole time and didn't know when to jump either." Terry came to Erin's defense.

"Y'all know I hate scary movies," Erin added in her defense. "I don't even know why you're making a big deal about it."

"Because you make a big deal of everything." Thad and Rachel said in unison, both tossing pieces of candy at her as they did.

"Personally, I don't know how you were scared, Terry. You didn't watch the last half of the movie." Van teased her playfully.

"Don't let him get to you, Terry. Erin would've done the same thing if Rachel or I would've let her." Ally's comment sent another round of laughter through all but Erin as they exited the door.

"I would have let Erin, no problem," Rachel added sarcastically. "If there had actually been anything scary happening in the first place."

What Ally saw outside, though, was more than enough to make up for not being scared in the movie. The moment she looked across the street and saw him, she froze. Across the street stood Raven Man staring at her clear as day, eyes glowing red under the brim of his hat. She felt herself moving towards him. She was completely unaware of what she was doing, but it didn't matter. Anger and fear overtook her. She wanted to confront him. Too many nights had she seen him in her dreams. Too many times had she woke, wondering if he or someone else would be waiting for her when she did. She heard voices, voices of her friends, calling to her, but they were slowly drowned out by the flapping of wings and caws from birds no one could see. There was nothing else but Ally and the Raven Man; the rest of the world faded away as she stepped into the street to close the gap between them.

The moment her foot hit the pavement, a car swerved to miss her, honking its horn loudly and shocking her back into reality. She jumped back in a late reaction attempt to dodge the car, but in her hurry, her feet caught on one another.

She fell face-first onto the asphalt, barely managing to get her hands up in time to stop her fall. She looked up to see that Raven Man was no longer across the street. Instead, he was crouched directly over her. "I warned you Death was coming, Ally Carver."

16
RETURN FROM NORMALCY

In the blink of an eye, Raven Man split back into a flock of crows and disappeared. In his place, Ally saw the bright lights of a truck barreling towards her. Ally felt the impact in her left arm. Time seemed to slow to a crawl. She closed her eyes and braced herself. She felt her body being thrown by its force. Everything in the world came to a stop. She didn't bother to open her eyes. Ally knew she was dead, and she no longer knew what awaited her when she opened them. So, she kept them shut and let the rush of the winds embrace her. She felt weightless in death's embrace as it led her onward to the afterlife. The thought of that put her at ease. She wanted to see what lay on the other side, so she opened her eyes and saw Win Browning.

"Are you suicidal or just lost?" His voice was too close, too natural. Something was wrong.

Ally looked around in disbelief. She saw Joshua and Van circled around where Win had pulled her onto the street. *This is not right*, she thought. *There's no way they could all be here.* Win's voice rang out again, jarring her senses.

"Do you want to die? Because if so, there are much easier ways to go about it than walking into slowly oncoming traffic." He pointed towards the street behind her.

Ally spun around to see the spot where she died; only she wasn't dead. She turned around again and saw the marquee of the theater. Behind Joshua, Win, and Van, she saw her friends and Terry huddled together in various states of confusion. Ally looked back at the street to see the truck she thought had killed her continue its steady pace down the road. She had been nowhere genuinely close to death, yet still, she could not help but feel that Win had saved her life.

"I," the words tripped coming out of her mouth, "I'm.... I'm sorry. I thought I s..." She looked over her shoulder where Raven Man had stood. "I just tripped. I don't know how exactly." She looked at the two brothers again. "Wait, how the hell are you here?"

"So I grab you out of the street to keep you from becoming a hood ornament on a truck, and your reaction is bewilderment at my presence. That seems rather illogical." Win's face was not mad. Now that Ally thought about it, his face had not been angry the entire time he was talking. Quite the opposite, it looked as if he knew something troubled Ally and was concerned.

"I'm sorry. I didn't mean it like that. I'm just surprised to see you, but grateful. Don't get me wrong. Thank you." She threw her arms around Win's neck out of reflex as she finally came back to herself. Then she jumped back, realizing how unexpected she had been, but Win gave her a faint smile, letting her know he was glad she was safe.

He released her to her friends, and they embraced her with hugs and a smattering of jokes. Ally looked back from them to see Joshua, Win, and Van chatting quietly with one another as they stared at the spot where Raven Man stood, and the feeling of relief slowly left her.

The three gentlemen slowly made their way over to the group as they were finishing their embrace.

"Glad to see everyone together and all in one piece." Joshua began, giving Ally a smile on the latter part. "Thad, it is good to see you again, sir, and Terry, I am thrilled you decided to join some outings finally. I hate that we have not been here for it." He gave Terry a knowing smile that suggested it wasn't the first time she'd been invited out.

"Hey yeah," Erin said, coming back around to everything going on, "I thought you guys were out of town."

"We were." Win replied plainly. "Our trip last weekend took longer than we had expected, unfortunately. We were afraid we would be hung up even longer, but we were happy to learn that Van was still in town upon our arrival. So we figured we would come down and see him."

"On that note," Van interjected with a smile, "now that everyone's calmed down, would it be ok with everybody involved if Terry rode back with the four of you? It would be nice to catch up with Joshua and Win for a bit before I have to leave for New York."

"Oh dear," Terry began in protest, "I wouldn't want to impose. My apartment is just up the ways a bit. I can walk home. That's totally fine."

"Nonsense," Ally said, refusing to entertain the idea, "of course, you can ride with us. It'll be a cozy fit, but with as short of a drive as we all have, everyone should be fine."

"Yeah, Terry," Rachel added, "you're not imposing at all. Trust us, Ally over here is the queen of 'oh I just don't want to be in anyone's way.' We're used to overcoming countless objections, so don't even bother."

Terry looked as if she might refuse again, but she agreed after seeing the friendly resolve in the group.

"Well, it's good to see you both back." She said to Josua and Win. "You three have a fun evening."

They each assured her they would, and Van charmingly kissed her hand before the three men turned and disappeared into the city. The groups stood for a bit, still laughing at the craziness of Ally's events. As they finally went to leave, Rachel felt her shoe skid across something. On the ground, where the commotion of Ally getting snatched out of the street had occurred, she saw one of the strange coins Van and Joshua had used before. The friends were already walking away, so she bent to pick it up, swiftly tucking it in her jacket pocket not to draw attention.

"Sorry, had some of Erin's popcorn in my shoe." She said to a chorus of laughter as she caught up to the group.

"Hey, Terry, if you want, you're welcome to come hang out at our place for a while. We won't be calling it a night for a bit still." Ally said, sensing a kindred spirit in Terry, who also struggled with being social.

"That's nice and all guys..." Terry began to object.

"Nope," Erin said flatly. "Gonna stop you right there. We already have to twist Ally's arm to do anything, so if she's initiating it, the rest of the group just has to go along."

Terry shuffled awkwardly as they walked, searching for an excuse to say no. Ally empathized with her. Most of her life was spent in the same mindset. Much to Ally's joy, though, Terry agreed to go with the friends, and so the group made their way to the house on Rock Street.

It was a pleasant evening for everyone involved. They all swapped stories about their adolescence while playing board games and laughing at one another's tales. The four friends told Terry all about the mischief they would get up to back home, which was very little at all, but they still had fun talking about it. Simple things like toilet papering a friend's house or driving through all the country roads to spot ghost lights had been the highlights of much of their youth.

Terry found it all most amusing. She could hardly relate as she grew up on bases in large cities. Terry told the friends of her family's life moving base to base. It meant never making many friends, she admitted, but it did bring their family incredibly close together. She talked about her brother Dante, who was supposed to be visiting soon. A few years her younger, he was her best friend and her pride and joy the way she told it. Constantly moving was tough on both of them, so she always looked out for him.

They asked Terry about Joshua's comments about her finally going out. She explained to them how she had been invited by Lili and the Brownings to dinner a few times but, as was her nature, had always felt like she would impose. It was only a handful of times, and they were very polite. It just felt to Terry that she would be taking too much liberty because she worked with them. Despite her never joining the family, though, she did have a standing invitation anytime she wanted. The friends couldn't help but hope she would use that, given they were spending time with the Brownings as well.

Feeling a second wave of hunger, Thad ordered some pizza and shared it with the group. They continued playing games well into the night as they worked through the pizza slice by slice. The friends asked Terry why she didn't move with her parents, to which Terry explained how she was just ready to stay someplace for a while. The three girls understood her feelings immediately, themselves being on the complete opposite end of the spectrum, having spent their entire life in one place. Thad understood in his light as well the longing for a change. It was the most normal any of them had felt in Little Rock, Terry included. For once, they were just a bunch of people who found themselves in the same place for similar reasons, and there was comfort in that.

It was well after midnight when the group finally began showing signs of fatigue.

After a few rounds of yawns, Terry finally spoke out, "It's been a blast, guys, but I really ought to be getting home. Thank you so much for not letting me back out. This was really fun. We should do it again."

With that, she grabbed her coat and made her way towards the door to the friends' confusion.

"Hey, wait," Erin said, "you're not walking home."

"I do it all the time," Terry said, facing the friends with a shy smile. "I don't even own a car. I've grown up walking around bases and cities all the time. It's really no big deal. I'm just a few blocks over in the downtown lofts. You'd use more gas turning your car on than you would driving me there. Don't sweat it."

"Yeah, but something could happen to you." Rachel objected.

"Sure, that's a possibility," Terry said with an unusual balance of innocence and confidence, "but that's not likely. I've walked home on these same streets every night for years now. I know crime's a thing, but so are car accidents. You're more likely to get in a wreck driving me to my apartment than I am to have something happen to me walking to my apartment."

"It feels like I'm breaking some sort of guy code not demanding we drive the lady home," Thad began, "but she's got a point. I gotta be the one to say 'cause I've been there. I was walking home from school by myself before I was a teenager."

"Thank you," Terry said, giving Thad a warm smile. "Truly, it's nothing."

"What about the murder?" Ally blurted out unexpectedly in an effort to stop her.

"You're genuinely worried about that?" Terry asked in confusion. "It was horrific, don't get me wrong, but there were four homicides last month. The month before that, there were three. Any is horrible, but one isn't going to make me lock myself inside. I don't know anyone who wants to kill me, and I keep pepper spray if some drunkard gets handsy. It's part of living in the city."

Ally, Erin, and Rachel were at a loss for anything else to say. They had no counter to Terry's rationale, they realized. They had been so taken aback by the terrible nature of Mr. Pruit's death; they hadn't put it into perspective. Despite feeling suddenly naive, though, the friends still didn't feel comfortable letting Terry walk home.

As if she sensed such, Terry spoke again, "Look, if it truly bothers you this much, you can give me a ride. I'd hate for you to worry."

The friends were beyond relieved as they grabbed their coats and headed towards the door. They all loaded into the car. Terry smiled comically at them but said nothing and let the friends have their moment. The drive to Terry's apartment was filled with little conversation, as the trip was even shorter than Terry even made it seem. She truly did live just minutes away from them. Terry thanked them again for having her and insisted they do it again before heading inside her apartment.

The drive back from Terry's apartment was even more silent than the drive there had been. Tiredness was finally setting in on the friends, but more than that, the normalcy of the night was fading as well. It had been an enjoyable evening, but something told the friends it was merely a distraction.

As the friends walked into the apartment, the actual level of their fatigue began to set in. They realized it had been some time since they had all stayed up so late. One by one, they filed through the kitchen, taking off their coats and hanging them on an empty chair. Thad began making his way to the couch, and Erin and Rachel were halfway up the stairs when Ally stopped at the base of them and spoke.

"Something's not right." She said flatly but emphatically.

The others turned to look at her with concern on their face, but no one moved to speak.

"Tonight, this week, everything that's been going on, something's wrong, you guys." Ally's voice had gone shaky, and she told herself it was just the lack of sleep.

"I don't know what it is." She said, knowing it was only partially true. She wanted to tell her friends everything; the dreams, the Raven Man, the strange wanderer who appeared with its cryptic message, the cities, the trees, the visions that were spilling over into real life. She wanted to tell them about what she saw that night at the theater that made her step out into the street, but she couldn't. She tried, but the words simply wouldn't form.

"I know we said we want to know what's going on, and I still do." Her voice was trembling even more. "I just can't shake this feeling. I want things to be normal, and I'm realizing now that I don't know what normal is any more."

Erin finally spoke and saved Ally from rambling endlessly. "Neither do I. So much has changed, just in us moving here alone. Then the Brownings, Idonia, and now Terry and Van, I'm slowly starting not to recognize my life anymore. The only thing that feels familiar anymore, the only thing that feels normal, are the people standing in this room."

It was an odd confession from Erin, and everyone in the group knew it. Erin didn't talk about her feelings. Even when she had a chip on her shoulder, there was never any indication of how it got there.

Yet there she was, confessing precisely what the rest of them were feeling.

"Erin's already got sappy," Rachel began, "so I won't go there. I'll just say I agree. I found this, though." She pulled the coin she remembered she had found on the ground earlier after Ally's incident. "I had honestly forgotten about it until now. I didn't want to bring it up around Terry, and then after a while, I just forgot."

"What is it?" Thad asked.

"I honestly have no idea. We've seen Joshua and Van both give it to someone as compensation now, so it's a valuable or maybe a currency of some kind. Doesn't help address any of what we're discussing, but since we're discussing things not being normal, well, this looks pretty not normal to me."

She held the coin up as the friends all studied it. Not normal was a fitting description, but that was as far as the friends could get. It was made of a heavy, black metal the friends didn't recognize. In its center was a pearlescent circle that looked to be the core from which the golden inlays formed. Three distinct patterns curved outward in perfect symmetry in what looked like circuitry that somehow had curvature unfitting of its nature. The lines swirled out to create three circles in equilateral formation where the golden metal pooled before spiraling further outward and encasing the edge of the strange coin. So the value seemed likely, but what it was or did the friends had no clues.

"Hold onto it with your life; I'd say," Erin said. "Till we know what to do with it, at least. Who knows what it might do. Worst case scenario, we hand it back to them one day and say, 'oops, uh, it looks like you dropped this.' Should go over fine."

The friends all laughed, feeling as normal with one another as they had in a long time.

"I've missed you guys," Thad said, catching the others off guard. "Ever since you moved, it hasn't been the same. It feels good being here. Even if something is, wrong."

He met Ally's eyes before looking at the others, and she couldn't help thinking back to that night. She had pushed it from her memories amidst all the other chaos they had experienced, but it was still a mystery in her mind. No more words were said that night. None need be. They still had things they wanted to say, things they needed to share, but what mattered for the moment is the group knew they were in it together.

Terry awoke at the sound of a soft knock on her door. She climbed out of bed slowly and pulled her robe on. The knock came again as Terry hurried to reach the door. She opened it to see Van's smiling face.

"I just wanted to make sure you were alright. I know tonight was rather strange. How are you?"

"I'm fine. It was pretty scary at first, but after I realized everything was fine, it all got better. After you left with Joshua and Win, they insisted I come over. I was just glad Ally wasn't troubled by everything." Terry pulled her robe tight as a cold draft blew into her apartment.

"I knew she'd be fine. She's a fighter. I can tell." Van smiled at her with a gleam in his eye.

"Do you want to come in?" She opened the door a little wider to give Van an entrance. "I could put on a pot of coffee."

Van stepped in and pushed the door closed behind him to eliminate the draft but didn't move further into the apartment.

"I really can't stay, sadly." He said, grasping her hand gently. "I just wanted to make sure everything was still good."

"It is." She said, giving him a faint smile. "How was your time with the Brownings?"

"It went very well. It was nice to catch up. Our work does really make things challenging."

"I'm sorry." Her words were genuine, even if they didn't mean quite what she said.

"No need to be," Van said, reassuring himself more than Terry. "Such is the nature of our busy lives."

"I know. It's still unfortunate, though." Terry let out a long yawn, which Van took as a sign.

"I'd better let you get some sleep. Plus, I must get back to work. My job is never done." He leaned in and kissed her forehead before opening the door and disappearing into the dark hallway.

The following day Ally made her way slowly downstairs, tired from the late night before, to find Thad standing in the kitchen with a solemn expression on his face.

"You're going to want to wake the others." He said in a flat tone.

"How long have you been up?" She asked.

"Long enough," was all he said, and Ally didn't bother saying anything else before going upstairs and waking Erin and Rachel.

Neither friend wanted to get up, but when she was able to get them moderately conscious and told them Thad sent her, they each came to. They were slow to rise, but they knew if Thad was up so early and signaling for the group, it must be severe. They shuffled downstairs to find him standing at the kitchen island, still wearing the solemn look Ally had seen him with moments before.

He slid his phone across the island towards them, "You were saying something wasn't right."

On his phone was an article from the local news headlined, "*The Ghost of Little Rock Kills Again.*"

17
REDUX

The group sat silently in the kitchen around the island. The article had explained how there were no apparent connections between the two men aside from the manner of death. The second victim was a man in his late thirties. Just as the first, there was no sign of a struggle and no signs that anyone had been in the house. Morning passed by slowly as the friends sat, unsure what to do.

"Shall we at least get coffee?" Erin said after some time.

No one could muster an objection. The friends were all lethargic, but they knew there was nothing they could do. The murders were horrifying, but the friends had nothing other than a strange dream none of them would discuss openly to connect them. Each friend was so focused on their personal apprehension they couldn't recognize the same feelings being reflected by the rest of the group.

So, they slowly dressed and made their way down the street to The Daily Brew without discussion or explanation. The walk was colder than usual. Autumn was taking over at a rapid pace, and the cold only served to dampen their moods further as the friends trudged along.

Much to their surprise, though, as they climbed the stairs to The Brew, the sight of the rich blue awnings began slowly warming them, inside and out. There was a peace and calm that emanated from the coffee shop. It was a stalwart anchor keeping all the passengers aboard its vessel in tranquil waters at all times, no matter their struggles.

Walking through the patio, the group felt their worries and frustrations fall away one step at a time. The aroma of The Brew cut through the cold air as it reached out to the friends, enveloping them, and drawing them inward. Their spiritual oasis had grown lush yet again, emanating peace and calm. It offered a sense of belonging and purpose. The fear was still there, the confusion ever-present, but The Brew offered assurance that someway, somehow, it would all work out.

Inside they were greeted with a warmth only The Daily Brew provided. Terry and Denise smiled at them from behind the counter like it was just another day. At the corner table, Joshua, Win, Van, and Lili all sat drinking their coffee as they gave the group a wave to come over. Everyone seemed genuinely calm, even if it was an active effort to remain so. The Brew provided that. It was a place to be centered and at ease.

The friends made a point to talk with Denise and Terry before joining the Brownings and their friend. It brought joy to each of them, the friends and the baristas alike. It seemed ages since they had first met. Even Thad, who had only visited a few times, fell right in with all of them; Terry, Denise, even the Brownings. It was strange how quickly the quaint coffee shop and peculiar family had gone from foreign to familiar. Such was the nature of The Daily Brew. Once it welcomed someone, they were family.

After visiting with Terry and Denise, they joined the Brownings and Van. Everyone mentioned the murder. It was impossible not to. Yet, somehow, in just a week, the mood of everyone in The Brew had gone from concern and fear at the first death to unfortunate acceptance at the second death. The situation was tragic and horrific, yet none of them could do anything about it. They weren't involved or connected; as far as any of them knew, they weren't at risk, so it just became an unpleasant truth. It was a surreal reminder for the friends that horrible atrocities were occurring at all times across the world. The closer it became, the more significant effect it had, but that did not change the fact that no matter how close or how far, horrible things happened every day.

"It's a grim reminder of mortality, sadly," Van said, sipping his coffee. "Anytime a massive terrorist attack occurs, or a tsunami or an earthquake kills hundreds, everyone looks up for a moment. They think about how tragic it is and how frail life is, and then after some time, people just go back about what they were doing. Less than a hundred years ago, the entire world was embroiled in a war that truly threatened to consume everyone, and now we sit here drinking coffee and never think about it until a new movie gets announced."

"I guess that's part of human nature, really." Rachel said solemnly.

"As individuals and a species, we fear our death, but we only think about it when something out of the ordinary happens. It's the fight or flight part of us, and then when the moment's gone, it's back to usual."

"Indeed," Van replied as he stood and put on his coat. "Well, friends, I truly must get going. I have a flight to catch after all. It's been a real pleasure, as always."

"Sorry to have to see you leave so soon, Van," Lili said, rising to give Van a hug. "Be safe out there, and come back soon."

"Always." He said, giving her a big smile. "I should be back in a couple of weeks, hopefully. We have a lot going on here currently. Ladies, Thad, it was great getting to meet you. I know we'll see each other again very soon."

They all said their farewells, and Lili went back to working with Terry and Denise, leaving Joshua and Win with the four friends.

"Van is certainly quite the character," Erin said after everyone settled back in.

"Oh, if you only knew." Win said with a smile.

"He and Terry seem to be hitting it off pretty well," Rachel added, unsure what else to say but not wanting silence to take over.

"So it would seem," Joshua replied coyly. "He spoke very highly of her, which he could hardly say anything to the contrary. Terry is a very nice lady. She's been a wonderful addition to our family here. If not for her and Denise, well, I do not know what we'd do."

"Is everyone family for you?" Ally asked, uncertain why she did so.

"I suppose it is different for us than most families." Joshua began as he set his empty mug down. "Van informed us, of course, that he told you a bit of our history. We may ward people off, but that aspect of our life is not something we keep from those who know us. To your point, that really is all there is for us. We do not get to know many people, not closely. We are very private. For us, there are only acquaintances, and family. If someone is not worth letting into our family entirely, they are not worth letting into our family at all."

There was an edge to his voice, a sharpness that spoke to the level of severity with which they held their family. The friends had been consumed with getting to know the enigmatic family from the first moment they met, and had never stopped to think that they were already closer to the Brownings than almost anyone got. It was a jarring realization.

As if on cue Terry arrived carrying a fresh cup of coffee for Joshua.

"I just want to say how amazing I think you both are for everything that you've done for your family." She blurted out as she sat his drink down. "I told Lili already, but I wanted to tell you two as well. I can't imagine what it must have been like for you before you came here, but I'm really glad that you did. I know what family means to me, and it's nice having something like that here."

"Thank you." He said with a sincere smile. Win grabbed her hand and gave a gentle squeeze to show his thanks. She blushed a deep shade of red as she smiled at them both before shuffling off.

"For what it's worth," Thad added sincerely, "I gotta say I'm with Terry. I'm sure there's far more than what Van told us, but as far as I can tell, you guys are pretty damn noble."

"I assure you, nothing about me is noble," Joshua's eyes were empty, and his voice was cold as he spoke, "but I thank you for your kind words nonetheless." His expression warmed as he glanced towards his family. "My family are very honorable people, and they deserve a better life than the one they once had. Hopefully, you can understand a little better now why we keep to ourselves."

"So it was all true then?" Rachel asked with compassion in our voice.

"I do not know what exactly Van told you, but knowing Van as I do, I cannot imagine it would be a lie. Not about my family or myself anyways, and if it were, it would only be to protect us." The seriousness on his face seemed to melt away as he took a drink of his coffee. "Now, I am sure that is enough tiresome conversation about family. Is there anything else you would like to discuss?"

"Van told us about how the universe came to be after the Sundering," Thad said, pouncing on the first opportunity, knowing it might be his only opportunity before he had to leave, and catching everyone at the table off guard. "He also said that Idonia was somehow rebuilt after the event as well."

"Is that so?" Joshua replied with a surprised and amused smile. "Well, that is an interesting development."

Thad was on a mission and refused to be deterred by Joshua's nonchalance. "It is. Almost as interesting as what we found in the library upstairs. Though, what was more interesting is what we couldn't find."

Thad was treading carefully, trying to get information without giving up more of what they knew than he must. They wanted the

Brownings to reveal more about themselves and Idonia, but they didn't want to throw all their cards on the table at once and let the Brownings then cherry-pick how to respond.

"My, my," Joshua began, his smile shifting from amusement to intrigue, as was mirrored by Win, "you are an inquisitive lot, and you have grown rather intrepid since our dinner. I sense a question forming. Do you wish to ask?"

The group was completely taken aback. They were watching as Joshua's entire personality seemed to shift before their very eyes. The man they had known had only ever been strategically elusive. He was calm, calculated, and strict. He gave them rules by which to discuss things, set boundaries of where they could and could not go. Even just moments before, he had been intentionally vague and deflective, and suddenly he was blithely inviting them to ask questions freely. Thad waivered slightly. He'd had a question in mind, but Joshua's response threw him off entirely.

Ally came to his rescue, "You described the Celestials, and Vox Ramus, as if they were beings, people, yet the, few, things we were able to find in the library referred to Vox Ramus as a star and Idonia as a system, or maybe a planet. It was a little confusing."

"Indeed," Joshua replied, not losing his playful smile. "It is interesting how often poetry can sound scientific, and how often science can sound poetic."

His answer was intentionally vague yet again, but his nature had changed entirely. He was no longer trying to divert the discussion but instead danced around the topic until the friends found the right thing to say.

"You're dodging," Erin said flatly.

"And you are making statements but asking no questions." Win replied coolly.

"Ok," Erin began, resentment at his sarcasm heavy in her voice, "were Vox Ramus and the Celestials people or not?"

"Well," Joshua began after taking another sip of coffee, "that is a tough question to properly answer considering whatever Vox Ramus and the Celestials were, have been dead or gone for billions of years."

"What?" Rachel exclaimed in shock.

"When Vox Ramus died, it did not merely shatter the world of Idonia, it also destroyed that which bound the Celestials to that plane and cast them off into the Void. Thus, the Ancients were left to rebuild

Idonia on their own, and this world was left to rebuild by itself."

"How were the Ancients able to rebuild something that took the Celestials ages to complete?" Thad asked, thrilled to finally be getting somewhere closer to the truth.

"Painstakingly. The Nuati and the Traco were fortunate to have been spared the brunt of the destruction and could rebuild with greater ease. The Davpyr, however, were not so lucky. It had been a generation since the Gurén Liber had set forth with the seeds of Leghtus and ushered in the Golden Age of Discovery. As such, the mantle was passed to the next generation. The two children from each family, mirroring their original creation, were tasked to journey from their cities back to the fractured heart of Idonia and renew the connection to Leghtus. The Salarinde, led by Urithina and Gabrize, were closest to Idonia and the first to rejoin their kin, the Traco and Nuati. Together they worked to open any possible pathways for the others to rejoin. The Resharim, led by Miria and Raphon, was the next to find this new pathway thanks to the others' help.

"The Netiziath were led by the siblings, Lithia and Locief, the latter of whom would become one of the most infamous beings in all the realms. Locief was the most beautiful and fierce Davpyr ever to live, showing overflowing power even as a child. Equal parts Netiziath and Resharim genetically created natural gifts in channeling Incarnum that paired with exceptional grace and agility would make Locief a being that commanded respect and admiration from everyone, everywhere. Each generation grew more potent than that which came before them, as is the natural order. Still, the massive evolutionary leap forward present in Locief was unparalleled by the other Ancients, save two.

"The children of the Daevon were led by the oldest sibling, the most powerful and purest of the Davpyr, Samias. Unlike any Davpyr that came before, Samias showed no natural affinity towards any Incarnum but instead was adept at all, much like that of Locief. They were the first Davpyr to be able to harness all the powers of the entire race for maximum capability. An evolution that proved more than necessary as the Daevon and Netiziath would have the most arduous journeys to reunite their worlds. It also proved to be most essential, as their generation would be the last in the Davpyr line.

"The task of reforming the world of Idonia was not merely a quest. It required sacrifice. As their parents had done before them, the children would carry with them a piece of Leghtus, but unlike the first generation of Gurén Liber, they were not taking a seed to be planted but to be returned. They took from each of their cities' Vash Leghtus a single seed for each Davpyr. That seed would journey with them across the treacherous expanse of the broken Idonic system until each member of the race returned to Idonia and rejoined it with Leghtus. To join the seed with Leghtus, though, and reforge the bridge that was broken required the seed bearer to channel their lifeforce through the seed and back into Leghtus itself, sacrificing a portion of themselves in the manner Vox Ramus had once done. It was an act that required more power the farther their city had been cast from Leghtus, and one that brought about the end of the Davpyr line as they sacrificed their ability to create life by pouring their own life back into Leghtus. The toll Leghtus took grew with each connection that was reformed, so the evolution that had taken place in Locief and the children of the Daevon had been one of unforeseen purpose as they needed every ounce of that new power to reforge Idonia's broken world. It was a task so demanding that the final mending took the youngest of the Daevon, pouring the entirety of their power into Leghtus, binding their entire being to the world of Idonia eternally, ending that lineage of Ancients with the Last Davpyr, Milas Daevon."

The group sat in stunned silence. Never before had Joshua been so forthcoming, and never before had he been so direct. All of his deflections had ceased. Even the quick little dance he had done around the topic and quip about poetry and science had been but a feigned diversion. The moment they struck the right chord, Joshua had poured forth the details without ominous warning or cautionary affirmations.

For a moment, the friends had thought he was toying with them, but the moment he spoke of Idonia's reformation, it was as clear and true to them as breathing. They took glances at one another and back to Win and Joshua, who, despite the solemn tone in his storytelling, had returned to the playful smirk that seemed so strange and foreign on him. In mere moments the friends had gone from being curious about the enigmatic Browning family to being completely confused as if they had no idea who the family was and were learning them all over again from the very beginning.

As if he sensed their confusion, Joshua leaned into his new playfully mysterious persona, "Well then, I hope that provides you with an adequate answer to your questions. I would love to answer more, as I am sure you have many, but Win and I truly must be going. We have a meeting we simply cannot miss. Hopefully, though, that will give you enough to go on."

He gave them a knowing smile as he rose, grabbing his blazer and folding it over his arm as his brother stood to join him.

Win turned his coffee up to drain the last of it, shooting a keen glance to the loft overhead as he did. "Best of luck to you." He said as he placed his empty cup on the table. "I look forward to our next visit." He gave the friends another charming smile that matched the coyness of his brother as he bowed slightly before they turned and exited The Brew.

The friends still sat in silence, glued in place by the sudden change in Joshua and Win. Slowly, in unison, their eyes all turned to the staircase leading upstairs to the labyrinth of peculiar books.

18
EVER VIGIL IS THE WATCHER

The friends had collected their drinks and belongings in no time and were upstairs at the kiosk, ready to begin their next search. Joshua had rekindled the flame in them that had been dwindling amidst all the strange occurrences. They stood at the kiosk running through queries in their heads, filtering through everything they had already searched and all the new things Joshua had said.

Slowly they began working through the list of names and races, working on spelling them as best they could. Words like Nuati and Traco came quickly enough but generated no results even after a handful of spelling variations. The races of Resharim, Netiziath, and Salarinde proved far more complicated as dozens, and dozens of attempts returned no results whatsoever. The friends were growing more frustrated by the moment, but they refused to give up.

Running out of options, they decided to try the names of the Davpyr upon which Joshua had placed the most emphasis. After a few attempts at spelling, the search for "Locief Samias Milas" finally gave them something. A book titled *Code of the Watchers* was the number one result, with several results following that referenced the book. The book had fewer possible locations than the elusive *Primus Stella*, but not by much. The friends split up the twenty-six potential areas and began their search.

Minutes turned to hours as the friends worked shelf after shelf, hunting down the book. One location proved fruitless, then another, and another as the group whittled the list down further and further. Erin was the first to finish her list of places, all of which had turned up nothing. Thad was just minutes behind her, an equally empty amount of results to show for his work. Erin quickly set off to help Rachel and Ally with the last of their possible locations, whilst Thad returned to the kiosk hoping to find something to help them. He rifled through page after page of results as the girls finished the last of their searches.

Just as the three friends had finished the last of the locations and all had begun thinking they were on as futile of a search as the quest for *Primus Stella* became, Thad, found another reference in the results. A single output with a digital excerpt from Ari Noach's teachings found within *Code of the Watchers*. The friends quickly took out their phones to access the digital library and read the passage.

We were not prepared for our first encounters with the forces of Idonia. We knew neither how to resist beings of such magnitude, nor what submission to them truly entailed. For that, we suffered losses we can never amend or avenge. This is the foundation from which we must build, and as such, there are certain truths we must accept if we are to be victorious.

First, when Idonia was shattered, and the making of our worlds was cast off, it was no accident. We must not treat ourselves as the victims of happenstance, for to do so denies the truth of our beginning and inhibits our path forward. There is no such thing as chance on the cosmic scale in which we meddle. Our worlds were cast out not by fault of our own nor malice by them, but by their carelessness. Malignancy can be anticipated, calculated, and countered. Carelessness strikes without rhyme or reason, and it is why we would always be in danger by their side.

Secondly, our worlds are imperfect. This is not a negative trait; it is merely a fact. They are but fragments of what made Idonia great, but we mustn't confuse greatness with perfection. For Idonia was, and is, great, but it too is imperfect. If we lose sight of that, we will succumb to the notion we need their world instead of ours. Ours are flawed, yes, but they are still mighty, and they are still free. Free for the citizens of our worlds to determine their fates, and free from the Davpyr determining it for them.

Part of that freedom, though, means letting our kind choose their own path. The Nalun may be a mortal threat, the Ana'si may be a lesser evil, but that is our cause, ours that we have chosen. The citizens of our worlds have not. It is our mission to enlighten them, educate them, and equip them to make the right choices, but they must be free to make the wrong ones. If we take this from them, we are no different than our enemies. The goal is not perfection. The goal is the most amount of freedom for the most amount of our people.

Thirdly, when Samias first led Locief and Milas and the might of the Nalun on their excursion into the stars seeking the remnants of their shattered world, they did so with sound purpose. Even now, as their methods have changed, even after the birth of the Ana'si, we must not forget that their intentions are ones that they believe to be good. It is essential that we remember, and pass on the truth, that there was a time before this; before they had turned to violence, and before some of them had given up on convincing our worlds or even helping them at all. We live much shorter than any in the Ana'si or Nalun. So we must pass down this knowledge, our future generations must carry it with them lest we forget, because they will not.

No amount of time will change that the Nalun will seek coercion before resorting to force, as will the Ana'si always work at subterfuge. We know their works to all be about one inevitable goal, conquest. We are not fooled by their methods, no matter how many of our brethren throughout our worlds may be. Still, we must never forget that while those are their methods, their motives are genuinely to help. They believe themselves just and noble in their cause. They must. For if they do not believe what they are doing is right, they will lose faith in it. If we forget this, if we begin to think of them merely as nefarious forces simply bent on destruction, we will fail. We will make mistakes because we misunderstand their motives, and it will cost us everything.

Their journey has been arduous beyond anything we can understand. To watch the world around you, the world you loved torn apart before your very eyes as your city stands impervious to the destruction but unable to stop the carnage, that is a horror few can fathom. They watched in terror as the world they had worked ages to build was brought low in mere moments, casting the Ancients in their mighty cities adrift in space, tumbling away from everything they ever knew. In an instant, the web they had woven across Idonia was undone, leaving them cut off from their family and from the heart of Idonia itself. The once paragon of their world laid isolated and battered from holding steadfast to its bonds throughout the decimation.

The unwavering devotion it took to reforge the connections between the great cities and Idonia, venturing out into the Void and dragging the broken fragments of their world back together, is unfathomable in any of our known existences. The realms of Bàofor, Euern, and Inverna may have fallen closer to Idonia than that of Kealfurm or the distant Nevadolia. Still, no journey into the Void is without immense peril. Their brutal battle against fate to restore the Idonic system was won at great price, and from the victor grew great powers.

Long before the Idonic races first set foot on our worlds, they pulled from the abyss the broken shards of their world created by beings even they couldn't understand and reforged those remnants into an empire even greater than the one that came before. Nor did they stop there. They were not merely satisfied to recapture their beloved Golden Age of Discovery, no. The Idonic system was bent on far more than that, seeking to lead their people into a brand new age that would one day overshadow the entire Idonic history before the Sundering. They reforged their broken cities into entire worlds more massive and vibrant than the worlds we know and reached out into the Void, stretching their empire to the stars beyond, bringing new worlds into their domain.

That is what first brought the Nalun inching ever closer to our doorsteps, leading the charge of the Idonic system. When they first discovered us, they were as gods in our eyes, and rightly so. To the first of our kind who encountered them, the Heralds of Idonia would have seemed as near to us as our cosmic creators. Our primitive minds and naive disposition allowed them to indoctrinate our kind world by world, and those who were brave or foolish enough to resist only hastened the transition of the Nalun. Our mistake was not merely trusting the Idonians, though but not seeing where that trust would lead. We were blinded by the possibilities of joining them and did not think of the opportunities to learn from them.

That was ages ago. We are no longer primitive or naive. We have seen the face of the true enemy. We were right to fear and admire Idonia, and we must do so still. For if we are to overcome our enemy, we must become our enemy. We must advance. We must evolve. We must rise. They play a longer game than we could possibly hope to. So we must play a smarter one. For it will not be our children, nor our children's children, nor even theirs that finish this fight. That is why we must remember these things, so that those who came after us will remember them too and finish what we started.

We are those who see, but are unseen.
We are those who know, but are unknown.
Patience is our process.
Strategy is our strength.
Wisdom is our weapon.
We are the eyes in the darkness.
We are the ears in the silence.
We are the knife in the shadow.
Ever Vigil is the Watcher.

19
VIOLENCE BEGETS VIOLENCE

Weeks passed with more study sessions with Joshua and Win, more zoo trips, family dinners, dinners with Terry, and visits from Thad, all in various assortments. The one thing there had not been more of over that time was victims of the Ghost of Little Rock, for which the friends were most grateful. They had accepted that it was something far out of their hands that didn't even pertain to them, but it still made them feel more at ease that no more deaths had been reported.

The only thing better than the Ghost's absence was the absence of Raven Man and the strange Wanderer. There had been vague moments where one of the friends saw a raven outside and felt like it was watching them more closely than a typical bird should, and on more than one occasion, one of them would wake from a dream certain they had heard the hour of the Raven and the Lion being whispered to them. While the weeks that passed had been essentially free of any otherworldly threats, they had also been disappointingly free of anything about Idonia. After Joshua's and Win's surprising about-face, the friends had hoped that meant much more was to come. Still, while Joshua and Win continued their inviting personas, the opportunities ceased presenting themselves. Moreover, the friends, and Thad when he was visiting, continued working tirelessly through the library, hoping to discover more about Idonia and the Davpyr, but it was to no avail.

After the discovery of the excerpt about *The Watcher*, the trail had gone completely cold. The friends had searched every single name and phrase they could try and searched through countless shelves still hoping to find the actual books of *The Watcher* or *Primus Stella*, but had found nothing aside from the initial references. It felt to the friends that the library was working in congress with the Brownings to intentionally entice them but not actually divulge anything until the proper moment.

Visits with the Brownings had given them minimal opportunities as they were often filled with schoolwork or mixed company that made the friends unsure about asking questions. The Brownings were still equally as inviting, almost drawing the friends in closer. Their discussions had become increasingly relaxed, more like old friends than obscure acquaintances still getting to know one another. The Brownings had invited the friends to dinner at Marc and Lili's and even to take a trip up to New York to visit Ceph and Lavy. Every time, though, something would go awry in the friends' plans, and they would be unable to attend. Working to get ever closer to the Brownings, the friends had returned the hospitality and invited them over for dinner. Still, Joshua and Win were busy those evenings, to no one's surprise.

What did surprise the group, though, was that Joshua and Win accepted, without hesitation, an invitation to Thanksgiving dinner with the friends' families back home. The group was utterly taken aback by that. What all of them were sure would be met with a polite refusal or an excuse for being unable to attend was accepted readily. There were no disclaimers or tentative addendums, simply an immediate agreement from Joshua and Win that they would drive down with the friends on the Wednesday before Thanksgiving to meet their families and have dinner. Amidst all the continued failures to establish and successfully carry out events with the Brownings, the friends were still skeptical but surprisingly less so than they had been about anything else.

Thus was the changing nature of their time spent visiting with the Brownings. When the Brownings were in town, that was. Despite many study sessions and dinners, Joshua and Win still seemed to be out of town almost every weekend. The friends had debated at multiple points whether they were dealing with the stuff that Harbilin needed, visiting friends, or working on some nefarious deal they didn't want to know about. At one point, they had even tossed around the notion they were going to sporting events or concerts.

While they had enjoyed a stretch of less chaotic days than their first few weeks getting to know the Brownings, by the time October had faded, the group was growing restless with the constant evasion and inability to discover anything new from the Brownings or the library. They had found no further information about Idonia or the family over that span, and every time they thought they were getting close to something, it would slip away from them. More and more so, the Brownings kept cutting visits short at night, either refusing to stay and visit after dinner or saying that they had something they needed to do after a study session. Every time the friends thought they were starting to figure the Brownings out, they would change yet again.

One Saturday night, the friends had finally had enough. It was the first time in weeks Thad hadn't visited as he needed to be home with his grandmother that weekend. Which was juxtaposed by the fact that Van had randomly appeared in town to visit for the first time since the Brownings mysterious week away. The evening was made even more strange by the quickly thrown together plans at Brave New Restaurant. Since meeting the Brownings, it was the one place that had guaranteed maximum dinner guests, formalities, and no discussion of Idonia. The friends couldn't help feeling it was done so intentionally.

The evening did at least give them a chance to visit with Lauren again, which they were coming to enjoy more and more. She and Terry were very quickly becoming commonplace in the friends' lives, one they realized they were coming to appreciate more and more. Still, the evening also brought with it an ominous feeling that loomed over the dinner. Despite the pleasantries, the friends couldn't escape the notion that something was awry, and just as they'd expected when dinner came to an end, Joshua and Win politely evaded, stating they were going to spend some time with Van before he had to leave again.

Something in the friends snapped that night. They were fed up dodging and were tired of chasing. It had almost been more manageable when the Brownings gave them the stonewall front. At least then, it was clear the friends needed to proceed with caution. That was gone, though. The Brownings had intentionally baited them. Joshua had directly invited them to ask questions, and then they took it all away. It's like the Brownings had started playing a game, and the friends wanted to know why.

As the dinner participants all went their separate ways, the friends circled the block and made their way to Terry's apartment. They parked on the far side of the next street over and waited. Van appeared shortly after to drop Terry off, and, as they had expected, Joshua and Win were right behind him. They waited outside while the two went upstairs.

"We sure about this?" Ally asked as the friends watched out the windows.

"I haven't been sure about a damn thing since we met 'em," Erin said, not breaking her stare from the back seat.

"Same," Rachel added. "Ever since that day, though, it's like they've been different people. Different than the different they already were."

"Least we're in agreement then." Ally replied. "Showtime."

Van had reappeared not long after, but instead of getting back into his car, he climbed in with the Brownings. Without hesitation, the three men set off, and the friends followed. The friends worked to keep a distance and not draw attention to themselves as they tracked the Brownings through downtown and toward the financial district. There was still some traffic to give them cover, but it was beginning to thin, making the friends anxious.

"Red light ahead," Erin called out, leaning upward into the front seat area as she pointed towards the light.

"Turn down this side road and then flip around real quick." Rachel said. "We can put a car or two between us. Give us some more cover."

Ally did so, and they were fortunate enough to have two cars roll ahead as they had hoped. They continued on the trail of the three men as they wove through town until they pulled into the covered parking lot of an old abandoned building.

"Keep driving past." Rachel said, sinking back into her seat.

"Yeah," Ally replied, "I'll double back and park."

She drove down to the next block and turned to come around the other side of the parking structure, switching her lights off as she did to avoid being seen. They parked but didn't get out so they wouldn't be noticed. The friends were surprised at how many cars were in the parking lot and thought they couldn't all belong to people in the abandoned building. They saw Joshua, Van, and Win as they vanished down a staircase alongside the building, but they continued to wait in the car to avoid being caught. For a moment, they wondered if they were at one of the countless buildings owned by the Brownings even more elusive employers, but after about ten minutes had passed, the girls figured they should make their move if they genuinely wanted to know what the Brownings were doing.

They crossed the parking lot calmly and slowly, hoping they didn't look out of place. No one else had entered or exited the building. Approaching the corner, they saw the staircase leading down where Van and the Browning brothers had disappeared. They walked down the stairs very carefully, unsure of what waited for them below. At the bottom, the friends found nothing but a steel door where the men must have entered, but the door was chained shut with a large padlock sealing it. They could hear yelling coming from inside, though. Erin gave the chain a quick, gentle shake to make sure, and the master lock came unhinged- a decoy.

Ally opened the door as the friends watched over their shoulders to make sure no one had seen. No one did, except the pair of eyes they didn't know were hidden in the distance. A chill crept down their skin, and they rushed into the door, afraid of being caught, slamming directly into a wall. Only it wasn't a wall. It was a man.

"You ladies look a little lost. The theater's a few blocks down." A large, barrel-chested man with dark skin stared down at them. His head was shaved so clean it shined, but a large, thick beard decorated his face and was starting to show grey in spots. He was frightening, but not intentionally. It was mainly just his size, stuffed into that tiny hallway, and the air of power emanating from him was intimidating.

The friends could hear the screams growing louder and louder from behind the doorway the man blocked, lots of screams. *Fifty, a hundred, two hundred?* They couldn't tell, but they knew they had to get in.

"We're friends of Joshua and Win Browning," Erin said, hoping she sounded more confident than she felt. "They just went in there with our friend Van, and they wanted us to come watch. We were a little behind in getting here, so they went in without us." Watch what they thought. They had no idea what was behind the door, but if yelling and cheering were involved, people must have been watching something.

"No, they didn't." He said flatly.

"Excuse me, sir," Rachel cut in, "but they did just go in there. We know that."

"I'm not saying they didn't." He replied, keeping his same level of calm. "I'm saying they didn't want you to come to watch."

"Why do you say that?" Ally asked incredulously.

He leaned down close to them so they could see his eyes clearly in the dim light. "Because, if they wanted you to come, I'd already know who you are. And trust me, ladies, if you're friends with those men, and I don't know who you are, you don't want to see what's going on in there." The man's bulging arms stayed folded over his burly chest, refusing to let the girls pass.

Not knowing what else to do, Ally reached into her pockets and pulled out two twenty dollars, turning to the rest to see if they had any cash. Almost a hundred between them. They hoped it would be enough.

"Does this change your mind?" Ally said, trying her best to sound like she'd done this before.

"A valiant effort," he said with a grin, "but it just further proves how out of place you are. Your money's no good here."

The friends were on the verge of accepting defeat. Ally and Erin didn't know what else to do, but the word money rang inside Rachel's head for a moment before it finally clicked into place. She quickly began searching through her jacket pockets, knowing she had it with her. She hadn't let it leave her person since the day she found it. Finally, her hand landed on it, and she let out a sigh of relief.

"What about this?" She asked, holding up the strange coin for the man to see.

"Well, well." He replied with great surprise. "You three are most unexpected, but then again, I suppose I should have expected that. Go on in. Keep the coin, though. You might need it."

He slid to the side of the hallway to give them access to the door, giving them a beaming smile as he did, equal parts proud and amused.

The friends paused for a minute, afraid to move forward. They had wanted to know what Joshua and Win were doing, why Van accompanied them that night, but after all the smoke and mirrors, they became uncertain. They questioned themselves, wondering if they were pushing too far. The abandoned building was clearly meant to scare people away. The lock on the door was clearly meant to deter people from seeing what was going on inside, and the large man with his tree trunk of an arm outstretched towards the door in front of them had given them every warning that they were not meant to be there. Yet, they were. They had to go on. They had gone that far, and they weren't about to turn back.

"Oh, and ladies," the man said in a cordial but solemn tone as the three moved towards the door, "let it be known, I did warn you."

They pushed through the door and were immediately assaulted by the scent of blood and sweat mixing in the air. The cheers echoing around them were deafening. There had been no people inside that building. They were animals, bloodthirsty monsters foaming at the mouth for their next victim. The friends feared for themselves as much as whoever the fiends' poor victim might be.

The three pushed their way through the people, afraid they might be struck at any moment from the cries for blood. The friends were blocked out at the back of the angry horde and had to walk around the outskirts until they finally found an opening. Bleachers formed on either side of them as they made their way through the crowd in the middle. Together the creatures looked like packs of feral dogs, teeth bared and gnashing at any and everything, yet they were ordinary, everyday people. Some of them still had on their suits from work, others were dressed up as if on a night out, but all of them screamed for the same thing.

On the far left end of the building, the friends could see a bar stretching across where the monsters placed their bets and bought booze to fuel their unquenchable thirst for blood. As the three moved slowly closer to the center of the circle, they saw a trail of crimson on the ground leading off to one side accompanied by two lines breaking up the dirt on the concrete that they assumed must have been where the monsters' last victim had been dragged out of the arena. *What were Joshua and Win and Van doing in a place like this?* They thought but did not want to know the answer.

The trail of blood thickened as the friends made their way deeper into the fray, and they realized at once that more than just a single victim had been dragged out through the path they walked. Between the bodies in front of them, they could just make out the edge of a wooden structure. Deeper into the pack, the hyenas seemed to grow even more vicious, salivating at the mere scent of blood that made the friends all want to vomit. They wanted to turn back, to run, but they knew they couldn't. Part of them pressed forward because they needed to know what was waiting in the arena, and the other part pushed forward out of fear the vultures would descend on them the moment they spotted an outsider that tried to flee.

They were almost to the center when the friends noticed the wooden object they had spotted before was a chest-high barrier keeping the buzzards from swooping on whatever prey was pinned up inside. The friends could smell the metal in the blood and the salt in the sweat at that point. They could taste it on their tongues when they breathed as if it were sweat dripping into their mouths where they just bit their lip. The friends turned to run away, but the crowd pushed them forward. The mob seemed to taunt them, screaming, yelling, cheering at the sight of it all. The friends had moved so far in they were but a single row of rabid dogs from the barrier when they caught sight of two men across the arena. Win and Van stood cheering, screaming over the edge of the railing, leading the pack of wild beasts.

The friends moved forward carefully to keep the front row of people blocking them from Win's and Van's view, though they seemed far too interested in what was in the arena to ever notice. Finally, the friends had worked up the courage to poke their heads through the front line and saw a monstrous man, shirtless, with blood covering his knuckles from an unknown number of fights as he bared his teeth at his and the crowd's next victim, Joshua Browning.

Joshua stood unfazed by the brute's attempts. The friends saw just how much muscle Joshua really carried on his once average-looking frame with his shirt off and wondered how he had ever kept it hidden underneath his suits. The muscles in his arms and chests looked as if they threatened to tear through the skin holding them back. Markings of some kind decorated his body with the same silvery glow the friends had seen on Win and Marc, but he moved too swiftly throughout the arena to tell what they were. One started from his upper-right rib and reached toward the edge of his chiseled abdomen as it stretched all the way down to his sculpted obliques. Something lay at the center of the marking, like a crest of some sort, from which an array of lines extended. Another stretched across his broad shoulders and crept down the crevice formed by his taut back. Despite Joshua's powerful, shredded physique, the man opposite him had clearly been the fan-favorite. Joshua kept his arms at his side, not even attempting to hit the man. Instead, he just dodged every swing the man sent his way with ease.

Joshua was a blur as he moved. His dark hair was pulled back and whipped wildly with each dodge. Such speed, such agility, and he did it with so much ease. Joshua hadn't even broken a sweat, and the thin strip of leather-wrapped double around his neck had barely shifted a single bead that adorned it.

The man's frustration had grown with every missed strike until he was throwing wild haymakers in desperation. He went in for a kill shot of a right hook, but Joshua merely slid underneath and around the man. In a wild fury, the beast reversed and spun around, landing a blow square on Joshua's jaw before he was able to adjust. The friends had seen the blood fly from his mouth and splash into the dirt as he took a step back to change his stance.

Somehow, though, Joshua seemed unhurt by the first hit despite the blood running down his chin. Before the friends could blink, the man landed a second blow to Joshua's nose, then a third to his ribs, lifting him slightly in the air. Joshua took a couple steps back and laughed at the man, his perfect white teeth stained red with his own blood. He spat the blood on the ground in front of him, continuing to smile, but the smile had turned wicked. The friends were not watching a sanctioned prize fight. There would be no tap-outs or victory by points from the judges in that den of jackals. The friends watched a bare-knuckle knockout battle unfold before their very eyes.

The man lunged for Joshua again, landing a fourth blow square on his temple and making him slow to step back. Slow enough that the man landed a fifth blow into Joshua's stone abdomen. The man pulled back his right arm again for his final killing blow.

The friends heard Win and Van yell in unison, "Just do it already!"

They buried their faces in their hands, unable to watch as they heard the sound of a fist crashing hard against bone. The crowd erupted. Screams shook the friends as they tried to regain control. Erin's and Rachel's cringing faces were buried in their hands. Ally's body began to wretch, but she refused to let herself vomit. Instead, she stood there dry heaving, refusing to let the beasts win and see her show weakness. Rachel and Erin fought back the tears as they huddled together over Ally. They would not give the monsters around them the satisfaction. Slowly, the friends stood and took deep breaths, filling their mouths with the taste of metal. They knew they had to look. The thought of Joshua lying broken on the ground hurt them in a way they couldn't explain, but they had to know how badly he'd been damaged. Locking hands with one another, they forced their eyes back towards the arena and let out a harmonious gasp.

Joshua stood, towering over the limp body of the man he'd just knocked unconscious with a single blow.

Every rabid monster in the room had gone insane. Those who had bet on Joshua were screaming in joy, while the others who bet on the lump of a body lying in the dirt cried out in agony. A bloody smile spread across Joshua's face making him look more sinister than the friends thought anyone could ever look. Yet at the same time, he was beautiful, a lion bloodied after a battle but still a lion no less. His rough years growing up had turned him into a machine, but underneath that, all the friends could still see the kind-hearted man they'd come to know and respect, who loved his family more than anything, shining through the blood in his smile.

Joshua made his way over to Win and Van, spitting out another puddle of blood as he went. Win and Van met him with open embraces as they shook their heads and called him a showoff. Then, to the friends' surprise, Joshua walked over to the man and helped him up. He was regaining consciousness as Joshua helped him over to his friends at the side. They quickly thanked Joshua before they rushed him out the side door. The friends were outright perplexed.

Back with his brother and their friend, Joshua climbed over the railing and clapped Win on the shoulder. Without even flinching, Win pulled his shirt off and leaped over the edge of the barrier. The friends turned to leave the second he landed. They couldn't bear the sight of him being turned all bloody too, or even worse, breaking someone apart like Joshua had. They shoved people out of the way, no longer caring what anyone thought. Ally slowly formed the head of the spear as her feet began to move faster and faster until she ran for the door with Erin and Rachel right on her heels. They busted the door open, shoving the guard aside as Ally fell to her hands and knees, gasping for air that didn't taste of blood and sweat. Erin and Rachel collapsed against the walls of the hallway beside her, eyes fixed on one another.

"Told ya y'all didn't wanna go in there." The guard said, closing the door behind him and retaking his post. "If any of y'all are gonna puke, please do it outside."

They rested there, Ally staring at the ground and Erin and Rachel at each other when one by one, the friends felt a giant hand grab them gently by the arm and lift them up. The guard looked deep into their eyes in turn, searching to see if they were alright. He brushed the dust off their clothes and smiled kindly at them.

"All those terrible thoughts swimmin' 'round in y'all's heads right now, just forget 'em darlin. He's a good man. So's Win and Van. Don't let what you saw in there tonight tell ya any different. You children go on home now. You look like you could use some rest." The gentle giant opened the door for the three girls as they exited.

They paused before leaving as they heard the voice inside announcing Win's fight. Part of them wanted to go back inside, but they couldn't bring themselves to do so. One horrific sight was enough for the evening.

"If y'all can get over the thoughts you're having right now, maybe I'll see ya again come some time. Drive safe. It's dark out." He closed the door behind the friends, and they headed up the stairs.

Back in the car, they sat for ten, twenty, thirty minutes. They knew they should start the vehicle. They needed to go home for one, but it also would only look more suspicious over time if they continued to sit in the dark parking lot. Not to mention eventually, the Browning brothers and Van would be out at some time. They didn't want to be seen there, not by them. At the same time, Ally couldn't bring herself to start the car, and neither Rachel nor Erin could get themselves to tell her to do so. They wanted to tell someone, feeling that somehow, if they shared the information, it would make it less haunting, but there was no one to tell. They were already in the car with one another. Everyone had seen. Then all at once, it clicked, and Ally took out her phone and called Thad.

"Do you know what time it is?" Was all they heard as Thad answered the phone.

"Thad, it's all of us." Ally said, hearing her uneven breathing as she spoke, and Rachel and Erin both greeted him as well.

"Oh shit. What's wrong?"

They launched into the full story of what had happened that night. Thad just listened in silence to the point Ally wondered if he had dozed off a few times, but they kept going regardless. Thad was silent for a moment after they finished recounting the night's events.

"You still there, Thad?" Erin asked finally.

"Yeah," he replied, "so when are we going back?"

"Back?" Ally asked, exacerbated. "Why the hell would we go back there?"

"Because we want to know why?" Thad's voice sounded genuinely confused.

His only focus was better understanding the enigmatic family, and it shocked Ally to learn how casual he was about it. Erin and Rachel, though, were beginning to understand him. What they had just witnessed was brutal, but it was still the same family they were trying to comprehend. Seeing the looks on her friends' faces, Ally found herself even more lost. The decision was already made, though. So, she put the car in drive, and they drove off into the night.

20
WE GIVE THANKS

The only thing stranger than the night in the fighting pits was that the Brownings seemed as if nothing had ever happened. They were their same overtly mysterious group the week after the fights as they had been before, and if the girls had not witnessed the event with their own eyes, they never would have believed that Joshua had recently spent a few moments as a punching bag. The girls half wondered if they had imagined the entire event, but given that they each remembered it vividly, that proved unlikely.

Still, they couldn't shake the fact that the Brownings were not only intentionally enigmatic, they were also the type of people who had no trouble maintaining clandestine double lives. That was a fact that troubled the friends most of all and one they carried all the way to the week of Thanksgiving. As the day neared, the friends grew more concerned about the two men they would introduce to their families. They were polite and charming without question. Their parents would all love Joshua and Win, but who exactly the mysterious men were was a question the girls still hadn't answered after months of searching.

Their classes on Monday before the holiday were all effortless. Being that they did not have classes Wednesday and Friday that week their professors had them discuss some reading prompts of various historical events to pass the day but still have them learn something. The friends were surprised to get an email just before lunch that stated History through War had been canceled for the day. It was the third time Edmonton had canceled class since the week both he and the Brownings were out of town, the week of the first murder.

The peculiar timing of both his and the Brownings comings and goings had not escaped the friends. They hadn't placed it yet, but they knew there was more to all the scheduling oddities. From visits with the Brownings being cut short or not happening because they were out of town to crunched classes to make up for the ones Edmonton had canceled, everything about the friends' schedules had seemed to shift in a manner that forced their time to rush by, only to find themselves suddenly alone with nothing to do but wonder.

That week, though, the friends were not upset by the fact class had been canceled. It was still strange, as had been the times before, but they were so anxious and excited about the break that they pushed it from their minds. They took Monday afternoon and all day Tuesday as an opportunity to pack and relax in preparation for their trip home. Even without Joshua and Win, it was already guaranteed to be an interesting trip. It was the longest they had been home since moving to Little Rock, and they weren't sure what almost a week back in South Arkansas would even entail. Much to the friends' confusion, though, the start of that week also had been devoid of the Brownings. Not only did they not see Joshua or Win on campus or at The Brew, but Lili had been absent as well. With no communication from the family by Tuesday, they had begun wondering if the last-minute dodge by the Brownings that they had been expecting had finally come to pass.

They woke early that Wednesday morning, fully anticipating such. The friends quickly worked to get ready and load their bags for the journey home, but they quickly realized it no longer felt like going home. The friends had only been away for a few months, but that short span had felt like ages. Their house, The Daily Brew, the entire city around them, and even the Brownings had changed their lives so much over those few months. Their house was their new home, and going back to South Arkansas was no longer a trip home but merely a trip to visit family.

After a quick lap through the house to make sure they hadn't forgotten anything, the friends drove down the block to The Brew to see if Joshua and Win would actually be joining them. They parked in the garage across from the coffee shop, scanning the other cars before making their way inside. Much to their shock, the two brothers were waiting at the counter holding the friends' to-go drinks.

Both men had taken their attire to another level. Win, who was usually wearing one of his assorted colorful t-shirts, wore a vibrant paisley button-down shirt that popped with bright greens and blues that danced in a rhythmic flow across his body. Over the fluid paisley shirt, he wore a soft grey suede motorcycle jacket adorned with a pink trimmed pocket square that popped against his outfit. His slacks were fitted perfectly for him as they hugged his sculpted legs. Befitting his flashy yet casual style, though, Win wore a pair of custom sneakers with grey suede outers to match his jacket, while the tongues were the same electric paisley of his shirt, effectively mirroring his upper body.

On the other hand, Joshua did not have a casual thing about him as he stood against the counter in a double-breasted silk blazer in a deep navy shade with pinstripes echoed by his grey striped button-down. His tie was intentional but straightforward, along with his pocket square in a bright green that matched his brother's more extravagant flare. All of which he had pulled together with a striking grey leather banded watch and matching monk straps that drew from the grey of his shirt to create an outfit of such intent only his brother could match.

The friends couldn't help feeling overwhelmed by the decision they had made. It was their decision, albeit provoked by some of their families' behest, to invite the Brownings to Thanksgiving. Their families had been inquisitive about their newfound friends, and as much as it confused them, they too had wanted to introduce the Brownings to their family. Seeing the two men waiting for them in The Brew that day, though, quickly reminded the girls how genuinely different the Brownings were from everything they had ever known. The friends were taking Joshua and Win to a dinner where the fanciest outfit might be a nice sweater with a pair of cute jeans and some booties. Meanwhile, the two men the friends brought to dinner looked like they had stepped off a Ralph Lauren runway.

It was a simple thing, really, one's attire. "Clothes don't make the man" was a phrase all three of the friends grew up knowing. It was more than that, though. Joshua and Win didn't just dress differently; they were different. Their appearance was merely an outward reflection of the undeniable truth that they were, without question, unlike everything else in Ally, Erin, and Rachel's world. It was a complex concept to rationalize, but the friends knew they had no other option as they moved towards the counter to greet the two strange men, speeding forward unto the collision of their two worlds.

Win greeted them with his usual effortlessly radiant charm as he handed out their drinks. "Good morning, ladies. I trust everyone is ready for a lovely trip. Joshua and I were unsure of what time you would want to leave since you did not specify a time, so we have been waiting here for you. Hopefully, we are not too early. You know it probably would be wise for us to exchange contact information at some point."

The revelation hit the friends suddenly. They had spent every bit of free time they could over the past few months with those two men and their families, and never once had they thought to get so much as a phone number. Even Van had offered his number the first day the friends met him, yet Joshua and Win had never even mentioned it. The friends realized at that moment that the entire time they had spent with the Brownings, they could count on one hand the time they had seen one of them even using a phone. What's more, the three friends, who spent as much time on their phones as anyone in their early twenties, had hardly even thought to use them when they were with the Brownings. It was as if when they were around the two men and their family, they existed within a bubble where the outside world became a distant reality. It was strange, bizarre, yet somehow it had not fazed them at all.

"You got a point." Erin began. "We may want to go ahead and do that now if y'all plan on following us down. Might have to call at some point if somebody needs to stop or anything."

"Smart thinking." Win said playfully as he took out his phone. "We did intend to follow you, of course. It seemed the simplest solution. That way, we can depart when everything is over. We assumed you would likely be staying for the rest of the break, naturally."

"Indeed," Rachel replied as she entered their contact details, "and y'all are welcome to stay as long as you like. Our families kinda just graze all day and come and go as they feel like."

"Yeah, it's basically an all-day buffet. We'll do actual dinner sometime in the evening once the turkey and everything is done, but up until then, everybody just hangs out and snacks. We're ready to head out whenever, though. Might be a little more peaceful for you to get there before everybody arrives." Ally added.

"Well," Joshua said, "after you then, I suppose."

With that, the friends set off on the two-hour, anxiety-filled drive to their families'. Every minute that took them closer to the inevitable meeting. They each were frustrated with themselves. They had presented the idea, orchestrated it, yet they couldn't help feeling apprehensive as the moment finally drew near. Every mile marker brought them closer to the meeting of their new life in Little Rock and the old they were steadily leaving behind. They wished they had been able to all ride together. At least that would have provided conversation to distract from the drive. With just the three of them in the car, no one could think of a topic that wasn't the impending event, and so they rode in silence as Joshua and Win Browning cruised along behind them, unaware of what lay ahead.

A couple of hours later, the friends pulled into Ally's house with the Brownings right behind them. Ally had taken note that they drove Lili's car instead of their Roadster and couldn't help wondering if it had been intentional to appear less ostentatious. Then it dawned on her that there would be no way for them to recharge it if they needed, and she hoped dearly they anticipated such. She had grown more nervous by the moment she realized and everything was stressing her. Rachel and Erin were on edge, too, she could tell, but the time had come whether they were ready or not.

Joshua and Win helped the friends grab their things before they began surveying the area. The two men took in all the sights and scents, acclimated themselves to the new location as they looked up and down the neighborhood at the houses and the flora that grew all around. Ally led the procession up the walkway to the house, but when she opened the door to go in, she noticed Joshua and Win were still at the foot of the steps staring off into the forest.

"What are you two doing? Let's go." Ally motioned into the house.

"My apologies," Joshua said, turning back towards her with a smile. "The trees here are beautiful, is all. You have to keep in mind we spend most of our time in the city, so it can be very refreshing just being around nature." He turned and took one last long look at the trees.

"You can look at the trees all day. Will y'all please come inside already?" Erin said as she chuckled at the two men. "Ms. Cammie's gonna come out here and get you if you don't."

Joshua and Win heard a voice from inside the house that could only be Ally's mom. She had not heard the door open but did manage to hear Ally's statement. Joshua and Win both made for the house with a smile.

The fair woman popped out from the kitchen with deep reddish-brown hair, followed by Lace in full trot. She gave her daughter a quick hug and took her bags as the dog circled them both. Then she turned to Joshua and Win, who looked strikingly out of place as picturesque representations of urban high society standing in Cammie's kitchen that looked like it belonged in a *Southern Living* feature. Lace immediately noticed them and skipped right past Rachel and Erin to begin sniffing the two men intently. Win reached down to pet her, and she practically melted in his hands.

"Well, look at you two. I can see why these gals are so hung up on you." She smiled and turned playfully to Ally. "You certainly undersold it when you said how handsome they were."

Ally's face turned beet red, "Thank you, mom." She huffed at her slightly as Erin and Rachel both chuckled in the background. "If you're all done now, this is Joshua and Win Browning. Joshua, Win, this is my mom, Cammie."

"Our mom," Erin interjected, giving Cammie a vast grin. "She's basically everybody's mom. We all practically grew up over here."

Joshua gently grabbed her right hand in his and cupped it with his left. "It is a genuine pleasure to meet you, madam. You have a lovely home, and you have raised a fine bunch of children."

Cammie blushed at his sincerity and charm.

"Could not agree more, my lady." Win said as he wrapped Cammie in a loving embrace. "I can see how your daughter got her striking beauty."

Ally's face only got redder. She should have known bringing home Joshua and Win would lead to such. Cammie was even blushing still when Win released her.

"And what charmers, yet another plus." Cammie smiled at the girls. "Better keep Mimi away from him, or may not be able to leave. You gentlemen look very nice, by the way. Handsome, well dressed, charming, now all you need is a small fortune, and you're practically a storybook character." The friends all look at one another, not wanting to address the elephant in the room as the brothers merely shrugged off the compliments. "Then, of course, you Win also have the whole fact that you saved my daughter's life going for you."

"I assure you she was in very little danger." He smiled beautifully. "To be honest, she easily could have stood up and walked out of the street in time."

"Well, there's no need to stand here and be awkward. Let's get those bags put up and get you something to drink. A little liquid courage before the masses arrive couldn't hurt. Now I'm a wine drinker myself, but Ally tells me you're a whiskey drinker Joshua, so I picked up a bottle from Spartan Distillery. It's a local spot here in town. I don't know much about whiskey, so I just went with what they recommended."

"I would love to try a glass then," Joshua said, letting Cammie take the bag from his shoulder.

"Sure thing." She replied. "Win, I believe Ally said you're a Gin drinker, but I don't know any gin recipes or even what a good gin is. We can run and get you something real quick if you like."

"Oh no, that is unnecessary. I will gladly have a glass of that whiskey you mentioned. I would much rather try something unique and local than something I can get anywhere.

"Now Ally, if you and the girls wouldn't mind settin' the tables, please. I already set the second one up on the deck."

Ally stopped when she said that. "Why did you need the second one up?"

"Well, how else would we fit Erin and Rachel's folks along with our crew? I'm sure Mimi, Pops, and the boys'll be here any minute."

"Oh dear God." Ally whispered under her breath. Thad was fine, of course. Mimi and Pops were sure to make things awkward, but Nick and Matt were an entirely different story. She couldn't believe her mother invited them too.

"Wait, does that mean Thad is coming too?" Rachel asked, thinking about something completely different than Ally.

"I mean, do we do any dinners where Thad doesn't come," Cammie replied rhetorically.

"Fuck me." Rachel said where only Erin and Rachel could hear. Introducing her parents to a guy she had a mild crush on was one thing. Her parents and Thad together in the same room was a completely different headache. Combining the two things into one dinner was enough to make her almost nauseous.

Ally rushed and put her bags upstairs in her room and flew back down. Then the three friends led Joshua and Win into the dining room and began nervously setting the table. The handful of forks Ally was carrying came loose as she approached the table, and two fell out of her hands. She listened for the clank but heard nothing. She looked down to see Joshua had caught both of them just inches off the floor.

"Is everything alright?" He asked with a bewildered look on his face.

The friends all stopped what they were doing and took deep breaths in unison.

"It's just my annoying ass cousins. I didn't realize my mom was going to invite them. They're great friends. They can just be a bit of dicks to outsiders, especially when it's guys. Lord, when Erin brought her first boyfriend over, they wouldn't even acknowledge his presence. Throw that in with the fact they love to embarrass me, and I'm just dreading them eating with us."

"Not to mention," Erin began, "Rachel's parents are still hung up on her and Thad getting back together. So anytime he's around, they continually drop blatantly obvious suggestions that they think no one gets but them."

"Yeah," Rachel said with notes of dread in her voice, "it gets awkward, to say the least. So, welcome to our families. Yay."

"I am sure they all will behave just fine. No need to worry." Win smiled as the front door opened.

"And here they are. Great." Ally sighed, setting down the last fork.

"It's just me!" They heard Thad call out from the hallway, and the friends let out a collective sigh of relief.

"We're in the dining room." Ally called back.

"What's up, guys?" Thad said as he reached the room. "I flew over here so I could beat the rest of the crew and hopefully help brace for impact. They're right behind me, though. Can we just all agree to at least not leave anyone alone tonight?"

"Fuck that," Erin said sarcastically. "You three are the ones that gotta deal with the shit. I'm gonna go sit out on the deck and drink by the old folks."

The friends all laughed, even Joshua and Win let out a chuckle, and the mood eased, if only a little. The calm before the storm had to end, though, as the doorbell rang, sounding the arrival of the first round of guests.

"Relax. It will be ok." Joshua said, following the friends from the dining room.

They entered the living room, and all eyes turned to Win and Joshua. Lace ran back and forth between all the people getting her hellos. Mimi and Pops made their way towards Cammie, but Matt and Nick stayed back, doing their best to intimidate Joshua and Win. Mimi and Pops both gave Cammie a quick hello as they studied the two men.

"Mimi, Pops," Cammie began the introductions, "these are the girls' friends Joshua and Win."

"It is a real pleasure to meet you both." Win said, giving Pops a firm handshake followed by a gentle one to Mimi as Joshua did so in reverse. "Ally speaks very highly of you. You have helped raise a very wonderful granddaughter."

"Well, she at least has good taste in men." Mimi winked at Ally as she held Win's hand tightly, sending Ally's face into a bright shade of red. "You seem to be quite the gentlemen."

Pops simply nodded his approval at both Joshua and Win.

Then Joshua took the forward approach and walked over to Matt and Nick. Neither said anything as they proceeded to stare him down. Unaffected, Joshua reached out his hand to Nick and introduced himself.

"So you must be the pretty little city boy Ally's been talking about," Nick said as he shook Joshua's hand, clearly trying to overpower him.

"I am truly flattered you find me pretty. You must be the annoying ass cousins she was just describing in the kitchen." Joshua smiled as he offered his hand to Matt.

"Zing!" Thad shouted as he and the girls all chuckled. Even Cammie cracked a smile.

The cousins both shut their mouths, obviously having no comeback. Instead, they just brushed by him and made their way into the kitchen. Win shook hands with the two young men as they passed by, not bothering to address Joshua's comments, preferring just to let it sit with them.

"Don't mind them. They're a couple o' punks, but they mean well. Most of the time, anyways." Cammie said as the door opened and Rachel's parents entered.

Rachel rushed over to greet her parents before they made it to Thad. "Mom, Dad, I'd like you to meet Joshua and Win, our friends from school."

"I would not even need an introduction to tell you are Rachel's mother," Joshua said as he took her hand gently. "A woman as lovely as she could have only been made by a vision such as yourself. You, sir, are a lucky man." He added as he shook her father's hand.

"Oh, trust me, I know." He replied. "I've been blessed just to have both of 'em."

"I could not agree with Joshua's assessment more." Win said, shaking both their hands in turn. "It is truly a pleasure to meet the people responsible for raising such a wonderful person."

"Well, Rach," her mother began with a big smile, "you said they were nice, but you left out charming."

Rachel was thrilled to see it going so smoothly until her dad finished shaking hands with Win and saw Thad.

"Thad, my boy," he began as Rachel cringed, "it's good to see you again. It feels like it's been ages since you came over."

Rachel turned to Erin and mouthed, "Just shoot me now."

Erin didn't have a chance to respond, though, as her parents came in right as Rachel's were walking into the kitchen.

"Hey, Er Bear!" Erin's dad said as he wrapped her in a big hug. "Missed ya' sweetie. I take it these must be your friends since they're the only people I don't recognize."

"Hey, sweetie." Her mom said quietly as she gave Erin a soft kiss on the side of her head.

"You guessed right, Dad." Erin began. "This is Joshua and Win Browning."

Joshua shook Erin's father's and mother's hands in turn as he spoke. "Mr. and Mrs. Cartwright, it is an absolute joy to meet you finally. Let me tell you; it has been a real treat getting to know your daughter. She is a truly remarkable individual."

Erin was surprised to realize she felt both flattered and mildly embarrassed by Joshua's words. His and Win's compliments about Ally and Rachel had felt normal, expected even for what she knew of the two men. His words about her, though, caught her off guard. She was the snarky one, constantly questioning and disrupting. She knew when she heard him speak, though, that he wasn't just saying that out of politeness. He truly meant it, and that struck Erin.

The introductions all concluded the friends braced themselves for the awkward questioning that would ensue as the day continued as the usual Thanksgiving pleasantries commenced. The various friends and family weaved in and out of the living room, kitchen, and dining room as they either helped make food, eat food, or get out of the way of the two prior groups. As with every gathering of the type, there was a television on in every room with either a ball game or local broadcast station on, all turned down so that no one could hear as no one but the older men occasionally.

The rest of the day consisted of everyone taking turns asking Joshua and Win questions and then grilling them about their responses. It was a repetitive process of "so what do you do" and "what brought you here" and "what line of work are your folks in" and so on as Joshua and Win graciously fielded the same questions over and over from different people as none of them would ever gather in one solid group at a time. Pops sat quietly and listened to Joshua's and Win's stories, while Mimi followed them around and "awed" at all the right moments. Matt and Nick did lighten up, but they still tried to work in jokes where they could. Erin's and Rachel's parents bounced back and forth between questions and talking about what they did for a living as they alternated between chatting and preparing food for dinner. Rachel's dad was always in charge of frying the turkey. Erin's mom had her dressing down to an art, while her dad would always have a variety of smoked meats and cheeses he'd prepared for his charcuterie board. Erin's and Ally's moms worked in tandem like seasoned partners getting broccoli salads, mashed potatoes, macaroni and cheese, and rolls all prepared. Mimi always had a dip and dessert that she prepared in advance, so she could just sit and chat with everyone.

The day continued like that. A naturally choreographed dance where all the members knew their roles, and somehow Joshua and Win fit in naturally. It stunned the friends. They had expected things to be awkward, and there was certainly no shortage of awkward moments. Joshua and Win, though, didn't seem fazed by it in the least. They took everything in stride, never letting a jab go unresponded or a compliment go unreciprocated. Ally, Erin, Rachel, and Thad all watched in amazement as the two men effortlessly handled the entire chaos that was their family gatherings. It occurred to them all as they watched it unfold that this was likely the most either Joshua or Win had ever had to entertain such a variety of conversations and answer such a list of questions. They were private and elusive intentionally, and yet there they were, sticking out like two sore thumbs and yet taking everything the day threw at them in stride.

"So Joshua, Win," Nick said when the group finally sat down for dinner, trying to sound as gruff as he could, "what are your intentions with our little girls here?"

All of the parents laughed, but Pops and the boys listened in seriously.

"Well," Joshua began, "I know I speak for both of us when I say we simply wish to be good friends to them and get to know them as best I can. Is that alright with you?"

The laughter began again as everyone enjoyed their food. The collection of families talked more about what was going on in their lives and finally let Joshua and Win off the hot seat. Towards the end of the meal, Cammie broke up the banter.

"Alright, ladies and gentlemen, I know this isn't technically a Thanksgiving dinner, but it is our Thanksgiving dinner as we're all together today and won't be tomorrow; I feel we should do the terribly cheesy thing and go around the table and say what we're thankful for. That is what this season is all about, after all, and with all the incredible people we have here, there's no shortage of things to be thankful about. I'll start. I'm thankful for my wonderful daughter and all my extended family." She smiled lovingly as she looked at everyone in the room, and everyone smiled back.

"Um, let's see. I'm thankful to be done with school and working finally." Matt said and looked at his brother to begin.

"I," Nick paused, thinking of what to say, "I am thankful I was able to get a new car this year and that the insurance isn't ridiculous." Everyone laughed.

Thad was up next. "I am thankful that I only have one year left on my current degree and can start looking for what to do next here soon."

"Oh, where do I even start," Mimi began, and everyone took a deep breath, fearing how long it might take, "well I guess mostly I'm just thankful to still be alive and in good health and to have so many people that I love in my life." She patted Pops' hand gently as everyone let out a sigh of relief that she kept it short.

Pops began without hesitation. "I'm thankful to have lived such a wonderful life with my beautiful wife, to have raised a beautiful daughter, who in turned raised a beautiful daughter of her own, and I'm thankful to have watched three young kids grow up to be young adults, and that they have the most important thing this life can offer, friends that care about them." He raised his glass to Thad and then to Joshua and Win.

The friends were surprised to see that Joshua and Win both seemed genuinely taken aback by the acknowledgment.

"Well," Rachel's dad began, "I think I probably speak for both of us when I said we are very thankful that next month we make our final mortgage payment and own our house outright after fifteen years now."

"Amen to that." His wife added. "I could say any number of things, but that one is definitely the biggest. So glad to finally be done with that."

A chorus of claps rose from the group at that.

"Well, I wish we were saying that as well," Erin's mom began, "but I am excited and thankful for my new promotion at work."

"And likewise, I am thankful for that and to be one year closer to my retirement so she can take care of me." Erin's dad added with a laugh.

Erin picked up right after her parents. "I'm thankful that Little Rock doesn't suck and that I'm doing well in all my classes even if I hate some of them."

Chuckles echoed around the table.

"My turn, ok," Rachel began, "honestly, I'm very thankful that our move has gone so well also. I know Erin was being cheeky, but it's true. We've been so fortunate with everything at our new place, and I really enjoy it."

The three girls all shared a glance that even Thad recognized. They had indeed found a new home, as strange as it may be.

"Guess that leaves me." Ally smiled as she began. "Well, I would definitely like to add to what Rach and Erin both said. I won't lie, I was nervous as all get-out about movin' away. I miss the dickens out everybody here every day, pretty much. I am so thankful, though, to have such wonderful people here and wonderful new people in Little Rock that make it enjoyable."

The response that followed was genuine and heartfelt. The family the girls had left behind was indeed glad to see they had found such an excellent new start, and the friends were so pleased to have one another on that journey. Fittingly, all eyes then shifted to Joshua and Win.

"I am thankful," Win began, "to get to know all the love that is in this room. You have made this a wonderful experience, each and every one of you, and I could not be more thankful for all the love you have shown."

Mimi became teary-eyed, and even Cammie was a little choked up. Erin's and Rachel's parents all exchanged glances as they let the beautiful words sink in. The friends couldn't help but feel moved by his words. Win was just as enigmatic as his brother, but he was also very openly kind in a way few people ever were.

"Win is far more poetic than I could ever hope to be," Joshua began with admiration of his brother, "so I will simply say that I am thankful I have made it through another wonderful year with my family and, even better, that I have gained some new family along the way."

Joshua raised his glass in appreciation as everyone nodded in acknowledgment. There were no "aws" or other outwardly expressive emotions. His words were simple, and the people at the table appreciated them in kind. Only Ally, Erin, Rachel, and Thad knew the weight those words honestly held, though. Joshua smiled at them knowingly, and the dinner continued in the same fashion. Their families laughed about Joshua's and Win's stories and asked question after question as they worked to get to know the two men. The four friends couldn't help but think how much they had grown accustomed to having Joshua and Win around. Elusive as they were, the Brownings had become friends, even family.

After dinner, Cammie and Mimi set off to cleaning the kitchen. Joshua and Win both tried to help, but they were very emphatically told no. Erin's and Rachel's parents were able to help a little but not much despite their best efforts. The assorted families and friends continued moseying about between the living room where the central television was and the kitchen where the second, third, or even fourth helping remained for anyone that wanted it.

Joshua and Win had managed to carve out a corner of the living room for themselves where Thad stood with them chatting. Mimi and Pops had already left as well as Matt and Nick, but everyone else remained, floating around the house and visiting. Everyone methodically made their rounds by Joshua and Win, but the initial shock and awe had finally worn off. After a spell, the three friends made their way over to Thad and the Brownings.

"Well, guys," Erin began, "this is our family. Hope today wasn't too crazy."

"Not at all." Win replied with a beaming smile. "You have such amazing people in your life, truly. Not everyone is so fortunate to have such an incredible family around them."

"Win could not be more right," Joshua began as he sought to expand on Win's compliments, but before he could finish, something on the television caught his attention.

"Breaking News." The alert flashed as the local news broadcasters addressed the bulletin.

"Police were shocked today to discover another victim matching the horrible patterns of the Ghost of Little Rock. What was first deemed an ironic description by locals due to the astonishing lack of evidence at the crime scenes has now manifested itself most horrendously. Police had hoped that the previous cases were isolated incidents and that we had seen the last of them. Tragically, they were wrong. This is now the third victim that matches the same horrible methods."

The broadcast continued as the reporters discussed the incident, but nothing they could say mattered. As Ally, Erin, Rachel, and even Thad watched in horror, the news reporters tried as best they could to document the death of someone the friends all knew, not as well as they wished they could, but well enough to be struck to their core at the revelation.

"We don't know the full situation yet as police are still working the scene," the broadcast continued, "but the fact that Denise Dearborne, a wonderful member of our community, is dead is a tragedy."

The four friends were devastated. Denise. Denise, the barista. The Denise they had come to know and love, had been murdered. Their grief, though, paled in comparison with that of Joshua and Win. The two men stood in stoic horror as they watched the screen unfurl the details. Tears began to fill their eyes softly. Joshua and Win both stopped breathing. They were lost in a trance from whence the friends couldn't possibly hope to pull them back.

A single, solemn tear slid down Joshua's face as he reached, robotically, into his inner coat pocket to grab his ringing phone.

Without even looking at the phone, he answered and said, "We're on our way."

He put his phone back into his inner jacket pocket as he turned towards the families gathered there.

"It was a genuine pleasure meeting you," Joshua said with a weak smile as he spun and headed for the door with Win alongside him.

PART TWO
THE HARBILINS

21
THE NEW GIRL IN TOWN

November had been cold, December was frigid, and by January, Little Rock had frozen. Ally parked the car next to their house, and the friends began unloading their stuff. It being barely eight in the morning didn't help the cold any, but they were too anxious to stay away any longer. They had decided to stay gone the entire holiday break. Something about Little Rock had felt wrong without the Brownings there.

They still had no idea where Joshua and Win went that day. For the rest of Thanksgiving break, the girls and Thad talked about the tragedy. Part of them felt they should return home, but they knew there was nothing for them to do. They had tried texting both Joshua and Win at various points over the break to see how they were, but after a few stiff replies stating they were fine, the friends didn't bother texting again. There was no development in the case over the weekend. As with the other two victims, there had not been a single shred of evidence.

The friends debated with their parents about going back to Little Rock as their parents feared for their safety, but after much discussion, the trio had finally calmed them. The friends were nervous about going back despite everything they had said to convince their family. The fact that someone they knew had been brutally murdered was a fact they couldn't ignore, but the group knew they couldn't simply stop living their lives either. Once they returned to Little Rock the next week, though, things grew even worse when they learned all of the Brownings had left town. The Daily Brew had remained closed the entire break out of respect for Denise, and when it had finally reopened, there was a strange emptiness to it with Denise and the Brownings gone.

Secretly each girl had kept hoping week after week that Joshua and Win would miraculously walk in the shop or Lili would suddenly be behind the counter, but week after week had passed without it happening. Every trip to The Brew began with them anxiously hiding their hopes and ended with their disappointment as they walked out the door. Terry had still been there much to their appreciation, but even she hadn't been quite the same. The friends could see that sadness in her at the loss of Denise, but more than that, she too seemed less alive without the Brownings around. It was as if they had lost an entire family on that one terrible day.

The few weeks they had left in the semester after Thanksgiving had dragged by with everything that had happened. Their classes, The Brew, even their home all felt as if they had been filled with a permanent melancholy air. Each day the weather grew colder, and the town and their lives had seemed to grow cold with it as if the city itself had fallen victim to the Ghost despite no new victims actually manifesting.

Their break had been a surprising retreat from the gloom that had settled over Little Rock. The friends enjoyed their time with Thad, and they had even been able to hang out with Matt and Nick for a change. At first, every news bulletin or phone notification sent a wave of fear through them, but as the weeks went by, it had slowly faded. It would never entirely leave while the killer was still loose, though. Despite their fear of the Ghost and the calm they had experienced while being away, the friends were very ready to return to Little Rock once January came.

Their time with friends and family had been a much-needed recharge, but the friends knew it was only that. Their new life in Little Rock had been patiently waiting for them, and with classes about to start back, the friends felt sure both that it was time to return and that the Brownings would be returning soon as well. The friends had gone the entire time since the Brownings vanished after Thanksgiving without the Ghost claiming another victim, without any visions of mythical cities or strange, cryptic books talking about them, and not a single sighting of the Wanderer or the Raven Man. Unbeknownst to the friends, though, the pair of eyes still watched them as they settled back into their home on Rock Street. The Ghost and Raven Man may have been absent for a time, but they would both soon have their day.

Within a few hours, they were wholly settled back into their room. They each sat in their rooms for a spell, soaking it all in. It felt good to be home for all of them. They had missed almost everything about Little Rock, but the thing they had missed more than anything was their house. It had become truly theirs in just the short time they had been in it, and every time they were away, the more they realized it. After they each took their time to let the feeling of being home washed over them, they went downstairs and got ready for the other thing they had missed the most about Little Rock, The Daily Brew.

It had felt cold enough for snow outside, but none fell as the friends each buried their faces within their coats. They had wondered openly if any of the Brownings would be back in town yet. Something in the air told them that the Brownings were near, but they couldn't explain why they sensed it or what it even meant. Still, the brisk walk they made to The Brew had their hope steadily rising as they drew closer.

They rushed inside the doors of The Brew, ready to warm themselves with a hot cup of coffee. There was no sign of Lili, to their disappointment, and the table in the far-left corner was still empty, reserving itself for Joshua's and Win's eventual return. They were very pleasantly surprised, though, to find Terry was in far better spirits than the last time they had seen her.

"Hey, ladies!" Terry said in her usual peppy yet soft voice. "It's so good to see you back. Man, it's gotta have been like a month, yeah?"

"Just about," Erin replied, giving Terry a polite smile. "We went back to visit our families for the break. Figured we might as well take advantage of the time off. It's good to be back, though. Can't lie, I've missed the place."

"Well, it's missed you too, and I gotta say, Erin, I absolutely love the hair. Wicked cool."

Erin blushed a little, a rare sight for her. Over the break, she had finally made the leap to do her hair how she'd been wanting, and she went ahead with the nose ring while she was at it. The tattoo, though, was still a way out, but she had been actively working with Lucky Bella there in Little Rock to design one. Her parents had put up a fuss over the hair at first, but with everything going on, they had let it go quicker than Erin expected. She was still getting used to receiving compliments on it, though. Not many people outside of the friends had said anything about it. More than anything, she was just glad to have people supporting her decisions for once. For most of her life, Erin had felt like she couldn't make any choices but the simple and safe ones, and she had finally begun stepping out of her comfort zone and doing the things she liked.

"Thanks, Terry." She replied, still blushing.

"So, can I get you, girls, some drinks? Still taking the same thing?"

"Yes indeed." Rachel said with a smile. "So, how have you been?"

"I've been great, honestly. Still have some rough days, but all in all, I feel pretty good. Van's come by a couple times while you were gone. I think I may be starting to like him, but don't say that to him!" She said, blushing as she worked on their drinks. "Lili should be back any day now as well, she said. I gotta say it's been rough her not being here as much. She's been by here and there, but it's not the same as when she's here regularly. So, I'm super glad she's about to be back, back. Guess that means Joshua and Win will be back here soon as well." She gave the girls a knowing smile as she said it. "You girls can feel free to have a seat if you like, and I'll bring these over. Your table is open, of course. Or are you getting your drinks to go?"

"We won't be staying for long," Rachel answered. "Gotta get ready for class to start back. We'll sit for a bit, though."

The girls settled in at their table, and shortly after, Terry had brought their drinks.

Erin smiled as she walked away and then turned to whisper, "Do you guys realize we haven't paid for coffee in like two months? They never ask us to pay. What's with that?"

"Either they like us a lot, or they pity us a lot. Regardless, it's free drinks, so you won't see me complain." Ally laughed.

The friends drank their coffees slowly, relishing the beautiful taste they had missed so much. They had almost forgotten how much they enjoyed it. The moments slipped by as the friends sat in the superb ambiance of The Brew. It still amazed them how a simple coffee shop could make them feel at home and at peace. They knew, of course, there was nothing simple about The Daily Brew. From the peculiar library upstairs to the enigmatic owners, it was undoubtedly a unique place, but The Brew would still make them feel connected even without those things. The whole place just felt as if it had been waiting for them to find it.

Abruptly, though, their trance broke, and coffee was the furthest thing from their mind as an aura seemed to fill The Daily Brew. The friends couldn't explain it, but they could sense something was coming;

no, someone, and they turned towards the door to see whom.

Time seemed to slow as the door swung open, and the friends saw a black heel strike the floor. All noise left the room, and every head turned towards the entrance. Her perfectly toned leg could be seen midway up her thigh where the hem of her silver dress that shone like stars in the night sky fell. Her skin tone was an even shade of golden brown, the kind that looked beautiful with any color and seemed to glow when she moved even more than her dress.

Her second heel struck the floor as she entered, and by then, everyone stared in amazed silence. Over her silver dress, she had a short cashmere trench coat in a soft shade of birch tied loosely at her waist by its sash so her radiant dress could easily be seen beneath. Her hands fell just below the pockets of her jacket where her nails could be seen in a deep, rich, near-black, purple that was breathtaking against the gorgeous platinum ring on her middle finger, beset with a diamond crest.

She took another step towards the counter. The perspective of the room shifted until it revolved entirely around her. The Brew was now her stage, and everyone in it was her audience. She was like water, a brilliant stream and a raging river flowing through that all the world might marvel. Her figure was petite but curvaceous, lean and efficient. She was built with purpose, elegantly wrapped in her cashmere. She would have stood around five feet six before the heels, and though she looked closer to five feet nine with them on, she might as well have been ten feet tall the way she commanded the room. Everyone looked up to her no matter the height, and every inch of her flowed in perfect rhythm with her step.

The collar on her trench was up when she entered, but she reached her soft, perfect hands up to lay it flat after leaving the cold. Doing so revealed her sleek, impeccable neck leading from her immaculately sculpted collar bones to her flawlessly shaped ears that were each decorated with a stunning brilliant cut diamond. Her jaw extended at a slight downward angle, giving her a dignified look of grace that was completed by her sharp yet smooth chin. Her lips were sized with perfect proportion, and their natural color gave the look of effortless beauty that was echoed throughout her face. Her nose had the same look of elegance and was delicately rounded at the end. It led seamlessly up to her brow bone that decorated her radiant eyes. They were both on fire with a lustrous grey that looked as if she had liquid platinum in them, and they were brought to life even more by the dazzling grey glow that adorned her eyelids and eyelashes. Her eyebrows arched in lovely harmony over them, completing the look of fierce, unbridled passion her eye line exuded. Her smooth forehead led exquisitely to her auburn hair. The closely cropped pixie cut was flaked with gold and set in soft, subtle spikes around her head.

The friends had never seen a more beautiful woman in all their lives, and they never would. No one else in the room was an exception, as no eye left her even when she reached the counter. Terry was unable to speak or even move. The woman flashed a smile that lit up the entire room until even the friends gasped for breath. Then all at once, everyone in the room went back to what they were doing, and the woman looked over at Joshua's and Win's table with a smirk.

"Dear God." Rachel said, breaking the friends' silence, her voice a whisper as she kept glancing back at the woman. "She is just mind-blowingly gorgeous. Like it almost hurts to look at her."

"I know, right. I mean, I've always been able to recognize if a woman's pretty, but I think I have a full-blown crush on her. I'm into girls now."

"That's not how that works, Erin." Rachel replied cooly.

"I'm fully aware of how it works," Erin began giving Rachel's hand a gentle squeeze, "but I could make it work for her. Damn. So, you think she's one of their crew?" Erin said, looking over her shoulder in awe.

"Judging by Terry's reaction, I think it's the first time she's ever seen her." Ally found her voice.

The three sat staring at the woman as she ordered her coffee. Every eye in the room kept shooting to and from her as if they feared what would happen if they looked but couldn't stop themselves. Terry spilled the woman's coffee twice and had to start over because she kept glancing back at the woman before finally getting it right.

The woman waited patiently, apparently unaffected by the stares and whispers. Every so often, she would smile as if she overheard a good comment from one of the tables. When Terry placed her coffee on the counter, the woman smiled another breathtaking smile and gave her a most gracious nod. The portrait of a woman looked towards the Brownings table for another moment before she leaned closer to the counter to speak with Terry. After a brief hushed exchange, the woman spun on her heel and made her exit, briefly catching sight of the friends at the table on her way out.

"So," Erin began, "did she, like, see us, or was she just looking through us?"

"Pretty sure the latter." Ally replied flatly. "I don't think people like her actually see people like us."

Terry walked over with fresh to-go cups and placed them down on their table. Sensing the tension, she tried to explain. "She's a vision, no?"

Ally did her best not to fawn. "I've never seen anyone or anything more beautiful."

That was all she could muster, and two friends could merely nod.

"Her name's Luci. I would tell you more, but apparently, you'll have to ask the Brownings about her. She said she was an old friend of Joshua's and to let them know she was in town when they came by next. Feel like I should probably text Lili." Terry's mesmerization suddenly turned to confusion as she considered the thought.

The friends did not say anything as Terry drifted away, clearly deep in thought. Something about The Brew had changed suddenly, if ever so slightly. The moment Luci had left the building, the vibrant life that was the shop dwindled. It wasn't a significant change they knew, but they no longer felt the sense of calm they had before the intriguing women's arrival. They finished the last sips of their first drinks and grabbed their to-go cups to head back home.

Outside it felt as if it had dropped ten degrees as they walked to their house. Each of the friends burrowed deeper into their warm layers as they walked and let thoughts of Luci and the Brownings dance in their heads.

"Hey, why don't the Brownings use phones?" Rachel asked, catching the other two off guard.

"What?" Erin asked in confusion.

"I mean, they hardly ever use phones. They have 'em. I could probably count on one hand the times I've seen them use 'em, though. Luci just now, and even Van back when we first met him, came into The Brew looking for their friends. Why don't they just text?"

"Huh," Erin replied incredulously.

"You know," Ally began, equally as confused, "that's a great question. Though not one I can come up with a great answer for. That's weird, though, right?"

"Is to me," Erin said as she pondered. "Guess we can add that to the list of millions of questions to ask them. Along with, you know, who the fuck they actually are, why they've been gone for over a month, what the hell Harbilin Corporation is, what the even bigger hell Idonia really is. You know, the more I think about it, them hardly ever using phones is actually, probably, the least weird thing about them."

Rachel and Ally scoffed humorously as they climbed the steps to their front door. They couldn't deny Erin's logic any more than they could Rachel's observation. They were both quite valid. The friends were glad to get inside from the cold, though, more than anything. Slowly they began shedding their layers and placing them on the chairs in the kitchen. Erin made for the sofa as Rachel sat down at the bar, and Ally started to make her way up the stairs when they heard a knock at the door. The friends froze at the sound. They had lived in the house for months and never had a single person knock on their door. Less than a dozen people even knew where their house was, and only three of them lived in the city. Terry they knew was at work, and from what they understood, Joshua and Win were still not in town, which left entirely no one who could know they lived there.

The knock came again. It was a soft knock, polite even, that made the friends feel as if they were the ones being invited into someone's home, as opposed to being asked for permission to enter. Possibilities ran through their mind, from someone with a petition to selling something and everything in between, but none of that made any sense. They had just come in from outside, and there had been no one out there when they did. *So, who was at the door*, they thought. Time slowed to a crawl. The friends slowly began to cross the room to see who it could possibly be. Another knock didn't come, but as they neared the door, they saw the figure silhouetted outside.

They opened the door wide, so it framed the woman's picturesque figure, the gorgeous auburn and gold hair, and the most beautiful face they had ever seen in the world. Luci.

"Good day to you ladies." Luci began with as much charm as the Brownings combined. "You're friends with Joshua and Win, no?"

Her voice was soft and sweet as she spoke with an accent that sounded somewhere between British and French. It was the kind of voice that made you want to be friends with a person because you knew they could be trusted in an instant. Only the friends didn't trust her, and no matter how lovely her voice was, they didn't think that would change.

"Um…" Rachel began at a complete loss for words.

"How would you know that?" Erin asked, sounding more impressed than she was disturbed.

"I would say it was merely intuition," Luci began with a caring smirk, "but that would be somewhat deceiving. They have told me a bit about you. When I saw the three of you in The Daily Brew, it was simply a matter of deduction. To be honest, I was only mildly positive when I knocked on your door and was fully prepared to leave, having been incorrect. Your reaction, however, gives me my answer."

"Wait," Ally replied, even more confused, "how did you know we lived here."

"Ah, yes, that is much simpler to explain. I was headed towards my vehicle when I saw the three of you leave. I tried to call out to you, but you did not respond. In trying to catch up, I saw you enter here, and, well, the rest you know already."

Ally didn't respond. None of the friends did. Her answers were indeed simple, conveniently so, and the friends were unsure what to believe.

With their lack of response, Luci began again, "I came by to see if you might like to get a drink." She stopped there and studied the friend's reaction. "I have a layover here in town and was hoping to see them; being as they are not here, it seemed like the ideal opportunity to meet you."

The friends were stunned. They couldn't imagine what Luci could want to talk to them about, but the chance to meet yet another of the Brownings' circle was an enticing opportunity, even if they were unsure if she could be trusted. After a brief moment of internal deliberation, the friends grabbed the jackets they had just removed and prepared to brave the cold once more.

Luci's black heels clicked as they walked along the sidewalk, and the friends couldn't help but notice how her hair seemed to glow in the sunset. The pair of eyes followed them from the darkness, the friends oblivious to the danger into which they were slipping further and further. Not knowing where exactly they were going, the friends just followed in step with Luci. They made it to the end of their block before Luci said anything.

"There is a lovely cocktail lounge just around the block here. Have you been to it yet?"

The friends merely shook their heads, still struggling to find their voices.

"You lot sure are quiet. Am I that unpleasant, or is it still just the shock?" Her voice sounded genuinely confused, but she in no way sounded weak. Quite the contrary, Luci evoked raw power when she spoke.

"Just not sure what to say, I guess," Rachel replied meekly.

"Fair enough," Luci said flatly. "I suppose I am not much for chatter myself. Small talk always was a struggle for me. Seems pointless."

They were a few blocks from the apartment when the friends saw the bar ahead tucked underneath one of the high rises where a staircase led down the side of the building to the entrance. Strangely enough, though, the friends had never seen that bar there before. They hadn't been down that road a considerable amount, but it had been at least half a dozen times that they had driven past without noticing. Luci, however, strolled right down the steps and in the door as if she owned the place.

The bar looked like the friends had stepped back into Prohibition. The dark room stretched deep into the underbelly of the building; a large, ornate wooden bar ran the length of one side with barstools all along it. Behind it was a couple of bartenders preparing drinks for the handful of people at the bar or in the booths tucked into the opposite wall, all of which spoke of intentional privacy with their domed roofs and deep benches. Two men in all-black business suits sat at the far end of the bar drinking a beer. The other two couples huddled in the booths avoiding any attention. Luci made her way past the patrons and took her coat off as she claimed the last stall in the back corner.

Without her coat on, the friends got a complete look at her for the first time. She was beyond stunning, more than beautiful. The friends searched and searched their brains to find a word that described the woman who stood in front of them. Only one word came to mind, perfection.

Her entire skin was the same gorgeous golden brown as her legs, and her figure was even more breathtaking without a coat to hide it. The strapless silver dress showed off her slim but perfectly toned arms and smoothly sculpted shoulders. Her exquisite collar bone and neckline formed two faint V's that led down to the subtly stunning curves of her body.

She sat her jacket down in the curved booth and positioned herself so no one else in the bar could see her, and the friends slid in around. There was a slight hint of annoyance in her eyes when the friends made contact with them that they couldn't help but guess was because of the continual glances from everyone in the bar. The friends realized she sat where she did with purpose.

It took the bartender a while to approach despite having had her eyes locked on Luci from the moment she entered, almost as if she had to work up the nerve to come over. When she spoke, her voice was shaky.

"May I get you ladies," she paused to take a deep breath, "something to drink?"

"I would like the oldest Macallan you have, double, with one rock, please," Luci said with a relaxing smile at the bartender.

"Um," Erin began in confusion as the waitress waited patiently, "just a nice Merlot, please."

"Rockhound would be nice if you got it, ma'am." Rachel's words were met with an affirming nod by the bartender that made her relax a little.

Ally froze as she tried to think of a drink. She hated trying to come up with orders on the spot when she drank so very little. Their entire time in Little Rock, she had felt like she was rushing to become more of an adult than she was and making essentially no progress in it whatsoever.

"I'll take a glass with her." She finally said, pointing at Erin.

Luci pushed a lock of her hair behind her right ear and rested her hand on the table as the woman walked away. The friends had seen the beautiful ring in The Brew, but they couldn't tell exactly what it was supposed to be. Up close and in the soft lights of the bar, they recognized the symbol on the ring in a heartbeat. It was the same symbol that Joshua had on his ring, his family heirloom, and yet his family was gone.

"So, you ladies are friends with my family now." Luci's sweet voice brought them back to reality. "Joshua and Win seem rather taken by you, and that is grounds for me getting to know you and vice versa. After all, if you are being brought into the fold, then we will likely be seeing quite a bit more of each other in the days to come. Judging by the looks on your faces throughout the evening, though, I would say you know nothing of me. That is hardly a surprise, mind you. I am not typically one of the first topics Joshua brings up. So, tell me about yourselves. What have Joshua and Win left out?"

The friends took turns discussing themselves, what they were into, and what brought them all to Little Rock. Luci was kind and listened compassionately, striving to understand the friends truly. They were surprised at how easy it was to talk with her. Her mysterious arrival made her a more enigmatic figure than any of the Brownings, and yet the friends could not help feeling at ease around her. Luci practically emitted a calming aura that made the friends feel safe. After the better part of two hours had passed along with a couple of drinks, the friends slowly realized they had learned hardly anything about this intriguing new woman. Finally, they turned the conversation towards her.

"I am an open book. What would you like to know?"

Her smile was so genuine and inviting the friends knew they could ask her anything, even if they couldn't understand her motives.

"Why haven't we heard about you?" Erin asked bluntly, voicing a question all of them had been thinking.

"Well, the answer is two-fold. For starters, Joshua and Win do not like to tell my story as they believe it is not theirs to tell because it's mine. Joshua is rather poetic like that." Luci's eyes grew distant as she stared off into nothingness.

"And the other?" Rachel asked, breaking Luci's stare.

"The other," she began solemnly, "is because I am a bit of a complication for them. A remnant of the life Joshua left behind when they came here. When Joshua found new opportunities for the family here, they asked me to join."

"But you stayed behind." Ally said, knowing it wasn't a question.

"I did," Luci replied with a soft smile. "I still believed in the work I was doing. I still do. I manage the family business back home in England. Since my mother died, I've pretty much had to step up and take over. Joshua and I have known each other our entire lives. We lost our mothers together, and our fathers left when they passed. Not physically, of course, but mentally they have been gone ever since." She paused for a moment as she read the friends' faces. "I am sure Joshua or Win or whoever told you a much more simplified version. Joshua doesn't like to talk about it much, still shouldering the burden of what happened to our families. I am a bit more direct. There was nothing we could have done, and I think somewhere deep inside, even Joshua accepts that. It is a hard truth with which to cope, however."

The friends sat in stunned silence at Luci's story. There was a simplicity in her words that made them seem like she told a trivial tale, but there was also pain they had never known.

"I," Ally's voice was trembling, "I had no idea."

"Yeah," Erin began remorsefully, "we knew he had built a new makeshift family with the Brownings, so to speak, but I didn't realize it was like that. I'm really sorry we brought it up."

"You're fine, trust me." She smiled at the friends again encouragingly. "Joshua and I have been dealing with it for a very long time, and to be honest, we are both well accustomed to it by now. I am just sorry that this has to be how our first conversation with each other goes. Hopefully, the next visit will be much more pleasant."

"So, I take it you'll be sticking around for a while?" Rachel asked, and the friends weren't sure whether they liked or disliked the thought of getting to know Luci better.

"Not right now, unfortunately. I do have a business to run and all, so I head out in the morning. Though part of that business entails a meeting with Joshua and Win later this month, so, I will certainly be back for that. As for now, I had probably best get checked into my hotel here soon. I have some reports I need to close out before my flight in the morning."

The friends had already finished their drinks and were reaching for their cards, but Luci refused to let them pay, a theme the friends were coming to recognize amongst the Brownings and their companions. Despite their best effort, Luci insisted they let her take care of it, and so the three friends rose and headed towards the door, never seeing the coin Luci placed on the table or the knowing nod she gave the bartenders as they exited.

The walk back was even colder, but Luci didn't seem bothered by it even the slightest. They exchanged no words on the trip back. Luci had sensed that the friends were done talking and didn't press them. It was strange, though, despite their apprehensions and Luci's generally intimidating aura, the friends felt ideally at ease walking back to their house with the recent addition to the peculiar Browning saga. They didn't think about the potential that lurked in the darkness, slowly and methodically working its way into the friends' lives.

"Well," Luci said when they reached the house on Rock Street, "it was a real pleasure getting to meet you, ladies."

"Likewise. Thanks for an interesting evening." Erin replied, and the friends echoed similar replies.

Luci did not even bother walking up the steps of their house and instead merely stayed on the sidewalk as the three made their way towards the door.

"I have no doubt we will see each other again sometime." She smiled politely and waved farewell to the friends before she disappeared into the night.

The friends gave returning waves as they smiled back before they turned and opened their door, hoping to find normality. They never would.

22
DEAD OF WINTER

In a cold apartment overlooking the Arkansas River, a woman rose from her lover's bed. Not even bothering to grab her clothes from the floor, she sauntered to the window and took in the sight. From a distance, the river looked peaceful and serene as it gently rolled through the middle of the city. Such was the deceit of rivers. They were beautiful and alluring. They were teeming with possibilities and carried with them the promise of new life, yet beneath their surface raged a mighty current that waited remorselessly to drag any foolish enough to underestimate down into its depths never to return. The woman was floating atop that river, where the current loomed just beneath her.

The coffee maker chimed, and she couldn't help but smile. Of course, he had set it to brew automatically, she thought. He was always one step ahead, always trying to be sweet. She grabbed a cup and sat in a chair by the windows, wrapping herself in one of the many blankets as she sipped her coffee. She continued studying the river that gave the city life. It had been the river that first brought people to the area, turning it into a principal port of the waterways that flowed from the west. People had made a life in that city and on that river, and she had done the same and forged a new life for herself in that city that once seemed so foreign.

She finished the last of her coffee and bid farewell to the river as she made her way to his shower. The hot water stung against her cold skin and brought her to life, breathing the heat back into her veins and vibrancy bank into her soul. Before long, the entire bathroom was filled with steam from the inferno of a shower that spilled out into the bedroom. She had the heat up as high as it would go, and every one of the five shower heads on creating a torrential downpour that woke the very depths of her soul. The glass walls of the shower had fogged, as had the mirror. She didn't even know he was in the shower with her until she felt the hands on her throat.

He gently kissed her shoulders as he massaged her neck. Then his lips moved to where his hands were as his hands slid down to her arms. He bit down softly on her neck as his fingers slid from her arms to her waist. She felt a tingle run through her body and the hair on her arm stood up. Grabbing a handful of her hair, he pulled her head back tenderly as his other hand slid down her hip.

"Well, somebody's awake." She said playfully as she turned around to kiss him.

She wrapped her arms around his neck and kissed him softly on his chest. The water beat down on them, adding a sting to every touch that sent spasms coursing through their body. She wanted him, needed him. It had been too long in the making, too long that she had been made to wait, and the wait was finally over. He was there in her arms, hers for the taking. As his lips moved to her, she felt a wave of exhilaration wash over her sending a tremendous heat coursing through her even stronger than the shower had. She ran her hands slowly down his chest as he continued teasing her with gentle bites and playful kisses up and down her neck. Her hand finally reached the spot, and she gripped him firmly but gently as she pulled him closer with each stroke, causing him to bite desperately into her neck, begging for more.

"Well, are you just going to stand there," she whispered gingerly into his ear, "or are you going to do something about this."

He granted her request and gripped her thighs firmly as he lifted her onto his waist. Her nails dug into his back, and she locked her legs around him as he thrust her against the shower wall.

An hour later, the man sat on the edge of his bed, lacing up his shoes as he got ready for work. He thought to himself it was starting off to be a wonderful day. He heard the water turn off as his lover finished what was left of her shower. Towel wrapped around her, she crossed the room and rested on the bed behind him.

She wrapped her arms around his neck again and kissed him softly on the head. The man didn't even have time to flinch before the warm blood trickled down his chest. He gasped for air but couldn't breathe for the laceration on his throat. The last thing he felt was the sharp pain as the knife entered his chest. His eyes went dark, and his body fell to the ground. Another soul claimed by the Ghost of Little Rock.

The girls were glad to finally reach The Brew the next day. The cold air had set all their teeth to chattering, and a warm drink was just what they all had needed. They were still at a loss with the events of the previous night. Luci had been the most unexpected thing to come from their time with the Brownings. She had given them even more insight into Joshua but also gave them countless questions about the strange life he left behind. It would have been easier for the friends if she had something about Idonia as Van had, or made it less obvious that there was still some issue at play between her and the Browning family, or even if she hadn't made it seem like whatever business endeavors she had might conflict with the work the Brownings did for the Harbilins in some way. Instead, the friends were left with yet another confusing piece of the Browning puzzle.

Inside The Brew, though, the aromas wrapped around the friends as if each girl were welcomed in by their long-lost friend, who made every care melt away. Eyes closed, the three stood, letting the sounds of the espresso makers rattle against their eardrums as the toffee and vanilla notes mingled in the air, dancing to the tune of the music as the friends breathed it in deeply. They opened their eyes to find an even more warming sight than The Brew itself. Lili Browning was smiling at them from behind the counter.

"Hello, again, ladies." She continued smiling as she prepped their drinks. "It has been quite a while. Fancy the usual?"

The girls nodded in unison, each too cold to talk and too stunned to form words.

"Terry told us you were gone for the break, so I guess you went home for the holidays. Did you have a good time?" She handed them their drinks expectantly.

Neither girl knew who should start. They each looked at each other until Erin finally spoke up, "We had a really good time. Just hung out and enjoyed not having class. We thought you guys were out of town, so it just didn't really feel right to stay."

"Oh, my apologies. After Denise's passing, Marc and I went out of town for the first part of December. We needed to get away, but we returned the week after Christmas and have been in and out since. I am sorry we missed you. Had we known you were out of town because of us, we would have sent word." Lili's face was genuinely sorrowful that she had missed out on seeing the friends.

"It's cool, really. We got to hang out with our family back home some, spend some time with Thad."

The way Erin spoke struck Ally. Ally had seen Thad a fair deal over the break. They all had, but the fact that Erin specifically mentioned it so intentionally made Ally feel like she was missing something. Over the break, Ally was slowly becoming convinced that Rachel and Thad might eventually get back together with the way they behaved. Ally suddenly remembered back to that first night Thad had come to visit. She had pushed the memory so far out of her mind she thought it had just been part of the dream. Months had passed, and suddenly Ally was unsure again. Unsure if one of her friends was sleeping with Thad, if she had imagined the whole thing, and uncertain if she was simply losing her mind as all the weird experiences of the last semester came back to her one by one.

Unable to control her thoughts, Ally had to change the subject, "So where did you and Marc go on vacation?" She said, sipping from her coffee.

"We were not on vacation exactly. We spent some time in the northeast doing family stuff. Not much to talk about it, honestly, but it was a nice change of pace. It is good to be back again and to have you back again, though. I trust we can expect you to join us for dinner Friday night?" Lili said as she headed back towards the counter to help a customer entering the door.

"Sure." Rachel said with a smile. "Will everyone be there?"

Lili didn't answer either because she was about to take the customer's order or because she didn't want to address the topic of Joshua and Win. As neither brother sat at their usual table and Lili hadn't mentioned them in any of their conversations, the friends couldn't help but assume the latter.

The three sat at their table warming themselves with their drinks for almost an hour. Erin finished hers somewhere around the thirty-minute mark and was ready to get her to-go cup and leave. Ally and Rachel, though, sipped very slowly, saying they just wanted to enjoy their coffee and tea. Erin knew they were lying but didn't bother pressing it further. She knew they both wanted some form of explanation from the Browning brothers, and they weren't alone.

After another thirty minutes, though, Rachel and Ally finally gave up and asked Lili for their go cups. Lili had them prepped in no time, and the girls were on their way to the door when Lili started saying something about making different plans for Friday's dinner. They were already turning for the door, though, and Ally slammed suddenly into a man trying to enter, nearly spilling her drink all over him.

"Well, it's good to see you again too, Ally. I didn't know we were to the hugging stage of our relationship yet, but if you're a hugger, I suppose that's fine." Van said with a smirk.

"Van!" The excitement in Ally's voice was evident. "What are you doing here?"

It did the friends well to see him. Seeing Lili and Van meant things were returning to normal, as normal as being friends with the Brownings could be, that is.

"I could ask you the same thing. School doesn't start back for a few more days, and from what I understand, you've been out of town."

"Ugh." Ally huffed in frustration. "Why do all of you keep saying that? We left because you guys were out of town. Lili said the same thing."

"Um, you do realize I live out of town, don't you?" Van's eyebrows dropped as he stared at Ally mockingly.

"Oh, shut up. You know what I mean." Ally couldn't help but smile slightly.

"Don't mind, Ally. We're glad to see you." Erin broke in with a laugh. "We're also standing in the doorway and should probably move."

"Valid point," Van said as he stepped further inside. "You're certainly welcome to stay and hang out if you want. I was just stopping in to see Terry. Her shift starts in about thirty minutes. I've had to be in and out of town over the past few weeks, so I've visited with her while I could."

"Aw, how sweet," Erin said playfully. "You better not hurt that girl. She's probably the most precious person on the planet. We would stay and watch her awkwardly, try not to show how into you she is, but we're just about to catch a movie. You going to be in town for a while?"

"Not this trip, but I'll be back up soon pretty regularly. I have some new clients here, so I'll be back and forth between New York and here from time to time for a while. We'll all do dinner the next weekend I'm here." Van smiled as he made his way towards the counter. "Oh, and bring Thad too."

The girls nodded agreement as they stepped out into the bitter cold and walked to the movies. None of the girls were ready for school to start back, so they did everything they could to draw the next few days out. The Brew and chats with Lili followed by movies each day was a start, but dinners at their apartment just weren't much fun. So on Tuesday, they invited Terry over, and the four cooked dinner, that is to say, Erin and Rachel cooked dinner as they were the resident chefs. After dinner, Erin and Ally roped the other two into playing video games. That gave Ally and Erin a decent laugh for the night.

Wednesday started pretty much the same, but after leaving The Brew to hit the theater, Lili invited them to have dinner with her and Marc. They gladly agreed, looking for anything to do that wasn't getting ready for class the next day. Ally and Rachel hoped that Joshua and Win would be there, but part of them had given up getting an explanation from them, which was good because when they arrived at Brave New Restaurant, Marc and Lili were the only two at the usual table.

"It is good to see you all again," Marc said, standing at the girls' arrival. "How have you been?"

The three girls each went into their explanation of their holiday breaks. Marc and Lili listened intently. Lauren even stayed and listened to part of their story when she came to check on them, and she did the same again when she brought them all refills. It wasn't until Ally mentioned Thanksgiving break without thinking that the conversation stopped.

She regretted mentioning it immediately, knowing that Marc and Lili had to feel pain at the subject still, and the friends couldn't help but think that was the cause of Joshua's and Win's disappearances. Marc's and Lili's eyes were laden with sadness and guilt as Ally stopped her story and looked at Rachel. Rachel just looked down at her hands, not wanting to press the topic either.

"Look, ladies," Lili began with the soft comforting of a mother, "what happened to Denise was horrible. There is no other way to describe it, but we cannot pretend like it never happened, no matter how tragic it is. That terrible truth is just a fact of our reality now. Ignoring it or avoiding it will not bring her back. The best we can do is continue living in a way that carries Denise on with us."

Her words were like a soothing ointment on a fresh burn, cooling and calming the friends' nerves. They had worked through it as best they could over the break, trying to process their emotions and cope with it all, but having clarity from Lili helped more than anything had over the holiday. They missed Denise. They felt horrible about her passing, and they knew that was ok. They could feel all of those emotions and still wake up each day, seeking to live the best day they could.

"I would like to apologize on behalf of Joshua and Win as well." Marc's words were lined with caution as he spoke, and they jarred the friends from the moment of clarity they had been experiencing. "Denise's death struck them as well, particularly Joshua. To be quite frank, we are surprised that they have remained gone this long, but their reasons are their own. That is for them to sort out as they deem fit, and we must respect their wishes. I would explain further, but that is something they should explain to you in person."

"That's understandable." Ally said with sincerity.

The friends let Marc's word sink in. It was true they had felt somewhat betrayed by Joshua's and Win's absence, but they also had to accept that if the Brownings were genuinely becoming more than just friends, it meant giving them the space and time they each needed to work through things. The friends knew they would get their explanation in time, and rushing to do so would only make things worse.

"Thanks for letting us know, though." Ally began again with more humor in her voice. "At least now we can expect an awkward conversation." She chuckled, trying to get off the subject.

Marc and Lili smiled in response.

"Granted, I'm sure it won't be anywhere as awkward as drinks with Luci was." Erin laughed as well, but Marc and Lili hadn't smiled at that comment.

"I'm sorry," Lili's voice sounded very concerned, "did you say Luci?"

The friends were at a genuine loss. They had thought the chance encounter with Luci was strange, but they had not realized it would cause such a reaction and only furthered their concern.

"Yeah." Rachel began cautiously. "She said she was a friend of yours, of Joshua's mainly, it seemed. She came into The Brew a couple days back and left Terry a message for y'all that she was in town. Were we not supposed to do that? We just had drinks at some old lounge not far from our house."

Marc and Lili exchanged nervous glances. They both sat in silence for a moment before Lili responded, "We did not receive the message, unfortunately, but I would imagine Terry was just distracted with everything going on and Van being in town as well. It's not that you were not supposed to do so, just that we would advise caution around Luci."

"Why?" Erin asked earnestly. "I mean, she seems alright, aside from the fact that she's perfect and maybe a little more ambiguous than is normal."

Marc shook his head with a nasty smile. "Luci looks perfect, of course, but that is where the perfection stops." Marc saw the questions on the girls' faces. He knew it was more than he should typically discuss. Still, the situation was an exception, so he went on to explain, "As I am sure you ladies have put together by now, our family was not the most respectable in our endeavors. In coming here, Joshua and all of us saw that we left that all behind. Suffice it to say that Luci has done no such thing."

Ally knew Luci had been too good to be accurate, but with Marc's confession, she couldn't hate Luci without hating Joshua and the rest of his family for what they had done. She kept telling herself that Joshua had changed and that he wasn't that person anymore, whoever that person was even. Her morals didn't work that way, though. She wasn't that quick to forgive and forget.

Erin and Rachel struggled with it too, but their thoughts were less direct than Ally's. They thought about the vague explanations and unexpected absences, about the underground fighting, and the strange stories he, Win, and Van had continued to tell that somehow crept in the friends' subconsciouses. Luci may be another piece to that obscure puzzle, or she could be the solution.

Erin feigned casualness about it, hoping to learn more, "So Ms. Perfect has some skeletons in her closet. Big deal. Who at this table doesn't? I know I'm no exception. Besides, Joshua apparently trusts her, so why shouldn't we?"

"Oh, we trust Luci," Lili said, trying to explain further, "but only because Joshua does. None of the rest of us, and I do not just mean our family, completely trust Luci. All of us just take Joshua's word for it. He is the only one who does not question Luci's allegiance."

"Because of their history together?" The pain in Rachel's voice was palpable. She felt abhorred that she would question Joshua's faith in Luci after learning what they'd experienced. She felt even more loathsome towards his family for it, yet she couldn't help thinking that if after all they'd seen from her, they were cautious and untrusting that she should be too.

"Yes." Marc's words were hollow as he spoke. "They went through a great deal together, as you must know, and for that, Joshua will never doubt. I know it may sound harsh of us to question Luci's motives, but in time perhaps you will understand. Though I truly hope not."

The friends were taciturn as they stared at Marc and Lili. Try as they might, no other words would form. Part of them wanted to know why Luci was not to be trusted, but every ounce of them also screamed that it was a terrible idea. Whatever Luci had done, it was enough for the two of the nicest people the friends had ever met to be afraid of her, and that was enough for Ally.

Erin sensed Ally's apprehension, though, and worked to take control of the conversation, "From the way you're talking, I get the feeling Joshua and Luci went through a lot more than just losing their parents together."

The Brownings exchanged looks, trying to decide what was best to say. "I see you know some of Joshua's history," Lili began, "which is probably for the best. You are correct in your assumption, though. They have been through more than any two people should ever have to endure. Joshua almost lost his life defending Luci on more than one occasion, and she has returned the favor multiple times as well. The things those two have seen," she paused as she tried to swallow the lump in her throat, and Marc took her hand, "with the things they have seen, it is a miracle they are still here today. Make no mistake, Luci is a great person, but great people are capable of even greater deceits."

There was a finality in Lili's last words that made it clear the three girls should ask no further questions. It was very evident that whatever was left to be told was Joshua's and Luci's story to tell. Defeated, the friends instead allowed themselves to sit and enjoy the food and drinks that Lauren had served, and they spent the rest of the night talking about Marc's work and the crazy weather and how Lili runs The Brew and the like.

As they drove home, none of the friends bothered to speak. Some unsaid thought between them all made it clear they were each concerned, and there was no need to address it. The friends shuffled inside their house, unaware and unwilling to accept the strange sense looming around them. Exhausted, they each tossed their winter layers onto the chairs in the kitchen and made their way upstairs for bed.

School, fortunately, hadn't come early that next morning, but the friends were still not thrilled about their new schedule given the fact they had class every day of the week for the rest of the semester. Despite being able to sleep in, they had barely slept the night before. No one had visited their dreams, and they had no visions of strange cities, but something tore at the three of them and kept them from ever reaching a deep state of sleep. They awoke late the next day with no idea if Joshua or Win would be in their second semester of History through War, no idea if they were even back in town and a strange sensation that something else was amiss.

They didn't have to wait long, though, as the notifications that went off on Rachel's and Erin's phones told them precisely what was amiss. Rachel sat hers down on the counter and began biting her nails, staring at it in horror. Erin had hardly glanced at hers before she placed it on the counter as well and slumped against the cabinets. Blank expressions stretched across both of their faces, somewhere between fear and shock.

Ally made her way over to look at the phone, but she didn't need to read it to know. Even Erin's words were unnecessary as she said, "He's back."

"*The Ghost of Little Rock Returns*," the headline read.

23
EDMONTON

Ally felt the life drain from her body. They had worked so hard to force themselves into believing the false security that Little Rock's serial killer was gone. It was how they dealt with the passing of Denise, how they rationalized that everything would be fine. They had convinced themselves it was over, but apparently, there was work yet to be done. Ally stood at the edge of the room, afraid to move into the kitchen, afraid to move anywhere. They all had frozen, locked in the terrible moment.

"The police are urging that everyone remain calm." Rachel said, finally reading the article out loud. "While the nature of the crimes is heinous, it is important to remember that they were not random acts of violence. People need not live in fear that someone is lurking on every street corner. Do your due diligence to protect yourselves, lock your doors, don't invite strangers in, everything you should already be doing in your daily life, and trust that we are doing everything in our power to apprehend the culprit. That was the police commissioner, obviously."

"Yeah," Erin interjected, "sounds about right. Says here the body was found this morning, but has been dead for a few days at least. Full details won't be available until the coroner report, of course. From what the article says, though, looks like another situation, just like the others. No evidence, no sign of a struggle, so on and so on. Guess it's a good thing we don't invite strangers into our house. Just promise me one thing, if it's one of us, we save each other for last, right?"

Ally and Rachel couldn't help but chuckle at Erin's macabre joke. That was Erin's method of dealing with anything. Humor and sarcasm were her ultimate defense. The friends appreciated it. Even if it didn't do anything to take away their fear, it at least made it easier to hide.

"So are we canceling the day, or carrying on and pretending nothing happened," Ally asked.

"I, for one," Rachel began, "vote for the pretending nothing happened option. Sitting at home all day is only going to make me go crazy."

"Yeah," Erin answered, "and if you think about it, according to the reports, they all occurred at the victims' houses here in Little Rock. If you asked me, I'd say locked in the house is probably the worst place we could be."

"Oh, fuck off." Ally replied snarkily.

The friends laughed off Erin's joke and grabbed their things to head outside and pretend like everything was fine. There was a harsher chill in the air that morning, a chill they recognized instantly; fear. The girls walked down the sidewalk, afraid of every shadow, every slight movement. They did their best to act as if they were perfectly fine, not scared of their shadows, not fearful of the pair of eyes they were unaware had been watching them from the darkness. Raven Man's words echoed in the friends' minds. "Death is nigh." The friends knew it was true. Death was coming fast.

At The Brew, Lili showed no signs of concern about the latest news. The girls wondered what courage she must have to appear so fearless, especially after Denise. They were pretending, but they knew they were doing it poorly. However, Lili smiled her usual smile, laughed her normal laugh, and even made their drinks without the slightest shake of her hand. She appeared genuinely unfazed by the horrific news.

Erin's hands, on the contrary, were practically vibrating as she grabbed her drink. She pretended it was just the cold as she stared up at the menu curiously. "Hey, Lili," she asked, searching for something to distract herself, "I've always wondered what this little symbol in the corner of the wood is. I can tell it's a bird of some kind, not really sure though with how faint it is, especially with the feathers all kinds of crazy like they are."

Lili smiled again at Erin's description. "That ma'am is an ancient symbol that has come to mean a great deal in our family. Part of having siblings who are incredible historians means coming across things throughout time that carries great significance. For us, it is a constant reminder that life is always moving forward. No matter how much we may enjoy living in the past, every second, minute, and hour is constantly ticking forward. It is a reminder to strive to be better every day. We do not always honor it, of course, but we certainly give it our best."

"Oh wow," Erin replied. "Well, that is something. That's pretty cool."

"Why thank you," Lili replied graciously as she handed them their cups. "If you stick around long enough, you will probably find quite a number of odd historical things our family collects.

The friends couldn't help but smile. It was a subtle thing, a simple symbol the Brownings had adopted that spoke to them. They thanked Lili as they grabbed their drinks and let her words sink in as they headed for the door. The crisp chill waited for them outside, but it strangely did not feel as frigid.

"Did anyone text Thad?" Rachel asked as the trio walked back down the street to their vehicle.

"Not yet." Ally replied regrettably. "Been too busy trying to brush it off."

"Same," Erin added. "Guess we can't put it off for long, though, huh?'

As if on queue, their phones all chimed with notification of their group text.

"Hey guys I saw the news. I'll be in this weekend. We all need to talk, in person. Hope everybody's doing alright. You can always call if you need."

The friends' hearts all skipped a beat. His timing was one thing, but the fact he had said he was coming up meant something entirely different. They knew it had to be about more than just the recent murder. That would have just elicited a message checking in on them. A trip up after they just moved back to town had to mean more.

The thoughts rattled around in their heads on their drive to campus, trying to grasp at any possibility of what Thad might finally know. They wanted to toss ideas back and forth, but everything that came to each of their minds seemed too preposterous to say out loud. So, they made the entire drive to campus in silence, wondering at what lay on the horizon when Thad arrived.

Their schedule that semester was not to the friends' liking at all. Having class every day of the week, was enough of a headache, especially given their drive. Having their second half of History through War be an afternoon class on a day that it was their only class was even worse, but that was the only time the course had been available. They were still perplexed as to how they even made it into the course in the first place, but given they had made it halfway through, largely with the help of Joshua and Win, they had been determined to finish it.

As such, the friends found themselves back in their familiar auditorium later that afternoon, feeling both right at home and completely out of place as always. Familiar faces had filed in around them, filling the room, all except two. Joshua and Win, to their dismay, had still been nowhere to be found. They tried to brush it off as inconsequential, reminding themselves that the two men had not been present on the first day of class the previous semester either. It didn't help.

"Welcome back, class. I see some of you are gluttons for punishment and wish to continue listening to me babbling on and on. Which is good, because I love to bore students with history." Professor Edmonton smiled as the class took out their devices.

"You can leave your notes in your bag for today. I'm going to digress from my normal routine because I want to discuss with you an assignment from last semester." Edmonton continued as the students put their devices away. "I'm sure all of you remember the paper you had to write about comparing two individuals or groups responsible for committing mass murderer of your choice, no?"

The class all nodded their heads, slowly sensing where he was going.

"Now, I'm sure many of you wondered even at the time why I would assign such a paper. I had intended for us to discuss immediately following my return, but given the two gruesome murders, I didn't think it would be apropos to dwell on such matters. In light of recent events in Little Rock, I feel both morbidly and horrifically prophetic for the assignment. More than anything, I am remorseful for my attempt to bring about essential discussions regarding what happens when people and groups commit such heinous acts. My initial reasoning, as this is a history course built around how war shapes our world, was to showcase the staggering difference between when an individual or a small group makes the horrible decision to kill another group or specific type of people systematically, and when a large, organized government or military apparatus which has dominion over a population of people do it. Both acts are terrible, both should be prevented at all possible costs, and both should see anyone who commits such acts be brought to justice.

"There is still a distinction between the two, and I think it is imperative to keep in mind now that we know what happened last fall was not an isolated incident but rather a pattern of whatever sorts. Many of you probably saw the destruction that an individual or small group could have on society in your papers. Some of the attacks in your reports claimed dozens, some even hundreds of lives. Each of those lives lost is a tragedy. As you each had most certainly seen in your papers, however, the numbers when an organized group in a position of power commits such atrocities, the victims rise into the tens or even hundreds of thousands, and in the worst cases even millions. Every death that occurs in a war or a genocide or a terrorist attack or even a gas station robbery is just as tragic as those victims of Little Rock's so-called Ghost. It is crucial as students of history to remember that each death is a tragic loss in this world, and each additional death makes the situation more tragic. As we look at wars and foreign occupations, or even simply natural disasters and famines, both natural and manufactured, throughout history, it is easy to see the total number of lives that were claimed and just catalog it like any other piece of data. Any life lost that could have been prevented is a tragedy.

"It happens. It happened throughout history; it's happening all the time right now. There's no point in avoiding the truth. We all know there's a killer in Little Rock, and not just one who killed out of greed or passion or survival, but out of some form of believed purpose. Just like the people and groups we study every day. I do not say all of this to put you in a state of fear or desensitize you. If your papers taught you anything, it should be that murder, even in large numbers, has been around for centuries, millennia even. No matter what it is labeled in the history books, death is a part of life in our world. We must recognize both that no one should ever have to die of anything but natural causes and that even though none should, people still die from horrible causes all the time. Only in accepting these two facts can we logically look at the world and not be detached from it, and trust me, as chroniclers of history, being detached from the world is very easy to do."

Edmonton had stopped pacing the floor to reflect on his words. He looked out at his audience of students who were all listening intently and studied their faces, looking from one to another to see what emotions lay in their eyes. No hand shot up with questions. No person opened their mouth to utter some deep introspection. Every student sat in silence as his words took root.

"Now that we have all that out of the way," Edmonton paused, letting the severe tone wash away from his voice and giving the class a moment to adjust, "the manner of these deaths has been most unusual. They seem more like something out of a mythic ritual than anything we normally see on the news, which leads me to our next assignment. Being that I've already given you one accidentally morbid project, and our course is quite literally based around warfare, I might as well lean into it and give you an intentionally morbid project. As I've already so thoroughly discussed, death is a common part of history, but the manner of death is something unique."

A pin drop could have been heard in the room as the students sat in anticipation.

"Everything about history serves as a lagging indicator. Often the patterns of events aren't recognizable until the situation has fully unfolded. In the current case the police are working, for example, they haven't found the pattern yet. Eventually, they will do so, catch the bastard doing it, and then in hindsight, the routine will make sense, even if in some strange way. The nature of the deaths themselves, though, is already very evident. You can't pull up the local news without seeing it. History is littered with strange methods of execution. The Huns infamously dismembered their foes. Throughout history, a victim might be decapitated and buried without their head to prevent their entrance into the afterlife. Humans, in general, are horrifyingly creative at coming up with ways to kill one another. Anytime a group puts that degree of thought into execution, though, it has a meaning of some sorts, even if the purpose turns out to be utterly ludicrous given enough time.

"So your first assignment for this new semester is to find a historical example of when a particular group used a particular form of execution that they believe carried some greater meaning or purpose. You could use the two examples I gave, if you can find enough information to make it an informed paper, but that's unlikely. You may also work in groups so long as you still produce at least three pages a piece of information. I would joke that if you find any executions that mirror those in the current police case, please contact the authorities, but I would hope, as you are taking this class, you're smart enough not to go looking for such danger. While we should not fear death, we would also be wise not to invite it to our doorstep. We must be ever vigil in times like these."

The words were a lightning strike in their veins. The friends snapped from their attentive trance and their brains kicked into hyperdrive. With fists clenched and hearts racing, they saw Edmonton in a brand new light. They had thought him just a fun, if not odd, teacher, one of their favorite new professors since they arrived at UCA even. It had never clicked for them that Edmonton was one of the very first people Joshua and Win had ever mentioned, and according to them, he was the very reason they had chosen to attend the school.

"That should do it for today," Edmonton said as the friends watched intensely. "You all know your assignment. Shouldn't take too much of your time, so be sure to enjoy your weekends, ladies and gentlemen."

The class rose from their seats and made for the door with a wave of his hand, but the friends lingered behind wanting to speak with Edmonton. They knew it was unlikely, but after what he'd said, they couldn't help thinking he knew more about the Watchers, and even more important to them, they hoped he also knew about Idonia. It seemed like a stretch, but they kept reminding themselves of his words. So, after the seats had emptied, they headed for the front of the class, where Edmonton was getting his bag ready to leave.

"Ah, if it isn't my favorite three grad students. I was glad to see you came back for another semester." He said without even turning around from the stage. "You have a question, I presume?"

"Um, yes, sir." Erin cleared her throat, hoping to find confidence. "It's about something you said. You said we must be 'ever vigil' in times like these, and well, we found a book, well, an excerpt of a book, and..." She trailed off, feeling like she was rambling and not making any sense.

"The excerpt of the book we found mentioned that exact thing as part of a creed or mantra or something." Rachel said, picking up for Erin. "Being that you're a historian and all, we thought you might know something about it, and whoever they are. It was an excerpt from *Code of the Watchers*."

Edmonton ceased putting things in his bag but didn't turn to face the three friends.

"And possibly," Ally continued, sensing his attentiveness, "if you knew anything about another world known as Idonia, or the Davpyr?"

Edmonton could have been made of stone from how still he stood. The friends were afraid to speak or even move. They held their breath for fear they might stir him. Silence had overtaken the room, and all light seemed to slip away.

"I see Joshua and Win have been filling your head with nonsense." His words were cold as ice.

"So you do know?" Erin barely managed to whisper.

"Yes, I know of them. It would be impossible to know of the Watchers or Idonia without knowing about the other with whom they warred." He paused, turning to face them as he considered his words. "You call me a historian. One does not become such without coming across things outside the purview of factual historical information. There are, of course, stories and myths which make up parts of our world's past that get left out of the history books.

"One such record is from a series of events some four to six thousand years ago. Writings of that time described a group or some secret society that believed themselves god killers. In those days, there were many beliefs as people worshiped various gods and goddesses from different religions or regions. However, this group claimed the deities were merely deceivers, and they hunted the so-called gods and goddesses that they believed had harmed the mortal races. They believed it was their calling to rid the world of the abomination in order to usher in a new day for humanity where they would evolve and rise to their rightful place. They were, however, steeped in much mystery, with some tales being claimed as proof they practice in some form of witchcraft or sorcery. It was said, though, that once the group had destroyed one of the beings they claimed to be false deities, they would record all the data at one of their temples to catalog their war against the forces of Idonia. One such record that discussed this in detail is the aforementioned *Code of the Watchers.*

"Of course, that's where it all goes crazy. No temples have ever been found, no records were documented of their actual existence, and obviously, anyone trying to hunt down and kill gods in the name of some higher power is a little absurd. Even the book you and I have mentioned has never actually been found; only excerpts or select readings pop up throughout history. Stories of them were at one time passed down for years somehow, but eventually, they vanished, and no one really kept looking. The few historians who stumble across the myth anymore consider it to be what would be the equivalent of an urban legend in current times. More than likely, people think it was something cooked up to scare people away from witchcraft and worshipping of false gods or whatnot. Humans in those times did have some very vivid imagination for explaining elementary things."

The friends stood locked in place. Everything they had read, everything they had been told, everything they had seen pointed to the strange groups which Edmonton had so intentionally danced around a truth he clearly knew. They were growing frustrated, anger rising at everyone and everything that, as soon as they neared some fragment of a reality they desperately yearned to grasp, suddenly tore the piece away from them as if it were all merely a game, a grand jest to which they didn't realize they were subject.

Edmonton only exacerbated those emotions when he said, "Unfortunately, ladies, that is all I'm afraid I can share with you. As your teacher and as a fellow historian, it is not my place to tell you such stories."

"Why does everyone keep saying that shit?" Ally's voice flared with a rage she didn't know she possessed.

"We don't give a flying fuck whose place it is to tell us anything. We just want some goddamn answers for once!" Erin exclaimed, Ally's fury having ignited her own.

The three friends stood with their fists clenched. Even Rachel's anger was at the point of boiling over as her heart raced. Their chests rose and fell with heavy breaths as their patience stretched ever thinner.

"Let me ask you this then." Edmonton's icy words chilled the fury rising in the friends as quickly as it had begun. "Have any of you begun seeing visions of their world in your dreams?"

The friends fell silent, frozen solid at his question. The silence stretched on for what felt like ages. Disbelief and confusion warred within the friends. They glanced from one another to Edmonton and back again as the edges of their reality began to fray. *How could he possibly know that?* They asked themselves as their uncertainty mounted at his perplexing observation. *Have they seen everything too?* Each friend asked themself, searching one another for the answers.

"Judging by your silence, I would say that's a yes. So again, I tell you, it is not my place." He spun and grabbed his bag, letting the words hit the friends with full force. "Just know this, ladies; once you learn something, you can never unlearn it. If you need me further, you know where my office is, and I would highly advise you to tell Joshua and

Win, and apparently each other, the things you've seen in your dreams. Good day."

He brushed by Ally, Erin, and Rachel effortlessly and was out the door before they could even turn around. The friends slowly left the room, Edmonton's words trailing behind them. They didn't care what was so dangerous about a dead race of immortals. They didn't care that he had warned them to show caution, just like everyone else had. They didn't even care that for every half-answer they found, they discovered countless new questions. They were determined to find out precisely who the Brownings were, what strange business they were in with the Harbilin Corporation, and what they really knew about the world of Idonia, the Davpyr that inhabited it, and why they had warred with the increasingly ominous Watchers.

Rach, Erin, and Ally did not speak a word on the ride home. Silence filled the drive as each friend questioned what they knew of their strange discoveries, what they had truly learned, and what had just been their minds getting carried away. The brewing storm overhead mirrored that which the friends felt within their own minds. Each had thought themself alone, surrounded by friends that cared but still completely isolated from the group. They had kept all the strange happening to themselves, at times afraid to share it, other times embarrassed. Every one of them had wondered more times than they cared to admit if they were, in fact, losing their mind, and all the while, the friends had each thought that they were alone.

The friends stood in the kitchen of their adorable house on Rock Street, spread out around the island, uncertain what to say or how to say it. None of them had even attempted to go to their room or start doing anything when the three had walked in. They all simply took their outer layers off and positioned themselves around the room, waiting for the conversation that had to come.

Winter's cold had crept into the house, accompanying the chill they all felt of the moment at hand. Even with their sweaters over their undershirts, the friends had still pulled themselves in tightly against their bodies, bracing against the frigid room and the tumultuous storm looming both outside the house and within. Only it was not cold in the room. It was only them, chilled to the bone at the thought of saying out loud what they had each kept so tightly locked away for months.

"Alright," Ally began with a resolve she didn't recognize, "I think it's high time we put all our cards out on the table, and discuss everything we've been keeping to ourselves."

The friends seemed to thaw from their frozen state as they each met her gaze in turn. Warmth and confidence spread through the room as they prepared to embrace the truth.

"Agreed," Erin began, "I…"

Before she could finish her sentence, she was cut off by a knock at the door. For the second time since they had returned to Little Rock, someone had mysteriously arrived at their house, and the friends moved anxiously across the room to see who.

Edmonton's words raced through their minds as they reminded the friends it would be unwise to invite death to their doorstep.

It was not death, though. It was Joshua and Win Browning.

24
SHELL GAME

Joshua stood on the landing of the porch with the collar of his grey double-breasted pea coat pulled up to guard his face from the bitter wind of the oncoming storm, and his hands were buried in his pockets as he gazed down the street. Win stood just beside him, facing the opposite direction in a slim-fitted, long pea coat buckled at the waistline that complimented his brothers. The friends stared at them, unable to speak. They both gave a slight smile that almost put the friends at ease, but they couldn't forget the endless warnings and cautions sounding off in their heads.

"We wanted to come by and offer you an apology in person as soon as we got back in town." Joshua's words were soft and kind as he spoke. "Our departure at Thanksgiving, well, the whole thing was a most terribly unfortunate occurrence. We would have been back sooner, but there was a…"

His words were cut off as the skies were set ablaze with a brilliant lightning strike followed immediately by a deafening boom of thunder. The storm would not hold off for much longer.

"Dear God!" Rachel exclaimed in response to the lightning.

"Yes, it does seem like we are in for quite the deluge tonight. Guess I should be brief then."

"Would you like to come inside?" Erin asked, realizing the rain could have started at any moment.

Joshua and Win shared a quick, inquisitive glance with one another before agreeing.

"Thank you, but we really should be going fairly soon. Hate to be stuck out driving in this after all." Joshua said as the two men stepped inside the house on Rock Street.

Inside the house, Joshua and Win took off their coats and hung them on the wall where instructed. Underneath his jacket, Joshua wore a plain grey v-neck that clung to his massive chest and stretched across his broad shoulder. His brother provided the color for the duo in a soft, thin coral henley that hugged every inch of his chiseled torso, showing every detail of his sculpted frame. Up close in the tiny foyer, Joshua and Win were even more imposing. The friends could not help but feel dwarfed by the two massive figures, but something about how the two men presented themselves made it seem as if being muscular was not even an intention of theirs but merely a natural state of being.

"This is a very nice setup." Win said, admiring the place as they moved to the kitchen. "I like the layout, but you took it up a notch with the decor. Very nice ladies."

"Thanks," Rachel said, slightly flushed, "it's kinda like a grab bag of all of us. We each brought things we liked from home and picked out new things to tie it all together. It's a bit eclectic, but we like it. Would you like to see around the place?"

"Perhaps next time." Win replied with a smile. "Joshua is right; we really must be quick. The rain should be here soon, and we still wanted to swing by and see Lili and Marc."

"You came here first?" Erin asked incredulously.

"We did," Joshua answered. "As I said, we wanted to apologize to you in person as soon as we arrived. Lili and Marc know we returned, of course, but we just got into town. The reason we were gone was at first because of Denise, of course. We wanted to be the ones to inform her family, but that meant tracking them down. A goal that proved largely fruitless. By the time we were able to locate the closest family, we were so far removed that they hardly knew her. We tried friends and connections as well, but it was to no avail. Denise very much kept to herself, it would seem, which makes sense why she felt at ease with us, I suppose.

"After that failed, we turned our attention to figuring out why someone would do such a thing to Denise. Denise may not have been family, but she was close. That made what happened to her personal. So, we spent the last month trying to figure out who Denise was for someone to want her dead."

"What did you find?" Ally asked, drowning in anticipation.

"Nothing." Win said with sadness in his voice. "That was the worst of it. When we learned of the latest incident this morning, it only amplified that. Denise does not seem to fit the other three victims in any way but being as another victim was discovered, and we had found nothing, we decided it was time to come back. We may not be able to assist the police with solving this, but at least we can be here to see when justice is finally served to the person responsible."

There was a bitter edge to Win's tone that was mirrored by the look on Joshua's face. Denise's death was personal for them. Even if she was merely a barista at their coffee shop, she was still as close to the Brownings as almost anyone gets. Joshua's and Win's emotions made even more sense of Lili's and Marc's behaviors. They weren't simply calm or at peace; they were resolved. There may not have been anything they could do, but they were determined to be present when justice finally came.

"We are very sorry for leaving as we did," Joshua began again, "and for not reaching out to you over the break. It was very rude of us. We lost ourselves in the task, but that does not excuse our behavior. Hopefully, you can forgive us. We are not exactly accustomed to having anyone else but our family around. So, it is an adjustment at times remembering that others are affected by our actions."

Joshua's grey eyes were honest and sincere, but the friends couldn't help noticing they also hid something. In that instance, the three girls began to wonder if they would ever honestly know the Brownings, if they would ever give up whatever it was they hid so preciously.

"It was pretty shady," Erin began sarcastically, "but I suppose hunting down the reason why someone you cared about was killed is an okay reason. We'll let it slide this time."

Joshua smiled at her tone. "Why, thank you. You are too gracious, my lady."

"Indeed," Win added with a curt bow. "We are humbled at your mercifulness."

The friends all flushed at the two men's unyielding charm.

"You are joining us for dinner with Marc and Lili tomorrow, are you not?" Joshua asked, changing the subject and catching the friends off guard.

"Um," Ally replied, "yeah."

"Yeah," Rachel said more emphatically, "tomorrow's Friday. That's right. We did tell Lili and Marc we would do dinner."

"We look forward to seeing you then." Win began again, still wearing his charming grin. "On that note, we really should take our leave. We would not want to impose on you, of course, and we must hurry if we wish to beat the storm."

Joshua and Win both smiled graciously as they made their way to the door, grabbing their coats and waving their goodbyes. The friends felt the cold air rush in from outside, which sent Ally's and Rachel's teeth chattering, but they remained on the porch to watch the two men get into their car. The moment they did, another clap of thunder shook the house as the sky flashed and the clouds opened up, unleashing the torrential downpour they had been holding back all day. Water fell so hard it splashed up the steps and onto the porch. The trees lining the sidewalk looked as if they might be blown away by the wind, and within seconds Joshua and Win had disappeared into the stormy night.

The friends sank into the chairs at the kitchen island back inside the house and had completely forgotten they were in the middle of an intense conversation before the Brownings arrived. A few moments later, they had devolved into a debate about dinner. As none of them wanted to go out in the rain, they opted to order pizza and tipped the delivery driver double the bill itself as a thank you and an apology for having to be out in the rain. They spent the rest of the night eating, laughing, and watching television, utterly unaware of how close they had been to finally making a breakthrough.

The friends all slept great that night, free of nightmares of serial killers or Raven Man or the Wanderer. It put them at peace to know Joshua and Win were back in town, despite not being convinced they had heard the whole story of why the two men were gone so long. Regardless, they awoke that next morning refreshed and excited to see Thad and have dinner with the Brownings that night.

The doorbell ringing at 8:30, though, made Ally bolt straight upright in bed. Panicked, she worked to postulate who could be at their door so early in the morning. The friends had already agreed to skip class that day, but that didn't give her any clues. Sitting up in bed and confused by the third person to approach their door in less than a week, Ally heard hurried footsteps fly through the hall, skip over a few stairs, and then clumsily slam their owner's body into the front door. She heard the locks being rapidly forced open, then the door banging against the door catch, but then no words were said.

Eager to know who was at their house, Ally raced through her morning rituals, putting on as little make-up as she was ok with and not even bothering to straighten her hair. She threw on a pair of comfy pants over her sleep shorts and tossed a hoodie over her head, so she didn't have to bother with her bra yet. Within minutes Ally was downstairs, but whatever excitement she'd heard had settled down as Rachel, Erin, and Thad all sat eating cereal.

"Look who decided to grace us with her presence this morning," Thad said with a sarcastic smile. "It's about time you woke up, but you're still not even ready to go get coffee."

"Ready to go?" Ally asked in disbelief. "It's not even nine yet. Why the hell are you here so early?"

"You told me to come early." He replied defensively over a mouth full of cereal.

"Yeah, I meant like lunchtime, not breakfast time." Ally began her trip back up the stairs to finish getting dressed.

"You should be more specific next time," Thad yelled after her.

Thirty minutes later, the four of them were on the sidewalk heading towards The Brew. The rain from the night before had drastically dropped the temperature making the cold so intense they were all surprised not to have snow on the ground, but they knew snow rarely happened in Little Rock. The friends stayed huddled close together as they walked to keep warm.

"So Ally, Erin, and Rachel said you guys were skipping class today, which is convenient considering I'm already here and had planned on just roaming around town. So is the plan, back to the house after coffee?" Thad smiled at the friends as he opened the door to the coffee shop.

The friends half-shrugged, half-nodded while they entered The Brew as if they had yet to remember why Thad had even visited.

At the counter, Lili greeted them, "Well, hello, Thad. It certainly is good to see you back. I trust you will be joining us for dinner tonight then?"

"I wouldn't miss it for the world." Thad smiled back at her. "I've been craving Brave New Restaurant ever since my last trip."

"Oh, the girls didn't tell you?" Lili looked slightly puzzled.

The girls' faces were even more confused. *What were they supposed to tell Thad?* They each thought as they looked at one another, hoping someone would have an answer, but no one spoke.

Sensing the confusion, Lili explained, "We will not be having dinner at Brave New Restaurant this week. We told the girls the other night at dinner that Marc and I were inviting everyone to our house to eat. Ceph and Lavy will be in town and everything."

The group stood frozen in shock. The three girls had somehow completely forgotten about their discussion over dinner. *How had they forgotten? Why had they not thought about it?* They had never seen any of the Brownings' homes. As they came to think of it, they had no idea where any of them even lived. All four of them were taken aback and rather nervous at the thought of it, but the girls were utterly lost as to how they had never managed to register the information for some reason.

Finally, Erin snapped back to reality and replied. "We would be stoked," she began awkwardly, "to join your family for dinner. Um, we don't know where you live, though."

"My my, well, of course not." She smiled as she handed Ally and Rachel their drinks and went back to work on Erin's and Thad's. "We figured you would just follow Joshua and Win there, but we live at 315 Rock St if you come separately."

"Oh yeah, that's one of the big complexes downtown," Rachel responded enthusiastically. "You literally live just down the street from us. We're just a ways up on Rock."

"Well, then I suppose there will be no need to follow Joshua and Win. You should be able to find it no problem."

"Definitely." Ally replied with a smile, choosing not to add that they could see the building from their front porch.

The friends all smiled at each other as she handed them their drinks.

Thad turned back to her in shock, "Wait, how'd you remember what I ordered? That was like months ago."

"What can I say? I have a good memory." She laughed jokingly as she went to help the next customers.

"Well, this should be a pretty fun evening," Erin said, grabbing her seat at their table.

"For real." Thad agreed. "I can't wait to see what their place looks like. I wonder what they'll cook?"

They all exchanged glances. That thought had not yet occurred to them. So many surprises lay ahead for them.

The four sat and finished their first drink. Then each went back for a second. Thad even grabbed a cream cheese Danish and ate it while they finished their second round. After almost an hour had passed of them just talking and hanging out, the four got up to leave, and Lili slid go cups over the counter.

They were almost out the door when Thad had a thought, "Hey Lili, in case we don't meet up with the guys, what's the apartment number?"

"2000" was all they heard as the friends stepped outside.

"2000?" Rachel said, confused. "2000 and what. That's not an apartment number. Wait, is that like the whole floor?"

"Guess we'll see," Thad replied with a laugh. "Least we don't have to worry about finding the place if so."

Within minutes the group was all back in the house on Rock Street, where they settled around the kitchen island, and Thad wasted no time getting to what he had found.

"Alright, everybody had enough caffeine for this?" Thad asked; all the humor and joy from earlier left his voice, and he waited until the friends each nodded before he continued. "So, let's get the elephant in the room taken care of, I don't know anything about the murders, but I am looking into it. With the fact, the cops have nothing, I don't know if I'll be able to find anything, but I promise I'll try. What I have found, though, is about the Brownings. Well, more precisely about who the Brownings work for. I did some digging, and I found some bizarre stuff."

"Strange stuff like what?" Ally asked, the fear creeping back into her mind.

"Well, we both know that Browning isn't really their last name. They took up that name when they came here. They also said that The Brew had been in the family for years, which didn't really make sense. So that's where I started. You guys saw the metric shit ton of paperwork that turned up. I've been going through it for months, and honestly, it still doesn't make any sense, but what does is a pattern I found, loose pattern anyways. So, once it all shakes out, everything ties back to that same Harbilin Corporation that basically owns the whole town. They semi-sorta own one thing in particular that will really throw you for a loop, but I'm getting off-topic. Looking through the property and company records shows each new building and business pops up almost systematically. Every couple years, a new business gets formed, new properties get acquired, and they all get rolled into this giant web of shell companies. Once I got to lookin' through all the records in New York, it was easier to see the pattern the further and further back I went because there were fewer pieces of the puzzle. Behind all the smoke and mirrors, Harbilin Corporation practically owns New York City, but it gets better. They don't even exist."

"What?" was all the friends could mutter.

"The company was originally founded by a family named Harbilin. No official records can be found of the family past, like, the 1820s. After that, it's all just the Harbilin Corporation with no known members or anything. I don't know if the family died off and someone else has just kept the name going with the business, or if they're just ghosts and can do whatever the fuck they want. We know that someone's still managing the family business nowadays, but no one has ever had direct contact with them. Not that I can find. It's always a phone call from some untraceable number or a piece of mail with no return address and no postmark, or a visit from someone who works for them. And we all know who currently works for them."

"The Brownings." Ally's words were a soft whisper as Erin and Rachel sat transfixed with her.

"Bingo. But, only in recent times, though. For the last few years, everyone who's dealt with the Harbilin Corporation has done so through the Brownings. It wasn't always them, though. They're just the latest spokesperson or figurehead or whatever you wanna call it. Before that, it was the Millers, and before them, it was the Smiths, and you get the idea. Every few decades, it changes. It's like the company, or the family, whatever it is, it's like it picks new people to represent them once one family passes away, or I don't know, gets too old? All the while, whoever actually runs the Harbilin empires stays invisible, putting everything into place. I'd bet the Brownings haven't even met 'em. I don't think anyone has, apparently. Whoever the front is just does what they're told and makes sure everything goes as planned."

The friends each took a deep breath and tried to regain their thoughts. One by one, they opened their mouths to speak, but no words came out. Instead, they sat in silence, letting everything Thad had said sink in.

"So, what, are they like the mafia or Illuminati or what?" Erin asked the group, trying to process the situation.

"Well," Thad began as the girls each held their breath, "not from what I can tell. I couldn't find a single thing that pointed towards them being involved in anything illegal, not that me not finding anything is evidence of their innocence, I guess. I mean, the fact that they virtually don't exist seems rather shady. On the other hand, though, the whole point of the mob is to obtain power and be untouchable. So what's the point of being powerful and invincible if no one knows you exist? Quite the opposite of that, though, it really seems like everything they've done is to remain hidden, and I don't mean the way the Brownings stay hidden. I mean truly hidden, but what could possibly cause a family to want to remain hidden for hundreds of years?"

"What if the stories Joshua's been telling are true?" The words escaped her mouth before Ally could stop them.

"You mean the stuff about Idonia?" Thad looked at Ally in astonishment. Each of the friends was thinking about it. They had been for some time. Edmonton's message from the previous day came rushing back, and the girls remembered the night before when they had stood in the same spots in the kitchen on the verge of discussing everything they had seen, only to have it slip away. *Why did it keep slipping away?* They each thought. Every time they got close to something, close to a truth of some kind, it would either slip away, or they would somehow get distracted and forget. It was as if their minds didn't want to find the truth any more than the truth wanted to be seen.

Ally, though, had reached her limit. "Guys," she began, her breath shaking with fear as her mind struggled to form the words and speak into being the truth she had been hiding deep inside, "Edmonton was right yesterday. I think we all knew it the moment he said it, but for some reason, we couldn't acknowledge it."

"Said what?" Thad asked, confusion and fear rising in his voice.

"Edmonton told us," Erin began but paused as she worked to steady her voice. "He told us that he knew of Idonia and the Davpyr and whatever the hell the Code of the Watchers is. Then, he asked if we had begun seeing their world." She paused again. The words were beginning to catch in her throat, and she had to fight to get them out. She had to say it, had to make it known. "I have. I've been having dreams about, well, about whatever Idonia is. Please tell me I'm not alone."

There was deep sorrow in her voice, fear at the thought of being truly alone. Erin had felt alone the entire time. So had Ally and Rachel and even Thad. They had each felt isolated from the rest of the group as if they alone were suffering.

"I have too." Ally said, grabbing Erin's hand for comfort. "You're not alone, Erin. I've seen their world, and other things too. Things I can't quite understand. There's this figure, two of 'em. One is hooded and cloaked, with nothing visible of his face but a pair of glowing eyes. The other is…"

"A man made of ravens," Thad said, finishing her sentence. "The flock follows you, watching you, and then eventually it forms into the haunting figure of a man whose words are darker than the feathers that make him, 'Death is Coming.' That's all he says. His words are like ice being poured through your veins, but it isn't a threat. He says it simply as a statement of fact. A truth that cannot be escaped. The only words harsher than his, are that of the other. The Wanderer. I can feel his words inside my head even now…"

"Nigh is the Hour of the Raven and the Lion." Rachel said, sending a shock down everyone's spines. Even coming from her, the words were otherworldly and felt like they might rip the friends apart as if they were being split atom by atom. "I've seen them too. I've seen Idonia, and, I think, other cities that make up their world. They were similar in ways, but certain things were different. The tree is the main thing I remember. There was always a great tree towering above everything. I saw something else too." Rachel paused, unsure if she even felt safe saying the other thing. Of everything else, it was the one thing that terrified her the most.

"You saw corpses murdered the same way as the Ghost, didn't you?" Ally asked, a mixture of fear and hope in her voice. Hope that she indeed wasn't alone, and yet fear that everything they had seen wasn't just her delusion.

Rachel nodded her head in agreement, confirming Ally's fears and hopes, and Ally noticed that Erin and Thad were nodding as well. It was done. They had all said the truth they were hiding deep inside, admitting it to themselves as much as to one another, for the first time ever. They weren't going mad, or perhaps they were, but if so, they were doing it together. That gave the friends some semblance of peace, knowing they weren't alone on whatever the journey was.

"So," Erin began, bringing the group back to reality, "either we're all losing our minds together, or…"

She trailed off, struggling to finish the sentence.

"Or," Thad picked up where Erin left off, "the Brownings are telling the truth, and we're stumbling into whatever next-level shit them, and the Harbilins are involved with."

The friends all let out a deep breath, feeling the weight of Thad's words.

"Well then," Rachel spoke for the group, "it looks like we have a decision to make. We can either go on the rest of our lives pretending like none of this ever happened. We walk away, and we never look back. It's that, or we accept that all of this is connected somehow. Idonia, the dreams, the Raven Man, the Wanderer, the Ghost, the Watchers, it's all connected to the Brownings and whatever the Hariblins are doing."

"I feel like we keep finding ourselves at this point," Erin added with a somber tone. "We keep having to make this decision, and I don't understand why. Joshua said there were secrets in this world worth dying, secrets worth killing. Something dangerous is at work here, and I think we're running out of chances to get away. If you ask me, I think we've already ran out of chances."

"I'm with Erin," Thad said without hesitation. "I know I was late to this whole thing, and I know I'm not directly in it like you guys are, but I'm in it too far to get out. My whole life has been spent waiting around, hoping for something spectacular. This is it."

"Agreed," Rachel added emphatically. "For my entire life, I just wanted the chance to do something great. I never knew what that something would be, but now I do. I'm not turning back. I'm scared shitless, I have absolutely no idea what's ahead for us, and for the first time ever, I am fucking ready for it. So what do you say, Ally?"

Ally's lips curled into a soft grin. "I say we need to get ready for dinner."

25
PENTHOUSE PARADOX

The friends opted to walk to Lili and Marc's condo since the River Market Tower was just down Rock Street, but the cold had them immediately questioning their decision. Bundled up, the four friends made their way a few blocks towards the river. The building grew more prominent and more imposing as they approached it. It was by no means an incredibly tall structure, but something about it gave the sense of power and grandeur as it towered over its immediate surroundings.

The River Market Tower was wealth and luxury, one of the most prestigious condos in Little Rock, and a rarity in a city dominated by houses spread out across the town. Little Rock was a city built horizontally, yet Marc and Lili chose to live in one of the few places that defied that norm, nestling their home up in the sky instead of sprawled out across the land. The friends were not all too surprised to learn that Marc and Lili lived there. The Harbilins may have been completely hidden, but the Brownings preferred to hide in plain sight.

The friends arrived at the Tower to find Joshua and Win waiting just outside the entrance that was nestled between a quaint local market that inhabited one corner of the building and a fantastic Irish pub named Dugan's in the other. The two men eagerly said their hellos to all of the friends, embracing Thad after the long absence. Erin couldn't help noticing how easily Thad took to them both. From the moment they had first met, it had been as if they were old friends, and it was in that moment she realized the same could essentially be said for the girls. Despite all the ambiguity surrounding Joshua and Win, and all the ominous occurrences, they swiftly became an eclectic group of friends. After the handshakes and high fives were done, the group turned and led the friends towards the inside.

The interior of the River Market Tower was sleek and efficient, with white tiles stretching endlessly across the foyer that was complemented by the rich walnut lining the walls and welcome desk. There were several seating options in the lobby for residents to entertain guests without going upstairs, all of which were wrapped in supple leather and accompanied by smooth metal tables. The greeter at the desk gave a polite smile and waved at Joshua and Win but said nothing as the two led the friends onto the elevator. Inside the elevator, though, the group noticed something incredibly unusual.

"There's no number 20." Rachel pointed out as all four of them were staring at the buttons.

"Yeah, I thought Marc and Lili said they lived on the twentieth floor?" Thad was just as confused.

"They do." was all Joshua said as he pushed the number nineteen button on the controls.

The four friends looked back and forth at each other and the Browning brothers as the elevator rose floor after floor. The elevator dinged nineteen, and the doors split open. Joshua and Win casually stepped out and, without a word, began leading them down a winding hallway. They saw room 1901 immediately on their right, followed by room 1902 on their left as they rounded the first curve. They began to wonder if the whole twentieth-floor bit was actually a joke, and the family lived at the end of the hall until they rounded the final corner and saw it.

A stunning mahogany staircase rose from the end of the hall and wrapped majestically back around to what could only be the elusive twentieth-floor. A giant glass window curved around the left side of the staircase, giving a full view of the city below as the river rolled patiently through. As they made the turn around the stairs, the four friends found themselves looking directly into a very simple yet gorgeous foyer. Two hand-carved white-wood tables like that of the menu at The Brew rested against either wall, each adorned with a vase of fresh yellow roses pointing up the high vaulted ceiling from which hung a small but ornate crystal chandelier.

The foyer had the same mahogany that flowed in from the staircase and led to the hallway at the end, adding natural warmth to the remarkable luster of the building. The friends could hear laughter coming from somewhere in the house, but it was hard to tell where as large as the floor was. At the end of the foyer, the hall split in two and wrapped around a wall holding a massive painting of a castle on a cliffside.

Once around the portrait, the hallway came back together and led into an enormous open room which stretched deep into the building that could have easily fit the friends' entire house within it and still had space leftover. Glass panels grew from the floors to vaulted ceilings high overhead on each side of the room that opened up to the lush terrace that incased the house, giving the friends the sensation they stood high atop the juggle canopy looking out over the city below. There were plants of almost every kind the friends had ever seen and some they hadn't growing in the beautiful balcony forest, and the interior complimented as with various flora scattered throughout the massive room as if the rainforest outside were slowly creeping in. Some hung from the ceilings high above while others stood tall in floor planters or nestled cozily on the various tables.

The wooden walkway continued the path, but the floor sloped downward on either side to the sunken marble floor below, making it feel like the friends were atop a levy. Faint neon lights were embedded on the edges of the wooden path bringing the wood vibrantly to life with an electric glow that complemented its warmth. On the left side of the mahogany trail was a collection of leather sofas and chairs in greys and browns that formed a social living room in a way that gave the appearance of stone and wood structures decorating the marbled landscape and leading up to the far wall where an ornate fireplace was nestled. The hearth covered almost the entire width of the wall, which stretched across the left half of the room, and it was adorned with an assortment of candles and trinkets that rested on it and a painting of a colossal tree with golden, fiery leaves mounted above it. On the right, a full wet bar stocked with every liquor one might ever need stretched in an L-shape along the opposite half of the back wall and wrapped out against the massive windows, and it was paired with the second section of a bar which curved outward from the corner for seating. Closer to the entrance, there was a pool table and a number of card tables in the recessed area that all fanned around a giant screen encompassing almost the entire wall of the foyer.

The mahogany levy led across the massive room to another hallway which cut the far wall in half and split the wooden walkway in two as it flowed deeper into the house. The friends followed Joshua and Win across the room for what seemed like ages before they reached the split and took the left path, which led by another vast, open area that was clearly Marc's office. Screens lined both walls, and a large touchscreen table sat in the middle, all powered down but still alluding to the sheer scale of the work Marc did. As they passed through Marc's office, the right wall gave way to a vast expanse of glass enclosing an aquarium that felt as if it should be in a museum. The friends had never known such a colossal aquarium could exist in someone's house. The glass wall of it curved slightly to the right before it cut sharply back to the left, forming a barrier of its own. Inside there were countless exotic fish of all different kinds, from vibrant Tangs to stunning Angelfish to hauntingly beautiful platinum Arowanas and even more, the friends had never seen before, all of which danced their aquatic waltz through the astonishing aquarium that seemed unending.

As they reached the curve in the glass, which served as a wall, the friends realized they could see through the tank into the dining room beyond. After they rounded the curve, they saw the jaw-droppingly huge kitchen where Marc and Lili stood cooking. A stunning columned refrigerator started the kitchen on the interior wall where the aquarium vanished into the wall and led into the bleached driftwood cabinets topped with black granite countertops that were flecked with white and gold. Hence, it looked as if a galaxy swirled atop the ashen wood. The mahogany floor gave a gorgeous warming contrast of rich brown against the black and white kitchen structure, bringing the entire room vibrantly alive. The island in the middle housed the sprawling cooktop with gas burners, induction surfaces, and electric griddles, all dancing to the tune of Marc and Lili's culinary concert. The cast iron chef's rack hanging well above their heads, with all the pots and pans one could imagine, completed the astounding kitchen that left the friends feeling as if they had stepped onto the set of a cooking show.

The island also doubled as a long enough bar to seat at least a dozen in the wrought iron chairs that matched the chef's rack, adorned with soft yellow cushions. That's where the friends saw the rest of the dinner crew seated, laughing with the cooks and eating the various hors d'oeuvres covering the bar in front of them; cheese plates with everything from gouda to chevre, freshly baked garlic bread, homemade hummus with carrots, cucumbers, and chips, roasted mushrooms stuffed with creamy pepper sauces, and skewers of lamb that were roasting in a lemon butter glaze on a small rotisserie which turned over the open flame of the burners.

Ceph, Lavy, Van, and even Terry all turned to greet the friends as they entered the room, along with another young man the friends had never seen before.

"Well, well, well," Ceph said as he stood from the bar with a massive smile on his face, "look who found their way back to us. Thad, it is a pleasure to see you again, and ladies, it is always a joy to have you around. I must say, I am quite glad that Joshua and Win have not scared you away."

The girls all laughed. Rachel's face was flushed. Thad just smiled his approval.

"It is always a treat to have you, ladies, around," Lavy said as she greeted the group. "As for you, Thad, it is about time. I hate that we are only in town for the night. It seems we get far too little time together."

"Aw, you aren't sticking around for the weekend?" Rachel said as she returned the greeting.

"Sadly not." Lavy continued. "We all fly to New York tomorrow for a few days to finish up a project Ceph and I started over the holidays. Sometimes things are just easier to get done with the whole family around."

The friends couldn't help noticing the strained tone in her voice, but they didn't bother to press her.

Thad shook hands and hugged the whole family before turning to Van in search of a distraction. "Van, I didn't know you were going to be in town for dinner. Here I thought I was special being invited over, but apparently, they'll have anybody up here."

Van laughed as he gave Thad a firm half-five, half-hand shake. "Well, I wasn't about to miss an awesome reunion with everyone. I got in town last night actually and ended up crashing at Terry's after handling some work stuff."

"Oh really?" Asked Erin, giving Terry her best "for shame" look.

"Oh no," Terry began as her face turned red. "It wasn't like that. He came over to visit. It wasn't like we were. We were just up late, oh dear."

Terry put her hand to her face and shook her head in embarrassment. Ally did her best not to laugh as she knew how Terry must have felt. Van put his arm around her, though, and gave her a reassuring hug.

"Terry is correct," Van said, stepping in to save her any further embarrassment, "and if you don't believe her, you can ask her brother who was there with us the whole time."

"Yes!" Terry exclaimed, regaining her awareness and coming out of her embarrassment. "Yes, of course. Guys, this is my brother Dante. Dante, this is Ally, Erin, Rachel, and Thad." She said, indicating each of them in turn.

The young man was tall and lean with smooth features that added to his youthful look. His face was slightly rounded, similar to his sister's, and his eyes had a softness like hers as well. He had the appearance of someone spry and athletic but still unpolished and raw, and he exuded a kindness that felt almost empathetic in a sense. Something about him made it apparent he was younger than Terry, yet he still carried himself as a person with youthful wisdom. Ally met his eyes directly, studying the softness within them as if seeking to understand what drove the young man. Erin and Rachel assessed him as well and found that, for some reason, they felt he was nice in the simplest of ways. He was simply a nice person, which only felt fitting to them given what they had learned of Terry.

"It's a pleasure to meet all of you," Dante said as he shook hands with each of the friends, and the friends couldn't help notice how completely out of place he seemed. Dante was meek and calm. He was diametrically opposed to the Brownings' strange brand of ostentatious ambiguity, and it showed. The friends greeted him with warmth, though, sensing a kindred spirit amidst the Brownings' eccentricity.

"Glad to meet you, Dante," Thad said with a cordial smile.

"Likewise," Rachel added. "The pleasure's ours."

"So, what brings you to town?" Erin asked, trying her best to sound amiable and not prying.

"Just visiting, sis," Dante replied, matching their smiles. "Been meaning to get out here for a while and see her, whole family has really, but you know how it goes. Just gotta make the time somewhere. I finally managed to get out here, though, so I took the chance while I had it. It's been nice getting to see the life she's made here."

"Well, we have been truly blessed to get to know her," Lili said with motherly warmth. "Thanks to you and Van, she is finally joining us for dinner. So we owe you for that as well. She has been outright invaluable at The Brew. Without her, losing Denise would have been..." Lili paused, unable to find the proper words.

"I am terribly sorry for your loss," Dante responded with a sorrow so deep it surprised the friends. "Terry told me everything. I… I realize I didn't know her, and I'm just now meeting all of you, but that doesn't change how tragic what happened to her was."

"That is very sweet of you," Lili said in a reassuring tone. "You have a kind soul. I meant to say that there is no chance we would have made it through that period if not for Terry. She was truly a soldier."

Terry seemed mildly embarrassed, but Dante smiled in thanks at Lili's kind words.

"You gonna be in town for a while?" Ally asked, looking to change the subject more for Terry than anyone else. "You two should come with us to catch a movie or something if so."

"I'll only be here for about a week," Dante replied, equally glad for the distraction, "but I've already promised Terry that I won't stay gone for too long this next time."

Terry gave him a loving smile which he returned graciously.

"Well then," Ally continued with a grin, "if y'all want to hang out while you're here, just hit us up. If not, there's always next time."

"Sure thing. Thanks." Dante said with a genuine appreciation that he was glad to receive such a warm invitation from them all.

"So I take it you lot were able to find the place alright?" Marc asked the friends as he chopped chicken into thin slices and placed them in an egg bath to prepare for breading. Next to him, Lili minced garlic cloves and tossed them into an oiled pan with onions simmering to start the base of a sauce.

"Ha. That's rich." Erin replied. "We never would've found the place if it weren't for Joshua and Win leading us around. I would have thought we were in the wrong building the second we stepped on the elevator if it weren't for them, and I certainly wouldn't have had the balls to climb up the random-ass, gorgeous staircase to who the hell knows where."

The whole family chuckled as if that were some kind of running joke.

"On that note," Rachel began softly, "this place is absolutely beautiful y'all."

At her words, the friends all looked around the room to study it even more as if talking to the Brownings had made them forget they were in a luxury condo the likes of which they had never imagined.

Across from the kitchen, the towering glass panels that wrapped the condominium in its concrete rainforest continued at least another twenty feet past the island area before a wall sprung out of it. The dining table sat in the middle of the room. It was a long white-wooden table that looked as if Marc and Lili had bought it from a castle, and it was big enough to feed a banquet of twenty with ease. The room itself was large enough that it stretched all the way to the glass panels on the other side of the condo, making the room feel even more open than its size. The aquarium reappeared on the other side of the cabinets, bulging out in points and curving in at others, making up pretty much the entire distance to the window on the far side except for a four-foot slice of metal between it and the glass. In the wall opposite of that on the other side of the table was a large archway through which continued the neon trimmed mahogany path that seemed to carve through the house. It split into two yet again, and the four friends couldn't help but wonder just how far the home stretched.

As if he had sensed this, Joshua spoke up, "Would you like a tour of the place before we eat?"

"That'd be great." Ally said with a huge smile, not caring if she sounded overly excited.

"Very well. Van, have Terry and Dante seen the whole place?" Joshua asked, to which Van shook his head as he took a sip of his Manhattan. "Well, why not bring them along then."

Van and Terry stood up to join the tour group as Joshua led them further into the house, pointing things out as they went. The left side of the path curved out and took them into a home theatre that could have easily doubled as an actual theatre. It had five rows of stadium-style seats, all decked in plush black leather. There were eight seats in a row, but the seats were all large enough they could easily seat two each, and there was enough space between the rows for all the chairs to recline comfortably. This was the only room in the house that wasn't lined with glass, but instead, a thirty-foot screen stretched out to cover the wall.

On the path again, the group walked a little further as it curved back in and finally showed the end of the house. The course opened up into another sunken room with a second visiting area and another group of lounge chairs and sofas for casual conversation. What made the room stand apart from the rest was that it was wrapped entirely in glass, walls and ceiling, aside from the side through which they had just entered.

Everyone looked up to see the stars shining brightly through the glass ceiling. The moonlight fell at their feet as it poured in from the right panel of windows. It was like the room was an aquarium of its own where they were the fish looking out at the beautiful world around them.

Outside the glass, the terrace wrapped around to show a lovely walking path on the roof with plants growing on all sides. In the left corner of the room where the glass touched the theatre, the friends could see a greenhouse extending from the building. The glass and stone all flowed around to a beautiful pool at the end of the house with two massive stone walkways leading off into the far corners, which the friends assumed were separate hot tubs decorated with beautiful stone archways. They stood for a time taking in the incredible view, letting it soak into their very beings as if they stood on the threshold of a new world just awaiting their discovery.

Breaking the silence, Joshua said, "Dinner is ready," as he turned with a smile to the group just before Lavy yelled it through the hallway.

The growing group sat down at the medieval banquet table to the plethora of Mediterranean delicacies, including a personal rendition of parmesan chicken with a creamy vodka sauce straight from Marc's homemade recipes and zesty salmon kabobs with fresh tzatziki sauce. Lili let them know how much of a treat they were in for as Marc was a master chef. According to her, they'd be hard-pressed to find better cuisine even along the Mediterranean itself. Marc just laughed and waved it off, but the comments from his family only furthered Lili's claim, and when the friends tried the succulent food he'd prepared, it was impossible for Marc to deny.

The evening went on in the same manner. Everyone laughed and ate and had a good time. After dinner was over, Marc and Lili ushered everyone into the theatre for a movie and dessert. Win made what the family called his specialty; a cream stuffed chocolate chip cookie pie served with homemade vanilla ice cream. Trays folded up out of the armrests in the theatre, and the friends couldn't help thinking they were in some spaceship rather than a home theatre.

Once everyone was full and the movie was over, they all went home, waving goodbyes and giving hugs. Ally had never felt more welcome in a place that wasn't her own home; none of them had. The walk home was filled with commentary and opinions of how amazing Marc and Lili's house was, how incredible the food was, how nice Dante seemed, and how much they had enjoyed the way everyone seemed to get along. The night had been a perfect evening in the friends' eyes, and by the time they arrived at the apartment, all of the friends were ready to drift off to sleep, completely unaware of the dangerous game that was being played all around them.

26
WAR OF THE ROSES

The weekend had gone in a flash. The friends had slept peacefully, undisturbed by nightmares, but they did repeatedly revisit Idonia in their dreams. They were calm visions, though. Treelit strolls through the gorgeous courtyards, down by the mighty river, and through the sprawling, otherworldly metropolis, left the friends feeling closer and closer to that world, as if they were beginning to belong. Ally woke one night to the sound of strange noises, but she immediately shut it out for fear the nightmares might return and fell quickly back asleep.

Sunday night came all too fast, and the girls were all a little sad to see Thad leave. He promised them all he'd be back the following weekend, though. He had hugged them all, climbed in his car, and drove off with the friends feeling even more like a piece of themselves was missing. Thad had not just been a little slice of home. He was a part of them forever, and the more time spent apart, the more the moments together made the friends realize how much they needed him in their lives.

With their hearts heavy, the girls had hurried back inside to warm up as quickly as they could, and each headed off to their own room to wind down before bed. They knew the first real week of school would begin the next day, and they needed to be ready.

Each day they had been back in Little Rock, the temperature seemed to drop even more, and that following morning had been no different. Dressed in as many layers as they could stand, the friends headed for their class, skipping The Brew entirely. The Brownings were still out of town, and none of the friends felt like walking that far in the freezing cold. Even the auditorium for History through War felt colder than usual despite all the heaters blazing.

Ally and Rachel didn't even bother taking their overcoats off when they sat down. Edmonton was back to business, unlike the previous week. They were already moving onto a series of dynastic wars between the houses of Lancaster and York for the throne of England between the years 1455-1485 AD. They did their best to pay attention but wound up mindlessly jotting down notes to be reviewed later. Despite being a long class, the furious note-taking had made it pass swiftly, and the friends were glad for the class to be over as they slowly dragged themselves out the door.

"Well, don't we just look riveted. Edmonton must really be getting into his lectures."

They hadn't even seen the person leaning against the door outside of the small auditorium as they walked through the doors. The voice made them jump at first, Erin especially, but they all relaxed once they recognized the ever-so-charming voice.

"I take it you and Joshua had a good trip then?" Ally said, turning to face the man. "Wait, where's Joshua?" She added when she noticed Win was standing against the wall alone.

"Ah, our beloved Joshua is not back in town yet. He is still helping Ceph and Lavy. That is why I'm here." Win pushed himself off the wall with his foot and threw his arms around Ally's and Rachel's shoulders as the group turned to walk. "I'm supposed to be checking on you, making sure you're ok, and seeing if you need anything. You know, being that there's kind of a killer on the loose and all."

"Ok, first of all," Erin began, unsure how to take another of Win's sudden changes of personality, "since when did you start casually traipsing about with your arms around people? Secondly, why the hell are all of you talking so normal all of the sudden?"

Win left his arm around the two as they walked across the lawn, and he replied in a mocking tone, "Well, first of all, I do not traipse. I always walk with purpose." He smiled at Erin with a playful wink. "As for your second question, well, sometimes it's ok to let our hair down, is it not. Besides, Joshua knows none of you really care for the way we typically speak, but he can't bring himself to communicate in any other way. Frankly, neither can we when we're around him. Interesting how adaptation works."

Ally had considered removing his arm herself, but in the bleak weather, she was actually glad to have his warmth around her. "He doesn't know that." She said, looking for some way to combat Win's sudden bravado. "None of us ever told him that."

"You are funny." Win said, straining to hold in his laugh. "As if Joshua needs to be told something. He's a great deal more, how would you say, perceptive than that. Now, what are we getting to eat? I'm starving."

"Um, I don't know," Rachel replied, trying to keep pace with Win's character change. "I didn't know we were getting something to eat."

"Well, of course, we are." There was a long pause as Win had stopped and released Rachel and Ally, smirking devilishly at the friends. "Because if we don't, how else are you going to ask me all those questions rolling about in your minds that you've been dying to know but somehow can't bring yourself to ask?"

The friends froze. It was that moment in The Brew all over again. Win was baiting them, daring them to dive deeper down the rabbit hole, not realizing they were already too committed ever to turn back. The three didn't have to bother discussing it. Their decision had already been made.

Without hesitation, Erin spoke for the group, "We're following you."

A short car ride later and the friends found themselves getting out in front of the same dimly lit basement pub just down from their house, where Luci had taken them. They paused at the sight of it. It felt even stranger in the daytime. At night it had been secretive yet inviting. By day, though, the place felt forbidden. Win didn't even bother to slow down. He opened the door for them and turned to see she was still halfway up the staircase.

"It's going to be rather hard to eat out there." Win smirked.

The friends snapped back to reality and continued to follow the charming man into the bar.

Inside, the bar was just as dark as it had been the night with Luci. Thanks to the no-smoking policy, though, there was no haze like in most twenty-one and over places. They glanced at the bar that stretched along the right side of the building, realizing it was stocked with more alcohol than the friends knew existed. They hadn't noticed before just how lovely the building was nor the collection of premium liquors. What they had first thought to be a simple speakeasy they quickly realized must have been one of the most exotic and exclusive places in the entire city.

"Hey, Win. Gonna be the usual for you and Joshua?" A heavy-set bartender called from behind the counter. "Oh, you got lady friends with ya. I'll get Jenny out here to wait on y'all then."

"Thanks, Tony." Win gave the bartender a friendly wave as he made straight for the same booth the friends had sat in with Luci.

"You and Joshua come here a lot?" Ally asked, taking her jacket off and tossing it deep in the booth.

"Anytime we want to get out of the house and have a drink, this is where we come. The food's pretty good too. There are only like three things on the menu, but they're good nonetheless. It's particularly nice on the nights they have a band playing. Nothing like smooth jazz and hard liquor."

"How do y'all drink so casually?" Erin asked, genuinely confused. "You act like you grew up in a distillery."

Win couldn't help but chuckle mischievously. "Maybe I did."

Suddenly a slim girl in a flapper dress that showed off nearly every inch of her long, perfectly tanned legs sauntered over, her six-inch black heels clicking against the hardwood as she walked. Her left arm was covered in a full-sleeve tattoo that stretched out onto her chest and connected down to a rib piece that could be seen thanks to the lace sides of her dress. The plunge of which reached so incredibly low it almost touched her navel. Her ears were gauged slightly, flashing a stunning red and black glass piece in each ear that matched her jet black hair, which was streaked with red. She was the embodiment of the roaring twenties turned twenty-first century.

"Aw, you didn't bring your friend along tonight, huh, Win?" Her voice was playful and sweet, but the look in her eyes made it clear the Browning brothers were both very much to her liking.

"No, ma'am. Sorry to break your heart, Jenny. He's out of town. I'm just having some dinner with my friends here." He extended his hand across the table towards the friends.

"Friends, eh? Well, aren't you lucky ladies in for a treat? Can I get you something to drink to get things started? A little liquid courage, perhaps." Her wicked smile made the girls' cheeks flush.

"I'll just have a water, please." Ally said, feeling suddenly innocent in a most awkward way and very out of place.

"IPA, please. Whatever's on tap." Rachel replied, resorting to her usual choice for safety and security.

Erin refused to back down from an awkward moment, though, "You know what, I'll take an Aviation. I dig your hair, by the way."

"Why, thank you." Jenny smiled, feeling genuinely flattered. "Same for you, my gal. The usual for you, Win?" The girl said, turning her seductive gaze on him.

"Actually, I'll drink what she's having." Win said, pointing at Erin and giving her a charming smile. "Oh, and two of the House Burgers, made my way."

"With pleasure, sir," Jenny said with a tone that suggested she very much enjoyed being bossed around by Win.

Ally waited briefly after Jenny left before she let the sarcasm enter her voice, "Well, she seems nice."

"Don't worry. She's harmless." He smiled playfully. "Jenny may come off like a firecracker, but she's really just a teddy bear."

The words were barely out of Win's mouth before Jenny was back with their drinks.

"Anything else I can do for you?" Jenny asked, eyes fixed longingly on Win.

"Just be sure you bring me another as soon as this one's empty," Win replied, tapping his glass, but he gave her a smoldering grin as well, "and continue being your wonderful, amazing self."

With a sultry smile and a soft pat on Win's shoulder, she disappeared from the room.

"Well, lay it on me." Win said to the friends motioning his hands for them to come forward.

"What?" Erin said, looking confused. "Oh, the questions. Shit, duh."

Win let out a very humored chuckle.

"Alright." Ally began, quickly working to cover for Erin. "Why are you so eager to tell us something when everyone gives us nothing but riddles and warnings, offering no more than just a tidbit at a time?"

"Because I am restrained by neither their own personal rules nor their morals. That being said, I cannot answer every question you ask. You see, Joshua is a big storyteller type, a loremaster, if you will. The type that has to tell the story from the beginning to the end." Win touched his left hand to his right and then stretched it out, demonstrating the story. "I, however, don't mind bending the rules a bit, but there are still certain things you can't know until the proper time. You wouldn't tell someone to start reading the Bible with the Book of Revelation, just like you wouldn't try explaining quantum field theory to someone just learning basic physics. Context is key."

"Fine, then." Rachel said, growing tired of the Brownings' games. "Then my first question is, what's with all the damn rules?"

A look of fake remorse crossed Win's face. "Alas, your first question is one I cannot answer. I will say this, though, do you know what happened to the first people to oppose Judaism and Christianity and virtually any other established religion? They were executed, and not usually in a simple manner. So, I think you can understand part of why we are cautious."

"You're not going to get executed in the twenty-first century," Erin said indignantly.

"Next question." Win replied sternly, closing the topic.

"Whatever." Ally replied sharply. "What can you tell us about the *Code of the Watchers* then."

"Ah, yes indeed," Win replied in a way that almost sounded like a sigh of relief, "now we're getting to the fun part. The better question is, what can you three ladies tell me about the *Code of the Watchers*."

"Practically, fucking, nothing," Erin replied, pausing between each word to emphasize her frustration. "You said you would answer our damn questions, and here you are just dancing around every one. We couldn't find jackshit on whatever the hell the *Code of the Watchers* is aside from one tiny little excerpt. Some speech or letter or something like that of a guy explaining how the Davpyr first found our world, worlds, I don't know. And how they had worked to reforge Idonia, and what that meant for the other worlds. It was worded in, like a memorandum or pep talk to get people prepared to face the threat that Idonia posed to the other worlds."

"Well," Win replied with a smirk as he took a sip from his drink, "that certainly is a great place to start."

"A great place to start?" Rachel asked incredulously. "What place to start? What other worlds? What the hell is going on with those other worlds and Idonia? The way the book made it seem they might as well all be at war, and what does any of that have anything to do with anything in our world?"

Rachel was panting, she realized. They all were. Fury burned within them, but it wasn't fury at him. It suddenly dawned on them that the emotion they were feeling was internal. A battle raged inside each of their minds, fighting to understand what was real. Their brains sought a simple solution that fits into the tapestry of the world they knew, but whatever the truth was, it was not straightforward, and it did not fit in the friends' reality.

"Now we're getting somewhere." Win said, his grin broadening in utter enjoyment. "The excerpt you found is but a tiny part in one of the many tomes regarding the Watchers. Their teachings tell of the human worlds that first came in contact with the realm of Idonia and its inhabitants. They describe the many things they learned about the Idonic system over generations and generations as more worlds overlapped with the cosmic civilization. What began as works of research seeking to catalog and understand Idonia and its people grew over time into a compendium of perceived transgressions and what must be done to stop them."

Win paused as he finished off his drink just as Jenny brought out two burgers about the size of her head on a plate loaded down with fries. The friends could see strips of bacon poking out from under the bun with sauteed mushroom and onions piled high on the Swiss cheese melting over the two meat patties. Jenny sat them down on the table with ease, then placed another fresh glass next to Win's empty one, which she swept up in the same motion. She had done that a lot. Without a word, Jenny vanished again from the table.

"So, is there any restaurant in town you don't have a usual at?" Erin asked, grabbing a handful of Win's fries.

"Quite a few. Our family, we're creatures of habit, as I'm sure you've noticed." Win smiled as he took a massive bite of his burger.

"Ok, next question then, how can you and your brother eat like that," she pointed at the burger, "and still be built like that?" she asked, gesturing to his entire body.

A giant smirk crossed his face as he chewed his food. He finished chewing politely before responding, "I would say good genes, but in truth, it's a lot of exercise. You wouldn't believe how active we are."

"You and your brother must've really been hated growing up." Rachel joked.

"You have no idea, sweetheart." The smile on his face made Ally realize how valid his words were.

"So," Ally began, not wanting to let Win drift too far from the topic at hand. "why can't we find any of these writings? Why only the one excerpt we found?"

"That's a tough question to answer." Win said, swallowing a mouthful of food and washing it down with his cocktail. "Not that it's something I can't answer, but rather the answer itself is complicated.

It is not merely about combing scroll after scroll in some ancient library in Mesopotamia or finding a cave with the entire tale written on the walls for all to see. The Watchers' works span across millennia spread out through different worlds and civilizations, so it means searching for tiny grains of sand across the beaches of antiquity. Even now, humanity is still discovering things about their history in this world, and only in the last hundred years or so have humans begun to understand even the most basic information about their neighboring planets. Yet, you ask why it is not easier to find the complex history of other worlds?

"There are tales strewn across this reality. Some speak of how Idonians wanted a relationship with humans, how Samias tried more than any to find the human worlds scattered throughout space and time so they could help the humans prosper and grow. Samias loved the human races with every ounce of his being. The only thing Samias loved more was the family; his sibling Milas, his true love Lithia, and his closest friends Gabrize and Locief. It was at Samias' urging that Idonia tried to reconnect with the humans. By the time of the earliest records of their encounters, the human races they found were thousands of years into their separate existences. By that time, whenever they encountered someone from Idonia, the humans would have just thought it was someone from a lavish nearby kingdom with tremendous knowledge to share.

"Samias urged his fellow Davpyr into giving the humans so much of their homeworld. They taught them everything the humans could comprehend, from better methods for hunting to farming techniques, even how to craft many of the things humans would need. Little by little, generation by generation, the visitors from Idonia would teach the human races more and more, pushing them to advance as swiftly as possible but always working to keep themselves cautiously hidden."

Win took a long pause as he looked down at his plate. Sorrow and remorse began to fill his stunning blue eyes.

"Even now, humans would likely react in fear or terror if they were to experience the true nature of someone from the Idonic system. So, you can imagine what people in ancient times would have done. A spark of lightning from Milas' fingertips, Samias moving entire logs to build homes, Locief conjuring a fire to keep the humans warm, there was no possible outcome but fear. The people would scream out in terror, fleeing from the very people who guided their lives."

Win stopped again, looking around the room. His eyes became vaguely misty. He grabbed his glass and finished the last of it just as Jenny brought him another. He waved her off just before she set it down, though.

"I think I'll stop there tonight." Win said, both to Jenny about the drink and the friends about the story.

"Well," Jenny replied with a seductive smile, "if you want something else to drink, you know where to find me."

Win smirked and nodded, his eyes still full of sadness as she turned to walk away.

"Somebody's got a bit of a crush going on you there," Erin said, holding back a laugh as she looked from Win to Rachel.

"No, no. She's always had a thing for Joshua. She is just playful towards me."

A wave of jealousy rushed over Ally, "Oh really?"

"Really. Since he won't bite, though, she turns her attention to me. It's all in jest for her. She's actually a pretty sweet lady. Don't let the look and attitude fool you. Deep down, she's pretty soft. She's just not Joshua's type."

"What exactly is Joshua's type?" Rachel asked, looking slyly at Ally as she did.

Win let out a soft laugh. "You wouldn't believe me if I told you." He laughed a little more. "Are you ladies about ready to get out of here?"

"How about one more question," Erin answered, "before we go?"

"Fair enough. What is it?" He asked, still smiling charmingly.

"This whole time, you've been talking about how the Watchers studied the people of Idonia, which they eventually sought to bring down the likes of Samias and Milas and Locief." Erin paused, searching for the right words. "I just don't understand. I mean, I get the fear aspect. That's an understandable enough reaction, but why would they want to go to war with Idonia when the Davpyr did nothing but try to help them?"

"Well, your problem is twofold." Win's eyes bore deep into the friends. "First, you mistake the power of fear. Fear is an emotion strong enough to make a group completely subservient or completely ruthless in their conquest; fear of destruction if they act out, and fear of destruction if they do not act. It is a compelling motivator. The second issue is you think the Davpyr did only good. I realize you may not have uncovered the whole tale just yet, but when Joshua gave you the conditions before he began telling you of the Idonia, did you really think they would all be tales of pleasant people? The Watchers can be a cruel, ruthless group of humans. They have done outright monstrous things, but that does not mean their hatred of Idonia is without reason. The Davpyr are not free of guilt either, for they have done truly wicked deeds. There are no white hats in war, especially on a cosmic scale. That is all I can tell you, though. I can only present you with the facts. Only you can choose what you believe."

The friends did not respond. Part of them felt foolish for not seeing what the forces of Idonia and the Watchers were. No war was black and white, yet another aspect couldn't help feeling the Watchers were misguided in their quest. Perhaps they didn't know enough yet, but they couldn't bring themselves to think going to war with a world such as Idonia was the wisest course of action unless it genuinely was the Watchers' last resort.

Win didn't bother saying anything as he rose from the booth and tossed another of the family's strange coins on the table. The friends barely gave it a second glance as they rose to follow him. Whatever the coin was, it clearly had great significance, but the friends were too busy thinking about everything Win had said.

The frigid cold shocked the friends as they exited the warm speakeasy, forcing Ally and Rachel to burrow deep into their coats. Even though their house was only a few blocks away, they were very relieved they had the car. Erin, on the other hand, embraced the bitter cold, leaving her jacket partially undone, inviting the chill. She loved the cold. No amount of time in it seemed to be enough, and that day with Win's strange behavior, the crisp air was exactly what she needed to feel alive again.

"Hey, Win," Erin began, feeling the life pulsing through her veins, "so, the Davpyr and The Watchers, are they still out there fighting somewhere?"

"I can only assume." A smirk spread across Win's face, and the friends knew he was back to normal. "Aren't you a little old to believing in silly fairy tales, though?"

"Do you think either of them will ever reach our world?" Erin continued, refusing to be deterred.

"Well," Win began, keeping his playful tone, "I would imagine some already have. How else would we have these stories?"

27
LIONESS

That Thursday was colder still than the days before, and Ally and Rachel were glad to finally arrive at the Brew for coffee just to have something to warm them. They chatted with Terry briefly, wishing they could stay longer, but they had to be quick that day. They still had not grown accustomed to their new school schedule, and the extracurricular activities in their life were growing more tiresome by the day. They were thrilled to have a good friend in Terry and were more than happy for their chances to visit with the Brownings, but their quest to understand the world of Idonia and its war with the Watchers was steadily consuming their lives.

As they left the Brew, though, a sight outside completely took Ally's mind away from everything else, though, and she nudged her friends to look. Before Erin and Rachel could follow her gaze, the person rounded the corner. At first, Ally thought she was seeing things. She tried to shake it off and pay no mind, but as they reached the main road, Ally scanned the intersection and saw the stunning figure of a woman with gorgeous auburn and gold hair that they would recognize anywhere walking off in the distance. Luci was back in town.

Without hesitation, the three friends made their way after the woman. They had no idea what they were doing, no idea how to tail someone, but that didn't matter. Everything about Little Rock only grew stranger each day they were there, but nothing was as unusual as the heavenly woman from Joshua's haunted past. She had only just made it a couple of blocks down Main Street before turning on Capitol Ave and headed toward the banking district. One block passed, then two, then three, and steadily the friends were beginning to wonder how much longer they could maintain their mission. They knew eventually their risk of getting caught would be insurmountable, but still, they couldn't pull themselves away.

Finally, after a half dozen blocks, Luci disappeared into one of the major bank buildings, and the friends stopped outside, discussing what to do.

"Should we go in?" Rachel asked, feeling it was a terrible idea.

"Too risky." Ally said. "There's no way we could follow her around without getting too close, and we don't even know what she's doing in there."

"So, do we have any kind of plan forming here?" Erin asked, but the other two had no answer. "Alright, here's what we do. We can't just keep following her on foot. Sooner or later, she's bound to either see us or get in a car. So, I'll head to the house, grab wheels, and meet y'all right back here, or wherever she goes next, I guess."

"Deal." Rachel said. "We'll keep our phones handy and be on the lookout. Speaking of, you should call Thad on your way. Don't know why, but this just feels like something he should know."

Erin agreed and darted off to get the vehicle while Rachel and Ally vanished into the corners of a nearby building, doing their best to keep a sightline on where Luci might exit but still working not to seem conspicuous, a feat that proved far more manageable than they had expected. Everyone coming and going was all either deep in conversations with one another or buried in their phones, one fortunate bit of camouflage the modern age provided them.

Minutes passed with no sign of Luci, and before Ally and Rachel realized Erin was back with the vehicle. The group decided it would be best to keep it parked but running nearby, so to stay on the same page, Rachel and Ally put their headphones in and started a group call with Erin in the car. Another half-hour passed with the friends growing worried they had somehow missed. Just as they were about to give up the pursuit, though, Luci reappeared out the same door she had entered accompanied by a very important looking, albeit very nervous, banker.

He walked behind her, frantically trying to keep up with her long, elegant strides. She was saying something to him still, but the friends could neither hear nor make out the words from their distance. At the sidewalk, she turned and faced the man with a smile that appeared to be meant as reassurance, but it hardly seemed effective given the look on the man's face. The two shared a brief handshake before splitting ways, the man heading directly across the street to another towering bank while Luci continued her trek up the avenue.

She remained on foot, which made Rachel and Ally thankful as they could easily keep pace at a safe distance behind her. Erin's situation, though, was a little trickier, so she waited in place until Luci and the friends covered another couple blocks before moving up on the next street over and finding another brief parking spot. Block by block, they moved further away from the business and financial district and closer to the state capitol building, which grew steadily more prominent on the horizon. The friends couldn't help wondering and discussing where the woman might be going, but given their general lack of knowledge about Luci, they realized anything was possible. They knew virtually nothing about her; no interests or hobbies, not what she did for work, and certainly not why she was even in Little Rock. Thus, the friends were faced with shock and confusion when they reached the Capitol Lawn, and Luci casually strolled up the walkway to the entrance.

"Ok, this is weird, right?" Rachel asked as Luci made her way to the main entrance.

"What's weird?" Erin said, still two blocks behind the others.

"Um," Ally began, "well, Luci just went into the Capitol."

"The fuck?" Erin exclaimed. "Who the hell goes to the Capitol aside from kids on school field trips?"

"I would venture to guess," Rachel answered, still heavily confused, "someone on official business perhaps?"

The friends grew silent at that, pondering what official business even looked like for someone like Luci. Erin made her way up to meet the others and parked in the nearby lot. Ally and Rachel climbed into the car with her, unsure of where else to seek cover, and there the friends waited. The minutes ticked by as the friends sat, growing ever more restless. Over an hour had passed. The friends wondered only briefly if somehow they had missed Luci's exit, but they figured she must still be inside as there was only one accessible entrance. After sitting for nearly two hours, the friends' patience was finally rewarded as they watched Luci glide back down the steps of the walkway before making her way across the street and back towards downtown.

Erin volunteered to walk so Ally and Rachel could enjoy the

warmth of the car. She stepped outside and embraced the cold like a long-lost friend as she sought off after Luci. The crisp chill in the air contrasted with the fire that blazed inside Erin at the excitement of what they were doing. It was a simple thing, following someone around that they knew, but something about the fact that it was Luci, that it was someone close to the Brownings, made it exhilarating.

She followed along, struggling to keep a safe distance as her excitement pushed her closer and closer. Despite her urges, though, she managed to maintain enough space between them that Luci never seemed to notice. She merely continued her steady pace back down Capitol Ave until she reached the adjacent banks and stopped. Erin assumed Luci was about to go inside one of them, but instead, she simply waited outside for a brief moment until a young man, an ambitious intern from the looks of him, hustled out from one of the banks. He handed Luci a small envelope, never daring to meet the woman's gaze, and quickly headed back inside. Erin saw the envelope disappear into the folds of Luci's jacket as she started off on her path again.

A few blocks from Main Street, the friends discussed what the chances were that Luci was heading to The Brew. It seemed likely that she had just left when the friends initially spotted her, and there was always the possibility Luci was meeting up with the Brownings there. The friends were puzzled by that, though, as they weren't sure if Joshua was back yet, and Lili didn't seem to care for Luci enough for either to fancy a visit. They did not have to wait long to discover the answer, though.

"Hey Erin," Ally said over the call as she and Rachel drove along the next street over from their friend, the road on which the speakeasy was located, "you can go ahead and cross over to get in with us. Pretty sure we know where she's headed."

Erin started to ask where, but something in Ally's voice made her hesitant. So, she quickly turned on the next street and walked as quickly as she felt it was socially acceptable to rejoin her friends. As soon as she reached to get in the vehicle, she saw ahead on the road what caught Ally's and Rachel's attention, Joshua and Win's Roadster parked outside the speakeasy.

The friends quickly turned on the side street and began making their way around to the road across from the basement bar, thankful that the Roadster had been parked facing away from them and hoping that Joshua and Win were facing with it or already inside the place. They saw the latter was not the case as they pulled into a parking spot just close enough they could see the two men get out of the car and walk towards the establishment.

Joshua and Win stood by the staircase to the bar when Luci rounded the corner and walked straight into Joshua's outstretched arms. The two embraced as if no one else was in the world, holding each other so tight it seemed they might crush one another. The world froze again with every visible eye fixed on this couple's otherworldly affection as if witnessing an event as rare as a total solar eclipse or Halley's Comet. The friends had never seen Joshua outright hug anyone, not Lavy, not Lili, not even his brothers, yet there he stood with that heavenly woman buried deep in his chest with his mighty arms wrapped around. The way the two held each other, it was as if their bodies had been perfectly sculpted to fit perfectly together, two pieces of an ageless puzzle rejoined.

After what felt like an eternity, the two released each other, both glowing with joy. The friends all felt a fit of jealousy eating away at them that they couldn't explain. Ally had a strange crush on Joshua, even if she would never admit it amidst Erin's teasing, but that wasn't the sense of envy that was welling up inside. Erin and Rachel both felt it too, and while they both couldn't deny they were attracted to Joshua, they held no romantic feelings towards him. As the feeling grew in each of them, they slowly realized that it had not been jealousy at all. It manifested that way at first because their emotions were struggling to process the foreign concept. It was longing. Not longing for Joshua, but longing for the love he and Luci shared, an insatiable desire to understand and feel a love that strong and pure and timeless.

It was Win's turn as they too embraced in a mighty hug. There was nowhere near the power, nowhere near the passion, and nowhere near the love in their hug. Time hadn't stood still, and only a few passersby glanced their way, but it was still clear beyond a shadow of a doubt that the two meant a great deal to each other as well. They held each other firmly, a sense of understanding and appreciation seeming to radiate from the two. They were kindred spirits, bound to a similar purpose and person, and they shared each other's journey in their embrace, the good and the bad.

After the three shared their hugs, they took a step back and stared at one another, taking the moment in. The looks on their faces were unmistakable. Every emotion that comes with seeing a long-lost loved one was there; overwhelming joy, surprise, relief, and most of all, consuming, unconditional love. After the brief moment of recognition and acknowledgment, the three disappeared down the stairs and into the speakeasy.

The friends sat in the car as time ticked by. They took turns running up the street to their house for bathroom breaks or to get drinks and snacks. Seconds turned into minutes and minutes into hours, and still, they waited and watched, all the while unaware of the other eyes that watched as well, watching them and the Brownings.

"Should we just go in there?" Erin said, breaking the silence after a time. "I mean, they've been in there for hours, so it's not like we just rolled up on 'em. Plus, Luci and Win both have taken us there, so it's not like we have to act like we don't know the place. We could just go and grab a booth and pretend we have no idea they're there."

"And if they spot us?" Ally asked, sure it would be a disaster if they went inside.

"We just act oblivious." Rachel said as she began a mock reply. "Oh hey, didn't see y'all there. We just popped in for a quick bit, ya know, since we live right up the street."

"And how about the fact we're terrible liars." Ally continued with her doubt.

"We're great liars." Rachel said defensively. "It's you that sucks at it."

"Their car is outside." Ally replied flatly. "We gonna pretend we didn't see that too?"

"I mean," Rachel began, hesitancy creeping into her voice, "maybe somebody else in town has that car. How would we know?"

"What about when they go to leave?" Ally asked finally. "We gonna follow them out and be like, 'oh, what a coincidence, we're leaving at the same time.' and just hope they buy it?"

"Shit." Said Erin emphatically, knowing Ally was right.

She hated being right on that too. Ally wanted so much to go along with her friends' plan, but they all knew it was pointless, even Rachel. So they continued to sit in the car, waiting as patiently as they could. They had ramen delivered to their house and sent a runner to bring it back to the car. A decision they immediately regretted because trying to eat noodles in a vehicle while being alert was quite the challenge, but they managed somehow. The friends had sat for the entire afternoon and evening before they finally had their patience reward.

It was shortly after nine when Joshua, Luci, and Win exited the building and immediately got in the Roadster to leave. Shuffling to get ready, the girls hurriedly buckled up and made to follow them. The friends were glad Joshua and Win drove such an ostentatious car as they struggled to keep a close enough distance to see them in the dark of night easily. They wove through the inner city streets, and in just a few blocks, the friends quickly realized where the group was heading.

The girls cut across a side street to allow them to come in the back entrance to the parking garage of the abandoned building they had visited just months before. They parked in the same spot they had the last time, quickly taking note of the Brownings vehicle to see that three individuals had already gone inside. They waited in the car until almost ten, trying to give themselves ample time to sneak in behind the Brownings without being detected. Quickly and without a sound, they scurried across the garage and down the basement stairs she had used before, accompanied by the eyes that stood ever watching.

Opening it, she stood face to face with the gentle giant she had met just months before. His dark lips parted in a smile.

"You ladies must be a glutton for punishment?"

Rachel quickly sorted through her jacket pockets, searching for the strange coin she never left the house without.

Just as her hand fell on the coin resting in her inner pocket, the man raised his hand and spoke. "If you're back a second time, don't worry about the coin. There's clearly more to you than we expected. The bracket's already been made, so you better get going quickly."

"Bracket?" Erin asked, unable to hide her confusion.

"The tournament bracket?" The man asked, studying the friends. "I would assume that's why y'all came back. Mr. Joshua and Mr. Win won't see each other until the semifinals. Mr. Van, however, is on the other side of the bracket, so he'll have to make it to the finals to face either of 'em. He's got some pretty stiff competition, though." He smiled as he emphasized the last words, clearly humored by his thoughts.

Ally stared at the man in confusion. "Why are you telling us this?"

His lips curled into a smile again. "Well, you must be rooting for one of them. Why else would their 'friends' be here? If I had to guess, it's Mr. Joshua. You've seen him fight before, so you at least know what to expect. That's who I've already put my money on. He's a great man despite all he does to the contrary. He'll make it to the semifinals, no doubt, but I'll decide my final bet that night. He may be great, but I'm also pragmatic. Y'all might be wise to place a bet as well, turn that one coin into a few more. Never know when they might come in handy."

"How do you know them so well?" Rachel asked, intrigued by the character. "How do you know Joshua's a great man?"

"I met him when I was at my lowest point. Homeless, jobless, and not a hope in the world. He fixed me up. Vouched for me to get me a job with his company. Found me a place to live. Then he did something I'll always owe him for; he introduced me to my wife."

A roar broke out from the door behind him.

"Enough about all that, though. You'd better get in there if you wanna see the show. Who knows, maybe you'll make it through more than one fight this time." He laughed a deep, burly laugh as he slid aside.

The friends couldn't help but like that guard whose name they didn't even know. Even though he was a bouncer for an underground fighting group, and almost certainly employed by the Harbilins, the friends somehow knew he was a good man. They each gave him a big smile back as they walked past through the open door.

Inside, the room was thick with anticipation. The fighting hadn't started yet, but the people were already on their feet screaming for violence. The friends felt their blood getting hot as the smell of sweat hit their nostrils. They remembered that room all too well.

Looking down at the walkway leading to the arena, they noticed no traces of the blood from the previous fights. They couldn't imagine how much cleaning that had taken. The betting booth and bar were outfitted with massive brackets this time around, but they were too far away for the friends to read all the names. It was what seemed to be a thirty-two-man bracket, though, and they couldn't help wondering how many of them would have the misfortune of going up against Joshua, Win, or Van.

For a minute, the friends started to make their way to the edge where they had stood the last fight, but something in them said not to get so close. Fortunately, the room wasn't completely packed yet, and they were able to grab a standing spot on one of the upper bleachers where they could be hidden by the crowd but still have a clear view.

Once there, they realized how much better they liked the view than the front row seat. They were much farther from the smell of blood and sweat. Up there, they could still see the arena, but it was far enough off that the realness wasn't as crushing, which made the friends question themselves. Even as they stood there, still disgusted by the events, they rationalized it in their minds, finding ways to make themselves accept what they witnessed. They looked across the room to where the brothers and their friend had stood the last time and found them again. Instantly they recognized the fourth member of their party. Her perfect features and beautiful face were just as discernible from the far-away distance where the friends stood as they were up close.

Joshua and Luci stood laughing back and forth, getting ready for the fights as the last few fans settled in. The friends couldn't understand how Luci could sit there and watch someone for whom she cared so intensely, preparing to do what Joshua was. Instead, the two looked like old friends playing their favorite game, and the girls had to question themselves again. They judged Luci, unable to understand her actions, yet they stood preparing to watch the same event.

The announcer called from his mic at the bar for the first two fighters to enter the ring. Apparently, everyone had already known the fighting order because, without hesitation, a man jumped over the ledge from the far right and made his way to the center of the arena accompanied by the yells of his friends. He clearly didn't know who his opponent was, though, because he scanned the crowd back and forth, waiting for someone to join him until a look of horror ran through his face when he saw who he had to fight. The friends' faces twisted in the same terrified manner. It was not another giant that jumped over the ledge, nor one of the fearsome Browning brothers. Instead, the friends looked at the family just in time to see a stunning coat fall as Luci leapt gracefully over the wall.

Everyone in the room had gone quiet in an instant. Even the man towering over her dropped his fists. Luci didn't look as if she was at all concerned, though. She wore the same jeans she'd had on earlier but had ditched her blouse for the fight, revealing a soft lace bra that only furthered her delicate appearance. Not a single eye left her as she walked to the center of the arena. The more of her body the friends saw, the more perfect she became. Her slim figure that was usually draped in a lovely dress, looked vivacious, sexy, and elegant all at once. Looks of terror and fright that filled the room were all mixed with those of jealousy, lust, and admiration at the stunning warrior queen.

No one was watching a fight anymore. Instead, everyone watched an angel, nay, a goddess, powerful and beautiful, walk across the room. Even Joshua's eyes were transfixed. They were aglow, burning a brilliant shade of grey that the friends could see from atop the bleachers. They knew it was clear he had seen Luci like that before, but still, he stood, ablaze with reverence, as if it were the first time he had ever laid eyes on her.

Studying her grace, the friends noticed Luci didn't have her ring on like normal and figured it wasn't allowed in the fight, but she still had the thin leather strip adorned with beads around her neck, just like Joshua, Win, and Van. What stood out the most, though, was the silvery tattoo adorning her ribcage that was nearly identical to Joshua's. The lion crest in the middle with lines wove around the symbol in the same pattern, only the friends could tell seeing hers for the first time that they weren't merely lines, but feathers. The feathers spread across most of her right side, but the friends couldn't tell where they stopped as the top feather was tucked under Luci's lace bra, and her jeans covered the bottom one.

Luci stopped directly in front of the man but didn't bother to bring her fists up. He was still entranced, but something finally snapped him free, and he began stepping back, shaking his hands in refusal to fight. Everyone else was still mesmerized by the deity in front of them, but what happened next quickly snapped them all back to reality.

Out of nowhere, Luci swung a mighty right hook and sent the man stumbling to the ground. All at once, the stands erupted, and the wolves were back crying for blood. There was no longer a gorgeous, delicate woman at the center of the ring, but a stunning, mighty lioness. Not wanting to be embarrassed, the man sprung to his feet and took his stance. It was clear he still had reservations about hitting Luci, though, because he kept trying to grapple and upend her instead.

He never even came close, though, as Luci darted around his every move landing a half-hearted blow every time, daring him to fight properly. After a dozen or so slaps to the head, the man finally started swinging, and Luci perked up. She sunk deeper into her fighting stance, dodged every swing without even trying, and before the friends knew it, the man was red with fury as he sent wild blow after wild blow aimed straight for Luci's head to no avail.

All at once, Luci gave a glance to the sideline where Joshua stood smirking, eyes still ablaze. Without warning, Luci turned on her opponent and connected a devastating right hook. The loud crack of bone filled the room as the man's jaw snapped, and he was sent into a headfirst dive for the dirt. It sounded like a bomb exploded in the stands as the cacophony of fans roared their approval.

The man lay motionless on the ground, completely unconscious, as his friends rushed over to help him out of the arena. Their eyes never left Luci, but the look of desire was gone, and in its place was a look of pure fear and admiration as the men dragged their friend away.

Joshua bounded over the side with open arms into which Luci ran. His face was beaming with pride as he lifted her back over the edge, wearing the biggest smile the friends had ever seen. Then, as if he'd conjured it out of thin air, Joshua extended his arm with a congratulatory gift for Luci.

A single red rose.

The friends left the room in disgust, not at the fighting or the animals craving for violence as they had the time before, but at Luci. Everything the friends saw and heard about the woman made the friends loathe and worship her even more. What was worse is they knew they had no right to hate her. Luci had been nothing but kind to the friends, and, from all they knew, she was the epitome of perfection. That's what infuriated the friends the most. It was easy to hate someone who deserved to be hated but to hate someone whom every fiber in your being wanted to love, to respect, and to admire was different. They wanted to know Luci, truly know her as Joshua and Win and Van did, but somehow their minds raged in protest.

The friends waved at the guard as they exited the building, who merely smiled knowingly in return, saying he would see them next for the upcoming round. Outside, the friends let the cold air brush against their faces and bring them back to life. It was a familiar feeling for Erin, one that she often did. In that moment, though, Ally and Rachel joined her in letting the cold, bitter air center their minds, and still, the eyes watched. They stood at the top stairwell for almost ten minutes before finally feeling calm enough to force their legs to carry them to the car.

Thoughts of Luci raced through their minds as they left the building. How before, they had thought that Luci was coming to watch the fight in support of her friends, only to find out she was just like them. The girls didn't know how they had let themselves become friends with such a group of people, beating men senseless and knocking them unconscious for sport. *What kind of monsters do that*, they thought. Yet still, the friends couldn't help being drawn to them even more.

It was an unusual ride home. None of the friends knew what to say. They had followed Luci the entire day, from the bank to the Capitol to the bar to the fights, and they still did not know what game the ferocious, resplendent woman played. In silence, the friends rode, contemplating what was truly at hand with Luci, Van, and the Brownings. They were timeless friends, but ones with a harrowing journey and clearly involved in something much more significant than themselves.

The car rolled to a stop in front of their house on Rock Street, and the friends exhaustedly stepped out into the cold air once more. They moved slower than they knew they should, something dragging them down. Their walkway was but a few paces, and yet it seemed ages before they reached the door, only to be met with astonishment when they did.

A small parcel laid against their door. No address, no note, just a slim, unassuming brown package marked "For those who wish to know."

The friends stood frozen on their porch briefly before they turned and scanned the night around them. The eyes were there, but the friends did not see them. They saw nothing but darkness. The parcel had to have been left recently, they knew. It had only been a few hours since they were last at the house, and yet there was no sign they could see as to who put it there, or why.

A growing sense of dread at being out in the cold, dark night forced the friends inside, grabbing the parcel as they went. They placed the item on the kitchen island, unopened, and stood around it, not even bothering to remove their coats. A minute passed, then another, and another, and still the friends stood.

At once, without word or warning, Ally reached her phone and dialed Thad, telling him to get there at once. He began to protest, but

Ally merely hung up the phone without another word, and Thad began his two-hour drive to their house. Not one of the friends moved the entire time they waited on him, save Erin, who had removed her jacket. When Thad arrived, no one even bothered to greet him at the door; instead, the friends stood rooted in place as he used his spare key to let himself in.

He began to comment on their strange behavior as he entered the room but abruptly stopped when he saw the package on the table that held the friends in their transfixed gazes. He wanted to reach for it, but something in his mind warned him not to. The three girls had been standing in the same place for hours, and Thad was suddenly locked in place as well.

Without warning yet again, Erin stepped forward and grabbed the parcel. She tore the end open with terrifying force and dumped the contents onto the countertop. A single, small book lay on the island in front of the friends, daring them to read it, asking them, if they truly wished to know, the *Remnants of the First World.*

28
REMNANTS OF THE FIRST WORLD

We were late in discovering the first world that the Idonic civilization had reached. We were too late, and they were too early. A single group of scouts was all that managed to reach the world and establish an outpost there. The citizens of that place were still relatively early in their development, leaving the scouts little room for error with their own resource management and even less in their efforts to remain anonymous. The data they were able to record and send back was minimal at best and far too spread out at worst. It is unclear from the information we have collected how much time the crew had before they met their end, and the transcriptions we received are scattered across that world's history. They worked diligently to translate the pieces they were able to locate while there and send them as clearly as could be done, along with additional explanations where they could. Some of the translations are believed to be loose estimations of what the original works would have contained based on the language barrier with the still unknown tongue spoken in that world. Some words are indicated as such.

What is clear from the collected works is a similar pattern we've already found in the worlds the Idonic civilization found later, with the apparent absence of the catastrophic end that befell the first world. From what we can gather, the Davpyr, which led the Idonic expanse, were much more cautious and uncertain in their early endeavors with this world. It is still unknown at what time in their considerably lengthy evolutionary journey Idonia discovered this world. Still, it would seem to be somewhat early from what the records transcribed indicate. Our best summation is that at this point, the Davpyr, and much of Idonia, were still unaware of the vast capabilities which they possessed. This is further supported by the nature of the early interactions with the citizens of that world, in how they worked to help the various groups with which they came in contact, but yet refrained from demonstrating as much as they could of their true nature. Some things, of course, with their kind are unable to be kept discreet, as will be noticeable in the descriptions contained within these historical excerpts.

Furthermore, it is essential to note that these fragments are collected and compiled within chronological order of the world as best we can determine. Due to the inconsistent frequency and content of the original transmissions, we cannot be certain that we have been correct in our assembly of this information. Any discrepancies should be considered with said context. The transmissions also did not include any explanation as to the origin of the individual translations themselves, which due to the limits of the crew reporting them should be expected, and respect should be given to the fact they were unable to return with their original records in light of their unfortunate demise. While their sacrifice comes with great sadness, we must appreciate the importance even this tiny glimpse into the first world provides. The collected works have not been adjusted in any way from their original transmissions, but they do include connotation as to our best estimate of when in the world's history they would have taken place based on the verbiage and descriptions used by the citizens. These are, as always, loose estimations, given we do not have any direct reference from the world itself. Lastly, before reading, it is imperative that all who seek to understand the records of the first contact with the Idonic civilization do so with reflection of all the aforementioned and do not seek to formulate opinions or explanations on the actions and behaviors of the Idonic citizens as these events occurred unknown eons before any current interactions.

First World - Earliest reference of Idonic presence (Believed to have occurred in ancient times)

It was late autumn when the strangers first arrived in our village. They claimed to be from a distant settlement. This was odd to us at first as they had arrived on foot, and yet our scouts and hunters knew of any neighboring tribes within walking distance and most that required horseback. None of our tribe recognized the individuals, however, which was especially odd given their appearance. They looked, unlike anything our villagers had ever seen. Even the stories our long-walkers had brought back of a massive kingdom far to the east had not seemed as astonishing as these strangers.

Their robes shined in a way no fabric we had ever known could. Even the most luxurious linens from the market in the 'distant neighboring seaside settlement' looked nothing like what the strangers wore. It looked soft and smooth, yet somehow rigid and impenetrable. More than that was the odd appearance of the material that was colored in ways we only knew from rare flowers that grew in the 'majestic' forests. Strangest, though, was the faint light that seemed to shine from the fabric itself, as if they had caught stars from the sky and woven them into their robes.

At first, our people were afraid, sensing we might be in danger despite outnumbering them considerably. They numbered only eight, four families, four couples, led by one who called himself Samias. He sought to calm our villagers, assuring they were no threat. The man and his kin stood well taller than anyone in our village, but he did not seem intentionally imposing. He looked so naturally with his height and solid build like chiseled stone, but he wore an appearance of calm compassion that made him feel safe. His hair was deep black, and though the front of his dark locks was pulled back, it still was long enough to fall to his shoulders, which were broad to the point they the stretched his cloak into a 'majestic' appearance. Magnificent wasn't a strong enough word for him. There was something about Samias that calmed all the villagers and spoke to them in some way. He felt pure, full of love and compassion, and powerful beyond belief. Not innocent, but sovereign.

He showed the village to his mate Lithia, who was more stunning than even he, his brother Milas and his mate Locief, both who look equally as powerful as they did awe-inspiring, and their brethren; Gabrize, Miria, Urithina, and Raphon, who each mirrored their kinsmen in regality and radiance. They were each beautiful in a way we did not understand. Their looks were unnatural, but somehow appealing to us all. Each of the strangers echoed the words of Samias, telling us we need not fear, telling us they were there to help.

Our harvest had been poor that year, not so much that we feared for winter, but enough that we all knew there would be hungry days. The herds of wild beasts we hunted had dwindled as well. They had done so each of the previous years, but they still numbered enough we would be able to survive the winter, we hoped. Samias presented himself and his kin as guardians, stewards there to help us grow strong and prosperous. They showed ways to use our crops to create foods that we had never fathomed, stretching our harvest from scarce to bountiful. They taught us ways to hunt with such potent efficiency we could fill our stores in a single outing.

Samias offered for him and his kin to stay with us through the frozen days and teach us everything they could. In return, they requested nothing but space to build themselves lodging. We thought them mad at first, seeking to build a shelter so late in the season. The frost was close at hand, and we thought it impossible they would be able to make safe lodging in such a time. To our surprise, though, they worked more swiftly than we knew could happen. They set off felling trees in ways we have not words to describe, clearing a small plot for themselves, and building a domicile unlike any ever seen. In what would have taken us countless hours laboring on end, they completed in a single afternoon, and they did not stop there.

Using their methods, they built us additional stores underground to which they said could be used to chill meat after it had been salted, keeping it fresh even longer. With the excess fibrous plants from their crafting, they showed us how to weave strong 'nets' that we could use in the river that ran through our village to catch fish swimming up and downstream. Being that fish was commonplace at the 'distant neighboring seaside settlement,' they suggested we store it for the winter and take some of our venison to the market along with the strange new wooden 'artifacts' they had crafted to trade for other goods that could help bolster our village. They helped us carry the goods to the market. Without them, there is no way we would have been able to transport everything, nor would we have had such goods to trade. The haul we returned with was unlike any our village had ever known. A dozen harvest would have hardly compared, and none of which would have been possible without the visitors.

The frost moved in, but our village was more than prepared. The visitors stayed through the frozen days as they had asked. They worked around the village by day, helping us build new structures that they taught us and reinforce old ones to survive even longer. They showed us ways to create systems that could harness the water of the river in ways we had never seen. Some of their kind taught us new ways to craft the wood we used in our spears and bows, while others showed us different methods to shape the stone in our tools to make them last even longer.

At night the visitors would stay outside around the mighty fires they built to tell us stories of the stars. Samias and Milas told of the cities of Nevadolia and Kealfurm, whose tales were written across the endless night sky. Lithia and Locief would tell of Inverna and Isirith, worlds so beautiful and magnificent because they were made from stars themselves. Wise and noble Gabrize and Urithina showed how the stars were maps of their very own, which humans could use to navigate the heavens, as had Bàofor and Gordäk. Miria and Raphon, ever compassionate, would teach of the healing that came from aligning Euern and Lascira.

Each night they would share tales they had learned on their travels and offered wisdom we could use to guide our people.

The visitors would join us for meals, but they would never partake, insisting they did not wish to take any of our excess resources. They stated that they could easily hunt for a day and eat for weeks on their stores, though they thanked us for our hospitality nonetheless. It proved most beneficial, for that winter was the harshest our village had ever seen. Snow fell so deep it trapped some villagers in their homes for weeks on end. The violent winds threatened to tear apart our town with needles of ice, and our harvest was nearly lost to the bitter cold.

The villagers began to question the nature of the visitors, wondering if they had brought the terrible winter with them. Some said it was merely the madness of the cold. Others claimed they could feel the visitors inside their minds, whispering things to them. It wasn't until the first days of the thaw that we witnessed but a glimpse of their true power. The frost had stayed longer than winter, and by the time it began to melt, the animals that had survived rose from their winter slumber with exuberant force. They had stayed asleep far longer than was safe, many had not made it, and they all needed to find nourishment soon. One such creature came to our village. The ferocious beast would never have come so close to a settlement, but the lack of food to hunt made him desperate. Desperation breeds danger. Two of our hunters made to slay the beast, but even in his weakened state, they were no match for him without the element of surprise.

In a blur of motion, Milas sprang on the creature. No one in the village even saw where he came from or how he managed to grapple the mighty beast. But, in a single instant, he had leapt into action and subdued the creature. It roared violently at first, trapped in Milas' unbreakable hold, but astonishingly the wild beast did not grow more vicious. Instead, as Milas laid there restraining the creature, it began to calm. Slowly at first, and then all at once relaxed. Locief went over to her mate as he released the beast. The two knelt on the ground next to the mighty beast petting him gently. When they rose, the creature turned and left the village peacefully.

Again the visitors had saved us from potential destruction, but the elders did not see it as so. They feared for the village, wondering what threat such powerful individuals could pose. In secret, they discussed ways to get visitors to leave, run them from the town if they must, but they knew not how without risking grave danger for the townspeople. Their conversations were all unnecessary. When the village woke the next day, the visitors were gone, vanished in the night, leaving everything built behind them. And so, we survived that bleak, brutal winter with the help of the strange visitors we would never see again.

First World - Second known occurrence. (Believed to have taken place sometime during the period of Classical Antiquity)

Something strange happened in the market square today, and I am unsure how to explain it. Father took us with him to the shops after we finished our lessons for the day as he always does. Anna was insistent on getting new fabric for a dress, claiming she had already used every kind she had and wanted something different. Father had obliged and told me I could pick out something as well. When we got to the market, though, we saw a group of visitors in our town that was unlike anything our town had ever seen. Father said they were surely just 'royals' visiting from a distant kingdom there to speak with the queen.

There didn't seem to be any rush to do so, though, as they browsed through the stalls and talked with the locals. Anna and I decided to follow them while father did his shopping. They bartered with each of the vendors trading strange trinkets and coins. I don't know what value any of it had, but all shopkeepers seemed more than eager to make the trades. There didn't seem to be any particular reason for what the strangers bought either. They simply collected random goods from various stalls as if they just wanted to buy stuff.

Anna talked about how she wished she could find fabric like they wore to make a dress, and I could understand. It was beyond lovely. It shined and flowed like clear, rushing water but looked almost metallic as if they had a blacksmith craft them breastplates from the finest silks. Their robes even glowed in a strange way like the braziers on the castle walls were ablaze in their very glows. The outfits moved fluidly with the strangers as they walked through the market like they were part of the people instead of just some clothes they put on. Everyone in the market stared in awe. Nothing like them had ever been seen in our kingdom.

They made their way to the edge of the market where the docks were with all the boats and fishermen gathered about. It seemed like ages that they sat talking with all the boatmen, but we were too far away to hear what they said. They just continued to gesture at the ships and the river that fed into the bay. At one point, the man who seemed to be their leader pointed far up the river into the mountains as he asked the men a question.

He was the fairest man I have ever seen and yet the toughest and most rugged. There was beauty in him, the way a vibrant fire or dazzling lightning or raging water is beautiful. It was a beauty that had power to it, fearsome power. They all did. Perhaps that is why everyone stared. They were a magnificent group, resplendent even. No doubt whatever these marvelous strangers had to offer the queen, she would want to hear. They were clearly not the type to be turned away.

Two of their group stayed very close together as they moved about the crowds. A man who looked as if he was kin to the gorgeous leader and a woman who was breathtaking beyond all description. It was as if a star had fallen from the night sky and was standing there among us. She was dazzling to the point she was almost terrifying. There was a depth to her elegance that made her outright intimidating, and it showed in the townspeople who all stood in marvel but did not dare go near her.

There was a rustle in the crowd suddenly, and it began to part as guards moved through the people escorting the queen herself. It is the first time I have ever seen the queen outside of her court, and she never greeted visitors on the streets. Yet, there she was, making her way steadily to the strangers from some faraway land. Even more surprising was when she reached them and bowed graciously. No one had ever witnessed such a sight. Not only had the queen gone out of her way to come to market and greet these strangers, but she had also gone as far as to show reverence to them in front of the entire crowd.

Remarkably, though, the strangers kneeled, humbling themselves before her and thanking her for the kindness. Each of the individuals greeted her in turn, introducing themselves and praising her beautiful city. They quickly began discussing something with her, but thanks to the guards, there was no way to get close. After a brief moment, they started walking with the queen through the marketplace, continuing their discussion. The queen would gesture to something in the town and comment on it to the strangers, and then they would do so in kind. None of the shopkeepers were paying attention to their stalls anymore, as everyone in the crowd was interested in the strangers walking about with their queen.

Suddenly, in the distance of the crowd, a commotion broke out. I was too far away to see exactly what it was, but someone was running through the crowd, knocking people over, with another figure in close pursuit. Everything happened so fast then I can hardly remember how. In an instant, the man who had been fleeing was descended upon by the nearby guards. He struggled to free himself and began climbing the scaffolding on one of the walls, looking to make it over the top and escape. The guards that were nearest began scaling the structure as well while yelling out for reinforcements to get to the other side. As they neared the top, the weight became too much, and the massive structure collapsed, pulling pieces of the wall it had been put in place to repair with it and sending all the men plummeting to the ground.

Except, they never hit the ground. None of it did. Where moments before a heap of collapsing rubble was falling down, it was all suddenly floating in midair. The mighty wooden beams of the scaffolding, the large stone blocks that had pulled loose from the wall, and the men who had caused it all were frozen midway through their fall. The crowd gasped in horror as they saw the woman, the unnaturally beautiful one, with her arms outstretched as if she was holding the collapsing structure in her hands. Her partner was right by her side and quickly raised his hands in a simple motion, and the pieces of the falling beams and dislodged wall each returned to their original place, reforming as if nothing had ever happened—another gentle movement from the woman and the falling men landed gently on the ground like a feather.

A look of horror and sorrow passed across the faces of the strangers at what had occurred. In an instant, the crowd went mad. People ran, screaming, knocking each other over, trying to get away from the strangers, trying to flee the market. Stalls began to topple over as the mob spread through the square. The boatmen started rushing to their ships as if it would offer them some measure of safety. Then something changed. Suddenly, I could feel a surge of rage and complete devastation in my mind, but it wasn't my thoughts. The thoughts were those of whoever was speaking to me inside my head. He screamed out for the crowd to stop, and everyone in the market froze where they stood. Only no words had actually been spoken, yet somehow, they were heard by all. There was nothing but silence, and I could still feel the hurt inside my mind that the silent voice had carried.

I looked to the strangers and saw the one who had reassembled the structure kneeling on the ground, a mix of exhaustion and sadness on his face. The leader of the group, his kin, stepped over to the man and placed a gentle hand on his shoulder. Then I could feel another wave of emotions pressing against my mind. Not my feelings, but his, their leader's. His brow was furrowed in deep concentration as I watched him. I could feel the same sorrow and disappointment as before, but this time was calm and resolved.

There was no rage, only pity. Three simple words entered my mind, 'You saw nothing.' No words escaped his mouth, though, and even though I heard them clearly, they did not take hold. I did see something, something extraordinary. The crowd, however, all went back to what they were doing as if the scuffle had never occurred, the wall had not almost toppled to the ground only to be put back together miraculously as if they had never panicked with screams of terror, and as if the strangers were no longer there.

The crowd moved around them unassumingly, putting their stalls back in order, and going about their day. The leader and his kin both knelt together for a moment before two of their group gently raised them, embracing them as they did. Then, as if they had never come, the strangers departed our city and never returned. Father says I have too wild an imagination, but I know what I saw.

First World - Historian Telemicus Hazop's recording of the first altercation. (Recording dated to the late years of Classical Antiquity)

Today I witnessed firsthand the horrible end of the terrifying events that have plagued our country as of late. Strangers arrived on our shores mere weeks ago. Some called them gods at first. Stories spread throughout the region of creatures from the heavens that descended before the very eyes of the Delphi townspeople. As they flew into the city, a calm spread throughout the people who stood in reverence. The people cheered, believing the Gods of Olympus had graced our lands with their presence. They learned all too quickly, though that was not the case. They rebuked the people of Delphi for monuments they had built to our gods, stating that they were false representations, inaccurate depictions based on the strangers and those that came before them. They called themselves Ancients and said our world was built from the fragments of theirs which had been made by the Celestials and that all of the deities we had formed were mere attempts to explain the civilization to which we once belonged.

They were met with confusion at first. The citizens of Delphi had never witnessed anything like the might and splendor of these beings, but their confusion and reverence shortly turned sour as the strangers' comments angered them. They lashed out at the visitors, chastising them for their lies only meant to deceive the people so they could sow conflict amongst the realm. Their leader, the one who calls himself Samias, expressed sadness and remorse that we would be so naive and unwilling to listen to reason that our idols were of him and his family instead. His brother Milas, though, was enraged, according to the townspeople. He wanted them to destroy their monuments and purge the fallacy, but Samias would not allow it. He insisted that we were all free to make our own decisions, even if they were the wrong ones, and they left the city to carry the message elsewhere in hopes people would see wisdom.

The one called Milas hid his anger as he followed Samias from city to city only to be met with different versions of the same refusal. At each city, they were at first met with the same confusion that eventually turned to anger. Fury began to spread throughout our lands at these false profits that would blaspheme our gods. Each city they came to met them with harsher and harsher responses. Soon our citizens were downright outraged at the strangers, nearing the point of violence. As the strangers visited new settlements, they didn't even have to speak before our villagers denounced them in outrage. Villagers began calling them demons, devils, minions of the Dark One, visions from Hades sent to trick us. Many began making offerings to the gods requesting that they strike down these horrendous visitors, proving that their message was indeed false. Still, though, the one called Milas devotedly followed his brother who insisted on peace with our kind, and thus Milas stayed his rage, until today.

They had been traveling for weeks when they arrived at our gate. When they approached the city, the sight was not unlike the others before, only this time they were not met with just words, for our people had grown weary of the strangers. Violence lay in waiting. Our city's Archon stopped them outside the gates and told them their lies and deceit were not welcome inside our walls. Without warning, archers sprang up on the battlements and loosed a volley of arrows at the strangers. Milas threw himself in front of the volley as three arrows lodged deeply into his chest. The others took flight as our soldiers leaped from the underbrush brandishing their swords, all except Samias, who remained perfectly still, awaiting the attackers. He refused to show violence or flee from our kind. Milas turned to his partner, demanding that she lead the others away, before darting towards his brother. Before he could cover the distance, though, a soldier lunged forward and buried his sword in Milas' back.

What unfolded next is a sight I could never unsee. The one called Milas was lifted into the air as light swirled around him. The wind bent towards him as if he was pulling the very air around us into himself. Trees shook all around, and even the walls shook from the force as our soldiers were nearly swept off their feet. The blade lodged in his back slowly slid free as the arrows protruding from his chest fell to the ground. A golden aura began to pulse around him as his body radiated with an inner light. His eyes swirled with a deep purple glow that looked as if they had stolen the stars from the night sky. The soldier who had stabbed him knelt on the ground in fear as Milas hovered above, and in an instant, the man was gone. Flesh tore from his bone so fast it disintegrated as his entire being melted away into nothingness. There was not a single piece of him, his armor, or anything else to ever acknowledge he had even existed. Only a blackened stretch of scorched earth remained around the spot where Milas and the man had been, and Milas had vanished along with Samias to rejoin their kin. It was the first time I have seen a god with my own eyes.

First World - Collected Notations on Idonic influence with respect to Milas (Documents discussed continue through the Early Middle Ages)

Descriptions fitting the Davpyr get very widespread and redundant during the period that followed the account from the Grecian historian. We are including them in all our original data storage, but we wanted to transmit a summary of the findings to have on record should transit back prove timely. Things seem to progress in a much more hostile direction after the incident with Milas and the Grecian soldier. We are actively searching for older records as well. Of course, we have discovered plenty of the usual markings and references in ancient depictions, which have been photographed and encrypted on the storage capsule. Still, at this point, our primary focus is on the uptick in Idonic interactions and the increasing severity.

Samias seemed resilient in his efforts to establish a harmonious relationship with the world, but the Davpyr continued to be met with resistance to their teachings. As polytheism gave way to monotheism in the Mediterranean regions, this appears to become even more intense. The Davpyr still worked to aid the people whenever the chance arose. At times they arrived in secret and at others in full regalia, refusing to hide themselves. At this point in the research, it is unclear why they took the two different approaches or what prompted each one. What is certain is that when they arrived in secret, the humans were more than willing to accept any help that was offered. They even began demanding more and more of the Davpyr. It appears in some situations even bordering on dependency of them, despite the Davpyr's best efforts to the contrary. In each scenario, though, when the true nature of the visitors from Idonia is made known, the human reaction is the same. Violence towards the Davpyr becomes even more common as the records progress throughout time.

From what the records show, Milas appeared to do his best to respect his brother's wishes; he continued to grow colder towards the humans. He controlled his hostility towards the humans for a time, but he began lashing out at the humans when they would attack the Davpyr. Some records say he 'cursed' them when the humans sought to exile the Davpyr, though it is unclear from the translations what that means and is likely just a reflection of the times from best we can tell. Other records state that Milas began striking the humans whenever they attempted to attack the Davpyr. Still, the translations describe a considerably milder form of violence than he is in fact capable of. A few records do state that Milas went as far as to use Incarnum on some of the attackers, but from the descriptions, it seems to be very minimal attacks.

Naturally, there are oddities in how subdued the actions of Milas were despite his abilities and the general lack of hostility from Locief in turn, especially given their future actions. Milas' efforts never went as far as to be fatal or even incredibly harmful after the first altercation recorded by Telemicus, which is vastly different from the records we have from other worlds. One possible explanation we have found is the presence of Locief. Despite his growing hostility, most records indicate that Locief, in some way, was able to calm him. It is possible that this kept him from his potential destructiveness. Some records even mention he and Locief arriving or departing with one another yet separate from the group. It is unclear at this moment if that has any bearing. One particular record poetically refers to her as "his morning star, a light that shined so bright no other light could drown it out and always ushered him into a new dawn." This is, of course, increasingly odd given the role Locief holds within the Nalun and her later actions on other worlds.

It is strange that in none of the ensuing records we've found, do any of them indicate the Davpyr using mind alteration despite the increasing hostility. It is unclear if they tried and the attempts merely did not take root or if the awareness in the human population had grown too widespread for the attempts to be effective. Over the course of nearly a millennium, the trend continued with human hostility slowly becoming worse and worse until suddenly it stopped entirely. All records of the Davpyr cease altogether from what we have found, even as far as to our current point. We are in uncharted territory now and unsure what exactly the Idonic system is doing. It seems unlikely they would abandon this world given their resilience with the others. Perhaps this was their first failure, a world upon which they gave up.

First World - Final Communication, Direct Transmission (Middle Ages)

We were foolish and naive. So strong was our hope that Idonia had abandoned this world and we would discover some rare truth about their failures, and that hope blinded us to the reality that has been in front of us since we arrived. The Davpyr did not give up on this world, nor did they leave it. They have been hiding in plain sight all along, and we have been too distracted to see it.

Word reached us that the mighty city at the heart of the Byzantine Empire was marching to war. What was odd was the war was within their own borders. A tale was being told of strangers from the eastern mountains that had descended upon the city in secret. None of the citizens of the empire had ever seen or heard of them before. The strangers dressed themselves like the townspeople and tried to conceal their appearance. Splitting up, they wove through the city streets, speaking to no one, and merely listening to the citizens going about their everyday lives. It was the innocence of a child that gave them away. Despite her best efforts to hide her beauty, Locief still caught the attention of a young girl who gazed in wonder. The child tugged on her father's robe and pointed at the woman, saying she must have been sent from heaven. The father corrected the girl at first, telling her that was blasphemy, but when the father saw Locief, he too stared.

It wasn't long before word spread through the market, and every citizen there was staring. It was merely Locief at first, but the town slowly recognized the other unnatural creatures. Crowds began to flock to them, pressing in upon the Davpyr, fawning over them or demanding they perform some miracle. The citizens were going mad. Their minds were unhinging at the sight before them. The Davpyr's time spent in hiding had shifted the people's minds to the point that their existence wasn't something the humans could process. The guards sought to quell the crowds, but they too were swept up in the pandemonium. The Davpyr worked earnestly to calm the minds of the people, but their numbers had grown too massive, and their emotions were too frantic.

Seeing no other options, the Davpyr made to flee, but the horde of people kept pressing in closer, tearing at their clothes as they sought to cling to the strangers. More and more people poured towards the group, until one snapped. At once, the mob clawing at the Davpyr were thrust backward in a mighty shockwave as Milas had sent them all tumbling away from the individuals. Fear rose in the crowd, and they panicked. Guards began to rush the Davpyr with weapons drawn. The Ancients leapt into action, but only to defend themselves. They disarmed and disabled attacker after attacker, urging even more people to calm themselves and hear reason. It was to no avail. The madness had already taken root. More guards rushed into the fray, and the Davpyr were running out of chances for a bloodless escape. A spear flew through the air with expert precision, aimed at the initial culprit, Milas. The spear never found its mark, though, as he caught it just before it pierced his head. Another shockwave shook the town as Milas sent the guards all tumbling backward and took flight along with his kin as they fled back to their mountain fortress.

For centuries the mighty castle has sat atop the mountains overlooking the sprawling empire humanity had built, and no one had ever thought anything of the strange fortress. From time to time, people would come down from the mountain to trade in the markets, their familiars, and not once did it occur to a soul in the whole massive kingdom that something was awry. The Davpyr had been hiding there all along, using their familiars to move throughout the world, spreading their influence, and remaining in the shadows, where even we didn't think to look.

By the time we reached the mountains, it was already too late to stop the destruction. Trebuchets and onagers had already taken formation around the fortress. We watched in horror as the first wave flew through the air, setting the night sky ablaze with their hatred and fury. It wasn't only soldiers gathered on the mountainside. Even the villagers had come to watch the spectacle, jackals eager for the bloodshed. Milas stood alone atop the parapets, shielding his kin that they may flee. He did not even flinch when the first volley fell, holding his shield firm.

We raced through the forces searching for their leaders and begged them to stop, urging them to understand they were no match for the forces they faced. It mattered not. Their bloodlust had grown unquenchable. They wanted nothing but devastation. We pleaded, warning them that there was no way they would win this war, that if they pushed too far, they would unleash the monsters within the fortress. Volley after volley struck the mighty dome Milas upheld, but the soldiers would not cease. The monsters, though, never showed. Whatever drove Milas, Samias, and Locief to lead Nalun on their conquest of world after world, it was not in them here. In this world, Idonia desperately tried for peace, but the humans that inhabit this world would not have it.

Hours passed as the volleys rained down upon Milas; slowly, painfully, his strength began to wane. The shield began to crack. Bit by bit, the mighty boulders set aflame tore through the dome and crashed down onto the once beautiful fortress. The sky turned red with fire, and smoke filled the land, choking out any hope that remained. The siege raged through the night unlike anything ever known. The ferocity of the humans was terrifying. No one slept. No one ate. No one drank. All they did was watch as the endless flaming balls rained down upon the Ancient and the fortress he guarded.

But it would not end there. Milas had stretched his avatar to its utmost limits protecting the gateway while his family fled. He continued pouring more and more of his power and himself into upholding the shield and maintaining the path between the worlds.

It was around dawn when he lost stabilization. Too much of himself had been spent. A devastating tremor shook the entire mountainside, leveling everything in its wake as Milas' power collapsed in on itself. This will be our last transmission, as this world is now imploding. We have launched our data cache on its return vector, but we cannot guarantee it will reach escape velocity in time. As for the crew, we are lost here. The gravitational fluctuations are too massive for us to depart. There was so much of this world we never even began to study, so much that will remain undiscovered. One thing we did learn, of everything that comes after this, all the horrors that Idonia brings our kind, here is where the war truly started.

29
A GHOSTLY TRUTH

He kissed the inside of her thigh gently. She was still scared; he felt it in the way she moved, the way she touched him. Terror gripped her body, and he was her release. He'd lost count of how many times she had reached her max, and after each one, he had brought her back down, letting her simmer with anticipation before beginning again. Such was their dance. A rush of emotions colliding together, swirling about them as the ecstasy rose and rose, then drifting apart yet again, so the longing begins.

His lips moved slowly up and down her leg, teasing her at what was to come but still keeping her waiting as long as he could. She wouldn't last much longer before she demanded release. She knew their days were numbered. The world outside that room was closing in on them, and the wolves were circling. They couldn't stop what was coming, but they could have that moment.

The danger only made the exhilaration more intense. Her mind screamed, part in fright and what lay ahead for them and part in the ecstasy he provided. Each time his lips touched her, each caress of his fingers, each stroke of his tongue, eradicated any terror she felt and filled her with calming waves of desire and love. She wondered why she could not feel his fear, knowing how strong her own was. He was merely lost in her. The only thing he could feel when they were together was complete. It scared him to no end when they were apart, the hold she had on him. When they were together, though, he could not be afraid, for he knew with every fiber of his being how right it was.

His lips worked their way up her thigh until they found the soft edge of her pelvis. She twitched violently as he kissed it, enjoying how much it both tickled and aroused her. He slid both arms under her legs, curling his hands around to grip her hips as he softly kissed her mound, sending a spasm up her spine that made her gasp. Gripping her hips firmly with his hands, he opened his mouth and kissed her innermost sanctum. With his lips on hers, he ran his tongue slowly up her, savoring every drop, drinking in the very essence of her being. Her breath quickened, letting out soft moans as she fought to control her breathing.

Sliding his tongue back down the length of her, he pressed it gently into her, pulling her hips into him and opening her ever so slightly. Reaching the spot, he rolled his tongue and pushed it softly inside her. She grabbed his hair in both hands, pulling him further into her as her back arched, and she gasped, desperately calling for him. That would be the last time before she demanded he join her, but he was not done with his fun yet. He slowly thrust his tongue in her three long times before sliding it out and running it teasingly up her until it reached her pearl. He closed his lips around her as it throbbed furiously, sucking gently as his tongue wove circles. Releasing her slightly, he began tracing her name smoothly over her pearl, accentuating each letter with another kiss that sent wave after wave of spasms through her body, driving him to grip her hips tighter and tighter as she grabbed his hair ever more firmly.

She'd had all she could stand as her body began to shake with ecstasy. She wanted him, needed him, and she would have him. Taking him by his hair, she pulled him up towards her until their lips collided with a force that could level mountains. Their lips parted as their tongues danced wildly with one another. He made to tease her even more, rubbing the throbbing tip of himself against her pearl, but she would have none of it. He had teased her enough, and she wanted what was hers. She slapped his hand away and grabbed it firmly, letting him know it was time. He did not protest as she slid him down to her, eased the tip in ever so slightly, and then grabbed his tight cheeks firmly, pulling every inch of him powerfully into her. She bit hard into his shoulder, screaming into him as euphoria took her. All at once, she was complete, and the dangers that awaited them melted away.

Ally woke late that morning. They had stayed up so late with the book, and by the time they did go to bed, her mind was too disheveled to rest. She'd slept terribly; everyone had. Visions continued to visit the friends every time they closed their eyes. From the magnificent city of Idonia to the tragic scenes of the first world, the friends were haunted all through their sleep. Everyone, except Thad. He had not slept at all. Unable to tear his mind away from the book or the Brownings or the broad swath of questions that surrounded him, he'd spent the entire night searching for answers, and thus he waited solemnly in the kitchen to tell the friends what he had found.

The look on his face when the three girls descended the staircase told them the terrible news without the friends even needing to look at his phone; he had slid across the island. The Ghost has claimed another.

"You guys should probably sit down." His voice was a gravelly whisper as he spoke. "We need to talk."

The girls all took a seat at the kitchen table as Thad stood and began pacing the floor.

"I found out some stuff that, well, to be honest, it's some pretty crazy shit. Ever since the second murder last semester, I've been keeping an eye on the killings here. At first, it worried me having you guys so close to something like that. As time went by, though, I took genuine interest in the case because of how impossible it all seemed. The lack of evidence, the lack of connection between the victims, it was just too weird. It wasn't until last night's victim that I put it all together, though."

"Wait, you've been accessing the police reports this whole time?" Ally asked in shock.

"Yeah, sure, it's technically illegal. Do you want to know what I found, or do you want to discuss the morality of the situation?"

"What do you know about the Ghost, Thad?" Erin asked emphatically but somewhat afraid of what his response would be.

"For starters, there have been some, um," his voice fell silent as he searched for words, "some inconsistencies in the murders. The papers say all the Ghost's victims have had their throats slit and then stabbed in the heart. That's what the police reports say too. That's not exactly true, though. The coroner's reports show that only a few of them happened that way. Some of the Ghost's victims' throats weren't so much slit as they were, like, ripped open."

Rachel gasped in horror.

"Ripped open how?" Erin asked.

"That's the thing; the cops don't know. They still list all the victims the same because the only thing they can guess is that the murderer just got sloppy with their knife work on some. Which would make you think that some of the victims put up a hell of a struggle while others it was like they died without ever knowing what was coming, right? Wrong. From what all the police reports say, none of the crime scenes really show any sign of struggle or anything like that. They maintain that all the incidents are the same"

"You don't think that's it, though," Erin stated, studying Thad's face.

Thad paced the floor in silence some more before finally sitting down at the table. He cupped his hands in front of his face and took a deep breath. "There are other things that don't match up between the murders. Things that the police don't mention but are there in the reports. Two things, in particular, stand out. The first is that the victims who had their throats gashed were all stabbed in the chest well after they were dead. The victims that didn't see it coming were stabbed almost immediately after having their throat slit. The second thing that doesn't line up is the third victim." Thad paused as he said. He'd mean to say her name, but he couldn't bring himself to do so.

"Denise." Ally said in a hollow tone.

"Yes." Thad's voice was full of sorrow. "So, I read back through all the case reports more thoroughly. Now the first two scenes were the same. No signs of struggle, clean slit, stabbed in the heart. Both times the body was found lying down with their hands at their sides and their eyes closed. Right away, the police saw the connection—identical scenes. Only problem, of course, was the two victims didn't have any connection to each other. Then the third victim, though, threw the first wrench in the system. The body was found exactly the same as the first two, but the cause of death wasn't the same. Denise died from strangulation; the throat slit and the dagger to the heart came after she was dead. What's even weirder is the lack of a struggle. I'm no expert, but I would imagine it's tough to strangle someone without them putting up a fight."

"That doesn't make any sense," Erin said softly. "There's no way that could happen, unless…"

"Unless, her body was moved." Rachel finished Erin's sentence.

"Exactly," Thad replied, "but still nothing linked the three together from what the cops could find. Then came the fourth victim, and that's when things start spiraling out of control. The fourth murder wasn't like the other three. It was the first one that had been gashed, and as it turns out, the forensics team noticed the lack of blood at the scene, but they figured from the nature of the lacerations on the victim's throat that most of the blood probably left the scene on the killer. So what the police have pretty much decided is that the times the victims suspected the killer, a struggle ensued, most of the blood got on the killer, and that would kinda explain the killer possibly stabbing them in the heart after they were dead and all the panic had died down. It still doesn't explain the absolute lack of evidence at the scenes, though. If there was that kind of blood being spilled, there would be splatter patterns, footprints, all that stuff. I mean, we've all watched enough crime investigation shows to know how this works, but there's none of that."

Thad paused to catch his breath, not realizing how worked up he'd become. The lack of sleep was getting to him as his movements grew jittery. He breathed deep, working to calm himself and stable his mind for what came next.

"The scenes alone would be enough for confusion," he began again after collecting himself, "but the fact that they still haven't found a connection or pattern between any of the victims is even stranger. I think I know why that is, though."

The girls stared at him in anticipation, but the look on Thad's face did not speak of good news.

"So the police haven't thought the discrepancies meant that much, but I think that's the key. The first thing is the little details. The eyes always closed, hands placed at the side—even the killing process. If you wanna make things quick and quiet, a full slit of both internal jugulars and a knife directly into the aorta less than a second later, that's a fast way to take somebody out without making a sound or even inflicting much pain. The person would be dead almost instantly. The Ghost of Little Rock isn't just systematically killing people; he's executing them."

"What about the other victims then?" Ally asked, her hands shaking with fear. "Why isn't the Ghost so meticulous with them?"

"That's just the thing," Thad's voice fell very low as he stared into the faces of his three friends, "I don't think the Ghost is killing those people."

Erin's words were a trembling whisper as she spoke, "You mean there's more than one killer?"

"That's exactly what I mean. It doesn't make sense otherwise."

"And how did you come to that conclusion when the detectives haven't figured it out with the same evidence?" Ally asked in horrified disbelief.

"Because I know the other thing the police don't, something only we know."

The room fell as silent as a tomb.

"Every, single, one of the victims the Ghost has been executing have first-hand dealings with the Harbilins."

The three girls stared at Thad in silence. All emotion left their body as a feeling of absolute emptiness took each over. The family with whom they had eaten dinner, been to the zoo, drank coffee, the family they had come to love, was connected to a series of killings, no, a series of executions. No one spoke. Words wouldn't form if they tried. Rachel's eyes sank to the table as she thought about each encounter, each time they had visited with the enigmatic family. Ally shifted her head towards the wall as her thoughts went to the elusive, guarded men that Joshua and Win were, how she'd become so fond of them. Erin's gaze stayed fixed on Thad's as they both thought about the entire Browning family, how caring and kind they were, and yet somehow so dangerous.

"Do you think they know?" Erin's words were barely a whisper.

Thad shifted himself in his chair, "They have to. Whatever they may be, the Brownings aren't fools. I'm sure they've seen the connection between the victims by now, at least after Denise. I mean, Joshua and Win straight up said they'd gone looking into her past for who would have done that. You can't tell me they don't know more than they're leading on. They've always known more about everything than they let show. At first, I thought maybe they were involved, or maybe the Harbilins were getting rid of loose ends. You know me and my mafia, shit. The more I think about it, though, all the precision and thought that went into each murder, that seems like a lot of work to put into covering up your trail. If somebody puts as much effort behind something as the Ghost has…" his eyes fell from Erin's and landed on the table. He took a long breath before looking back up, "That seems like someone trying to send a message."

"Do you think..." Ally's voice cut off, unable to voice the terrible thought in her head.

Thad knew what Ally was wondering even without her saying it, "I don't think the killer's targeting the Brownings specifically. Just like I don't think the murders so far have been about the victims. I realize I'm no detective, but something inside just tells me the Ghost's message is for the Harbilins. Trouble with that is," his voice fell soft again, "there's only one way to the Harbilins."

Rachel's eyes filled with tears. If what Thad felt was true, the Ghost would be after their newfound family sooner or later. Ally felt a lump swelling in her throat, and Erin's had gone hollow. All too soon, the visions of Raven Man flashed before their eyes. They remembered the terror of not being able to escape him, how everywhere they went, he was there. A small part of them knew what the victims of the Ghost had felt. Only the Ghost's victims hadn't seen their killer coming. They'd had no warnings that Death would come for them. Or had they? Their minds raced with the thought that perhaps the victims had been warned but did not heed their warning. The group had no way of knowing if the victims had been haunted by nightmares as they had, but somewhere deep inside, they knew that Raven Man's words were not just an empty threat.

"Should we tell them?" Erin's words were shaky as she spoke. "I mean, in case they don't know. Should we warn them?"

"I want to. I don't know what to say, though." Thad was torn on what to think.

"You don't need to tell them." The words came from Ally's mouth without her even knowing.

"What? Why shouldn't we tell them?" Rachel turned to Ally with tears in her eyes.

"When the Ghost first started killing people, Joshua, Lili, Win, each of them tried to calm us down. They told us that we didn't need to worry, and every victim since they've had the same tone. They always had a look in their eyes of absolute certainty. I thought it was just them trying to keep us from panicking, but now it all makes sense. They've known from the beginning the killer was coming for them."

Silence overtook the room again as eyes darted from one face to another, looking for an answer. Erin and Rachel wanted to argue Ally's point, but they remembered all too well the look of which she spoke. There was nothing for them to say. If the Brownings did know, then none of them could imagine trying to discuss it with Joshua or Win.

"I need air." Erin's words were simple, but their meaning carried so much weight for everyone at the table.

As if by command, they all rose from the table, grabbed their coats, and followed her out the door. The air outside was as cold and bitter as it had been the day before, but the wind gave them a strange comfort as it nipped at them while they walked. No one bothered to speak, not even to discuss where they were walking. They'd already said enough that day, and so they let their feet carry them, unaware of where they were headed.

Despite the silence or oblivious walk, the friends found themselves fittingly in the one place that always made their world feel right. They quietly flowed inside The Brew, and a wave of relief hit them. Terry served their drinks as cheery as ever, not even stopping to notice the friends' mellow mood. She never mentioned the recent victim or even acknowledged anything was awry. Terry simply busied herself behind the counter as the friends drank in peaceful silence.

Thad stayed the rest of the weekend, which passed in a haze. Everyone had been locked away in thought. Their dreams were filled with nightmares of Raven Man and the Wanderer or the Ghost, or visions of other worlds. No one got much sleep. They had ordered pizza and watched movies, but no one was really involved or even paying much attention. They had even discussed inviting Terry over to visit, but everyone's minds kept wandering back to the horrible revelations of their so-called Ghost of Little Rock.

Ally woke in a cold sweat. She had been running through a forest, but the moment her eyes opened, she couldn't remember what pursued her. It could have been Raven Man, or it could have been the collapsing mountainside of the first world. Either would have befitted her sleep the past nights. She checked her phone to see it was just after 3:30. Her cup was empty, so she went to her bathroom sink and filled it up. The water tasted strangely stale. She poured it out and went downstairs to get a fresh glass from the dispenser. It was crisp and refreshing, thankfully.

She downed one glass and refilled it, but before she went back to her room, she stopped and stared out the front window. Frost had settled, and it looked like it might snow. Ally loved the snow. Arkansas rarely saw any, but when it did, she had always enjoyed it. Something about it made it feel like time had slowed down for her. She continued to stare out the window, praying the flakes would fall. Out in the frosty night air, Ally couldn't help but feel as if eyes were staring back at her. She couldn't see them, but somehow she felt them. She closed her eyes briefly, feeling like her dreams were finally getting to her.

A sound to her left made her jump, and she turned to see Thad lazily descend the stairs, half asleep yet trying in earnest to be stealthy. He was so out of it that he didn't even notice Ally was in the kitchen as he shuffled towards the couch. Ally froze in the spot, not wanting to alert him yet also wanting to scream at him. She couldn't believe what she was seeing. It hadn't been her imagination before. She had heard the sounds, more than once. Thad had a secret.

The rage began to build in Ally, furious that he had just spent the night in one of her best friend's rooms, that he had been for months, and worse, she, his closest friend, had been kept in the dark the entire time. She suddenly felt like she didn't even know him. Then, as soon as the anger came, it began to fade into doubt and confusion. Rachel was practically in pieces, stressed over school, missing her family, and fearing what was to come of the Brownings. Erin was completely lost, unsure what dangers were ahead and not knowing what to do as a friend. And, amidst all that, her concern was that Thad was sleeping with one of her friends. They weren't kids anymore. The two girls asleep upstairs were well on their way to being adults, whether she wanted to admit it or not. Who was kissing whom under the bleachers at school no longer mattered.

He was her closest friend, but they were his friends too. All of them were. They were family. Maybe that is what she feared. Rachel and Thad had been together before, and they had all made it through when they broke up. That was different somehow, though. That was kids, and they no longer were. Ally struggled with her emotions. Thad was allowed to be happy and dating someone, and her friends were allowed to be happy and dating someone, just so long as those didn't intertwine. That didn't feel right. Thad cared about both of them, just as he cared about her. She tried to rationalize it from their perspective. They may not yet know who they were as a couple or what they wanted that to mean. Ally began to resent herself. She would have hoped that if her friends were in a relationship, she would support them. She only felt betrayed, but she couldn't figure out if it were simply because she hadn't been told or because she didn't, in fact, support them.

Thad was an incredible person. He always had been, to her and all of them. Erin and Rachel were both two of the most amazing people she had ever known. Rachel and Thad had a past. She couldn't deny that. Even Rachel had said how she still cared for him. He and Erin had been friends just as long. They flirted, but they were both just flirty people. Erin flirted with everybody, even Joshua. It's just how they were. They constantly teased, of course, but they wouldn't be around each other if they didn't get along. Rachel was attracted to Win, but Ally knew she was foolish to think a crush would keep her friend from a real relationship, a relationship with someone she loved. Erin was a hard-ass, independent girl who took no shit, but that didn't mean she wasn't also a woman wanting to be loved. Rachel always seemed like the innocent little girl who flushed at the slightest compliment, but she was also a sage, driven woman willing to take what she wanted. And Thad, sweet Thad, was also very much a man; ambitious, focused, and most of all caring. Ally's mind turned somersaults as she sought to analyze and break down her three best friends' love lives, but it only found one possible solution; relationships were complicated.

Her original feelings of betrayal and disrespect were replaced with guilt and embarrassment. The whole time she had wondered about Thad's involvement with one of her friends, she never stopped to think what would drive them to such secrecy. At some point, all of her friends had started growing up, and she stood there in the kitchen feeling more like a child than ever. She walked to the edge of the kitchen, where it met the living room. She wanted to say something to Thad, but instead, she just stood in silence. An inconvenient truth hit her at that moment. She realized that Thad and whomever of her friends held a secret; it had nothing to do with her. For whatever reason, they kept it secret because of them.

With that, she returned quietly to her bed, feeling it best if she simply closed her eyes and let go of the whole thing. Much to her surprise, no nightmares found her, and she slept peacefully well into the late hours of the morning. When she woke again, Ally wanted to sprint downstairs and announce her full support to Thad and her friends, but she was resolved not to make mention of it. Instead, she made her way downstairs and found her friends, all still in a general state of fear and gloom, and the reality of the world around her crept back. In place of words, the friends only exchanged glances, not wishing to share any of their thoughts.

The group dragged themselves to The Brew, afraid to go anywhere else with what seemed to be multiple killers in the city of Little Rock, killers that had the Harbilins, and thus the Brownings, squarely in their sights. As always, a calm settled over them the moment they entered The Brew. Their fear was not removed, but an overwhelming sense that they would find their way through that dark period spread through each of them.

They sat, drinking their coffee, and finally, they began to talk. It was idle chat, but it was progress. Much, much-needed progress after the few days they had just endured. They talked about every trivial thing they could to prolong the day and keep the sense of hope alive. Thad and Ally talked about games. They both had several titles they hoped would get announced that year. Erin spoke about her idea that was slowly solidifying for her next tattoo. It was going to be a big one, and beautiful at that. Rachel talked about a couple of career fields she had begun researching, some largely thanks to Edmonton's class. She very much wanted to study abroad for her doctorate to use for her next step.

The friends felt at peace for a time. They even laughed some as they drank their coffees that their sweet friend Terry kept filled without fail. Slowly, despite their best efforts to find peace, a horrible realization crept into the friends' minds. The friends had all felt a certain level of unspoken safety for the Brownings somehow. Even though the Ghost was incredibly skilled, the Harbilins and the Brownings did not get where they were without knowing how to abate danger, but eventually, a harsh fact took root. The Ghost was trying to send a message to the Haribilins. It was killing off people who were connected with them, including the Brownings. The Ghost, however, had already sent a message by claiming the life of one employee of The Daily Brew, which meant they could claim another. Terry.

30
WOLVES IN SHEEP'S CLOTHING

The friends were relieved that getting Terry to hang out with them had proved so easy. They didn't have any false pretenses that Terry spending time with them made her any safer, but it made the friends feel like they were at least doing something to help. All it took was a simple question of if she had evening plans, and as soon as she got off work, they had all gone back to the house on Rock Street. Thad stayed as late as he could that night, but knowing his grandmother would need him home, he eventually made himself leave. Terry, though, stayed well into the waning hours of the night and did so again the next night and the next.

Each day the friends felt more and more at peace. It was the effort of trying to do something, the mere act of normalcy, that let them shrug off the feelings of dread. Terry made them feel even better as well. She was a genuine friend, sweet and funny, but still very real. The friends loved how quickly they fell in step with her as if they had never even left for the holidays and simply picked back up right where they left off. In the middle of the week, her brother Dante arrived, and the friends worried that might be the end of their visits. Much to their surprise, though, both Terry and Dante were more than willing to come over, stating that it beat just sitting around in her apartment.

Dante was like his sister in so many ways. He was a gentle soul but still had a toughness to him that spoke of a challenging life, making him one who'd seen hardship but not been jaded by it. Though he didn't talk a lot, he was very well-spoken, as if he was very comfortable in conversation but simply preferred not to. That fit in just fine around the friends and quickly made for common ground between him and Ally. It was nice for her to have someone with whom she could be quiet and at peace. It was odd to the friends how they had gone through all of their high school and undergraduate years without adding any numbers to their flock, yet just a few months in a new place and their group had practically doubled, but it also gave them a comforting reassurance in their new home.

Night after night of having Terry and then Dante over to their house, though, put the friends in a predicament when the next fight came to pass. Despite the horrifying sights they had experienced before, the friends still wanted to attend, earnestly so, as if something was drawing them there. The same something that was persistently drawing them to the Brownings. They had only seen Joshua and Win sparingly that week as they had spent so much time with Terry, who fittingly was at the center of their predicament. To go to the fights, the friends had to avoid a long evening with her and Dante, but they also didn't want to abandon their new friends. That led the friends to their plans for dinner and a movie, forcing the group out and creating a window for them to slip away afterward quickly.

The window was tight to fit dinner in between when Terry finished working and the movie started. They had insisted on an early show stating they didn't want to be out too late, and so the group decided on a quick burger and fries downtown before the movie. It wasn't until they sat down that the friends realized it was the first time they had been out somewhere with Terry and Dante without the Brownings or Van present. They had always seen how shy Terry was, but they had often assumed it was simply her timidness towards the enigmatic family and their friend. Even as she gave her order to the cashier, though, she was awkward and quiet, standing well away from the counter as if she were scared it might attack her. The cashier made a flirtatious comment, and Terry's face turned bright red. She gave an innocent giggle as she handed him her money and quickly shuffled away. Dante, on the other hand, was calm and resolved. It was a stark contrast for the three girls who had thought him shy from the moment they met him to see he was someone else, someone reserved and private but not bashful.

Ally couldn't help feeling relieved by Terry, knowing she wasn't the only awkward and shy one, but she was also intrigued by the increasingly complex character of Dante. As they walked to their table, Ally found comfort in the fact their group had somewhat ushered Terry in. It would be nice having another girl like herself around.

"So you never really said how you like working at The Brew, Terry. How'd that all come about?" Ally asked Terry.

"I love working there," Terry replied quietly. "The Brownings are super nice. I'm pretty certain Lili is an angel somehow," she giggled softly, "and all of their family and friends are really cool. It kinda just fell in my lap, though. When Dante and our parents were getting ready to move, I knew I'd need a place to stay, which meant finding a job as well. I'd been into the Brew plenty times, and I just happened to be in there talking with…"

Terry paused as sadness filled her eyes, and the friends knew immediately with whom she had been talking. Dante grabbed her hand and gave it a soft, compassionate squeeze of reassurance. She wiped her eyes to keep any tears from falling.

"Sorry," she continued, taking a deep breath. "Anyways, I mentioned in passing that I was going on a job hunt, and out of the blue, Lili asked if I wanted to work there. It was kinda perfect, honestly. The hours are solid, it's in downtown, which I like, and the pay is crazy good. I don't think I could have found a job paying even half what they do without some degree or certification. Plus, I get to work around fun people."

"And the eye candy known as the Brownings is pretty damn nice too." Erin teased playfully, which made Terry turn a deep shade of red. "Not to mention Van."

"Van's a sweet guy." She replied in a hushed voice, still blushing immensely.

"Yeah, it's been nice having him around," Dante said, stepping in for his sister. "Terry's a tough one, but it's comforting knowing she's got people like him and you folks around with us, not around."

"So why'd you move Dante?" Rachel asked, curious to know more about their new acquaintance.

"I help my parents with a lot still, taking care of the family business with them looking to retire soon." He replied with a subtle note of disappointment. "It's not exactly my thing, but it's what's best for the family."

Terry took his hand in return, giving him her thanks and support.

"I'd like to maybe make it back out here at some point to be closer to Terry, but in the meantime, she at least has all of you and Van. So that's nice."

"I don't know if I would call myself nice," Erin replied sarcastically. "Van, however, is all the nice a girl could ask for."

"That he may be," Ally tried quickly to take the embarrassment out of the situation for Terry, "but that is Terry's business."

Terry's face continued to redden, "Oh, no. I mean, I like him and all. He's one of the nicest men I've ever met. I just don't think he wants something like that from me. I just mean that he probably has plenty other choices, and I don't know why he would choose me when he could have any girl he wanted."

"Because you're awesome." Ally said in an attempt at encouragement that turned Terry's cheeks a soft shade of pink.

"I'm nothing special." She denied the compliment despite being flattered. "Van does keep coming around, though, so I'm not complaining. Coming around to visit, that is. Like coming to Little Rock to visit the Brownings and do work stuff. It's just that he stops by to hang out. Just hang out. I mean, like we watch movies and stuff. Oh, dear."

Erin wanted to laugh, but she saw the embarrassment in Terry's eyes and felt compelled to console her. "Relax, Terry." She said, smiling encouragingly. "It's all good. Look, I make jokes all the time, but they're just that. Jokes. Nothing more. You don't have to sweat it with us."

"Thanks." She smiled thankfully at Erin. "I'm not really used to having friends to tease me aside from his punk self, but that's just siblings for you. I've always been the shy, loner girl, I guess. It's nice having people to visit with like you and Van and the Brownings, and Luci, of course."

"Luci?" The friends all asked in harmonious shock.

"Wait," Ally began, "you're friends with Luci?"

"I wouldn't say we're friends," Terry replied with confusion in her voice. "She spends days at The Brew from time to time when she's in town working or waiting on Joshua and Win. We just chat a lot while she's there. It's sad to know so many bad things can happen to such sweet people. Did you know she and Joshua saw their moms die?"

"Yeah, it's just terrible," Dante added with pained remorse. "God, the horrors that must bring you. Nobody should have to go through that. My heart breaks for them anytime I think about it."

"They never told us the details," was all Erin could manage to say.

Ally and Rachel both sat in sorrowful silence.

"Oh, they didn't tell us either," Dante replied in a sorrowful tone. "I doubt that's something they talk about."

"Yeah, I can't imagine you'd want to," Terry added. "Van let us know when we were asking about them. Luci never mentioned anything bad about their life. None of 'em do, really. She always just smiles and laughs as she asks questions about me and what's going on. Aside from Van, I don't think I've ever met anyone so caring. She even sent me a card on my birthday with a sweet little poem in it."

Again the friends' perception of Luci was muddied. They had no idea when Terry's birthday even was, yet this person they were so skeptical of had been thoughtful enough to write Terry a poem. Luci was quickly becoming as much of an enigma as the Brownings.

"That was pretty cool of her." Ally said as she stood to throw her tray away. "We'd better get going, though, if we want to catch the movie."

Neither Terry nor Dante took note of Ally's dodge of the Luci topic as they followed suit in throwing their trays away, but Erin and Rachel agreed with Ally as they headed towards the door. The group set off on the short walk to the theatre through the streets lined with couples mingling about in a steady flow. The friends knew the Ghost wouldn't dare attack in such a large public group, and that had been their primary goal in keeping Terry close. The resurgence of Luci, though, brought them back to the complexities of their situation.

"Terry, how well do you really know the Brownings?" Erin asked, trying her best not to sound conspicuous.

"I don't know, really. I mean, I just know them from work and the few things I've overheard. I had concerns for a little while there, but after Van cleared them up, it was all good. To be honest, I guess I don't really know them all that well. I've been working for them for over two years now, and I pretty much only know the things I've learned about them recently. Huh, that's kinda weird. I'd never really thought about it till you mentioned that."

After the movie, the group walked back to where they had parked Ally's and Dante's cars, laughing the whole time about the terrible acting in the film. They exchanged horribly scripted quotes from it and swore they'd never see another movie with those actors in it again. The three girls were thoroughly glad that Terry and Dante had joined their circle, but that night was about far more than just their two new friends.

At their cars, the group said their goodbyes and agreed to do it again soon. Part of them wanted to stay and spend more time with Terry and Dante, but their entire being pulled them towards the violence at hand. So the friends hopped in the car and sped off towards the abandoned building.

Traffic dwindled the closer the friends got. They had the path memorized by then and made their usual route looping around the back of the parking garage, turning off their lights as they rolled into the same spot they had used the times before and turned the car off. They scanned the garage but saw no car they recognized as one of the Brownings' or Van's or even Luci's. That thought made their minds stop. They had no idea what Luci drove, if she drove. They'd only ever seen Luci walk everywhere she went. As they scanned the lot again, searching for a vehicle that looked like something she might drive, they saw the Roadster gliding in with an all-black twin right on its heels. Without warning, all four doors shot up, and the friends slumped in their seats, trying to hide. Win and Van came laughing out of the Brownings' car while Joshua and Luci stepped out of its blacked-out counterpart wearing matching grins.

The four friends pulled the collars of their coats up to guard their faces against the wind, and the girls sat waiting for them to enter the building. As always, they didn't get out immediately. They wanted to give themselves time to sneak, convinced that would help maintain their secrecy. Five minutes passed, then ten, then fifteen before they finally made to exit the vehicle, only to find two figures waiting for them. They jumped back against the car, expecting the strike to come at any moment, but they only heard the soft, sweet voice of Terry.

"Um," She began in confusion, "what exactly are y'all doing?"

Neither Ally, Erin, nor Rachel could formulate an answer. The truth was too much to explain, but their confusion at Dante and Terry standing before them was even greater.

Unsure of what had just unfolded, Erin asked, "Better question, what exactly are y'all doing here?"

Terry's face contorted with hurt as she spoke, "Well, you said you were going home, but I couldn't help notice you drove off in the complete opposite way of your house, which happened to be on our way to my apartment. I thought you must just not know the city all that well yet, but then when you got to the last turn to cut back to your house and went the other way, we thought maybe it was something else."

"Sorry we followed you," Dante added with remorse, "and even more sorry if we startled you. We've been waiting here to see what the heck was going on. We just wanted to make sure you were ok. I mean, it's not exactly safe to be out this late, especially in this part of town, and especially when there's a serial killer on the loose."

"We're sorry too." Erin began again, feeling guilty. "I didn't mean to seem like a jerk. You just scared the shit out of us, is all, and we didn't mean to be all sneaky. Ok, well, we did mean to sneak over here, but not, like, to sneak away from y'all. We just came here because, well, we came here to –,"

"To see what Joshua and Win and Van and Luci are doing?" Terry's words cut Erin off and froze the friends solid. "That was them that went into that building just a bit ago, wasn't it?"

The friends nodded their heads.

"So what's in there?" Dante asked. "Do y'all know?"

The friends nodded their heads again, but they couldn't bring themselves to explain. Terry and Dante were already there, and they certainly wouldn't be able to explain the situation away. The friends looked at one another in unspoken agreement. Not knowing where to start explaining, they simply took Terry and Dante by the hand, led them across the garage, and down the staircase to the basement.

"Enjoying it so much you had to bring friends this time, huh?" Asked the burly guard, they had grown to enjoy.

"They don't know yet." Ally said as the man opened the door.

"Well, in that case, I'll see y'all back out here fairly shortly." He smiled playfully at the friends.

They led Terry and Dante through the door and climbed immediately to the upper rows to be far from the fighting. No one bothered sitting down. In fact, Terry and Dante stood on their seats to see better and began looking around to figure out what was going on, so the friends did the same.

"It's a fighting tournament." Ally whispered into Terry's ear but still loud enough so Dante could hear.

Terry let out a gasp, "That's horrid. They're really beating people up? What if they get hurt?"

Erin was slightly unsure of how to respond, "Well, it is a tournament. They kinda have to beat people up to win. As for getting hurt, we've only seen Joshua and Luci fight, and trust me; they ain't getting hurt."

"Luci's in it?" Terry's voice was laden with terror. "Dear God, no."

"Relax, Terry." Rachel said, putting an arm around Terry. "Luci can handle herself. She already won last time we were here. I'm not sure about Win and Van. We haven't seen them fight yet, but I would imagine they're capable enough with how they act."

Terry didn't speak. There was a look of deep disgust in her eyes, and the friends knew exactly how she felt. They recognized the face they had the first time at the fights. Dante, however, was almost pensive as he studied the arena. He did not speak, as was his nature, but his eyes were ablaze with thought.

The evening had only just begun, though. The announcer called out the first set of fighters, and all noise seemed to be vacuumed from the room. The friends looked over at Terry, not even hearing the deafening shouts from the crowd. The look of terror on Terry's face made the friends' hearts swell in their throats almost as Van took off his coat and blazer before jumping over the ledge.

Terry and Dante could not have picked a worse night to follow the friends, and the group hated themselves instantly for putting the evening's events into motion. Terry just stared down at the floor, shaking her head, not wanting to see what would happen. Dante's eyes shifted back and forth from his sister to the arena, fearing for her and apprehensive about seeing what would unfold.

Van unbuttoned his dress shirt and tossed it back over the ledge to Win. He stood only in his slacks, his entire tattoo visible as it adorned his lean, sinewy figure. He was not built like the Brownings, but there was a lethal efficiency to his body. There was muscle on his frame clearly, but it wasn't overt. Its subtlety, though, gave him a quietly ferocious air. The circuit board-like design of his tattoo continued from his neck outwards to his shoulder, where a massive circle formed like a power center. From the ring on his shoulder, the circuits spread out across the right side of his chest, over his right shoulder blade, three-quarters of the way down his right arm, and even downward over part of his rib cage. Unlike the others, his markings bore no symbols like that of Joshua, Win, or Luci. He did, however, have a similar thin leather strip wrapped double around his neck, adorned with beads that the friends had seen on Joshua and Luci during their fights.

The friends desperately wished they understood it all. They wanted to know what the markings meant on the four friends and what purpose or meaning their odd jewelry carried. They knew Van wasn't family, but his attachment to them ran deep. Deep enough that something about his markings must be connected.

Terry had finally looked up, and Ally glanced over to see her face was a soft pink as she stared at Van. Ally shifted her gaze back to him and realized why. She'd never taken much interest in Van aside from him being nice to her, but as she saw him in the arena with the light illuminating his toned body and the youthful grin on his face, Ally couldn't help thinking he was somewhat beautiful in his way.

Each of the friends began to see him differently. He was not built the way Joshua was. He didn't have the powerful presence of Win. He wasn't unnaturally gorgeous like Luci or even Lili. He had always been handsome and charming, but he became something more as the friends saw him moving across the arena. Even Dante watched with an estranged admiration of the man in the arena who was far more than a man. He was elegant. Van's charm quickly gave way to the monster within in a flash, though.

Terry clasped her hand to her mouth, and Dante jerked in surprise as Van struck his opponent with a swift left blow. The man stumbled back, but Van was too quick and caught him with another left hook. Terry let out a scared squeak as she covered her face with her hands, peeking between her fingers. Dante's eyes grew wide as he watched the masterful artistry unfold. Van danced around the man, still grinning but with a sinister look in his eyes. His opponent stumbled around, dazed by the two quick hits. Van let fly another jab with his left hand catching the man square on the jaw. The man swung wildly in defense, not even coming close to Van, who just laughed in return.

The three girls realized all at once they weren't watching a fight but rather an animal playing with a toy. Like a cat with a ball of string, Van pawed at the man doing no real damage as the ball of yarn swung wildly, trying to defend itself. Win jeered while Joshua and Luci watched with pleased smiles. The crowd ate it up. Everyone knew how it was going to end as Van battered his toy with one left jab after another, but they were all still enthralled to watch it transpire. Van's smile grew crueler and crueler as he fought until a malicious grin decorated his face.

Finally, the friends had heard the chants from the first time they saw Joshua fight. Win was leaning over the ledge screaming for Van to end it. Joshua and Luci had leaned on the railing as well but only watched intently. Van glanced over at them, and his crooked grin broke into a full smile. With a mighty left hook, his opponent went completely limp and crashed to the ground. Terry almost knocked Ally over as she started jumping up and down, screaming for Van in chorus with the crowd as Van stood over his unconscious foe.

The friends couldn't believe their eyes. Where a few minutes before had stood, an innocent, scared little girl, another crazed fan in the pack, had taken her place. Out in the arena, where earlier a handsome, sweet young man had been, stood a wild animal with his fangs bared at the body of his prey. The friends stood in disbelief, looking back and forth between Terry and Van. They realized in that moment how much like her they truly were. For months they had thought themselves more righteous, more wholesome than all the people at the fights, yet each time they had entered the door. They had ignored the warnings, witnessed the spectacle, and still had gone back again. They may not have yelled and screamed as the others did, they may have placed no bets, but as much as the friends tried to hide it, they enjoyed watching their friends win the fights.

The only one who seemed genuinely removed from the events was Dante. He had watched. He had even clapped for Van's victory. He had not engaged, though. Dante had not let himself become a part of the moment. He had observed, studied, absorbed the events happening before him. Van's fight, the arena, the entire situation was something he was trying to comprehend, data he needed to collect to understand the family with whom his sister was involved.

Van made his way back to where his friends waited. In a few swift motions, his suit was back on, and his gentle demeanor had returned. To look at the sweet man standing amongst his family, no one would have ever believed the animal that lay within. Joshua wrapped his arm around Van's shoulder and gave him a firm shake; Luci gave him a simple kiss on the cheek, and then Win locked him in a gripping hug as he patted him forcibly on the back. Violent or not, all the friends could do was admire their love for each other.

Win released Van from his powerful clutch as the announcer called his name. He dropped his coat and pulled off his v-neck before jumping over the railing. He landed gracefully in a way none of the others had. He was a different sort of nimble, like a gymnast preparing his next routine. He wasted no time starting the fight the instant the bell sounded, landing a swift jab on his opponent's jaw. He lacked the power of Joshua, the playfulness of Luci, and the ferocity of Van, but he was equally as dangerous. His moves were smooth and graceful. Win was a dancer, not a fighter. Each step of his dance, though, was a lethal strike as he glided across the floor. It was evident to the friends he wasn't putting his full strength into his blows, but he wasn't toying with his foe as the others had either. Instead, Win was putting on a show for the crowd, the routine he had prepared.

A quick dip to dodge a right hook from his opponent led into a simple twirl as he spun around to plant a jab into the man's ribs. Win floated back as the man stumbled around to face him. His opponent charged headlong at Win, who delicately swirled off the man's shoulder in a blur of speed, and whipped around into a knee tuck directly into the man's abdomen. Win gracefully slid away again, leaving the man in full charge to the ground.

His opponent clambered to his feet as fast he could, struggling to regain balance. Gripping his rib cage, the man stumbled around the floor, keeping his eyes fixed on Win's dance. Win swooped in again, gliding across the floor and landing a swift two-step set of jabs into the man's jaw. The opponent swayed, fighting not to lose consciousness. Win became a blur, circling him. With the last of his will, the man swung wildly at Win, bringing about the crescendo of Win's performance. Win brushed off the haymaker with a left strafe, raising another high-step knee into the man's rib cage, lifting him into the air. As the man rose upward, Win leapt high above and brought his elbow down forcefully into the man's skull, his grand finale.

The man hit the ground unconscious. Win raised his hands to the cheers of the crowd and began a series of deep bows. The room erupted with excitement at his performance while his friends clapped softly in playful approval as smiles spread across their faces. No matter their different methods, the family was all lethal.

"Alright, guys, let's get out of here." Ally said to the group. "We don't wanna risk getting caught."

"But we're gonna miss the other fights?" Terry asked, unable to hide the thrill in her eyes.

Dante's eyes cautiously studied the family of fighters, making sure they were still unaware.

"Well," Rachel replied with conviction, "Joshua and Luci win their fights if they even fight tonight. Look, we don't know the schedule or whatever. Okay? We're just figuring this out ourselves, but I can assure y'all, whatever else happens, they'll all still be fighting next week. Trust me; they got this. Ally's got a point, though. We're playing with fire here. So let's skedaddle before we get burned."

"So we're coming back next week?" Dante asked. His tone was straightforward, a matter of fact. Terry, however, was actively listening in anticipation.

"Well," Erin began, voicing something the friends had only thought, "I don't think we plan on missing any of the tournament. It's not something we've, like, openly discussed, but I'm pretty sure that's just kinda where we are. Amiright girls?"

Ally and Rachel nodded without even thinking. They had committed. They knew that even if it wasn't said. Dante acknowledged them with a nod, Terry with a grin, and steadily the group climbed down from the bleachers and made for the door. The screams of the crowd followed them and drowned out the goodbye from the loveable doorman. The cold air greeted the group again as they exited the building. Erin took a deep breath, embracing her friend, letting the air fill her lungs. The others didn't share her sentiment, bundling up as they met the chill. The three girls, though, were beginning to enjoy the fights they once loathed, and somehow that knowledge let an ensuring peace wrap around them.

The friends said their goodbyes to Terry and Dante, both of whom seemed far more at ease with the night's events than the girls would have imagined. They each loaded up into their vehicles and drove off their separate ways into the night. Snow began to fall as the friends went home. Small flakes landed on the windshield only to melt away in an instant. They pulled up to the house and parked the car, but they didn't bother to go in. Instead, they sat and watched the snowfall out the window. Things had changed, and they were beginning to grow comfortable with that.

31

THE FIRST & SECOND RULES

By the next week, the snow had settled, and Little Rock was covered in a thick sheet of white like never before. Cold gripped the town, and the girls found even the Brew couldn't fully warm them any longer. That had not stopped their routine trips, though. They would spend their time outside of class drinking coffee while they visited with Terry. Joshua and Win began showing up more and more, but there was always too much commotion for any meaningful conversation. Either Marc or Lili would be in the shop talking with everyone, or Van and Luci would suddenly appear.

Everyone in the Brownings' circle, though, acted as if nothing out of the ordinary was occurring, which was even stranger. The family was nothing if not good at keeping secrets. Joshua, Win, and Van even joined the girls at dinner one night with Terry and Dante, and still, nothing was mentioned regarding Idonia or the violent, nightly adventures. The friends had grown too cautious and concerned to bring up any of the strange topics, and Terry and Dante certainly weren't looking to stir the pot. It was as if they were all playing a game for which no one knew the rules except the Brownings.

The week had passed even swifter than the last, and the friends found themselves ready for yet another trip to the abandoned building. What was odd for the friends, though, was that they looked forward to seeing the fights for the first time. Thad had driven up to go with them, still frustrated he had missed so many already. Terry and Dante were going again, with planned attendance that time. In a sense, their secret was finally out. The Brownings may not have known, but the fact their entire group was going meant the friends no longer had to be so stealthy. They didn't have to secretly follow Luci or slip away from their two newest friends. For once, they were going to enjoy a seemingly ordinary night out with friends watching a simple fight, except it was anything but a simple fight. Because it was the enigmatic family who believed in Idonia that might very well have a serial killer after them. Try as they might, the friends couldn't keep from thinking about it.

Ally walked downstairs, wondering if her roommates were ready, only to find them waiting by the door along with Thad. Erin and Rachel were both excited, but their eyes also reflected their concerns. Thad looked enthusiastic but still very apprehensive. None of the friends said anything as they made their way out the door. The car ride to dinner was silent as well, and even Terry and Dante were quieter than usual as the group sat eating their dinner. Everyone was focused on what was to come.

The group did their typical wait after arriving at the parking garage before they hurried across the lot and down the old staircase. The abandoned building was already roaring with excitement as they reached the door. Ally slid the fake lock off and opened the door to see the friends' giant of a buddy handling his post at the door.

"Geez, there's more every time y'all come here." He chuckled. "You keep it up, and we're gonna have to find a bigger building."

"Good thing this is pretty much all the people we know then," Erin said, giving the man a big smile. "Has it started yet?"

"No, ma'am, you're just in time. Mr. Joshua and Mr. Win are about to start in just a few."

The friends froze at his words. They hadn't been keeping track of the tournament. It dawned on them that they had somehow missed a round. They'd never even stopped to look at the bracket after the very first night and had shown up thinking they still had another round before any of the Brownings' group would face one another. Instead, they stood before the guard, trying to prepare for the scene inside. It would no longer be someone they knew against a nameless foe, and suddenly it no longer felt like a simple game for the friends.

"Go on in." The guard said, smiling as he opened the door for them.

The four walked robotically into the packed room as the announcer called out the first two fighters and told everyone they had only minutes left to place their final bets. The group clambered up the bleachers as they all took a seat on the top row, looking down on the pit. Win and Joshua were both getting ready as they handed their clothes to their friends and fellow semi-finalists, Luci and Van. Though Win was a few inches taller than Joshua, he didn't have quite the heft of his older brother's massive figure, but they both were the physical embodiment of the pinnacle of strength and agility. The three girls knew from seeing them both fight it would be a battle of speed and finesse versus raw power and precision. Win had the upper hand in his reach and how easily he evaded opponents, but if Joshua could get a hit or two in, it would be over. Ally, Erin, and Rachel, however, were the only ones who had seen both men fight. Dante and Terry had only seen Win, and Thad was entirely new to the entire event. Each of the six individuals that stood atop the bleachers had come to the event with different perspectives, but they were all there for the same reason.

Joshua and Win walked out to the center of the pit, their necklaces dangling on their necks and their hair slicked or pulled back, respectively. Anticipation had overcome the crowd as they prepared to watch the two brothers duke it out. Everyone else in that room had seen them fight multiple times. They knew what Joshua was capable of, and they had seen Win's dangerous dance. All the bets had been placed, and the moment of truth was at hand.

"Ding!" Rang the bell loudly, and the battle began.

Win took to his feet and began circling his brother planning his strike. Joshua bobbed slightly as he studied Win's movements. Both had fists pulled to their chins, waiting for the first chance to strike. Win made the first move as he took the lead in the dance. Joshua ducked under Win's right jab but was caught by his swift left counter as Win's fist landed hard against Joshua's ribs. Joshua stepped back, smiling at his brother despite the pain.

Win made to strike again, not wanting to lose his advantage. Joshua strafed left to avoid his brother's right hook, and though he managed to turn quickly enough to prevent the punch aimed for his jaw, Win's strike still caught Joshua on the shoulder, causing him to turn in his step. Win wasted no time pouncing on Joshua's mistake and began a series of jabs to his abdomen.

Joshua was not about to go out quickly, though. He swiftly darted out of Win's range before swooping back with a one-two punch to his face. Win didn't break his dance, but it was clear the hits had taken their toll as redness began to spread on the right side of his face, and he shook his head to maintain focus. Joshua was on him in a flash, pelting his ribs with jabs. Still, before Joshua could land too many, Win quickly bounded to the left and brought a heavy elbow crashing into his brother's spine as he spun away from Joshua to begin his dance again.

Joshua spun around to face his brother, but Win was waiting with a powerful jab to his jaw, followed by a left hook, then another right jab. Joshua absorbed the blows, planted his feet firmly, reared back his fist, and threw a mighty punch into Win's chest. Win stumbled back briefly as Joshua shook his head and spat a mouthful of blood onto the floor.

Joshua balled his fists up and brought them up to guard his face, still shaking his head. Win saw his brother's lack of focus and lunged around to catch him off guard. Joshua shook his head again, regaining his composure as he followed Win's dance. As Joshua turned to track his brother, though, his gaze found the group of friends atop the bleachers. Their eyes locked on Joshua in a terrifying moment, right as Win's fist came crashing into his skull.

Joshua collapsed to the ground as the friends all gasped. Ally and Terry clasped their hands over their mouths. Thad and Dante mirrored one another in stunned stances with their hands on their heads. Erin had closed her eyes, not wanting to see the sight in front of her. Rachel had frozen in a state of horror. Win stared down at Joshua in brief confusion about why he'd dropped his guard before glancing over at Luci and Van in concern. Win didn't even bother to wait for the announcer to announce the winner, though, before he knelt to the ground and lifted his brother's limp body. He slung Joshua's arm over his shoulder and led him to the barricade.

"We should go now," Terry said, snapping the others from their trance.

No one bothered to argue as they rose to follow Terry out the door. The girls and Thad looked back in to see Joshua slowly regaining his consciousness as he and Win reached the barricade. Luci and Van both leaned in to hear something Joshua was saying. Then all four of them turned to the door to see the girls and Thad leaving the building. Terry and Dante were already outside en route to their car.

The friends tried to relax as they said good night to Terry and

Dante before they headed home. Erin made jokes the entire drive in hopes of easing everyone back into their normal moods. They had played with fire. Not only had they gone back to the fights each week, but they kept bringing more and more of their friends. It had only been a matter of time before someone noticed. They couldn't have possibly expected to keep it a secret forever, and at the end of the day, the Brownings were doing that for sport in the first place. There was nothing else to be done about it.

By the time they were inside the house on Rock Street, the four friends had accepted the situation. They would talk with Joshua and Win the next time they saw the duo, and that would be it. There was nothing more to be done. So they rested in the house for a time, talking about everything that had occurred, unready to go to bed right away. Ally thought of seeing Thad come downstairs in the middle of the night. She wanted to say something, but she didn't. Thad was still trying to process what he had seen along with everything they had learned. It hardly felt like the appropriate time. Erin and Rachel filled Thad in on the events of the previous fights as well, and the group all talked about their increasing time with Dante and Terry.

Part of them wished they would have invited the two over after the fights, but after seeing Joshua knocked unconscious because of them, it had just seemed best to call it an evening. It helped that Dante was in town. His being there as well at least meant she wasn't alone, and with Van in town as well, they hoped it would be enough barriers to keep the Ghost at bay. So the four friends let the time pass into the late hours of the night, resolved that there wasn't anything else for them to do until eventually, they were all desperate for sleep. The girls had been about to walk up the stairs when a knock at the door made them all jump.

Fear crept through the house, gripping each one of the friends. They huddled together instinctively, but no one moved towards the door. A silhouette was visible through the glass, but it gave no inclinations as to who was outside. The friends would have to figure that out on their own.

"Why the hell is someone knocking this late?" Ally asked rhetorically as the group grew more frightened.

"Fuck if I know," Erin said, steeling her nerves, "but I'm not about to sit here and wait for it just to come in."

The group moved slowly to the door, Erin leading the way. They froze for a brief moment upon reaching it, the last hesitation running through the group. Finally, Ally opened the front door to see Joshua Browning standing there with his eye slightly swollen and cut on his cheek where Win had struck him. His hair was still pulled back, and the collar of his pea coat was raised, casting shadows across his face. The snow had begun to fall again and flaked his dark ensemble making it shine in the streetlight. Snow had fallen in the soft waves of his hair that he didn't bother to cover with a hood or beanie. He looked at home in the cold, like it belonged to him.

"May we enter?" His words were smooth and soft, and it wasn't until that moment that the friends realized Win waited outside behind him.

"Uh, sure." Ally replied. "Just let us move…"

Ally's words were cut off as Erin pulled her into the house, making room for Joshua and Win. Rachel and Thad had already slid further back inside so the brothers could enter.

The two men, however, did not move swiftly into the house. The cold didn't bother them enough to rush indoors. They removed their coats as they slowly entered the house on Rock Street, taking care to knock them off outside before going in to hang them up.

Joshua waited until they were all inside and seated around the island before he began, "If you wished to watch us fight, you could have just said so. There was no need to sneak around all of Little Rock just to come."

"We," Ally paused, completely thrown off by his calm

"Well," Erin began, stepping in for Ally, "we honestly didn't realize you were so chill about it. I mean, you did kinda disappear off to a random abandoned building. I guess we just thought, I don't know, that you might not want us knowing."

"We're not ashamed or secretive about it. It is not like we do it for a living. Just every once in a while, when we feel like it. The abandoned building is merely easy to use."

"So, are you, like, ok?" Thad asked, more concerned than he had realized he was.

"Oh, he is fine." Win laughed softly. "Trust me, he and I have put each other through far worse."

"And what about Luci and Van?" Rachel said, suddenly realizing that they had not stayed to see the two fight.

Win laughed again, "Now that is even funnier. Luci is excellent.

She is way too quick for Van. He has a few cuts and bruises, but he will be okay in no time. He went to Terry's to visit with her. A good night's sleep, and it will be like it never happened."

"Hey, wait," Ally began as Joshua's first statement finally clicked, "how'd you know we were sneaking into the fights before?"

"Well," Joshua began with an amused grin, "if you make friends with a guard, you should probably make sure it is not one we know. After I saw you there tonight, all it took was one question."

"Oh." Ally said, feeling silly she hadn't already guessed that.

"Makes sense," Erin said, feeling just like Ally. "So, what gave us away tonight? I mean, we've been to, like, three or four other fights; how'd you just see us this time?"

"It is hard to explain properly," Joshua said as a studious expression overtook his face. "I just sensed I was being watched, not just being watched as I fought. Obviously, there are always people watching. No, I felt someone genuinely watching me. The entire fight, it kept gnawing at me. As I turned to catch Win on his strafe, I caught sight of your group, and it all clicked. Granted, it was a hard price to pay for figuring it out."

"Yeah, I see your gash there," Thad said as he pointed to the cut on Joshua's cheek.

"Oh, that?" Joshua asked rhetorically as he touched the cut. "That is nothing. It will heal in no time. As Win said, we have had much worse battle wounds, I can assure you."

"So why all the secrecy with your little underground fighting ring?" Erin asked, growing more curious by the minute.

"Oh, we do not orchestrate it." Win said, slightly surprised at her thoughts. "We merely happened to learn about it this past year, so we decided to have a little fun. Once we told Van and Luci about it, well, there was no stopping it. I doubt we return after the next fight, though. All things must end."

"Are you really going to fight Luci?" Rachel asked with genuine sadness in her voice.

"I do not have much choice." There was a resoluteness to his voice that was foreign to the friends. He truly was decided, through and through. "She and I are opponents. We have sparred before, so it is familiar. I cannot just let her win, but it is pretty much a foregone conclusion. I was fortunate to catch Joshua distracted as I did. Barring similar luck with Luci, I do not stand much of a chance. She could easily handle any of us."

The friends paused at his words. There was a definiteness to them. His assessment of Luci was not one of conjecture. She was indeed capable. The girls had seen her fight, knew she was lethal, but they didn't realize just how fierce she was.

"Does that mean you are not coming next week?" Joshua asked, mildly confused. "Given that the secret is now out, we had planned on inviting the lot of you over to our house afterward for a little celebration of sorts. It matters not who wins at this point. One of our number will regardless, but if none of you are coming, then we completely understand."

The four of them all looked to one another for an answer."

"You mean," Erin began, being the voice for the group, "you actually want us to come? To the fight?"

"As I said," Joshua replied with more confusion on his face at their lack of understanding, "we are not secretive about it. Our family knows and will be there next week. They would have come to others, but they have previous obligations naturally. It is not an important matter, but if you do not like the whole situation, I would see why you did not wish to attend."

"We'll be there," Thad said with a smile.

"Well, it would seem all is settled," Joshua said, smiling charmingly. "Now then, I am sure you have each had more than enough excitement for one evening. We really should take our leave."

"You're welcome to stay. You don't have to rush." Ally said, not even considering how late it already was.

"With all due respect," Win replied with a comical smile, "it would be most inappropriate for us to keep you up any longer on this already late evening. Plus, we do head out of town tomorrow. Plans must be made."

The friends all nodded their agreement, Ally realizing just how much she had spaced out. It was well after midnight when the two men arrived on their doorstep, and they could all use some rest. They each bid their farewells and expressed relief that everything was alright and out in the open finally. Only, everything was not alright, nor was it all out in the open. Merely one tiny thing was. Everything else still loomed overhead.

After Joshua and Win left, the friends finally resumed their treks to bed. Dragging themselves to their rooms, they each kept thinking of how good their beds would feel after such a long night. When they finally made it to their respective resting places, their eyes were closed before anyone's head hit the pillow. No dreams visited them. No one snuck upstairs. There was simply sleep.

The rest of the weekend passed in peace. Thad stayed the entire time, not to anyone's surprise. They had Dante and Terry over again for movies and pizza, and no one spoke of the two Browning brothers. It was a calm weekend that they had each desperately needed. Dante and Thad both had to depart on Sunday, but they assured the friends they would return before the next fight. Ally, Erin, and Rachel felt yet another unfortunate sadness as the two boys department. Dante was new to their group, but they were quickly growing accustomed to him. Thad was Thad, of course, and the friends had begun to accept how much a part of their family he was.

The week continued just as the previous one had. Class, Terry, and The Daily Brew were their routine. The friends were happy to see Joshua and Win again during the week, both seeming to be in lifted spirits. They talked openly about the upcoming fight; even Lili joined in on the discussion when the group was at The Brew. It was as if one of the many layers of the Browning mystery had finally been removed. They were closer to the peculiar family than they had ever been. Close enough that it felt like the friends truly knew them. Except, they didn't.

"We need to get to class," Erin yelled up the stairs when the day had finally arrived.

"Yeah, yeah, I'm coming." Ally said as she rushed to finish getting ready. She was never late. She hated being late. Yet, for some reason, that morning, everything had gone awry. Ally had significantly overslept her alarm, hadn't realized it when she finally woke, and then had lost track of time as she was putting on her makeup. Something snapped in her suddenly, "Fuck it, I'm not going."

"What?" Rachel shouted up the stairs in exasperation.

"Look," Ally said in frustration, stepping out onto the staircase, "I don't know what the deal is this morning, but it ain't happening. I'd rather just not go than be late. Y'all go ahead. I'll handle my shit and meet up with you in a bit."

"Okay," Erin said plainly as she set her bag down. "Then we don't go. No big deal."

"What?" Rachel said even louder with shock and disbelief in her voice. "That's it?"

"Yeah," Erin replied, shrugging her shoulders. "Fuck it. Why not? Let's go to The Brew."

"What are you…" Rachel sputtered in frustration. "We're not just… I mean… Ah, fuck it. Whatever."

Rachel threw her bag down in defeat and sat down at the island. The friends were each all out of sorts that morning. The day was finally upon them, and they could not mentally prepare themselves. It had been one thing to be visited by Joshua and Win late at night to open up about things. It had been another thing to talk casually with them about it throughout the week, but to be partaking in an event with the Brownings that they had long since been hiding was entirely different.

Terry gave a huge smile and an elaborate wave the moment the girls walked through the door of The Brew. Despite themselves, they couldn't help smiling and waving back. The group took their usual seat in the corner, and Terry was there in no time with their drink.

"Hey, you!" Terry said to the group, still smiling her sweet smile. "How the heck are ya?"

"We're fine, Terry." Ally gave a soft smile back. "I see you're in a good mood."

"Well, of course. How could you not be in a good mood today of all days? Plus, it's freakin' snowing for cryin' out loud. It couldn't get any better. We're going to the fights tonight, and I get to spend the day watching the flakes fall. Ah, I just love the snow. I can't believe we've had so much. It's never snowed like this here. Not since I've been here anyways. This year just keeps getting better. Do y'all like the snow?"

"Uh, yeah," Erin began, surprised at Terry's exuberant joy, "I mean, I love snow. We all do. I guess I just haven't ever seen it like this to fully take it in."

"Yeah," Terry continued with a strange calm, "it sure is something."

The friends followed Terry's gaze as she stared out the window, watching the flakes fall and cover the ground. Terry was right. It was a beautiful sight, a sight, unlike anything the friends had ever seen. No snow had ever lasted that long in Arkansas. It was a special treat for them. Terry sipped on a drink of her own, still watching out the window, while the friends slowly drank from their mugs. It was peaceful being around Terry. Something about her just made the friends feel safe and at home.

"You know something, Terry," Ally turned from the window and looked up at her, "I'm really glad we met you."

Terry turned a bright shade of red. "Oh, dear. I don't know why you'd be glad to meet me. I'm nothin' special. Just a silly girl who likes snow."

"Nah, she's right, Terry," Rachel added. "You've been hanging out with us for a few months now, and ya know, I'm really glad you have. We all are. You're alright in our book."

"Well, thank you, ladies, very much. Y'all are pretty awesome too." Terry smiled, still blushing. "I'd better get back to work. Super excited for tonight! If you need a refill, just let me know."

They spent the rest of the day at The Brew visiting with Terry, all of them working to prepare themselves for the night's events. Dante arrived in town in the early afternoon, and Thad was there a couple of hours after him. The group was finally back together. Once Terry finished her shift, they made their way to the restaurant, laughing and talking about their weeks over dinner. It wasn't long before they were walking into the movie late and having to quiet down. It had been Ally's night to pick the flick, so the group saw a new slasher film that had been released the previous week. Ally and Dante loved it. Erin and Terry spent the whole movie making disgusted faces. Thad and Rachel merely laughed at the terrible acting. After the show, the group all piled into Thad's vehicle and headed off for the fights.

"Any of you wonder why we're still doing the dinner and a movie thing before we go to the fights?" Erin asked as they turned onto the street of the abandoned building.

"What do you mean?" Terry asked.

"Well, correct if I'm wrong, but wasn't the whole dinner and a movie thing the original cover so we could sneak off afterwards?"

"Yeah," Rachel added, "that was why we started doing that."

"Exactly," Erin continued, "and now that the whole sneaking around part is over with, we still keep up the same routine."

Ally thought for a second. "You know, I'm not sure. I guess it's just become tradition."

"Well, what are we going to do next week when there's no more fights then?" Terry asked with a worried voice.

"I guess we'll just do dinner and a movie like boring, normal people." Ally laughed.

Thad parked his vehicle on the street by the garage, not worrying about sneaking in as the group had always done before.

"That's weird." Ally said as she scanned the old parking garage. "I don't see any of their cars. Hell, there's hardly any cars in there."

"Huh. Guess they parked somewhere else this time. Not sure why there's so few cars, though." Rachel responded.

"Yeah," Erin added, "wonder if the turnout isn't going to be very big since it's just the one fight."

Ally nodded her head, but an ominous feel began to creep into her mind. Something felt wrong. The feeling only intensified when they reached the top of the staircase and saw a man leaned against the wall outside the door taking a slow drag from his cigarette as he stared at the ground.

"Had to grab some air before the fight?" Erin asked sarcastically as they walked down the steps.

"Ere's no fight t'night." The man replied in a scruffy voice, not bothering to look up.

"Then why are you here?" Erin asked again.

"Ta tell folks ere's no fight."

"Why isn't the normal guy here telling people that then?" Ally asked with confusion.

The man looked up for the first time showing tired, weathered eyes. He spoke with a strange hollow tone in his voice, "Ya mean JJ? You folks must not read da news."

"What news?" Rachel said, incredulously. "I read the news all the time."

Erin, though, had already yanked her phone from her coat. Panic was spreading through the friends. Something was wrong. Horribly, horribly wrong. It didn't take Erin but a few seconds to find the report.

"JJ," Erin replied as the terror hit her, "as in, Jeremiah Joseph?"

The man took a long drag from his smoke as if he was trying to hold onto some life left in it. "Yes'm. Dat's JJ for ya."

"Erin, what's wrong?" Ally said, looking to her friend.

"Are you ok?" Terry asked.

"What's in the news about Jeremiah Joseph?" Rachel added.

Thad and Dante moved closer to Erin, afraid she might faint. It was all too overwhelming. Erin couldn't begin to find the words.

"Da Ghost got 'im." The man said to no one in particular as if he was speaking to the night itself. His eyes grew misty as he stared up at the sky.

"Oh, dear God..." Terry whispered.

The weight of it hit the friends like a ton of bricks. Rachel sunk against the wall. Dante moved to steady Ally as she nearly fell. Erin continued to stand in frozen disbelief. Thad put a hand on both Rachel's and Erin's shoulders, letting them know he was there. They each thought about their friend, the guard. They'd never even learned his name, but uniquely, they still saw him as a friend of theirs. He was there for them the first time they witnessed the other side of the Browning family and every time after that. Tears filled the girls' eyes, and lumps swelled in their throats. He was gone forever.

"Let's just you get girls home," Thad said gently as he guided the friends up the stairs.

The ride back to the house on Rock Street was silent as a tomb. Even when the group dropped Dante and Terry off, no words were said. Terry hugged each of them, and to their surprise, Dante did as well, giving them each a soft pat on the back to bid them farewell. The friends sat for a time in front of their house, not wanting to go inside. Going in meant accepting it, making it final. They didn't want that. The four friends felt all at once naive. For the past week, they had been so relieved, thrilled even, that their secret fight night adventures were out in the open. They had thought everything was beginning to come together, when in fact, it was about to fall apart. They had played with fire indeed, and playing with fire meant getting burned.

They finally managed to pull themselves from the vehicle and began trudging through the powdery snow. The wind outside battered with an unforgiving ferocity, reminding them of the horrors that were unfolding. The eyes watched the friends from deep within the snowy night as they made their way to the door. Slowly, laboriously they made their way across the sidewalk and up the steps to the house on Rock Street. Landing on the porch, the friends were met with a new horror waiting for them; a small white envelope resting on the windowsill of their front door. There was no inscription on it as the package with the book had. Like the book, though, there was no address or stamp, nothing to mark it as a piece of mail. It was hand-delivered.

The friends grabbed the envelope and moved swiftly into the house, looking to escape the cold and the growing fear that was welling up within them. They made their way inside and gathered around the kitchen island, placing the envelope down on the countertop. They studied it for a brief moment. It was no simple number ten envelope. It was a special one, chosen specifically for them. They opened the envelope slowly and tipped it over, sending a thin piece of paper folded in two sliding out onto the countertop. They unfolded it to see the message scrawled neatly inside.

"*Ever Vigil is the Watcher.*"

32
THE HOUR OF THE RAVEN & THE LION

As the friends laid their heads on their pillows that night, the room began to slip away as they drifted off. The walls peel back, and a gentle breeze blew through, wiping away what remained. They opened their eyes to find themselves in a deep, black forest. This was not the beautiful orchard they had seen in their dreams before. This was a place of terror, and they were there together. It was not like any of the visions they'd had before. They could each make sense of one another, feel the actual presence of each other in that horrible place.

It was so dark they could not see more than inches in front of them. They stumbled to their feet, working to orient themselves with the darkness, and began slowly walking with hands outstretched, feeling for objects in the pitch black around them. One of the friends' hands landed on a tree trunk, and they worked their way around, reaching for the next tree with the other hand. Their foot struck something hard and sent them tumbling to the ground.

Erin reached down to find what had tripped her, and just as her hand landed on the cold metal object, a flock of crows flew through the canopy of the forest. The other three friends ducked their heads down, hoping the birds wouldn't see them. Erin quickly snatched the metal object, pulling it tightly against her chest, and hugged close to the tree as the birds flew away.

It was a flashlight. Erin had a flashlight. She clicked it on and a bright beam of light shot up into the trees. She made her way to her feet again and let the beam spill out onto the forest floor, illuminating a slight stretch of the forest ahead for the friends. Ally, Rachel, and Thad quickly moved to her side, huddling together, shielding themselves against the dread that filled that dark place. With light in hand, Erin began leading the group through the thick trees. They could hear the sounds of the night woods as crickets chirped and owls hooted in the distance. A cold breeze ran over the group, sending chills down their spine and setting their hair on end. The group could feel the danger close by, closing in on them. Erin had no idea where she was going. All she knew was they had to get there before whatever was lurking in the woods got to them.

They shuffled along for what seemed like years, slowly weaving in and out of trees with no sense of direction. After ages had passed, they finally noticed some sort of path in the forest floor and began following it through the woods. Every strange noise that came from the darkness made them tense up, fearing it would be the end. The friends heard a twig crack in the distance, and Erin turned her light in its direction.

Nothing was there, but they couldn't shake the feeling they were being watched, being stalked, like prey. A hoot came from their left side, and Erin spun around to find the owl. Again, though, nothing was there but the trees. The other friends began to scan the darkness around them, searching for whatever could be out there, until they distinctly saw a pair of red eyes glowing in the forest. They grabbed Erin, turning her towards the eyes, but when her light shined in that direction, it was gone.

Erin relaxed slightly and let the light slump to her side. In all their spinning, the friends had lost their footing on the trail. Erin knelt with the flashlight, and the friends all began looking for the slightly beaten path again. It only took Rachel a few minutes to catch the trail, and when she did, they wasted no time moving forward. After just a few steps back on the track, though, they heard a chorus of twigs snapping on all sides of them. Erin spun slowly as the friends huddled tightly against each other, letting the light flow through the trees. There was nothing to their right, nothing behind them. They were almost wholly turned back around when an odd shape caught in Ally's peripheral. She grabbed Erin in fear, pulling her close. Erin turned back to the left where Ally was looking as the light illuminated the figure in the distance. There was a man in the woods.

Immediately the friends turned to flee, trying their best to stick to the path they had been on, but caring not for the light that guided them. They were in a frenzy. The friends ran in a dead sprint, not pausing to look back, not slowing down, just ran. They could hear the crows flying in the distance, feel their heart beating in their ears. Minutes seemed to turn to hours and hours into days, and still, they sprinted through the forest. They could feel the sting setting into the muscles in their legs, the veins throbbing in their head as their body called out for oxygen. It felt like years had passed in that brief moment, but finally, they had to stop. Their bodies could weather no more. Quickly, they ducked behind a tree to catch their breath, massaging their legs in an effort to remove the stiffness.

Rachel, most of all, was perplexed. She had trained for this, practiced for it. The whole reason she spent hours at the gym and running every week was to be ready if something like this happened. Yet, she was just as exhausted as the others. In that dark place, her work had meant nothing. *Surely, they had lost him in the woods*, she told herself. They couldn't take the chance, though. Rachel was the first to stand, but the others followed her cue as they forced themselves back onto their legs and began walking forward again, still trying to catch their breath. Suddenly, in the distance, they could see a faint light through the trees ahead of them. It must be the edge of the forest, they thought, but as Erin looked down at the flashlight, she noticed it had grown dimmer. They had to hurry. Time was running out.

Erin pressed forward again, pushing the group towards the light. She tried jogging for a spell, but she was still too out of breath. Thad came up beside her and helped her along as Ally and Rachel marched behind them, pressing them forward, forcing them to move as fast as they could. They each wanted to look over their shoulder to see if the man still followed, but something told them not to. Doing so would mean losing their hope forever. A few steps further, though, and they heard the crows again. It was quickly followed by a rustling of leaves and cracking of twigs all around them; to their left, right, behind, and even in front of them. They froze. Erin made a quick spin of the woods, and the light caught the man far down the path behind them as she passed over him in her spin. She whipped the flashlight back to make sure what they had seen. He was still just standing in the path, but somehow considerably closer than he was just seconds before, with red eyes glowing from under the shadow of his hat. Only it wasn't a hat; it was a hood. Then it was hat again. The eyes shifted as well. Their dreams of Raven Man and the Wanderer were crashing together all at once.

The friends turned again to run, terrified at what they had seen, making their way towards the edge of the forest as fast as they possibly could. They could hear the crows flying behind them, and their heartbeats grew louder and louder. One by one, their legs began to give out, slowing them each to a brisk jog, as fast as their legs could move. In unison, they pressed on, drawing nearer and nearer to the edge of the forest. They'd been driving through those woods for decades, they knew, and suddenly they could see Erin's flashlight beginning to flicker.

The light at the edge of the forest appeared no closer than it was when they had first started running. Genuine fear swept over them; a terrifying thought crept into their minds as they wondered if dying in a dream would mean dying in real life. Even more frightening than that thought, though, was their greater fear that what they were experiencing may not be a dream. Erin knew it was futile, but still, she turned to see if Raven Man was still following them.

The light flickered as she turned and lit up his figure dimly to show that Raven Man was standing in the distance but much closer than he had before. He stood perfectly still, not moving towards them, with his hand on his cane and his eyes glowing in the shadows. The light flickered, briefly removing all sight of Raven Man, then it clicked back on again, and he stood perfectly still, only he was the Wanderer, hooded with his glowing eyes staring at them from the darkness, and he was somehow even closer to the friends.

Erin dropped the flashlight, not even caring to see what was in the dark. With every ounce of will left in them, the friends sprinted towards the edge of the forest, but the harder they ran, the further away it seemed to be. The crows were right behind them, and their hearts beat so loudly it echoed through the forest like drums. They dared not turn around or slow down, for they knew that either Raven Man or the Wanderer was right behind them.

All at once, they each stumbled and were sent flying forward, carried over by their momentum. Pain shot through every part of their bodies, but they didn't stop to even think about it. The friends all leapt to their feet as fast as possible and made to run again. Only they couldn't move. Each of them tried to force their legs forward, but their bodies were entirely out of their control.

The crows stopped flying. The woods went silent. The only sound that could be heard was the loud thumping of their hearts echoing through the forest. Their bodies slowly began to turn by no control of their own. As the friends spun around, they saw the creature just feet away from them cloaked in shadows, shifting back and forth between the two horrors that had haunted them, red eyes aglow in the darkness. His words were painful and distorted and ripped at their minds as they resounded through the forest.

"Nigh is the hour of The Raven and The Lion.
The Frost sets in, the Storms coalesce.
Slow, steady doth beat the Drums of War.
The Mountain rages as the Great Tree beckons.
With fire and fury beat the Wings of the Wind.
The River rises and carries forth unto Oblivion.
Stars will fall. The Heavens will burn.
Gods will crumble as the Void reaches out.
Seek not the end. The Rising is at hand."

The friends writhed in their sleep. The words poured through their veins like molten magma. Unable to sleep, unable to wake, they were lost in the space between worlds as their minds sought to understand the words that had been said. Their eyes opened and closed and opened again. They faded into a haze as their eyes grew heavier. Repeatedly, each of them looked around their rooms, unsure if they were awake or asleep. Their minds were unhinging, slipping between realities. They would let their eyes close, begging for rest, but a loud cawing sound made them open again. They blinked several times, trying to clear the blurriness. They each heard the sound again. In each of their rooms, the girls in their beds, Thad on the couch, they all turned to see a raven staring at them from across the room.

A strange series of events was replicating through each of their minds; they shared the same moment. Separated though they were, the friends were all living in a single existence together. They each rubbed their eyes, not believing what they saw, but when they opened their eyes again the bird was still perched in its stance. They each heard the flutter of wings as all light was sucked out of the rooms. Suddenly, the wings' flapping began to slow, and the light gradually returned to each friends' room. All the light except for a deep black shadow in the corner of each room. All at once, the shadow took form, and it was clear a person was standing in the rooms with them.

The girls each leapt from their bed and raced to the doors, knowing it could be only one man. Thad jumped up from the couch, darting around in panic, unsure of how he would escape. Ally, Erin, and Rachel flung their doors open and lunged from the room so fast that they each slammed headlong into the wall and fell to the floor. Not bothering to check their bodies and not caring about the various stings that cried from within, they pulled themselves up as best they could and bounded down the stairs. As they reached the last step, the girls looked back towards the hallway to see if their tormentor pursued, but all they saw was darkness.

Thad raced into the kitchen. He had been frantically running shuffling through the living room, trying to evade the horrifying figure that clung to the shadowy corners. Upon seeing the girls descend the stairs, he quickly made his way towards them, hoping somehow that being together would bring them a safety he simply couldn't feel.

The friends embraced one another at the bottom of the stairs, huddling together for safety once more, but as they did, the group turned again, looking at the kitchen, and saw Raven Man seated in one of their chairs. He turned to face them with his head bowing and resting his hands on his umbrella cane. Slowly he wrapped the fingers of his upper hand against the lower, creating a haunting rhythm. The friends each felt an icy chill run down their spine.

All at once, though, Raven Man was gone, disappeared from his seat. In his place stood the even more obscure Wanderer. His robes billowed unnaturally as if a breeze from far away was blowing them. He made no motions and gave no gestures as he stood staring across the room at the terrified friends, but his fiery glare burned into them. Refusing to face the horrid figure, they spun to run up the stairs, but a flock of crows flew across the room, and suddenly Raven Man stood, leaning against the wall, blocking their path.

His face was not particularly evil. He was neither ugly nor particularly handsome, but he possessed a certain rugged appeal. There was a weathered charm to him like that of worn leather, but there was also a peculiarity about his face that hid something sinister. His greying mustache and goatee showed he was aged but not old. He was wise, seasoned, and the reddish-orange eyes reached into the friends' souls from under the shadow of his hat.

They looked back into the kitchen to see the Wanderer had shifted positions, but he was still there waiting for the friends. Their visions had finally come to a head. The Wanderer stood in the corner of the kitchen, his shadowy figure melding with the darkness of the room itself, making it unclear where the house ended, and he began. Unlike Raven Man, nothing could be discerned about the hooded figure. He offered no appearance at all aside from the glow of golden locks that flowed onto his chest and the fiery blaze of his eyes that peered at the friends from the endless black of his hood.

The friends wanted to run, to flee from the horrible place, but it was as if their feet had been bolted to the floor. Their eyes darted back and forth between the two ominous figures, unsure which posed the most significant threat or might strike first. Yet the visitors made no moves towards them, locked in their stares as if waiting for the friends. Locking arms together, the group found courage in one another. They focused all their might and began slowly turning towards the door in hopes of escape.

"There is no point in running." The Raven Man said. His voice was cold and empty yet held none of the malice their dreams had.

"This is when we die, isn't it?" Rachel asked both the friends and the visitors, searching deeply for bravery within herself.

"My sweet children," the Wanderer's voice began from across the kitchen in a familiar metallic tone, but yet it felt much closer and more precise than ever before, 'if we wanted you dead, you would be so."

"But you said," Ally paused, afraid of the words as she looked to Raven Man, "you said Death was coming."

"Oh, Death is coming, dear ones." Raven Man continued as he began descending the stairs. "Death comes for all."

His cane struck the landing with a resounding echo. At once, the Wanderer was no longer across the room but right next to the friends. Raven Man stepped past them, his cane clicking against the hardwood, as the Wanderer ushered them forward.

"We do not come to kill, though." The Wanderer said, his metallic tone warming with each word as the friends turned to see Raven Man leading the group forward.

"We are merely the messengers." Raven Man opened the door and gestured to the friends to exit. "Come, we mean you know harm."

The friends walked out the door of their house and saw they were no longer in Little Rock. Their door opened to a lush pasture stretching as far as they could see, vibrant green and blue blades of grass whipping in the breeze. In the distance, a cloud danced above a beautiful mountain range that dazzled with the glowing aura of a sunset horizon. Suddenly all their fears and horrors that had gripped them were gone. The only thought in their mind was how majestic it looked and how the Raven and the Wanderer could ever have wished to show them such a thing.

"This way, my dears." The Wanderer said as he led them across the pasture. "There is much for you to see."

The great sea of blue and green grass mixed with mossy stones as they walked with boulders lining their path. There was a gap in the grass ahead, and over the expanse, glorious swirls of red and orange danced against the black night sky. As they neared the edge of the gap, it became apparent they were walking towards a towering cliff that overlooked a mighty valley at the center of which was nestled a massive object emanating all the vibrant colors they had seen painted across the stunning sky. The object took up almost the entire valley and became more distinct as they reached the edge. Tall lines rose from the ground and created the outline of the structures. They were woven together like a maze with a myriad of colors shining through all parts. In an instant, the blurry lines and shapeless figures came into focus. They weren't structures. They were buildings. The friends were overlooking a colossal city, a city on fire.

The giant buildings rose well into the sky but were drowned out by the red and orange swirls of flames the friends had thought to be the horizon. They tilted their heads up to see the black sky was not of nighttime but rather thick clouds of smoke consuming the world. Looking down at the city again, they could see the plethora of colors coming from the city's denizens at war with one another.

"What is this?" Ally asked, turning to the two messengers. "Why are you showing us this?"

The two figures stood facing the friends, not even bothering to look at the city engulfed in flame and sounding like demonic tour guides as they spoke.

"It is the end," Raven Man stated flatly, "and we are showing you so that you will know what is to come."

"Where is this?" Erin felt the panic rising in her voice. "When is this happening?"

"Where and when are immaterial." The Wanderer answered with

a hollow animosity to the event the friends watched in horror. "It could be Ancient Rome or Alexandria. It could be your modern-day London or New York. It could even be some city far in the distant future that has yet to come into existence, or yet it could be an entire world, an entire system that your minds can merely imagine as a city. None of it matters. All that matters is this will come to pass. It always comes to pass."

"Do something to save them, to stop this!" Rachel shouted in horror.

"My dear child," Raven Man responded with a note of sorrow in his voice, "no one can save them, and no one can stop this. Death will come."

The friends wanted to yell, but the visitors' placid demeanor made them realize it would be to no avail. They turned and faced the city. Together the friends stood, feeling the heat of destruction, the death and decay of that once great city which they had never known. An hour passed, then a day, then time fell away entirely. All that existed was that city, that civilization being torn apart.

No one spoke. The Raven and the Wanderer had both said their piece. The friends had no other questions for them. The visitors simply watched the friends as they witnessed humanity give way to extinction. The war raged on yet somehow never began to dwindle. It was as if civilization was forever locked in its demise. Everything else in their world seemed to melt away, and there was only that moment the friends were in. After years of standing, watching the civilization unravel, the group noticed another cliff across the gap from them where two hooded figures stood cloaked in grey overlooking the city.

"Who are they?" Thad asked. "Other messengers?"

"Not at all, my dear." Raven Man answered with reverence and awe in his voice. "Those are the harbingers themselves. They are Order and Chaos."

"Which one is which?" Erin said.

"Does it truly matter?" The Wanderer answered solemnly. "Are they not the same thing? Can one exist without another? There can be no light without the dark. Together they bring balance to the world."

"So, they did this?" Rachel asked.

"Yes, and no." Raven Man answered ominously. "They are neither the cause nor the solution, but rather the Revelation."

"Why show us this?" Thad asked in confusion. "Why Us?"

"Because change is coming," the Wanderer replied in pained tones, "change in which you will each play a great part. Events have been put in motion that will shake the very foundation of your world, and the first move has finally been made."

The Raven Man turned for the first time to look upon the city. The Wanderer placed a hand on his shoulder as he did so. He gave a brief glance at the Wanderer's hand before turning back to the friends with resolve.

"It is time for you to awake now."

33
DEATH & MOURNING

Ally's eyes shot open, and she found herself back in her bed. She looked at her nightstand. No raven. It was all just a dream. She couldn't explain, though, why she could feel a throbbing in her shoulder where she had crashed into the wall. She thought back to the dream. Her friends had been there with her. Truly with her that time. She had been aware of them, as they had her. Ally rubbed her eyes, trying to shake her confusion, and she heard a soft sob breaking through her confused haze.

She rose from her bed and walked over to her door. Opening it, she heard the soft sob a little stronger. Someone downstairs was crying. Ally jogged down the stairs as fast as her tired legs could carry her, not even carrying what she looked like. The moment she reached the floor, the sight made a lump swell in her throat though she knew not why yet. Across the kitchen, Erin stood with tears running down her stone-clad face. The soft sobs, though, were coming from Rachel, who was pouring tears into Erin's shoulder as Erin held her. Thad stood rubbing both their backs calmingly. His eyes were red from recent tears, but they showed his resolve at taking care of his friends before himself.

At once, Erin's and Thad's eyes found Ally's, but they held nothing except pain. It was something too terrible for their eyes to explain. Erin forced her eyes shut hard, refusing to say the words. She gently kissed Rachel's head and hugged her tighter as the sobs grew worse. The horror was fresh. They had only just woken before Ally and learned the news. Ally's eyes followed Thad's as he looked down at the table.

On the table, Ally saw Erin's phone, still unlocked with the window pulled up. Afraid of what news it held, Ally slowly walked towards the table. Thad peeled himself away from the other friends to come to Ally's side. Ally circled around the phone until it was upright, and she could read what had caused the tears. Her hand went to her mouth without warning. Thad caught her as she fell backward and held her as she slumped into a heap in his arms on the floor. She didn't have to read the article to know. She recognized the beautiful, smiling, innocent barista in the headline instantly. Another soul claimed by the Ghost of Little Rock.

"Though I only knew Terry for a few months, it was a most wonderful few months. Regardless of what was happening in my world, she was always able to bring a smile to my face. She was one of those people who never seemed to have a bad day, but unlike most people like that who are incredibly annoying, Terry managed to spread her good day to everyone she saw. That was her gift; I guess you could say. I remember the day I first met her. It was our first day here in Little Rock, and I was not looking forward to it at all…"

Ally paused and patted her eyes with a tissue trying not to ruin her make-up.

"Erin," she yelled into the other room, "does this sound fake, or am I doing ok?"

Erin walked into the bathroom where Ally was practicing her speech, "You sound great, Alls. You mind tying this dress up for me real quick? And you're gonna do fine."

"You know how much I hate speaking in front of people, though. Dammit, why'd her family have to ask me to speak! How the hell could I say no to that." Ally took a deep breath and let out a long sigh. "You're right. I can do this. I have to, for her."

Rachel came into the bathroom, her eyes red and puffy, "Be honest guys, how bad do I look without any make-up on right now?"

"Rach, you look beautiful." Ally said, hoping to cheer her up.

"You always look beautiful," Erin added, "and no one expects you to have dry eyes at a visitation Rach."

"I know. I tried putting make-up on three different times, though. Every time I got it on, I thought about Terry, and then I started crying and smeared my make-up, and finally, I just gave up. Why'd the Ghost have to kill her of all people?" Rachel's eyes began to fill with tears again.

"Shhh. It's ok, Rach." Erin said, taking Rachel in her arms. "It'll be ok. I promise."

Ally took Rachel's hand in hers, "We'll get through this Rach, together."

Ally and Erin stared into each other's eyes. They knew their statements were going to be a lot tougher than they seemed. They had to stay strong, though, for each other.

"Alright, how close are you girls to ready?" Ally asked. "We're supposed to meet the Brownings there in like forty-five minutes."

"I just need to put my heels on. Any update on Thad?" Erin asked in reply.

"Can't make it tonight. Gotta help his grandma, but he'll be here first thing in the morning for the funeral. Rach, what do you have left to do?"

"I'm ready now if you guys are."

"Ally, are you ready?" Erin asked, showing the concern in her eyes.

Ally sighed, "As ready as I'll ever be."

The day was colder than it had been in weeks. The girls weren't sure if it was actually the cold or just them feeling so empty, but they could all feel the chills deep down in their bones. The drive to the funeral home was silent. They all knew if they spoke, it would only lead to more tears, and there was already plenty of that ahead.

The Brownings were all standing by their cars when the girls pulled up. One would think they were in the middle of deep conversation from their appearance, but no one was speaking. Every eye turned to the girls' car as they parked, though. Ally couldn't shake the feeling something was wrong, something more than just Terry's death.

That was the first they had seen of the Brownings since news of Terry's murder. They'd spoken to Joshua on the phone briefly the day of, but he only offered his condolences and let them know he would be there for them soon. They had a similar conversation with Win when he called a day later to check on them. He seemed more upset than Joshua had been, but the conversation had been equally as brief. Seeing them that day, though, the girls couldn't help feeling relieved to have their support.

"How are you doing?" Joshua's question for the friends was

simple, but they could see the sincerity in his eyes.

"Been better," Erin said honestly.

"Same," Rachel added. "A bit up and down is all."

"Yeah, I'll be better when this part is over," Ally answered softly, "but I'm ok for now."

"That is good to hear."

"Where's Van?" Erin asked, noticing he wasn't with the family.

Joshua turned and looked at his family like he was searching for the answer.

"Perhaps inside," Win said, stepping in for his brother, "which is where we should be going. Some people will want to meet you."

The girls followed the Brownings inside the small funeral home. The lump began to swell in Ally's throat as she realized she was on the verge of meeting the family she had only spoken to via email, a family who she never knew but shared so much with already.

Ally saw them waiting at the door of the viewing room, Terry's mother and father. Though they looked nothing like Terry, Ally could tell it was them by the way they waited to greet everyone. They shook hands with two young ladies ahead of the group and thanked them as they entered the room. Then they turned and saw Ally for the first time.

"You must be the Brownings and, let me make sure I get your names correct, Ally, Rachel, and Erin, right?" Terry's father said, pointing out each one of the girls in turn, who all nodded in response.

"Terry told us a great deal about you all." The mother said with a soft smile. "I'm sorry our first meeting isn't under better circumstances. My name is Elizabeth, and this is my husband, Victor. We're happy you could come."

The parents shook hands with the girls and the Brownings as they each introduced themselves and their relation to Terry. The friends glanced inside the room as the introductions were made and noticed how empty it was. The realization that they numbered more than all the rest of Terry's friends and family combined made the lump in Ally's throat swell even more. They had known Terry was shy, but the thought had not occurred to the friends until that day that they may have been Terry's closest friends.

"So tell us, Ally, how did you and Terry become friends? She talked about you probably most of all." Victor asked with a polite smile.

Ally was taken aback, "Wow, I um, I didn't realize she talked about me that much. I don't really know how it happened exactly. I mean, we'd seen Terry at The Brew tons of times, but we first hung out with her the day we met Van. All of us got together for drinks. After that, we just kinda clicked."

"That's usually how it goes with friends. They just seem to happen. We were very sorry to hear that Van wouldn't be able to make it today. Terry was quite fond of him. I daresay she may have even loved him." Terry's mom said with the smile a mom gets at the thought of her child growing up and finding someone special.

The friends, however, were more taken aback by a different part of her statement. Van wasn't at the viewing at all. They turned to Joshua, searching for answers, but the look he shot them only said, "not now." The friends turned their eyes from him swiftly, not wanting to draw attention, but their feelings from before were confirmed. Something was wrong, very wrong.

"Ah, and of course, there's someone else already here that I'm sure would like to see you. Dear, would you come over here?" Elizabeth asked, calling into the room.

The young man with sandy brown hair that fell just above his eyes, whom the friends had grown to like, rose from his seat and walked over to them. Unlike Terry's mother and father, there was evident sadness on Dante's face. His eyes were red from where he'd been crying, and he had to work very hard to keep even a weak smile on his face. He, too, had no resemblance to Victor or Elizabeth, but they could still see Terry all over him.

Elizabeth put her arm around Dante as he spoke, "Thank you guys for coming. It would've meant a lot to Terry, I know."

He gave a brief smile and nodded at them all before leaving to return to his seat. The friends were immediately struck by the distantness in Dante's demeanor. There was great confusion mixed with the sorrow the young man felt. The friends couldn't help but feel sympathy for their friend. Losing someone as close to him as Terry in such a horrible way was debilitating.

"This has been hardest on him most of all. We should probably start the visitation now. We'd love it if you joined us for dinner afterward, though." Victor said as he motioned them into the room.

The Brownings and the girls all took their seats together, filling up an entire row in the middle. Dante sat at the back as far from the casket as he could. Ally couldn't help wanting to join him, partly because she, too, didn't want to look upon the coffin, but mainly because she didn't want him to feel alone in that room. Too many emotions were fighting inside the friends' minds as they tried to keep their grip on reality. One thought, though, stood out more than any other, fear.

"Why isn't Van here?" Erin whispered to Joshua.

"We'll discuss this later." His voice was laced with concern, and the friends' fear only grew.

"Thank you all for coming on such short notice," Victor said as he took the podium. "It means a lot to Elizabeth, Dante, and myself that you would be here. I know this caught everyone off guard. It certainly did me." He paused, searching for the words he had prepared as he fought back the tears. "No parent ever expects to have to speak on their child's death, so I've asked a few of you if you would say some things about Terry instead. I thank you for doing what I could not. After those who have prepared speeches say theirs, we'll allow time for anyone who wants to say anything else. Ally, if you would start us off, please?"

Ally felt her legs go to noodles as she stood to walk. A cold sweat broke out on her forehead, and the room began to spin. She climbed the steps to the podium, and the lightheadedness hit. Grabbing the podium for support, she put her paper on it and tried to calm herself. She looked out at the room as her vision started to fade to black. She gripped the podium tightly and stared down at the closed casket. She forced a deep breath into her lungs and let it out slowly. She had to do this, for Terry.

"Though I only knew Terry for a few months, it was a wonderful few months. Regardless of what was happening in my world, she was always able to bring a smile to my face. She was one of those people who rarely had a bad day, but unlike most people like that who are incredibly annoying, Terry managed to spread her good day to everyone she saw. That was her gift; I guess you could say. I remember the day I first met her. It was our first day here in Little Rock, and I was not looking forward to it at all.

"Terry, though, somehow managed to brighten our mornings and made me actually enjoy my day somewhat. I had no idea then that we had just met someone who would become our good friend, but I'm so glad that we did. Rachel, Erin, and myself were blessed to have known Terry. Everything from her smile and her laugh to the things she would say so innocently that everyone would just laugh, she was just awesome. For us, Terry was more than just a friend; she was an escape. Rachel and Erin can tell you as well as I, that this has been a rough year for us. Moving away from home, away from our family, it was a daunting experience, and Terry was always there when we needed her.

"I know if she was here now, she'd be smiling and laughing at how silly we all are for being sad, and I'm certain she's up in Heaven doing that just now. I'm glad to have met more of her family today and to see more of her friends. It makes me happy to know I'm not the only one whose life was touched by this beautiful person. A person like Terry can never be replaced, and she will certainly always be missed. I'm proud to have known such a wonderful friend."

The cold outside was only worse by the time they exited the funeral home. The only dry eyes left were the Brownings, along with Victor and Elizabeth. Ally could feel the sadness on them and wondered how many tears they had already cried over Terry's life.

"Thank you all again for coming," Victor said to Brownings and the friends. "If you would like to join us for lunch, we are heading to this restaurant Terry said she heard about from you. Brave New Restaurant, I believe it's called."

"Thank you for the invitation," Joshua spoke for his family. "It is very kind of you, but we have some family matters of our own to which we must attend. Perhaps tomorrow, after things are done."

"Totally understandable. Take care of your family matters. Trust me; I know how important they are, especially now." Victor replied, locking eyes with Joshua intensely. "Ally, Rachel, and Erin, you are welcome to join as well. If you're unable, though, we will see you tomorrow morning. Enjoy your days."

Dante came by and hugged each of the friends firmly, thanking them again for being there. With that, Terry's family climbed in their car and drove off towards Brave New Restaurant. The friends stared after the family for a moment, wondering what it was like in their car now that the world wasn't watching them. Then they thought about the other family who was being watched by the world.

Ally turned to Joshua swiftly, "Where is Van?"

"We are not exactly certain." He replied with a sad truth in his voice. "We believe the people responsible for Terry's death have him, but where they have him, we do not know."

The girls were overcome with terror. Rachel clung to Erin in desperation. Erin stared at Ceph and Lavy as if trying to say she was sorry but not knowing how. Ally just stood in shock as their world continued to unravel even more slowly.

"What do they want with him?" Erin whispered.

"We are trying to figure that out currently." Win said plainly. "They have not contacted us or anything, so we are merely working on conjecture. It is best if you do not worry, though. What is important is that you and Thad are all safe now. This has finally made its way to us. We can deal with it from here."

"Is Luci ok?" Erin asked, fearing how bad things may indeed be.

"Luci is fine," Joshua replied. "She is far away from here right now. She wanted to come today, but after the news of Van, we decided it was best if she stayed away. You three should get home, though. We have to handle this ourselves."

The girls sat at their kitchen table. No words were spoken. There was none to be said. They had lost a friend, were perhaps about to lose another, and they were powerless to stop it. Ally had survived her speech, but she didn't know how she could survive what was coming. Joshua's words rang in her head. They were safe, but, for the first time ever, they didn't want to be because being safe meant people they cared about being in danger. The friends thought about what it would be like to lose the Brownings and Van. Though they had only known the group for a short time, they had already become almost as close to the girls as they were with each other. The emotions began swelling up in Ally all at once.

"Ok, you guys, I can't take it anymore." Ally began as her fear and sadness overtook her. "With Terry dead, Van gone, and God-knows-what about to happen to Joshua and Win and the whole family, well, I don't know what I'd do if we lost them, which makes me think of what would happen if I lost y'all or Thad. I can't. I won't. I'm not about to lose any of you, for any reason." Tears were welling in her eyes. "You guys, y'all are my family. You always have been. I don't ever want to know a life without you. I want to know you better in five years and ten years and so on, and I don't even want to keep anything from you again. The dreams, these visions, all year I've felt like I was losing y'all, like something was tearing us apart, and I can't have that. I don't ever want a life without all of you. Whatever y'all need from me, I'm here, forever."

The girls both stared at Ally in silence for a moment.

"Thad and I have been sleeping together for the last year and a half." Erin's voice was resolute in a way it had never been before.

Ally stared at her friend in disbelief for a moment, and slowly all the pieces came together. The things she had seen, things she had heard, Erin's behavior, it all clicked at once.

"How?" Ally asked, trying to sort it all out. "Why?"

"I don't know at first, honestly." Erin began as she worked to come to terms with her own emotions. "It started one night we had all been over at your house watching movies, after Thad had finally turned twenty-one and celebrated the occasion a bit too much to drive safely. I gave him a ride home, remember? When we got to his house, though, he couldn't find his keys."

"He left them at my house." Ally said, remembering the night. "I had to run them to him the next day."

"Yeah," Erin continued, "and given that it was late, he didn't want to wake his grandmother. So, I told him to crash on my couch. His car wouldn't be there, and since I'm up over the garage, nobody would ever know anything. We wouldn't have to deal with rumors or jokes—no big deal. Just one night on the couch. Except he didn't sleep on the couch. I don't know how, we just…"

"I understand how that part happens well enough." Ally said, sparing Erin from anything embarrassing she might say. "What about Rachel?"

"She called me that next morning." Rachel said dismissively. "I tried telling you Thad and I were for sure not a thing."

"Yeah, I couldn't just not tell her,' Erin began again, trying to explain to herself as much as the group, "not after everything her and Thad had been through. Plus, it was nothing. Just a couple of dumb friends one night." She paused; her eyes stared deep into Ally's, where she suddenly found a truth she'd been denying. "Only it wasn't one night. It happened again and again, and it's been happening ever since. I wanted to tell you, Ally, honestly, but no one but Rachel knew and telling you meant it was real. If we kept it secret, it was just that, a secret. Rachel and I never really talked about it, so it was like no one knew, and as long as no one knew, then it wasn't really happening. I couldn't say it out loud because then I would have to admit that I, I'm…"

Erin paused again, tears welling in her eyes as the words caught in her throat. She couldn't lie any longer. For so long, she had refused to say the words, to admit it to herself, but amidst everything unraveling in their lives, she could no longer keep the secret, not from herself and not from her friends. They were family. He was family, and it was time for her to admit the truth.

"I'm in love with him," Erin stated factually for all to hear, especially herself.

Ally wrapped Erin in her arms, tears filling her eyes to match her friend. Rachel joined the group in tears and hugged Erin tightly as she smiled at her friend.

"Thank you, Ally," Erin said as she squeezed her tightly. "Rachel, you're the best. You two have no idea how much this means to me. I've wanted to say it so many times, but I just didn't know how. I didn't know where things would go with us. All I knew was he made me happier than I've ever been, and if I made it real, things could only go one way or the other."

"You have to tell him." Ally said as she released Erin and sat back down, smiling as big as she could with tears in her eyes.

"I do, don't I," Erin said, gasping as she sought to calm herself. "Let's get through this first, though. Love can wait a bit. We have a lot going on."

Ally couldn't help smiling herself as she felt the soft tears rolling down her cheeks. At that moment, she didn't know why she had ever been bothered by the fact or how she could have ever kept her friends from being together. She loved them both separately, and she would love them together, but Erin was right. They still had significant hurdles ahead.

Even though they were all heartbroken over Terry and dreading the next day, the three friends couldn't help how happy they felt to have each other still. Losing someone had that effect. The day was long as the coming funeral loomed over them, but none of the three could avoid smiling every so often as they thought about what they had been through together. Ally was hopeful again; they may be ok after all.

The morning of the funeral came early the next day, and though the girls missed Terry, the feeling of release began to set in. They told themselves she was in a better place and that she would want them to be happy. They even managed to relax some about Van's disappearance. As much as it scared them, they trusted Joshua and

Win. The Brownings all seemed confident they would get him back, and the girls had to support them in their confidence. It was that, or admit defeat and let the gloom take over.

Thad arrived not long after they awoke. All three girls raced down to see him. They all wrapped him in a mighty group hug. He meant something different to each of them but at the same time the same thing to all of them. He was Erin's lover, Ally's closest friend, Rachel's first crush, and all of their best friends. Weirdly, he completed them all and their group as a whole. It wasn't until that moment that they realized how much better him being there made them all feel. They all truly thought they would make it through it all.

"Well, it's good to see you, ladies, too," Thad said as they released him. "If I knew I'd get this much attention, I'd have come up yesterday. For real, though, how are you guys holding up?"

"Better today." Ally said

"Not too bad at all, actually," Erin added.

"Definitely better than we have been." Rachel agreed.

The three girls all smiled faintly at each other.

"Ok…" Thad said, unsure of what he'd missed. Erin had informed him that Ally knew about them, but she left it at that for the time being. "Well, I'm glad to hear it. So what time are we meeting up with the Brownings and Van?"

The girls fell silent in response. After Erin's confession the previous day, they had completely forgotten to tell Thad about Van.

"Are we not meeting them first, or are we just like meeting them there instead?"

Still silence in reply.

"Van's missing." Ally said after a long pause. "Joshua and them think that the Ghost or the Watchers or whoever the fuck they are, took him.

"Yeah," Erin continued, "they said they had it taken care of and for us not to worry. So, we've just been busy, you know, worrying."

"I see," Thad replied. "Well, this shitshow just gets more fucked by the day. I don't know how I'm supposed to respond. Like, I feel like I should be absolutely freaking out and losing my shit right now. So, why aren't I? I don't get it. I don't think my brain can process calamity."

"We know what you mean," Erin replied. "It's weird, really. I feel like normally, I would still be in shock at Terry's death. Maybe that's what this is, shock. Maybe too much has happened lately for any of us to really react."

"Yeah," Thad said with confusion in his voice. "Let's just get through the funeral. We'll figure out what the hell's going on later."

Terry's funeral was held outside even though she wasn't being buried. Her family was taking her back with them to bury her at their family home. Terry had always wanted her funeral to be at a graveyard, though, even if it wasn't her final resting place. She just wanted a traditional burial. The snow hadn't fallen since the previous week, and the ground had cleared up. It was still bitterly cold in the air, but the grounds were green the way Terry wanted.

The service was a simple one. All the people from the visitation gathered around with the addition of Thad. Victor and Elizabeth seemed much sadder than they had the day before, but still, no tears fell. Their final goodbyes would come when they got her home. Dante was dry-eyed, and the redness was gone from his face. Instead, his face appeared angry, as death often causes. The line of black suits and black dresses surrounded the casket. The only one who truly stood out was Joshua. He still wore his standard shade of grey. From his grey blazer and tie to his grey and white oxford wingtip shoes.

Strangely enough, he seemed to be in mourning more than any person there. His entire family looked on in sadness as Terry's final service was spoken. Tears began to fill the eyes of the four friends. Thad wrapped his arm around Erin, not caring who saw. All that mattered was she knew he was there for her. Rachel and Ally held each other's hands firmly as the tears rolled down their faces. Their friend was truly gone, better place or not, they would never see her again in this life.

After the service, Joshua, Win, Ceph, Thad, Dante, and Victor loaded the casket up in the van, which would carry Terry on her final ride home. The family repeated their thank yous to everyone, shaking hands and hugging the necks of those who had come to pay their respect. Dante lingered for a moment, thanking the friends for everything they had done and promising he would return soon. With sadness in their eyes, Terry's family climbed into the van and waved goodbye to their daughter's friends as they rode away into the unknown.

34
MEET THE HARBILINS

It had been a week since the funeral as the friends sat staring at the letter from the Watchers. They hated the faceless monsters for taking their friend, but they couldn't throw the letter away for some reason. Each one of them wanted to rip it into shreds, burn it, destroy it forever, yet they sat there running their eyes over the ridges the ink had made on the paper.

Ally's and Erin's phones both buzzed and jolted the girls from their daze. They picked them up to see Thad had texted, saying he was on the way to visit. Surprise and confusion swept over them suddenly at the random turn of events, but they were excited about the development. It seemed sudden, granted the girls had just lost a friend, and he was worried about them. That was plenty of reason for him to make a surprise trip.

The girls hadn't spoken more than three sentences to any of the Brownings since the funeral. They had yet to find Van, but they were still trying. The friends' confidence was beginning to falter. Nothing in the friends' life made sense anymore, and they had begun to feel they were just floating along. The emotional rollercoaster of the previous week had finally come to a halt. The relief at Erin and Thad finally not being a secret and their grief at losing Terry were all beginning to settle, and it left the girls in a state of lethargy. It did them well to see Thad when he arrived. They appreciated just how much they had grown to enjoy his visits. The three girls that had been floating along for the past week felt Thad's presence, bringing them back to a normal rhythm. Something about Thad was just that to them, average, but no amount of ordinary could lighten their moods.

Thad saw the group sitting around the island, staring at the warning from the Watchers. "You guys feel like getting out of here?" He asked.

The friends all nodded in agreement, glad to have any kind of distraction. They quickly fell into their typical formations as they grabbed their coats and headed out the door into the cold. The chill had faded, if only a little, from the city, but the ominous revelations of their dreams and the Ghost's presence still kept a frigid feeling in the air. The friends did their best to shake it off as they walked to The Brew, but they had grown to feel they were being watched anywhere they went. They had no idea how true their fear was.

The draw to the warmth that emanated from The Brew had grown to an aura that stretched blocks away. It had become a beacon in the city for the friends to come and seek shelter within its calming embrace. If only its power had grown along with its reach. The friends still felt better every time they got near, but even their family being back together and the warmth of The Brew was not enough to fully erase the growing sense of dread that mounted every day Van remained in the clutches of his captors.

"Well, hello, there, Thad," Lili said from behind the counter. "And to what do we owe the pleasure?"

"Hey, Lili," Thad replied, matching her smile, but they could feel the sorrow that remained in her voice. "No news yet?"

"No news indeed. We'll let you know as soon as we find out, though. So what brings you to town?"

Thad shuffled his feet in disappointment, "Ah, I was just coming to see the girls. Figured with everything going on, we could all use some time together. Make things feel a little better."

"That is very thoughtful of you. I know how important you are to one another. We understand that kind of connection. It is good to have your family together in times like these. Will it be the usuals for everyone today?"

"Actually," Erin began, a sudden wave of spontaneity taking her, "I want something different. Doesn't matter what. Dealer's choice. Just something new."

Lili smiled softly at Erin as the others agreed to have their usual drinks. "And will you want these to go?"

"To go?" Rachel asked in surprise. "You trying to kick us out already."

"Well, of course not," Lili said in a dismissive tone. "I just thought you would be going to the movies. It is Thursday. You lot usually go to the movies on Thursdays, correct?"

The thought had not even occurred to the friends until that moment. It was Thursday. It had been two weeks since they found out about JJ's death, two weeks since they had last seen Terry. For whatever reason, Ally felt compelled to see another movie.

"You know what," Ally answered for the group, "we will take them to go."

"We taking them to go and catching a movie?" Thad asked, making sure he was following Ally's train of thought.

"Why not?" Ally said, trying her best to force them out of the rut. "It is a Thursday."

"It is a Thursday," Rachel repeated, giving Ally a supportive nudge.

"Well then, here you go," Lili said with a soft smile to the friends as she handed them their drinks. "You lot enjoy your movie."

"So, what movie are we going to see?" Erin asked as the friends stepped back out into the cold Little Rock air. "And if any of you shits vote horror movie, I'm punching you right in the dick."

The other three each let out a mild chuckle.

"You can laugh all you want," Erin continued, not being deterred. "Our life is a fucking horror movie right now. I don't need that shit in my movies too."

"Fair enough, fair enough," Rachel conceded, "We'll find out what's playing when we get there and go from there. No horror movie, though. Scout's honor."

"Good," Erin replied in relief. "So, we driving or walking?"

"I think I'd like to walk." Ally replied, surprising even herself. Of the group, she hated the cold most of all. She loved it in theory, but actually being in the cold was not for her. That day, though, something about the cool air just felt right.

"How far is the theater from here?" Thad asked. "I don't think we've ever gone straight from The Brew."

"Eh, it's only 'bout a half-mile." Rachel said, knowing the area better than any thanks to her running. "Easy enough if my toes don't freeze on the way."

"I feel you, Rach," Ally added, "but if I can make it, I know you can. I'm liable to be a popsicle by the time we get there."

"I believe in you both," Thad said to the two girls mockingly. "So you guys think you'll stay here once school is done?"

"Um," Ally began, caught completely off guard, "I don't know."

"Yeah," Erin said, realizing what staying through summer meant for her, "I haven't really thought about it."

"I've thought about it a little," Rachel added, "I may. I mean, I do like it here, alright, and if I stay over summer, maybe I could take another class or two. I don't know, though. If y'all aren't staying, it'd be a little weird. Not sure I could do that."

"Well then," Ally said to the two girls, "I guess we have something we need to figure out, huh?"

"Sounds like it," Rachel replied as they made their way through the city streets. "Better question, Thad, when are you moving up here?"

"Whoah, now," Erin said before he could answer. "Let's not go getting carried away there. That's a loaded question, young lady."

"Well," Thad began with the most straightforward answer he could, hoping to divert from the implications, "the bigger issue, as you guys know, is Grams. Can't really move anywhere until things change with her."

That flattened the conversation without him or Erin having to deal with the topic entirely. He didn't have to say what things would have to change with her. They all knew.

"Hey Ally, isn't that new movie with your boy in it out?" Erin asked, trying to lighten the situation again as they drew closer to the theater.

"That new movie with my boy, very descriptive there, ma'am." Ally replied sarcastically. "Let me just check IMDb real quick to see what upcoming movies 'My Boy' is starring in."

"Ha, ha," Erin said sardonically, "you know good and damn well who I'm talking about. It ain't like everybody here doesn't know who you be flickin' the bean to."

Ally simply rolled her eyes in response.

The friends were nearing the theater as they turned into the alleyway that cut across the two blocks to their destination. The sun had just begun setting, but the alley seemed to suck what little light there was left, plunging the friends into darkness as they made their way through. A hauntingly cold wind blew, sending a shiver down each of the friends' spines. They knew the feeling all too well. It had visited them too many nights in their dreams. They were almost halfway through the alley when they heard the rustling behind them.

They turned to see the shadowy figure of a man. He was ambling towards them, and the friends felt their heartbeat getting stronger. He was no common mugger. This person wanted something more. The friends felt a cold chill run through their bodies as if their veins had turned to ice. They were familiar with that feeling. They'd felt it every time Raven Man or the Wanderer had entered their dreams, but those strange visitors had changed. They weren't after the friends anymore. They were a warning, and the friends couldn't help feeling that shadowy figure moving through the alley was part of that warning.

Without any hesitation, it charged headlong at them with blazing speed. It closed the distance instantly, throwing Ally to the ground and knocking Rachel and Erin to the side. Thad never even had a chance to react as the man flung him against the wall of the building. Ally felt a rush of life coming back to her, shaking her from her daze as her brain kicked into fight or flight mode, knowing she might be nearing her end. She climbed to her feet, desperately wanting to save her friend. Erin and Rachel had stumbled into the trash cans along the side of the alleyway from the attacker's blow and were working to free themselves. Erin screamed for her love as she flung herself forward, joining Ally in the center of the dark passage. Rachel was quick on their heels as three began to advance on Thad's attacker, hoping desperately to save him.

The sudden screeching of braking tires shot through the air, and the friends' eyes all darted to the end of the alley where their rescue vehicle pulled up, and the two men jumped out in a flash as the wing doors on their evac unit lifted. The girls knew in an instant who the men were flying through the alley towards them.

"Get them home," Joshua commanded, darting past the friends as Win grabbed the three girls and raced them back to the car.

Their movement was a blur as they flew through the alley towards the open wings of the Model X. Win flung them in the car, wasting no time as he darted to the driver's seat. The three girls looked back down the alleyway as Joshua's fist slammed against their attacker's head, sending him flying off Thad. At once, the wing doors closed, blocking their view, and the car sped off into the night.

Win said not a word as he drove nearly ninety through the streets of Little Rock, weaving in and out of cars with terrifying efficiency. The friends couldn't have kept track of his turns if they tried the way he blazed through the city. The friends slipped back into their daze as the city lights became a blur, wondering what would become of their beloved friend; no, not just friend, family. They could see the man charging at them again in their heads. They knew that man somehow. Though they couldn't tell how or from where, but somehow they knew who he was. Only their minds couldn't make sense of it.

Tears had filled Erin's eyes and rolled down her cheeks as she looked out the window of Lili's car. She hadn't told him. After all that time, she had finally said it, finally admitted to herself, but she hadn't told him. That truth she had ignored for so long was finally absolute. *They* were finally real for her. Erin and Thad, Thad and Erin. It wouldn't just be one and the other anymore; it would be *they*. The two of them, friends for so long, newfound lovers, would finally be *they*. Only she hadn't said it, not to the only other person that truly needed to hear, and as she rode through the blurring city lights, she wondered if she would ever get to.

At once, the friends were each yanked from their separate hellish realities and brought back to their shared present once, as in an instant, the car was power sliding into the driveway of an old cement factory, snapping them back to the horrors around them. The friends didn't know where they were. None of them had been able to follow the drive. They were still in the heart of the city somewhere, as tall buildings towered all around, but none of them recognized a single thing around them. They were startled yet again as the driveway suddenly opened up in front of the vehicle, and Win drove down into an underground parking garage.

"We should get you inside." He said to them as the car came to a stop.

The friends exited the car, not knowing what to say, and followed Win over to an elevator in a haze of confusion.

"Where are we?" Ally asked as the elevator began to rise.

"Our house." He replied simply.

"What" Rachel began with weighted breaths, "the hell just happened out there?"

Win paused for a moment as he considered what to say.

"You were attacked. Joshua will explain when he gets here."

"What the fuck are you talking about?" Erin exclaimed with more fire in her voice than she had ever known she possessed. "Our friend is still out there. My… My…" She choked on the words, unable to say them. "How can you be so goddamn calm?"

To their shock, Erin's especially, he pulled the frantic, hysterical young woman into a gentle, loving embrace. He soothed her gently as he reached out to Ally and Rachel, drawing them into the union to give Erin the comfort she needed.

"Joshua will do everything in his power to save Thad. If it is possible, he will do it. What matters, for the moment, is that you are each safe." Win said as he pulled Erin's face up to look at him, forcing their eyes to meet. Then he looked to Rachel and Ally, in turn, to stress just how valid his words were.

"Welcome," Win stated as the elevator doors opened and he gestured for them to enter, "to our house."

Joshua and Win's house was nowhere near as lavish as Marc and Lili's, but it was most certainly as intricate and possessed a certain charm to it. The clean, sleek hallway from the elevator led straight into a sunken living room on the right with a giant projection screen built into the windows and a small bar and kitchen adjacent to the left of the living room. Soft, neon lights trimmed every edge of the room, giving the home the feel of a futuristic spaceship.

"Welcome home, Winston." A silky female voice said as they entered the building. "I notice we have visitors."

The friends looked around, trying to see who was speaking.

"Not now, Artelli. We have a problem."

"Very well. Should I initiate emergency protocols?"

"Absolutely," Win said, looking back at the friends. "Also, Artelli, tell Lavy not to dawdle, just in case, and start a couple of pots of coffee, please. I fear we may need it."

"Right away, Winston."

"Um, who was that," Rachel said, deep in confusion, "and who the hell is Winston?"

"Artelli is her name. She is our house's computer. Joshua did tell you she was rather sophisticated, and Winston would be, 'Win' for short."

Ally's head began to spin. "What on Earth is happening right now?"

"I know you have countless questions running through your minds. Truly, I do, and all your questions will be answered in time." Win said to the group, urging them to relax. "For now, is there anything that you need? Were any of you hurt? Do you need anything to drink, do you need anything at all?"

"I need you to cut the shit," Erin said softly, but still with the fury burning deep within her, "and tell us what the fuck is going on."

"No time now." Win said, looking towards the elevator. "He's here. I'll return shortly. Artelli, these ladies have full visitational privileges of the facility. Please make sure their needs are met."

"Certainly, Winston," Artelli replied calmly.

Win exited the room, not giving the friends any chance to speak. They walked down into the sunken living room and looked out into the city from what they guessed was the fourth or fifth floor at least. Their heads were spinning, trying to piece everything together. None of them could make sense of it. Ally and Rachel both held one of Erin's hands, unable to let go of their friend. All Erin could think, though, was how much danger Thad was in. She sank down in a chair and buried her head in her hands as Rachel and Ally slumped beside her and threw their arms around her.

They were all back in the alley at once; the man had Thad pinned against the wall with one hand around his neck, choking him. A familiar voice came through the alleyway. *I warned you Death was coming. I warned you Death was coming for all. Yet still, you did not believe me. Already the dead are mounting, and many more will die before this war is over.* Erin squeezed her hands against her head, trying to force the voice away. Ally and Rachel held her tight, letting her know they wouldn't leave. They didn't want anyone else they cared about to die, but it was all too clear to them that things were far beyond their control now.

"Excuse me," a familiar voice called, but the friends didn't stir. "Erin, Ally, Rachel, are you each alright?"

They looked up to see Joshua standing at the corner of the room, his shirt covered in blood.

"Are you ladies ok?" He asked with deep sorrow in his voice.

"What…" Ally asked in terror at the sight of the blood on him, "what happened?"

"There was a struggle when I tried to save Thad," Joshua began. "That is what caused the blood, you see."

"Is he ok?" Erin asked as tears filled her eyes, fearing she already knew the answer.

"I am sorry we were not there sooner, Erin…" Tears began to pour from her eyes. Erin's world was crumbling around her. "But there is still hope." Joshua continued, hoping to give Erin and the others some semblance of peace. "I've done everything I can here to mend the damage, and Artelli has stabilized him. Lavy should arrive any moment now. For the time being, that is the best we can do."

"Can I see him?" Erin asked shakily. "Please?"

"I do not know if it would be wise for you to see him like this," Joshua said with deep pains of empathy in his voice.

"Thad," Erin began, her shaky voice rising, "means more to us than I know how to express." Rachel and Ally hugged their friend, adding their thoughts to her confidence and her voice. "We don't care what state he is in," Erin's voice continued to rise, and the three friends stepped forward, "and you will let me see my fucking partner." Erin exclaimed the words with a force deep within her soul, owning the title with every fiber of her being.

Joshua gazed at Erin in admiration and understanding. "Very well," he said.

Joshua led the friends from the open living area down a dark hallway to a set of stairs descending deeper into the house. Erin could feel the lump growing in her throat, and her palms began to sweat as they descended. Ally and Rachel held her tightly, reminding her she was not alone. The stairs opened into a hallway that split into two directions. Joshua took the split to the left that led into what looked like a medical operating room, and the friends tried not to think about how strange the existence of such a room was in a house.

In the middle of the room, Thad's pale, cold body lay on the table. Erin felt her knees growing weak as she walked across the room. Ally and Rachel had to work to support her, unable to leave their friend's side. His hands were stiff as Erin took one of them in hers. He was barely clinging to life. Ally and Rachel reached out to him as well, tears filling their eyes. He was not the dear friend they each knew and loved in their own unique way, but there was still a remnant of him clinging on.

Erin turned towards Joshua, refusing to believe it could indeed be the end, "You said there was still hope."

"There is," Joshua said plainly as Win entered the room by his side, "but I fear you may not be understanding my words correctly. It is difficult, this process. Thad is stable. He is still in there, but it will take time to bring him back to you."

"You mean," Ally said, holding onto Erin and speaking for her, "like, what? Like a coma?"

"You could say that," Win said, looking at Joshua as he searched for words. "Look, these situations get a bit tricky to communicate what exactly is going on. You have to understand, that attack in the alleyway..."

"What was that?" Rachel asked emphatically, cutting Win off.

Win shrugged, searching for words to explain, "What happened in the alleyway... Look, you do not have to go through this right now." Win paused with a sad expression on his face. "Not if you lot are not ready yet."

"I think we know what we're ready for, and what we're not," Erin said as the fury rose within her to all new heights, and she could feel the raw power tearing at the fibers of her being. "Now, how about you tell us exactly what the fuck is going on here."

"My friends," Joshua began, earnestly wishing to calm the group, "you truly do not have to do this now. You can rest if you wish. We can deal with this later."

"Tell us, Goddammit!" Erin screamed at Joshua with tears pouring down her face.

Joshua's face was hurt and full of sorrow as he turned to his brother and gave a slight nod.

"Very well," Win said with sorrow in his voice as he made to exit the room. "Come with us."

With clenched fists, Erin followed Win and Joshua back into the hall, Ally and Rachel at her back, bolstering her emotions, as the friends walked across the hall to the other side into another operating room. On the bed in the middle lay Thad's attacker.

His clothes had been excellent at one point, a business-like suit and overcoat, but they were tattered and distressed from the quarrel as he lay motionless on the table. Rips and tears showed different cuts and breaks all over his body from what Joshua had done in his efforts to save Thad. At first, the friends believed him to be unconscious, but then they realized the horrifying truth. He was dead. Strangely, the friends didn't know what bothered them more; that Joshua had killed someone or that they were glad he had.

"I give you one of Little Rock's so-called Ghosts," Joshua said, pointing at the body.

The friends scanned the monster from head to toe, thinking about the things they had learned from Thad's detective work. On the table laid one of the men who had been terrorizing Little Rock. Perhaps he was the one who had killed Denise, maybe the one who had killed JJ, or maybe the one who had killed Terry. The monster before them could be one of them, but they knew it could only be one. Erin was still at a loss from the state of her love, but Ally and Rachel quickly understood what Joshua had just said.

"You said one of," Rachel stated emphatically as she and Ally turned to Joshua and Win.

"He did indeed," Win replied plainly. "The rules by which we are bound are beginning to lose their hold, and the illusion is beginning to fade."

Even Erin was forced from her previous state at his words. The three friends stood, staring at the lifeless body on the table as the rest of their world began to unravel around them entirely.

"He's one of them, isn't he?" Ally said, turning to Win and Joshua. "One of the Watchers?"

Joshua said nothing as he walked across the room and stared at the body.

"Yes, he is," Win said in a calm voice. "They have grown very brash as of late."

"And they're after you because you believe in Idonia." Rachel continued, all of their experiences of the past year finally clicking into place. "You know of their world, because of your connection to the Harbilins. You've been dragged into this feud, and you believe we should be part of Idonia."

Joshua and Win solemnly looked at one another.

"They are not at war with us because we are connected to the Harbilins, or because we believe this world should be part of Idonia." Win's voice had turned ominous. "We are the Harbilins, and they are at war with us because we are part of Idonia."

The friends' world, which had been unraveling, finally came undone. Rachel froze in shock. Ally grabbed the edge of a table for support. Erin grasped onto her friends' hands firmly, desperately clinging to the last remnants of the life they had once known. All that time, the friends had believed Joshua and Win to be two strange men who were simply involved with something much bigger than themselves. Even after learning the Watchers were real and after contemplating whether or not there was truth behind all of the legends two men had told, they had never stopped to consider how they could know such things. Said knowledge could only come from the source.

Win began again, sensing their realization, "The stories we told you are stories passed down to me from my ancestors. That is why I know as much as I do about Idonia."

"And you?" Ally asked as the three stared at Joshua in horror. "That's why you know so much, isn't it? You're older than him, brought into this, whatever this is, first, so you've learned even more from your ancestors."

His gaze rose from the body on the table to the three friends, and he stared at them with the strangest look they'd ever seen. They had missed something somewhere, and they didn't know what. There was something else about the enigmatic man. His eyes studied the group, deep in thought about something worlds away. He glanced at Win and then back to the friends, planning his words carefully. He had asked the group upon the first discussion if they were prepared. His family, his friends, everyone around that man had warned them to be careful. They had ignored every warning, believing the entire time that they were indeed prepared. They were wrong. The friends had never been ready for the truth he held.

"This is not how you were supposed to learn of our kind." He said as he looked down at the body again. A silence fell over the room that marked the turning of their reality. Ally, Erin, and Rachel existed in a vacuum for that brief moment, before their world was remade.

The man looked back at the group with a powerful, fierce glow in his eyes, "You are right about one thing. I am older than Win, but these were not the stories of my ancestors. These are the stories of my people. I have not been forthright with you. My name is not Joshua Browning. It is but one of many I have held in this world. In this realm, I am the head of House Harbilin and Avatar of Nevadolia. By choice, I am the Throne of Nevaolia and leader of the Ana'si. By birth, I am the heir to the Davpyr Lordship and the Throne of Idonia. My name is Milas Daevon."

35
IN THE LION'S DEN

Artelli's voice carried through the house in her polite tone, "Lavyrja has arrived."

"Thank you, Artelli," the man they had all known as Joshua replied, "Ladies, I know this is overwhelming, and I know you have a great many questions. I promise that you will get your answers in time, but there is much to do right now. This night will be a very long one. I need each of you to be strong, stronger than you have ever had to be, and bear with us."

The friends didn't speak a word as the man led them from the room. Erin took another painful glance back at the space where Thad laid on the verge of death. She had to be strong, for him. The friends stared at the floor, watching their steps, as they walked back upstairs, unable to raise their heads. All the stories Joshua had told them about Milas and the Davpyr and the world of Idonia, all the stories Win had told them, they weren't simply true; they were his stories. They felt betrayed that he would be so dishonest with them. At the same time, though, they knew he could never have told any human being who he truly was without them thinking he was mad. He had asked the friends that very thing before he began slowly reshaping their world, and they had agreed without question.

The three young women crashed onto the loveseat the moment they reached the living room, clinging tightly to one another as if holding on to their own sanity. They sat there staring back and forth at the two brothers. Only they weren't merely brothers. They were Davpyr. They began to question everything they had ever known about them; Van's story of how their family came to be, Joshua, no

Milas, being an orphan, even the mystical goddess known as Luci. The young women knew nothing about the men who stood before them.

The elevator door opened, and two pairs of feet shuffled down the hall.

"Good evening Cepharis and Lavyrja," Artelli said as the parents entered. "I've prepared plenty of coffee in the bar. Let me know if you need anything."

Lavy wrapped her arms around Win, "Are you ok, Stoni? You were not hurt, were you?"

"I am fine, mother," Win said, patting her gently. I was not even involved."

"Mothers will be mothers." She said, smiling back at him.

"Thank you for the coffee Artelli," Ceph said as he poured a mug.

"And I trust you're ok, Milas?" Lavy asked, looking much less concerned at the older brother.

"Never better. Grab some coffee, Lavy. You are going to need it. We have work to do." The man called Milas spoke with the purpose and efficiency of someone commanding troops.

"I assume that blood belongs to someone else?" Ceph asked, seeing the bloodstains all over Milas.

"Two someones, both Thad and his attacker."

"How is the poor lad?" Lavy asked, her tone shifting to match Milas'.

"Not good," Milas replied plainly as if near-death was simply a routine procedure. "We have him stabilized in the med-bay, but you will need to tend to him before he can be ready for transport. I have done all I can in this form, but Win and I must take care of our other issues before we can move him as well. I have not yet had a chance to change. I was waiting for everyone to arrive for us to begin. Speaking of everyone, I believe Lili and Marc just arrived."

"That is correct, Milas," Artelli confirmed politely. "Emergency procedures are already well underway. I daresay, I will be ready before you are. Marcus and Liliandra have entered the building and will be with you momentarily."

"Very well," Lavy took a large chug from her coffee and headed straight for the friends. "Are you dears alright? Have you been hurt in any way?"

Ally was still locked in shock. "No, no, ma'am. He didn't attack me."

"We were knocked aside," Rachel began holding Erin's hand firmly, her voice quivering as she spoke, "but it's just some bumps and bruises.

"Let me see your arm, child," Lavy said, pointing to Erin's right arm.

Erin offered her arm forward, and the friends noticed the large bloodstain on her coat for the first time. Lavy pulled the jacket off her to reveal a sizable gash Erin had yet even to feel. Erin was in such a state of shock over Thad the wound had not yet registered. She faintly remembered feeling a sharp pain when the man had barreled through them, but she had been so terrified by everything that happened afterward she had forgotten about it altogether. Lavy pulled a small pouch from her pocket and poured some dust-like powder into her hand. She sprinkled the dust onto Erin's wound. Erin braced for the pain to finally hit her, but much to her surprise, it never came at all. Quite the opposite, she felt a soothing sensation running through her arm. Lavy then placed her hands around the cut and began muttering words softly under her breath, eyes closed and brow furrowed in deep concentration. Another wave of shock rushed through the friends as they watched the wound slowly stitch itself back together.

"There. Now let's get you some chocolate." Lavy's words were cut off as Milas handed her a bar. "Why, thank you, Milas. Here eat on this for the next little bit. It will help you feel better."

Erin took the bar of chocolate and began to nibble on it in silence as Rachel and Ally moved in closer, holding on to their friend for dear life.

"Poor child has been through far too much already. They all have, the sweet lot." Lavy said as she returned to her family, soft tears in her eyes of compassion for the three young women. "No one should have to learn this way."

"I know, Lavy. I know." Milas said, looking at the friends with a pained sorrow in his eyes.

The friends didn't look back. They were transfixed on the couch across from them, unable to keep any thought in their minds and barely able to hear what was being said about them. Erin sat still nibbling on her chocolate with Ally and Rachel rubbing her back and petting her hands gently. The elevator doors opened once more, and another pair of footsteps made their way down the hall as Artelli ushered her greeting.

"Good evening Marcus and Liliandra." She said with a tone that sounded as if she might be smiling. "There is coffee in the bar for you."

"Thank you, Artelli," Lili said as she approached the family. "How are they?"

"They're in shock," Lavy replied, still compassionate but with her intense efficiency returned as well. "Erin suffered a mild abrasion, but I patched it up. She is strong, that one. They will be ok, though. They are a tough lot."

"And Thad?" Marc asked as he took his first drink of coffee.

"Stable," Milas said, a note of sorrow still in his voice. "Lavy will have to tend to him while we handle the matters before we can transport him."

"I see," Lili replied, understanding what Milas expected. "What of the attacker?"

"I took care of him. He's downstairs. He was young, probably no more than in his fourth decade of this life."

"And you are certain he was the other so-called Ghosts?" Ceph asked.

"Absolutely," Milas began as if giving a debriefing. "Before he left this world, I read through him. It was definitely his work, but this attack was different. All of his others were premeditated. This was an impulse attack. He had been following the group for some time. He was the one keeping watch for her. Something triggered in him with this attack, though. They are getting desperate; it would seem."

Suddenly the elevator clicked as it reached the floor, and the family all turned to see who had surprised, all except Milas.

"Relax." He said simply.

A blur of motion moved through the room before Artelli could even greet the person, and instantly a woman was wrapping her arms around Milas, not even caring about the blood that covered him. The friends recognized the auburn and gold hair without even leaving their trance.

"Are you ok?" She asked softly, holding Milas' face close to hers. "Your call was very troubling."

"I am," he replied reassuringly and gently kissed her forehead. "Thank you for coming, Locief."

The name shot through the friends' state of shock like a bolt of lightning. They should have realized it the moment Milas confessed who he truly was. The friends were in such terrifying confusion at all the events unfolding; they had not even considered the obvious fact that Luci was but another fake name the family threw about. The friends should have known the moment they found out who Milas was; there was only one woman he would ever look at that way.

"And the girls?" Locief whispered in Milas' ear where only he could hear.

"They will be, in time." He whispered back before they released each other.

"And Stoni," she said, turning to Win, "I trust you were careful?"

"You know me, m'love." Win replied with his devious grin. "I'm always careful."

"So, where do we stand?" Locief asked to the room at large.

"Now that everyone has arrived, we can begin," Milas said, taking command of his unit. We have precious little time, so I need everyone at their best. I have already contacted Control and informed them of the situation here. Lavy, you know what I require of you. Ceph, see that she has any support she needs, and get him ready for transport. Luci, I need you to do a quick sweep of the town. Make sure there are no Davinum or Nephilus left scattered about aside from the coven. Once you have done that, tend your lot as needed. Marc and Lili, you are to take care of Thad's grandmother first, and then tend to clean up. Make sure you cover every known acquaintance you possibly can, but be timely. Win begin your preparations right away, and then get the ladies back to their house shortly. I will take care of my responsibilities, and then I need you to meet there. We have to settle this before we transport him."

"If they do not understand?" Win asked in a worried tone.

"Make them understand as best you can for the time being. The rest will have to wait for later. We have no choice. I will need you there as soon as possible. The coven should not be long now. Does anyone else have any questions?" Milas paused to give his family time for clarification. "Alright then, everyone to it."

Lavy and Ceph headed towards the staircase while Win disappeared down the hall. Marc and Lili made for the elevators. The elevator revved into motion, and then the room was left with just the friends and the two Ancients.

"Is there anything else you need of me before I depart?" Locief asked Milas.

"Will you lot be ok by yourself for a minute?" Milas asked the friends.

They were still lost in their trance and barely managed to nod their head yes.

"Very well," Milas said, turning back to his partner. "If you would please come with me, Locief."

Milas led Locief from the room and down the staircase. He first walked down the left hallway to check on Lavy and Ceph. After seeing that they had everything they needed, he led Locief down the other hall and into the room with the dead attacker, closing the door as he gestured to the dead attacker.

"Is there anything specific you need me to see?" She asked as she approached the body.

"You will know when you see it."

Locief studied the body closely. She lifted his hand and examined the lines. She opened his eyelid to see his iris and the nature of his veins in his eyes. There was something Milas wanted her to see, but she wasn't finding anything that stood out. Flipping the body over, she took off the overcoat to reveal the tattered shirt underneath. She saw at once what Milas had meant as she pulled back the shirt to reveal a symbol tattooed on the man's shoulder.

"Do the others know?" Locief asked.

"No," he replied flatly, "and it shall stay that way until the situation is resolved. Do you know of him?"

"I have never seen him before. Have you informed…"

"Indeed," Milas replied, knowing her question before she even finished it. "After Win and I resolve the other matter, we will convene."

"Good," Locief stated simply, matching the focus in Milas' eyes. "Please keep me informed as best you can. Did you get the man's name?"

"Thomas. That was all I was able to retrieve. I have not seen a new bearer of that crest in countless years, and I have never seen a child this young be a Crest Bearer. We agreed to peace so long ago. We have maintained it, and everyone in the Four Orders has prospered under that peace. The Ana'si have acted in good faith. I have made certain. Can you assure me you have done so with the Nalun?"

Locief stared deeply into Milas' eyes, not even bothering to speak what was already known.

"I knew as much," Milas said, relieved that Locief had confirmed his thoughts but disappointed at what that meant. "Then I fear our current predicament is much worse than I had thought. Before he left this world, he informed me he was here in Little Rock on a mission, to end House Harbilin."

Locief stared at the man on the table with hatred.

Milas continued, "You and I both know whoever sent him did not think he was capable of such. They knew how it would end. He was merely a pawn, sacrificed in hopes of retaliation."

"Do you truly believe this group is who you said?" Locief asked plainly.

"I feel almost certain."

"Then we both know what to do. I will see what I can find out, and I will make sure no one in my Order moves too quickly. We must be extremely diligent henceforth. For now, you had better prepare. I sense they will not wait much longer. If you are right, if those four young friends are who you believe, we know what is coming."

"Of course," Milas replied painfully as she took him in her arms. "Do be careful, Locief."

"Always," she assured him, gently kissing his lips as he wrapped her in his warm embrace, "I look forward to finally seeing you. It has been too long, my love. Until then."

"Until then." Milas echoed as the two sorrowfully bid farewell and released one another.

Locief flew through the house in a blur of her shimmering dress. The elevator clicked, and she was gone. Milas stood looking over the friends as they still sat in their trance. He sat down on the ottoman in front of them and leaned over, so he was directly in their gaze. The three young women stared at him in confusion for a minute before snapping back to their fragmented reality.

"How are you ladies feeling?" Milas asked with the most profound compassion in his voice. "Erin, has the chocolate taken effect yet?"

Erin nodded, but none of the friends spoke, still lost in confusion.

"Still not ready to talk, I see. Understandable. This always takes a minute, and given the situations, it makes sense it might take longer." He reached down and gently lifted the young women to their feet. "Very well. Follow me, and I will begin explaining things until Win is ready."

Milas led the friends down a separate hallway, which Win had used, that led to a staircase going up. The halls split off at the top of the stairs, and Milas led the friends down the left corridor, which ended with two doors. He entered the door on the right, which the friends realized instantly was a massive walk-in closet the size of their rooms. Milas tossed his bloodstain shirt in a trash can in the corner and grabbed a soft v-neck t-shirt to put on for the time being. His muscles rippled as he pulled the shirt on and turned to the friends.

"I am truly sorry this is how you had to find out the truth about our kind. This is not how it is supposed to happen. There were to be many more conversations over a great length of time as we introduced you to our world. Normally the process takes years, but our hands were forced. The rules I told each of you when we first began our discussion are laws to which I am bound, and I could only tell you certain things before their proper time. We had to bend the rules given recent occurrences, though. As such, I at least need to give you the basis of where things currently stand. Idonia is, of course, real. It is the world from which I hail. The Watchers are indeed at war with our world, but they are not the whole of this story. The Watchers are merely a small subset within one of The Four Orders involved in an eons-long conflict, but as of right now, they are the most important for the three of you."

"Why?" Ally asked, finally breaking the silence that had held the friends.

"Because they mean to hold true to their letter. The Watchers are ever Vigil. I am sure you have already pieced together it was them who have hunted us these past few months. Their signals to you no doubt caught your attention. It is hard for me to explain their motives regarding you with the short time we have. I daresay you may even think them monstrous. You would be wise not to jump too hastily to any conclusions, though. Things are far more complex than that. Members of both our Orders come in many forms, and the three of you have even considered yourself friends with some of both our kinds."

"What…?" Erin tried to ask but was cut off by Milas before she could.

"Come now," Milas said, leading them towards the door. "Your ride is here."

Win seemed to appear out of thin air, "All set on my end." He said to Milas. "Are the ladies ready for me to take them home?"

"Indeed, they are," Milas said, turning to three friends. "I will see you ladies on the morrow. I promise. Win will see you home safely and answer what questions he can on the way."

The friends simply nodded in confusion.

"Win," Milas said, turning back to his brother, "I will be waiting. Do be quick."

"Certainly," Win answered.

The three tried to speak, but no words came as Win grabbed them gently by the arm and led them from the room. There was silence in the elevator as they rode down to the garage. The friends wanted to ask Win all of the questions that were tripping over one another inside their minds, but they weren't sure where to even begin. Instead, they just strolled to the vehicle.

"You lot are tranquil," Win began, "are there truly no questions, or has the shock not worn off yet?"

Erin finally landed on the question she had tried to ask Milas before they were ushered from the room. "Your brother said we already consider ourselves friends with a number your kind and the Watchers. What did he mean?"

"Ah," Win began calmly, "I see you haven't quite worked it all out yet. Well, obviously, you know us, but you've also spent a considerable amount of time with some of their number. Until recently, you even counted one of them to be one of your best friends."

"What are you talking about?" Ally asked in horror as the revelation dawned on her.

"Terry was not killed by the Ghost of Little Rock." Win answered in a profoundly apologetic tone. "She was the Ghost, one of them at least."

"No," Ally said emphatically. "You're lying. I know you're lying."

"Terry," Rachel began with tears filling her eyes, "was a wonderful person. She would never do that."

"Terry was indeed a wonderful person. The world is truly less fortunate without her." Win stated with respect and sadness in his voice. "That doesn't change the fact that she was a Watcher, and that she was sent here to kill our family. One does not have to choose if they want to be completely evil or absolutely pure. There is good and evil in all of us, and for most of us, the difference between good and evil is what we believe. Terry believed that killing us was the right thing to do, and that doesn't take away that she was a good person. She was merely a soldier on the opposite side of a seemingly endless battle. The real tragedy is how she was blindly led to do what she did by her superiors."

"Well, if she was the Ghost of Little Rock," Rachel asked, not wanting to believe it to be true, "then why did Van disappear after she died?"

"Yeah," Erin added, hoping against hope he was lying, "Joshua, I mean, Milas said the Ghost took him, but if she was the Ghost, where'd he go?"

"Van went to inform her family, of course."

"What?" Erin exclaimed. "Why the fuck would he do that?"

"Because Van belongs to the same Order they do."

Ally was too stunned to get her thoughts out properly, "Wh… why, why are you and he so close?"

"Why are Milas and I friends with someone from a different Order?" Win asked with genuine confusion in his voice. "Because Orders do not define us. Our family extends beyond lines drawn by our beliefs. We like Van, and he is a great friend. Did we know eventually the day might unfold which would force him to try and kill us? Of course, we did. Such is the nature of war. It doesn't change who we are, or who our family is. Van wasn't at the funeral because Terry's family insisted he not be there because of his connection to us. I would venture to guess he is probably with them now as they ready their attack."

"Attack?" Ally gasped.

"Yes, ma'am. The only reason her 'family' had the funeral here was so they could meet the three of you and make a connection, and so that they could study our family. Now they plan to finish what Terry did not."

"That's why they didn't cry," Erin replied simply as the pieces came together for her.

"I beg your pardon?" Win asked, unsure of whom she was discussing.

"At the visitation and again at the funeral," Rachel added, following Erin's train of thought, "her parents didn't cry."

Suddenly the lack of resemblance between Terry and her parents clicked in Ally's mind, "They didn't cry because they weren't really her parents. Were they?"

"You are correct." Win replied, the sadness still in his voice. "The only family member Terry truly had was her brother Dante. I'm sure you noticed there was no shortage of sadness in him. Terry's death devastated him, and no doubt he will be with them in full force."

"When will they return?" Ally asked as the fear began to set in.

"Return?" Win said, the surprise noticeable in his voice. "My dear, they never left. They have been in Little Rock planning their attack ever since the funeral. We would have taken care of them already, but with each of you still in the fray, it was too risky, which is the same thing that was keeping them at bay. Now that their other scout is dead, they will attack in the morning."

"So, what will you do?" Erin asked, sure she already knew the answer.

"Well, that's simple, really," Win replied nonchalantly. "We strike tonight. Milas is already in position at the building in which they're hiding. As soon as I get you home safe and sound, I will join him, and we will take care of this."

"How can you be so calm," Rachel asked in detest, "when you're about to kill someone?"

"After a while, you sadly become accustomed to it."

Hundreds of questions rattled around in the friends' minds as the gravity of everything began to sink in truly. Despite their hatred for the Watchers, their heart went out to Terry's family. The friends knew if what Win said was true that Watchers deserved whatever was coming to them, but then again, so did Milas.

"Do you ladies need anything else?" Win asked with worry in his voice as they arrived at the house on Rock Street.

The friends shook their heads. Of course, they needed something. They needed explanations. They needed all of it to go away and life to go back to making sense, but Win could do none of those things at that moment. So, the friends didn't bother asking.

"If you need anything, you have our numbers." Win said as he walked them to the door. "We'll be back to check on you as soon as this is resolved."

"Thank you." The friends each said as they opened the door to their house and walked inside. They truly meant it. Win had been nothing but pleasant and helpful to the young women ever since they met. Even if what he was about to do was horrible, they couldn't forget that.

"Ladies," Win said as the friends were about to close the door.

"Yes?" They answered in unison.

"It will be better in time." The kind man said, giving them a reassuring smile. "Trust me."

"Thanks." They said once more. They closed the door, and before they could even get their coats off, Win was gone.

The friends fell into each other's arms. No one spoke. The hug said enough. They were all scared, all lost, all wanting answers. The three young women's eyes began to water, as again they were reminded just how important they were to each other. Slowly, Rachel, Erin, and Ally finally released each other and stared at one another with the same looks of confusion. They wanted it to make sense, but they knew none of them could do so. The only answers for them lay outside in that dark, endless night.

"Is this real?" Erin asked in a whisper.

"I wish it wasn't, but…" Ally's words trailed off as she stared down at the floor.

"I keep trying to understand, but it just all seemed so unreal." Rachel said, staring at the door as if she was waiting for her normal life to come walking back in.

"I know," Ally replied. "If I woke up tomorrow on Mars, I don't think I'd be less confused than I am now, and to think right now Josh… I mean, Milas and Win are about to risk death at the hands of the Watchers and aren't even worried."

"Do you think they'll live?" Rachel asked with tears in her eyes.

Erin felt the anger and frustration of the night swelling inside her; anger at what happened to her partner, anger at everything that had happened around them. The courage that comes with rage began to fill her. She wasn't standing around to find out the answer when the Brownings came back in the morning.

"I don't know," Erin said, the fire burning inside her, "but we're gonna find out."

"How will we find them?" Rachel asked, throwing her coat as her courage grew too.

"I think I might just know where they are." Ally said as she opened the door into the cold, murderous night.

Milas stood on the street across from the abandoned building downtown as Win joined him. Thunder drummed in the darkness, sounding off the coming storm. Lighting flashed in the distance as Win's eyes began to glow an even more brilliant blue. Milas' were ablaze with the grey of the storm as he studied the building intensely.

"Less than twenty of them," Milas began debriefing his partner with the assessment of their foe. "With the None even in their second century. One of them is a patriarch."

"You must be seeing it wrong." Win replied in shock.

"No," Milas replied succinctly as he accepted the fact himself. "I thought so too at first, but the eldest is, in fact, one. That would be the second youngest we have encountered, I believe."

"Indeed," Win replied as the thunder clapped again and the rain began to fall.

"They have already drawn the circle around the building and activated the fulcrum inside too."

"Good thing I left my sceptres at home then." Win said with a mischievous grin, ready to begin the game.

"It would seem so. We will do everything we can, but I fear they will not yield." Milas gave the instructions simply, not needing to explain anything to Win. "Get the storm going as best you can before coming inside. You know what to do, Win."

"Yes, sir." Win flashed him a dazzling smile, letting Milas know how ready he was. "See you inside in a few."

Milas walked across the street, letting the rain soak into his pulled-back hair. He crossed the Circle drawn by the Watchers and stopped just outside the door. He pressed his mind into the building again. None of them had noticed his presence, so he continued inside the door and down the stairwell to the basement with which he was all too familiar.

Rain leaked in the broken windows that lined the tops of the walls flowing down the stains on the walls from previous rains. Nine of the Watchers, Elizabeth and Victor among them, stood around a workstation with a map of the city pulled up on it. They were going over the buildings owned by the Harbilin Corporation, trying to finalize their strategy. While they did, Dante and the others went through double-checking their supplies in the armory. Daggers, crossbows, spears, swords, and axes lay on the table, all with diamond-lined edges gleaming in the light. They were amateurs, barely outfitted for a skirmish, sent to the city either as a feint or a provocation, as to which Milas was still uncertain. He made no noise when he entered the room. The entire group was all taken off guard when Milas spoke.

"There is no need for any more of your number to die here, Frederic," Milas said to the one he had identified as the patriarch. "Terry's death was a terrible loss, but you pressed on. Now another of your flock has fallen, and it is time you accept defeat. Let it stop with them. No more blood need be shed over a battle you cannot win. You are already on the verge of breaking the terms of the treaty, but it is not too late to be stopped. This can still be forgiven. Do not force my hand."

The one called Frederic spat at Milas, "Not a chance, you Davpyric…"

"Stay your tongue, child," Milas commanded in a powerful voice that echoed through the room, silencing any who would lash out. "Do not dare speak to me with such arrogance. I am giving you a chance at peace. I am offering to let you leave now with the rest of your coven intact, and you treat me with hostility. I could just as easily have ripped your head from your shoulders the moment I entered the room. You struck first. I am well within my treaty rights to retaliate, but I do not wish for this to end in violence. You may leave here tonight, never pursue my family again, and we will be at peace once more."

"Even if I were to become weak and cowardice," Frederic continued with a more evenly controlled temper still laced with hatred, "even if I were to betray the holy Order, I follow and walk away from here, leaving you alive, I assure you my coven would not. None of us will leave this room while you still live."

"This man speaks as your leader," Milas began, addressing the entire room, "but no one, not this man nor any man, can choose for you to lay down your life without your permission. It matters not if you chose to follow him before. It matters not if you swore to do as he commanded, even if it meant your life. Your life, your liberty, is yours and yours alone. No one can tell you what to do with it, not even this man who leads you."

Milas scanned the entire room, locking eyes with each and every one of them as he did, pressing his message upon them, pleading with them to listen.

"You are faced with a horrible choice this evening," Milas said to everyone in the room with a mighty sorrow in his voice. "You believe your actions to be just and noble, and you think there is honor in giving up your life for that cause. I cannot convince you otherwise, and thus you must each make the terrible decision of abandoning your beliefs or dying for them. I do not wish harm upon anyone in this room. The only thing I want, is for each of you to leave this place and live beautiful, wonderful lives."

Milas paused, lost in the painful sadness of what was unfolding and torn by the monster beginning to wake within himself.

"This choice is yours, and only you can make it." Milas continued saying to the room, pleading with the last ounce of his hope. "Lay down your arms, and leave this place. I assure you, no harm will follow." He met each of their unyielding gazes one by one. "If you choose to pursue your violent delights unto their violent ends, though, there is no other alternative. If you choose to stay here, if you take up arms against me and my kin, every single one of you will die here tonight."

None of the coven moved to leave. Expressions of excited hatred moved through the coven as they each grabbed their preferred weapon tightly and prepared for the ensuing battle—all except one.

Patriarch Frederic scanned his flock with exuberant pride. "You see, Davpyr," he began with malice dripping from every word, "there is no place here for Idonia, or any of its kind. You and your kin are a blight on our world, and we will remove every heretical trace of your kind from our existence. None of us will leave this room alive, while you still stand."

"Then none of you," Milas replied, his words turned cold as he spoke, and a demonic grin spread across his lips to reveal the monster had been unleashed, "will leave this room alive."

Lightning struck as the lights flickered, and Milas dashed across the room in the strobe of the lights. His first blow connected with one of the Watchers surrounding the workstation, sending his head crashing into the table and fracturing the screen. Milas swung a brutal left hook into the Watcher on his right, knocking him into another, and then spun in full force with a right hook to the Watcher on his left that sent the man to his knees, all before any of them could even react. Not realizing Milas' tremendous speed, the Watchers were all stunned as they saw three of their number hit the floor, incapacitated. All at once, they sprang into action, raised their weapons, and raced towards Milas, all except the one.

A crossbow bolt whizzed past his head as Milas dodged a sword strike from a Watcher leaping over the table. Milas brought his elbow down hard into the woman's back, sending her crashing into the floor. Two more crossbow bolts flew across the room, with Milas barely dodging the second before a dagger cut into his side. He slammed his fist into the attacker's head, knocking the man back several feet as he pulled the dagger loose without flinching.

The Watchers were in full tilt as four of them brandishing swords charged at once. Milas dipped under the first horizontal stroke and sent a fist into the woman's abdomen just as a second sword came flying down from an overhead strike. He rolled right with the blade of the sword cutting the tail edge of his coat as it struck the floor. Milas leapt through the air and delivered a devastating blow to the attacker's cranium while his sword was lodged in the ground. Two more sword swings approached from both sides as Milas barely had time to duck before the swords clashed together, but the moment he ducked, the first woman lunged forward with her sword, sending Milas leaping backward to dodge the attack. Just as he landed, two crossbow bolts finally found their mark, both lodging into his left shoulder. Milas ripped the wood and diamond bolts loose from his shoulder as one of the behemoths charged at him with an axe. Milas swiftly strafed to dodge the downward strike, delivered a massive jab to the man's ribs, doubling him over, and as he did, Milas rammed the two bolts into the man's chin and up into his brain. The giant man collapsed on the floor. One dead.

The Watchers were unfazed, and Milas quickly grabbed the axe from the ground as defense against the oncoming sword strikes. He parried left, then struck the man in the jaw. Milas caught the woman off guard with an advancing strike, then thrust his knee deep into her abdomen. Another bolt flew towards his head, but Milas snatched it from the air in front of him. Parrying another strike, Milas closed his fist tightly and jabbed the man square in his nose, sending blood down his face as Milas stabbed him in the throat with the bolt. The man stumbled back and ripped the bolt from his throat, but as he did, the blade of a sword burst through his chest, dripping with blood. The man collapsed on the ground in front of Milas, revealing the hidden blade-wielder behind him.

"That's two, I believe." Win said with a devilish smirk.

Two bolts flew at Win's head as he strafed through them both, advancing on the shooters, and the battle resumed. The three Watchers firing crossbows stood next to the armory, grabbing more and more bolts to throw at Milas and Win. Frederic stood, winged by Terry's family, guarding the crossbowmen as Win made his way toward them. Two Watchers wielding daggers both leapt towards Win simultaneously with their blades slicing through the air. Win began his dance again, spinning around them with ease. He reached over the top of the first woman's head, grabbed her by the chin with both hands, and rammed his knee into her spine, sending fractures into her vertebrae. She dropped to her knees, coughing blood onto the floor while her partner swung wildly at Win, catching him in the arm. Her dagger slung blood across the room as it tore through Win's flesh, but she wasted no time reveling in her strike before plunging her other blade into his side. Win caught the woman's wrist before she could pull the blade free and swiftly caught her second as it swung wildly toward his face. Win lifted her hands into the air, twirling his dancing partner around before bringing her own daggers stabbing down into her chest.

Diamond blades clashed against each other as Milas parried another swing from one of his attackers. Three of them were circling, sending stroke after stroke at him while Milas parried and dodged his way through. Two swords flew down on him in a dual overhead strike. Milas raised his stolen axe and caught both blades, swiftly kicking the man on the left directly in the chest, sending him flying backward. Milas then stepped back, bringing his axe down quickly to let the other sword fall, and as it crashed against the ground, Milas brought his axe overhead and sliced down through the wielder's arm, ripping through the flesh and severing the bone. The sword fell motionless, gripped tightly still in its owner's severed hand. The man stumbled back, clutching his arm as blood spilled onto the floor. Milas grabbed the sword from the floor, wrenching it free of the dead hand, and ran the man through, piercing his heart. Milas stared into the man's eyes as the life left them.

Pulling the sword from the man's chest, Milas spun to face his remaining attackers. With sword and axe in hand, he took the offensive, jabbing with the sword and sweeping with the axe. The two

Watchers parried and swung back, then parried and strafed, then parried and swung back again, but Milas had taken control of the fight. In a desperate plea, the man lunged forward in an attempt at Milas. Milas ran the blade of his sword across the man's thighs as he lunged, strafing to dodge him, then lowered his axe into the man's back, sending him face-first into the ground. Milas flipped the sword around in his hand, gripping it like a knife as he raised it into the air, and then brought the blade crashing down into the man's head, cleaving his skull in two.

Switching the hilt back around in his hand, Milas pulled the blood-soaked blade from the man's skull and began attacking the watcher still standing. Milas could see the fear in her eyes as the woman tried to defend each advancing stroke, but she was more ferocious and powerful than any of the others in the room he'd dispatched thus far. Despite the fear, the woman refused to yield. She parried swing after swing, then began to fight back with thundering blows. Forsaking her form, the woman swung more wildly and powerfully with each lunge. She made broad sweeping strokes left and right until Milas managed to catch the woman's sword with his own, pinning it to the ground. Milas raised his other hand and jabbed the woman in the throat with the blunt end of the axe's shaft. The woman stumbled back, gripping her throat with her off hand and gasping for breath. Milas advanced upon her, slicing his sword across the woman's knee, sending her buckling to the floor. As the woman fell, Milas brought both his blades swinging in a high overhead arch and crashing down through the Watcher's shoulders. The sound of flesh ripping and bones shattering echoed through the room as the blades tore through the Watcher's collar bones until the blades met deep in the Watcher's chest. Milas wrenched the blades free. The Watcher's spine snapped as the blades dislodged, ripping the head off and sending it across the floor behind Milas as the headless body collapsed.

The friends pulled into their familiar spot in the parking garage next to the abandoned building as the rain poured down.

"You really think they're here?" Erin asked, staring at the building.

"I mean, where else would make sense?" Ally asked rhetorically. "Only one way to find out, though."

Ally hopped out of the car and ran across the lot, Erin and Rachel right on her heels. They crossed the garage and made their way down the staircase as they had done so many lifetimes before. There was no guard at the door. The lock still came loose without effort, though. The friends opened the first door and made their way inside. They could hear the commotion of violence within. For a moment, they almost felt back in their old lives. Reality took hold, though, as they opened the interior door and saw the horror within. Seven bodies lay on the floor with blood pooled on the ground around them. Terry's family was huddled together at the back of the room, and three others were slowly getting up from the floor as Milas and Win made their way across the destruction. All the friends wanted to do was run back to their car and escape the terrible sight before them. That was a different life, though, a life that was no longer theirs. Their life, as much as they did not understand it, was within that violently blood-soaked room.

Win and Milas split as they dissected the room. Win attacked the three Milas had initially incapacitated as they rose from the floor, and Milas worked his way towards Terry's family. Win began his dance again with the poorly armed Watchers. Without their weapons drawn, they were barely even sport for Win's skill. Hooks and jabs flew from body to body as Win weaved in and out of the three. The sounds of jaws beginning to break and noses fracturing created the beat for Win's dance, and the sprays of blood from their faces added to his subtle flare until suddenly he caught one with a shattering blow that sent them sliding across the room towards where the friends then stood, with Ally at the lead.

She didn't remember leaving the corridor; none of the friends did. They didn't remember walking across the room, yet there they stood staring at the Watcher laying mere inches from Ally's feet. Win and Milas still hadn't noticed the friends were there amidst the fighting. The Watcher on the floor took notice, though, as he grabbed Ally's feet and yanked them from under her. Ally's world upended, sending her toppling back as her head smacked against the floor, making her mind spin and her vision blur. Her eyes slowly came into focus just in time to see the Watcher bringing his dagger down at her.

Erin and Rachel raced across the short distance. They lunged forward in desperation, wishing they could stop their best friend from being the next victim of that heinous night. Erin and Rachel's screams of fear alerted everyone in the room to what was happening. Every head turned to see the Watcher bringing his dagger down on Ally and the two sweet girls lunging after him. Frederic screamed for the Watcher to stop, but he was already lost in the act. None of them had any time to react as he brought his blade down.

Ally gazed into her attacker's eyes as the dagger drew nearer. Of all her nightmares and her close calls with death, none of them affected her like that one. She refused to close her eyes, and no part of her even wanted to. She was unafraid, unmoved by her coming death. A rush of adrenaline shot through her as she stared at her attacker, daring death to defeat her.

A hand came into view as it stretched over the Watcher's face, pulling his head back. Time caught back up to itself in an instant as a dagger slid across the man's neck, opening him up. The second the blade left the skin, the dagger spun wildly in the wielder's hand, which closed tightly around the hilt once the blade reached its position, and swiftly plunged the dagger into the Watcher's chest draining what little life was left in him. Ally's savior tossed the body off her and reached his hand down to help her up. The friends were all, Ally especially, beside themselves to see Van's smiling face.

"Next time," Van smirked as he lifted Ally from the floor, "please be a little more careful. Now you lot stand back and let us finish this."

Too in shock to speak and too overcome with joy, Ally just nodded her head as her friends pulled her back into the safety of the corridor, wrapping her tightly in their embrace. As Van turned to join Milas and Win, the three young women could see that Milas had used the distraction to finish off his two attackers, and Win had pinned the three crossbowmen to the wall with spears thrown violently through their hearts. All that remained was Terry's family and Frederic.

Frederic motioned the family to fight, and the three each charged at one of the friends. Elizabeth lunged at Win, who swiftly dodged the blade and began a final dance. Victor made a sweeping strike at Van, who ducked under his sword as Van's favorite game began. Dante advanced on Milas with half-hearted but meticulous strokes, doing his best simply not to lose ground as his fellow Watchers had. Frederic didn't join any one fight. Instead, he tried to thwart each of the three men. He made stab after swipe after stab at each of the three attackers as they tousled with his coven. Win thrust his knee into Elizabeth's abdomen, spinning away under Frederic's sword. Van laughed as he delivered a swift one-two jab to Victor's abdomen while his blade glanced off Van's shoulder as he strafed away from Frederic's stab. Milas parried Dante's swing, then caught him in the stomach with the hilt of his sword, causing Dante to double over as Milas leaned back, both of them missing Frederic's stroke.

Milas grabbed Dante swiftly by the back of his cloak and flung him into the water-stained walls. Then he leaped forward, catching Frederic with a clean stroke across his back. Frederic spun around wildly with fury in his eyes. He swung madly at Milas, who only parried each attack with ease. Milas hit Frederic with a left jab as he dodged a stab, then struck him across the face with the sword's hilt as he parried a strike. Frederic stumbled, but Milas gave him no time to recover as he ran the blade into Fredric's thigh. Rage overcame Frederic as he stepped back, pulling his leg off the blade, and he charged forward, raising his sword for a killing blow. Milas switched the sword swiftly to his left hand, spinning away as the strike crashed to the ground. In full force of his spin, Milas brought his elbow crashing into Fredric's nose, sending him tumbling backward. Milas whirled back around and jabbed the hilt of his sword into the ground and held it there with the blade up as Frederic fell back onto the blade.

Win connected another powerful knee to Elizabeth's abdomen, doubling her over. He grabbed the Watcher's head swiftly and spun it violently around, snapping the Watcher's neck and sending the woman's limp body to the floor. Van flung Victor against the wall. He bounced off and raised his sword to head height preparing his swing just as Van's fist sent his skull smashing into the wall with his blade lodged in it. Victor's body slumped to the floor. Milas rolled Frederic over, sliding the sword free from his back and letting him collapse again. Milas stood over the dying Frederic, holding the sword at his throat as Win and Van joined his side.

"I warned you that your coven would fall here tonight," Milas began, working to calm his fury, "if you did not accept my offer of peace."

"I would still rather die," Frederic replied as he coughed out blood, "than accept anything from a Davpyr."

"So young, so foolish," Milas said as a deep sadness crept into his voice. "One of your own Order stands here against you, because even he knows the terrible mistake you made. Who sent you on this impossible quest?"

“God,” Frederic replied with a fiery gaze.

“Do not hold to such ignorance,” Milas replied, his sadness growing as he pleaded with the dying man. “You cannot know of my kind and still view things with that type of zealotry. No Watcher with any sanity would ever attack my family. So, tell me then, who sent you?”

“Just as arrogant as every other Davpyr I’ve killed.” Frederic spat a glob of blood at Milas’ feet. “Always think you rule the world. My coven and I may have failed today, but we will not be the last to come for you. Those who sent me will send more. Your days are numbered, Harbilin.”

“I assure you,” Milas began, rage welling up, “you have never met a Davpyr. They who sent you, deceived you. I am not of this world. My days number well into the trillions, and it will be trillions more before a Watcher ever harms my family. I know not what they told you of me, but it was not enough.”

“Oh, they told me enough about you,” Frederic spat, injecting venom into his words, “*Vox Milas.*”

Milas buried the sword into Frederic’s throat, choking out his last words with coughs of blood.

36
THE END BEGINS

Milas turned to Van and Win, who stared at him with concerned looks at Frederic's dying words. Milas released the sword, letting it fall to the ground, and he walked across the room towards the unconscious Dante.

He shook the young boy whose head only rolled back down. Milas shook him again more forcefully to rouse him, and the boy's eyes shot open. He fought to free himself from Milas' grasp, but to his surprise, Milas released willingly. Dante tried to slide away from Milas, but his back was already against the wall, so Milas stepped back and raised his hands to show he intended no harm. Dante looked around the room in horror at all his dead comrades before returning his view to Milas' calm face.

"First fight?" Milas asked plainly.

Dante only nodded his head.

"Have you ever even faced one of our kind before?"

"Once," Dante replied in a shaky voice, "but he was younger than you, clearly."

Milas couldn't help but let out a soft laugh, one that Win and Van echoed, "Dear child, there are few you could ever meet who are not younger than I, and not many you could find younger than my kin. They truly did send you out for slaughter. How old are you?"

"In my second decade," Dante replied, still struggling to control his emotions.

"I see," Milas said, turning to Van and Win to see the sadness in both their faces, "and did they tell you anything of my family or me?"

Dante's voice grew a bit stronger, "Just that a Davpyr family had been hiding in Little Rock for some time and that they were a danger to the town. That's what Frederic told us, at least. I've never actually been to a Convocation."

"No, I wouldn't suspect so." Milas continued as his sorrow grew at the thought of the misguided youth and his coven. "My dear lad, I am afraid you have been terribly deceived, but you have seen us now. You met my family. Do you believe we are a danger to the town?"

"I think you're a danger to anyone who gets on your bad side."

Win and Van both let out a laugh.

Milas smiled softly as he spoke, "That may be true, but it does take a great deal to get on our bad side. What you witnessed today was an attempt by your Patriarch to break the Accords. Do you even know what those are?"

"No, sir," Dante replied simply, feeling as if his entire life was a lie.

"I see," Milas said as he turned to Van and Win. "I assure you we are no danger to you. We do not wish you harm. I could have very easily killed you earlier if I chose."

"I believe you." Dante cut in. "So why didn't you?"

"Because you do not wish us harm. Unlike every one in your coven, you did not wish to do this. We knew from that very first night you came to dinner. You never wanted this life. From the very first moment they introduced you to this new existence, you have felt something was wrong, that something did not quite make sense. That is because you were not given the full truth, but you have a chance now to learn it. You have an important calling yet to do."

"What calling is that?" Dante asked, his voice mixed with fear and confusion.

"Well," Milas began purposefully, "eventually, you are going to carry a message. When the time comes to begin our voyage, you will go with Van to those who sent your coven here, and you will tell them what happened this night."

"With what took place here, it would be the perfect opportunity for me to check in on things," Van said to Dante reassuringly. "Whoever sent you, Dante, did so hoping to start a war, one that has been brewing for longer than you can understand. You and I are going to find out why."

"Yes, sir," Dante replied weakly.

"Before that happens, though," Win said, stepping towards the young man with a smile, "there is much we have to do. First, however, we must tidy up some things. If you would, please follow us."

Dante rose and followed Win as he, Milas, and Van walked across the room to the three young women.

"I know I should be asking if you ladies are ok right now," Milas began in a calm voice, seeming completely untroubled at their arrival, "but what I must first do is ask you to go home. This building will collapse soon, and you need to be safely away from here. If you would, take Dante with you and wait at your house. The three of us will come by when it is done."

"What?" Ally asked, still huddled together with Erin and Rachel.

"Leave now," Milas commanded, and the young women hurried from the room with Dante in tow, no one bothering to question the command.

The building burst into flames as Ally, Erin, Rachel, and Dante sped down the street. Milas, Win, and Van watched from across the road as the fire grew and grew, engulfing the abandoned building with an unnatural fury until it was consumed and collapsed on itself. The rain began again, even more heavily than before, as it slowly squelched the flames, leaving the smoldering rubble to fade into nothingness.

The ride home had been silent for the estranged group. The friends had not objected to Dante accompanying them given the severity of Milas' command, but in the vehicle, they knew not what to say. The friends were riding with one of the people who had been actively hunting them and the Brownings, yet he was also the same young man who had just lost his sibling and whose world had been upended just like theirs. The confusion they each felt before the events in that horrible basement had only multiplied. None of their questions had been answered, and they had even more to ask. Nothing about what was happening made sense to any of them. They watched as the sun began to rise, shining through the horizon of the turbulent storm clouds. It was hard for any of them to think that just a day before, their biggest problem was the death of their friend and sister, and instead, they found themselves amidst a world of supernatural beings they didn't understand.

The four sloshed inside, removing their soaking coats, but making it no farther than the kitchen before they plopped down in the chairs. Blank stares were plastered across each of their faces as their minds tried to process what they had seen and learned. Dante wanted to apologize to the friends for what they had endured at the hands of his family. The friends wanted to apologize to Dante for all he had been through, but they all struggled to find the words.

"Is this," Erin said softly, "is all this really happening?"

Ally and Rachel stared at Erin, wishing they could comfort her, but there was no comfort to be found in that moment.

"I wish it wasn't." Ally replied, exhaustion and sorrow in her voice. "I keep hoping I'll wake up, and it'll all be gone, but it's not working."

"I'm scared," Erin said with barely a whisper.

Ally and Rachel turned to her, unsure of how to help or what to say.

"I'm scared," Erin continued as tears began to fill her eyes, "I'm scared for Thad. I'm scared for us, and, most of all, I'm scared it's only going to get worse."

"Me too." Ally and Rachel both responded, reaching their hands out for Erin's. "Me too."

"You each," Dante began, but his voice cracked with pain, "each of you deserves apologies I cannot even give you. Apologies from people who are no longer alive to give them. I don't know what my family was anymore. I don't know if I ever did. I don't know what family even means. I feel betrayed by them, but at the same time, I feel like a traitor. To them and you, and those cannot both be true. You have all been wonderful people, some of the most pleasant people I have ever known. Each of you, and the Brow… Well, whatever they're called. I don't understand how the people I thought were my family could have been far worse of a family to me than all of you have been. I realize none of you will ever be able to trust me. I'm not even sure that I want you to, but I do wish so much that I could somehow make this right. I can't, though. All I can do is work to be a better person than I was, than I am."

He fell silent as his head slumped in defeat, staring at the floor. The friends wanted to comfort him, console him. He had been their friend, but he had also betrayed them from the very first moment. They could see the anguish and confusion on the young man, horror at what he had done, and sorrow at who he had been. Ally, Erin, and Rachel each wished they could forgive, but the words simply wouldn't come. Denise, JJ, all the other lives lost that the friends did not even know, and even their dear friend Thad, whose life hung in the balance, were all because of Dante's family. He bore not all the guilt, but the friends could not deny he bore some.

A soft knock came at the door, rousing the friends, followed by the door swiftly swinging open. Milas, Win, and Van calmly strolled through the hallways and into the kitchen. The water barely dripped on the floor beneath them as if they'd only walked through a slight drizzle. There were prominent dark spots on each of their coats from where the blood had stained them. Milas had a few dried splashes along the left side of his neck and jaw.

"Are any of you hurt?" He softly asked.

The group all looked to one another, unsure of what to say or who should say it. Hurt was such a loose term at that point. Everything about them hurt in some way, but it was not the kind of hurt Milas had meant.

Ally's voice was shaky as she replied for the group, "We just watched the three of you slaughter an entire room of people, and your first question is just making sure we aren't hurt?"

Milas' had a tone of slight offense when he spoke, "I apologize for not asking the appropriate question. After what occurred tonight, I figured your safety was the most important thing. Would you have preferred I ask 'are you ok'? I believe we all know the answer to that. I would be foolish to expect any of you to be even the slightest thing resembling ok after what you have endured the past couple of weeks. What is important, though, is that you did endure them."

The girls exchanged glances as his words soaked in.

"I know this is more than you knew you were in for when you began spending time with my family. I assure you this is not how any of us wanted you to find out either. We did warn you, though."

"You warned us alright," Erin said indignantly. "You and your friends and your family warned us that we should be cautious around you, that you had troubled lives and whatnot. You all came off as the dark, mysterious types. If we'd known from the beginning…."

"If you had known what, that we were, in fact, of Idonia? That we were immortal? That I am Ancient? To what piece of knowledge do you refer? Had you known from the beginning our stories were true, you would have done what? Stayed away? No, you would not have, Erin. None of you would. You might not have known what we were, but all of you saw the signs. You knew there was something much larger occurring than anything you had ever known. Still, though, you refused to stay away."

"Alright, fine," Ally exclaimed, her exhaustion reaching its max. "Why can't we? You're right, Josh; I mean Milas. Whatever the fuck your name is. You're absolutely right. Any person in their right mind would've ran away from you screaming months ago if they'd seen what we have. So why can't we walk away?"

An ominous look spread across Milas' face. "The same reason he could not bring himself to hate us truly." He said, pointing at Dante.

A confused look spread across Dante's face. He had no idea why he couldn't hate Milas and his kin, no idea why he had never been able to believe what his coven had taught him entirely. Yet Milas made it clear there was some greater truth there.

"I cannot fully answer that question for you. That is an answer you must each discover for yourself. You are wrong about one thing, though," Milas continued, turning his gaze back to Ally, "people in their so-called 'right mind' would not have run away in fear. They simply never would have been able to see the things you have each seen or learn the things you have learned. I cannot tell you why you are able to understand when others are not. That is a question you each must ask yourself. All I can tell you is how. Our existence in your world is a very sophisticated one. After many attempts, over many generations, to build a connection between the various worlds failed, or resulted in violence, we developed certain safeguards to make sure that people could not discover our kind unless they were capable of truly understanding.

"It is impossible to fully explain when you still know so little of our world. Were you each unable to see the truth, none of the things you have experienced would have even registered for you. You would not have been able to truly speak with us, to hear our stories, even to see the books. Anyone whose mind is not ready when they enter The Daily Brew does not consider going upstairs. People come and go all year long and never even register that Lili is there. They do not even see myself or Win."

"That day you first met me," Van interjected, hoping to make the friends understand, "you saw people pass in front of me to place their order, and then you called out to me to start a conversation. Never mind getting drinks later; if you could not know more, you would not have even made it to that point. If you were like everyone else, like the couple who stepped passed me, I would have simply been another stranger in the room. There for a moment, and then gone from your lives, never to be remembered.

"And you, Dante," Van said, turning to the young man with sadness in his voice, "you are the inversion of these ladies. Your upbringing in the coven is what happens when people take the stories of Idonia and strip away the deeper truths, warping them into simplified narratives they can use to dement the minds of everyday people. The others in your coven existed with religious fervor for the mission they were given because their minds could not see through the veil being placed over their eyes. You, however, could. You knew that there was something more, and you questioned the nature of the reality you were being told. Were you not able to comprehend the greater truths, you would have been no different than the others of your coven."

Silence fell over the room as each of the four individuals sought to process everything they had just learned. For the friends, it slowly all made sense. Their hunting for information through the library in The Brew, their ability to find out about the Harbilins, even being able to see the connections in the Ghost's victims, it had all been in plain sight. The friends thought back to the days after their dreams, how they would almost forget or move past them as if it had never happened. Time and time again, the friends had reached a point where they questioned themselves and what they were learning, each time clearing another hurdle that allowed their minds to be open to more. For Dante, it was all the teachings he had been given from his coven. Stories of how the forces of Idonia had moved through world after world, destroying everything in their path, how their Order rose up as guardians of the sacred realms to stop the monstrous advance of Idonia, all of which were stories meant to shape them into mindless soldiers. Only for him, they hadn't.

"So, how old are you truly?" Ally asked, bringing the group around to the moment at hand. "All of you?"

The three men looked to one another, searching for words to explain.

"Age is a difficult concept to explain with our kind." Win answered in an apologetic tone. "Our years number to the amount people from your world struggle to understand, but there is also the problem of time. You see, time functions differently for each of us and each of the worlds. The easiest way I can explain it is that we are each older than humanity."

"What are you then?" Erin broke in, trying desperately to understand.

"Well," Van began delicately, "Milas, as you know, is a Davpyr, one of the Ancient races. We are both," he continued, gesturing to himself and Win, "something that came much later. We were once human, both from the mortal worlds. Many terms exist for what we are now, but in proper terminology, I am a Nephilus, and Win is a Davinum. That's getting a bit ahead of things, though, so for the time being, just consider us both Human 2.0. It'll be easier to understand that way until you're ready for more. That will come soon."

"What about all the other stuff you told us?" Rachel asked. "The Watchers, Idonia reforming. What about Locief and Samias, and your family? What role do they play in this?"

Milas' words were tense as he spoke, trying earnestly to help the group as much as he could, "There is so much about our kind you do not yet know, so many things you were supposed to learn before we reached this point. The reforging of Idonia was eons ago. Our people have grown and evolved, our society has spread throughout the stars alongside the human worlds, but through it all, lines have been drawn, sides have been made. Wars were fought across entire systems, and from those battles rose the Four Orders, each adopting certain beliefs on how things in our cosmic society should be governed. Entire civilizations were born and died as each of the Orders fought for control of Idonia and the mortal realms, until finally a peace was established, at great cost. Since that time, the Four Orders have maintained their stances, but no battles have been fought. Idonia and the human realms have flourished under that peace. The entirety of humanity here in this world has been within that time. Skirmishes have popped up from time to time on the fringes, but it has never escalated beyond that. What you saw unfold tonight was one such event. Which is why, the three of us are working to ensure it remains just that, a skirmish that does not escalate. This time of peace has been the most prosperous in our entire existence, but it is only the calm before the storm. The resurgence of The Great War still looms ahead, and we are doing everything we can to prolong its arrival as long as we can."

"We've had dreams," Ally cut in, "these two men, two creatures, one hooded and cloaked, the other a flock of ravens, they showed us what they said would be the end of the world. They were showing us what you're talking about, weren't they?"

"In our world, they are referred to as the Raven and the Wanderer," Milas responded in an ominous tone, "and yes, they were showing you what could happen."

"Who are they?" Rachel asked.

"They are both beings I cannot yet explain to you," Milas replied with an apology in his voice. "There is more you must see before you can understand what they are. The vision they showed you, though, there is no certainty that it will happen, nor is there any certainty at when it could happen."

Milas grew quiet as he looked into each girls' eyes. His eyes explained what his words could not. It was not a time for them to feel fear, but a time for them to prepare, to prepare for what their lives would become.

"There will come a day, when you each must choose what you believe and to which world you belong. The three of us have each taken a side in this war, and we cannot try to sway you. We may only inform you. That is why our stories have such strict rules. In the coming years, though, you will learn everything you can of our world and the beliefs of the Orders. You will be taught the history of each of the worlds and all the wonderful races that inhabit them. Only then will you be asked to choose."

"How?" Rachel asked. "How will we learn these things?"

Milas smiled a radiant, exuberant smile. "I am going now to make the final arrangements for your journey. Win and Van will be staying for the next few months to make sure no other situations arise and to help you prepare. My family has already begun our preparations. That is what the three of you saw us doing last night. I will not see you again until you return to Little Rock next autumn, when we will collect you and your things. Thad, however, will be departing with me immediately."

"What?" Erin exclaimed, horror swelling inside her.

"His damages were severe," Milas began in a calming tone, "we can heal him, but we cannot do so here. We do not have the tools nor the resources. Here he would have to remain in a coma indefinitely, left to hope that his body would mend itself."

Tears began welling in Erin's eyes as Ally and Rachel moved to her side, wrapping their arms around her. To their surprise, Win moved forward and placed a hand on her shoulder, and Milas knelt, taking

Erin's hands in his. He met her teary gaze directly.

"Erin," he said softly and reassuringly, "I give you my word, Thad will make a full recovery. We have the power to mend him, but we have to take him to our world. It is the only way we can ensure he is healthy and whole again. Lavy is already with him now, making certain of that. I know what he means to you," Milas continued, surprising the friends yet again, "and I promise you he will be with you again very soon. You have to trust us. By the time I return for you and your friends, Thad will be waiting for you on the other side."

The friends couldn't explain it, but his words soothed them in a way no amount of time could. They weren't simply words of reassurance, they were reassurance itself, and despite all the fear within the three girls, they felt peace move through them.

"Where are you taking us?" Ally's words were but a whisper.

"To Idonia," Milas replied with a smile.

Ally, Erin, Rachel, and Dante each stared in disbelief with mouths agape. Idonia, the birthplace of all life. They were going to see it with their own eyes: excitement, joy, fear, sadness, and every emotion the group could imagine flowed through them. There were tears in each of their eyes, both at the absence of their dear friend Thad and at the thought of what it would be like to see him again on the other side of the veil. They weren't tears of just sadness or hope; they were tears of everything.

Milas stood, and his group moved towards the door.

"We must go finish taking care of everything," Milas began, giving the group another assuring smile, "but Win and Van will be around soon. I know each of you is scared and confused about a great many things. I cannot promise that it will go away soon, but I can promise that it will go away in time. Take care of yourselves and each other while I am gone, and be ready when I return."

The three men smiled and bid the group farewell as they left the house on Rock Street. Erin, Rachel, Ally, and Dante all looked at each other, an entirely new group formed in a mere night. It would take time for them to heal and trust one another, but they were forever bound by their journey. With Thad gone, Dante was the closest thing the girls had to a friend who knew what they had experienced, who understood what they had learned. Thad would be with them again soon, though. It would not be long until they made the journey to Idonia to be reunited with the other member of their family. Their time in Little Rock had been rough thus far, but as the sun rose outside the window of the house on Rock Street, so did their hope that there was good yet to come. They each stared out the window, watching the sunrise, embracing the dawn of their new life, and the friends couldn't help but smile, knowing it was only the beginning.

ACKNOWLEDGEMENTS

Were I to name every person who has impacted my works and described their impact, this section would be longer than the book itself. Every person I have ever encountered has contributed to this book somehow, as they have contributed to shaping me as a person. Whether I name you directly or not, please know that if you have ever met me, you affected this story as you have affected me. Every encounter I have ever had taught me things and introduced me to some existence outside my own, which in turn fueled my creativity.

Those of you who know me somewhat probably think of me as the smiling, jovial extrovert, the guy who has never met a stranger. For the few of you who know me best, though, you understand the deeper truth. You each know that underneath the smile is a mind constantly at work, studying the world around and analyzing every last piece of data in an endless quest of comprehension. Even if I'm always alone inside my mind, though, lost in my own little world, I am still incredibly grateful for the beautiful people in my life.

I wouldn't be the person I am without so many of you. I can't begin, though, without thanking my parents, all of them, and my older brother. We've been through some times. I don't have to say anything else for you to know how true those words are. Even through the roughest parts, though, I know, to this day, the love you each have for me. That love, and all that came with it, forged me into the person I am today. The lessons you taught, however they were taught, guided me on my way.

My younger brothers, Micah and Malachi, I know our journey was different. At times we were very close, at times far apart. I never spent as much time with you as I wish I could have, but I hope you know anytime I wasn't around, I wanted to be. I still remember reading pieces from this story to you boys before bed so long ago you probably have no memories of it. Those bonds can never fade.

Frank, my other brother, I've said this to you off the page, but I still have to say it here as well; our time together was awesome, even when it wasn't, and I wish so much we'd had more. I'll never forget those first few days at a new school, completely flipping roles and tripping everybody out. Those are but a few of our incredible memories. You are a great brother, and you're an even better dad.

Many others shaped my journey, though, both close and distant. There is no shortage of writers I can thank for the wonderful worlds that inspired me. From Tolkien to Tolstoy, my entire life has been impacted by the power of prose. Were it not for Rowling or Stine, who knows where I would be. It was not merely books either. Fiction comes in many forms, and I wouldn't have the imagination I do without the works of Lucas and Lee or even more Bioware and Bethesda. As I grew, so too did my literary adventures, shaping my world through the words of Martin and Corey, and I cannot thank enough of them.

The creative works that have shaped my mind are almost as numerous as the people who have, and I can't express enough words to thank them. This entire book and everything I do after it is a testament to their influence, and while I wish I could personally thank each of you, there are some I can't write this work without mentioning.

To my teachers, growing up with educators as parents, I know the work so many of you put into molding young minds. Some of you did even more, though. Mrs. Murdock, who is now gone from this world, you were the first, and you will always be missed. Ms. Hansen and Ms. Burkhart, (I don't think you even still have those last names, but that is always who you are inside my memories.) you challenged my literary curiosities and pushed me to discover works I would have never imagined. Without you, I may have never truly known Don Quixote or Pip or Pierre or Lear. You may not have known it then, but your instruction shaped my journey in ways few could.

Mrs. Mitchell, Shannon, I cannot say enough words about you. I don't know if I ever disliked a human being so much, who would come to mean such a great deal to me. I do believe you are the only teacher who ever kicked me out of their class. I'll never forget that day, just like I'll never forget when you cast your vote for me as Student of the Year in a school that didn't even want me to be eligible for the award. You pushed me to be a better student than any of my coaches pushed me to be a better athlete, save one. This book never happens without you.

Jeremi Finn, you may not have been my teacher in the classroom, but you are a teacher inside and out. You were the very first person who gave me hope that the fantastical world inside my head and all the zany things I was into could actually coexist with having a full, vibrant life. You taught me that classic tales of true love and high adventure could be more than just words on a page. At a time when I was drifting further and further away from my true nature, you guided me back to who I really was, even if you didn't know it.

College was much different, but there were still professors who stood out. Ms. Niswonger, you gave me the best advice anyone could ever give a young writer. You believed I could write if I wanted, but you also kept me from being a "starving artist." Were it not for your words, I never made the journey to New York and expanded my horizons. Dr. McKenzie, your classes were some of the toughest I ever took, but the things you taught me and the encouragement you gave instilled in me the faith to run a business. You're the only professor I've ever had on my resume, and it was for good reason. David McLeane, you helped make Tech some of the best memories I have and the closest thing I ever got to an authentic college experience. You gave me a fresh start and brought so many people into my life that would forever change it.

There were many beyond my teachers that impacted me in profound and different ways. Chris Storey, my journey to New York wouldn't have happened without others, but it most certainly wouldn't have happened without you. It was a dream of mine to move there, but I could never have done it without you moving with me. I hate we both worked such insane hours that one year we had there together, but we certainly had some fun when we could. Even if I wish it had been more, I wouldn't trade the time we did have for anything. Of course, I'd be remiss not to mention all your help with the book itself. You gave me more direct feedback while living in our shoebox apartment than almost everyone. Without your input, my characters never found their voice, and their interactions with one another have nowhere near the connection. So thank you, for everything.

Michael, Kerrian, you helped shape the world of Idonia probably more than any one person. Our endless chats about all our stories, tossing ideas back and forth, and coming up with entirely new worlds was absolutely invaluable. I would never have explored the inner workings of my worlds and figured out how everything actually functioned if not for you. All the economic government systems, the currencies, the technology that fuels the world, and so much more were discovered as you pushed me to expand on my creation. I know music is your focus now, but I do so hope that one day you finish some of your novels as well because I for one cannot wait to read them.

Ryan and Amanda, a lot of our experiences aren't appropriate to write here, but I still love them all the same. From our days in that tattered apartment to your wonderful wedding at Bethesda Terrace to the beautiful families we're now raising, a part of you is with me always. No matter how much time we have apart, there are still few closer to me than the two of you. I was so thrilled to finally see you together and get married and have two beautiful girls (and now a son). Rare are those that have a love as special as yours. I still have our notes to-do list, and we've managed to check a few things off. There are many still to come, though, and I can't wait. I love you guys.

Moon, Brian, and Dillon, part of me thought to mention you separately, but you're all one to me and one with me in a sense. In a way, we're always that group of kids at Tech dreaming of creating fantastical stories to tell the world. Our journeys have taken us so many different places and down so many different paths, but we'll still always be those dreamers. Moon, your help with the designs of the book and feedback, Brian, your constant push driving me forward to build my empire, and Dillon, your fantastical and wonderful outlook helped make this work a reality and make me who I am. I can't thank any one of you enough.

Lera, you probably don't think it, but your influence on me has been some of the most profound. While all our road trip conversations are some of my fondest memories, along with the happy calves, your views and insight encouraged me to explore the deeper thoughts and spiritualities of my characters and my lore. You challenged me to expand my mind and pour myself into my work to create something greater than I imagined. While I'll always miss the fun drives, and New Orleans, I look forward to wonderful new memories to come.

Levi, what can I even say on these pages that hasn't been said a million times better over our time together. When I began writing Win as one of the other sides of my personality, I worked to imagine what that person would be like, and then a few years later, I met that person in real life. Win finally existed because you existed, and it's still surreal to this moment. I can't explain how much I appreciate everything you've come to mean in my life and my family's life. The journey that we have been on together as I forged this story and we forged ours, in turn, has been beyond incredible, and it's only just beginning. From Calexico to Alexandria to the stars, I'm so grateful that we are on this journey together.

There are countless others too. To all of my extended family who have shaped my life, I can't say enough. Todd and Tammie, I am so fortunate to have you as another set of parents. I always feared the sitcom in-law situations, and I cannot express how thankful I am to never know that life. Tommy and Laura, the love you have shown Tiff and me, and most especially Rue, is beyond exceptional. Thank you for taking us in as your own and introducing us to some new best friends. Evan and Margaret (and now Easton as well), you are one of the brightest spots of our new life, and we could not have asked for a better addition to our family. Our journey together is just beginning, and we couldn't be more excited about it. To everyone who read pieces of the book early and gave me your thoughts and to everyone else who influenced my life and creativity - Greg & Emily, Tia, Hunter, Jimmy, Allie, Rachel, Stu, Rebecca, Bobby, Matrika, Zakiya, Jon, the trio of Rachel & Meg & Letha, Lisa & Daniel, David, Easton, Jessica, Wes, Kyle, Keith, Steve, Carrie, Ken, Britt, Holly, Herb, Pat, Jared, Brandon, Morgan, Thomas, Angie, Alex, Eric, and so many more people that I know I'm probably leaving out, I wish I could thank you each properly. All I have, though, is this book. This book is my thank you to everyone I mentioned and everyone I left out. You all made this possible.

It's not all people that influenced me, though. Little Rock and New York, I'm not me without you. I was born in Rock Town, raised by it, but I was made in Manhattan. When I finally took all my loose ideas and concepts, people and places, all swirling around in my head, and wrote the first actual words of this story, I did so in New York. I may not have been there physically, but my mind was, just like it always is - my same mind that is always in Little Rock. The entire time

I was writing the first draft, I placed it in New York while using Little Rock as my reference. Then when I was in Manhattan, I began the final draft, placing it back in Little Rock while using New York as my reference. They couldn't be more different, but for me, they are the same - the two sides of me that are always present. Little Rock and New York, I love you both, and I could never do this without you.

And now, for the ones closest to me. Tiff, I know you wish I would keep this part brief, and I will try as best I can. It's hard to silence such an integral part of yourself, though. I'm still me without you, only I'm not at all. All the best qualities in me are the ones you bring to the surface. Without you, I'm the worst version of myself, and, more than anyone, this story quite literally never happens without you. Without you, there is no Ally, no Locief, and there is no Milas. If not for you, I never watch that terribly wonderful movie and read that terribly wonderful book and come away thinking I can actually write something like this story. It doesn't stop there, though. You have always been a guiding light in my life. From when I wrote the first words of this novel to when I released it unto the world, you have been there. I've tried off the page to explain what you mean to me, and now I've done so on the page, and neither will ever fully capture it.

Averly Rue, my sweet darling girl, it will be a decade and more before you even read this, and it will be another decade and more before you can even begin to fathom what you mean to me. Your mother may bring out the best qualities of me, but you, my love, are the best qualities of me. You are everything I wish I could be and more. You are that which drives me to late nights and early mornings, giving every ounce of myself to create something greater than I could ever be. You will never know a time before this work existed, but said work would never have reached existence if not for you. I could do countless numbers of great things in my life beyond this point, and not a single one of them would ever be as great as raising you.

Lastly, to all of you reading this who dream of a world beyond our own, it doesn't matter whether that world only exists within your own mind; it is as real as anything else that has ever existed. For that world, the world in which you live, is yours. Cherish it and hold it dear, but know that you are never alone there. We are all there with you, all of us who live in our own little world.

www.ingramcontent.com/pod-product-compliance
Lightning Source LLC
Chambersburg PA
CBHW020603310726
48979CB00008B/1324/J
9780998883328